"You have to ask the question: where have we come, and how?
'Cause the end's in the beginning,
And the beginning's in us now."

~ Tyler McCloud

a Mackenzie Wilder/Classic Boat Mystery

BOOKS IN THE
MACKENZIE WILDER/CLASSIC BOAT SERIES

BOOK 1

Where The Bodies Lie Buried

BOOK 2

Sweet Corn, Fields, Forever

Sweet Corn, Fields, Forever

a Mackenzie Wilder/Classic Boat mystery

by

R. J. Minnick

Wingspan Books
1513 Briarwood Lane
Fayetteville, NC 28303

Printed in the United States of America
First edition
ISBN- 13: 978-0692729878 (WINGSPAN BOOKS)
ISBN- 10: 0692729879

about this book

Sweet Corn, Fields, Forever is a work of fiction. Any resemblance to real people or incidents, other than historical, is purely coincidental. Kings Hill is a geographic and topographic counterpart to an actual town, but not identical to the original. Any perceived similarities or dissimilarities is the result of the author's active imagination.

References to real places have been made with an attempt at respect due the places and their real-life inhabitants. Characters throughout the book, even those with historical reference, are fictional.

My gratitude to all those connected with antique boats and antique boat societies who have had a hand in introducing me to these fabulous boats. In addition, I am grateful for 24 years of living in Nashville, and the unequivocal friendliness of country musicians and songwriters.

Sweet Corn, Fields, Forever

Sweet Corn, Fields, Forever

R. J. Minnick

Sweet Corn, Fields, Forever

·C·H·A·P·T·E·R· 1

·T·O·R·Y·

"Sometimes a new beginning is someone else's end,"

from "The End's in the Beginning" by Tyler McCloud

When I met Mackenzie Wilder, I knew for a fact we had things in common; mostly the privilege of bein' acquainted with Jason Fields.

Come to find out, we also shared a fondness for good lines. 'Course my lines had to do with songwritin' and hers had to do with tying up boats, but even that little wordplay was common ground for us. We wound up being part of a common story as well, made up of lines from my life, and lines from hers.

We're going to share the story-tellin' here, and I reckon I'll start off, even though I really don't come into the story right away.

My name's Tory McCloud.

Some days before I pulled into Albany with my band, Jason Fields and his friend Mackenzie Wilder walked the halls of his fancy new Research and Design Center. Jason was showing off his new building to her. Mackenzie is his company doctor. He's a bit sweet on her, too, but nothin' serious.

As Mackenzie told me, they were on the last leg of their little tour and headed back to meet up with the press when they noticed a problem with one of the conference room doors.

Now, I should tell you all that Jason Fields is a detail person, and he designed most of this complex himself. A door having a problem, however tiny, wasn't something Jason would accept. He had to check it out.

Jason reached out to pull it shut, but as he started to grip the knob, his movement pushed the door inward. It bounced back. Jason pushed it again, harder.

It bumped against something and held, sounding exactly like someone bumping a door with his toe. Now, no one bumps toes against doors in silence, says Mackenzie, unless they are hiding. Or unconscious. Or maybe dead. She started worryin' right then.

Jason put some force behind things and pushed the door open enough to get through. He slid into the room, flipped on the light, and turned to look behind the door.

It was Mackenzie who saw the toe of the cowboy boot first. Saw that it lay at an angle that meant it was still on someone's foot. I thought later about how I would have known what was what a lot quicker if I'd been the one to see that boot.

She pushed in alongside Jason as he squatted down beside the young cowboy dressed in a twill jacket and jeans. He lay face down, palms pressed against the floor like he was ready to do some push-ups, knees bent like he was pulling them out of the way of the door.

Mackenzie checked his pulse but got nothing. She hurried to check his neck, and her fingers found what her eyes had missed: a silver strand embedded in his flesh. He wore his hair styled long and colored blonde, and it covered that part of his neck pretty well. The first thing she did when she felt that strand was to brush his hair out of the way. Then she saw the color of his face.

"Jason! Help me here!"

They rolled the young man over, and regretted it right away.

It's one thing, Mackenzie told me, to see someone dead. She's a doctor; she expects it now and then. It's another thing to see someone who's been strangled.

I closed my eyes when she told me. I didn't want to picture it.

Then she realized that he was barely dead, or newly dead, however she put it. Point is, whoever murdered this cowboy had to still be in the building.

Jason turned away from the contorted face. He reached for a wall phone with a 'possum pallor on his cheeks.

"Security. This is Fields. We've got a problem in Conference Room L24. Call 911 and secure the building and grounds." He listened as someone protested. "Foster, we have a dead body in here. Do what I said."

Mackenzie smoothed the jacket back over the man's shirt. A shirt that didn't belong on a dead man, she said. A Western shirt, red and black and white with silver threads shot through it. Silver threads that seemed to match the wire cuttin' through his flesh. She stood up.

"You okay?" She rested her hand on Jason's wrist; his pulse hammered.

He nodded his head to the questioning tone but didn't seem to hear her words. His head began to bobble as he stared at the body spread out on the carpet. She stepped in front of him.

"Jason. You've got guests out there that are going to want to know what's going on. Chamber of Commerce. Media people. Can your men handle it? Do you need to go out there?" She snapped her fingers lightly in front of his nose.

He seemed to come back. "I'll handle it, Mackie. Excuse me." He moved her aside and knelt beside the figure. With long fingers he brushed strands of hair away from the forehead and eyes, eyes bulging from the blood-suffused face. He pulled his hand back and stared.

His face reddened and tears began to appear. Mackie took a step forward, reaching towards him as footsteps sounded down the hallway, heavy muffled thuds rushing closer. Jason rose, shaking his head.

"I know this guy, Mackie. He has - had a distinctive face. His name's Tyler McCloud."

"Tyler McCloud? The country music singer?" The footsteps halted outside the door. Someone grasped the door handle.

"I knew him some years ago. A solid performer. Good songwriter. A little tricky to deal with. Real star personality even then. He's the guy - "

The door swung open.

"He's the reason I don't write country songs anymore."

A New York State Trooper stepped into the room, his face as grim as his uniform was gray.

·C·H·A·P·T·E·R· 2

·T·O·R·Y·

"a circular relationship where time begins to blend,"
- from "The End's in the Beginning" by Tyler McCloud

M atheson!"
Trooper Ted Matheson's eyebrows twitched into briefly held arches, his gray eyes taking in the scene, including Mackenzie's presence. He nodded to Jason then turned to gaze up and down the length of the victim.

"Did you move him?"

"I - we turned him over. When we came in, he was lying face down, feet near the door. We didn't know for certain he was dead until we turned him over."

"Thought you felt a pulse, did you, Dr. Wilder?"

"No, of course not. But you don't leave it to chance. It was just too late."

Matheson sighed. "He hasn't been dead long, has he? It's my guess you've probably destroyed evidence here, Dr. Wilder."

"Hey - "

He held up his hand. "I understand. It's inevitable when civilians find a body. Doesn't make my job easier." He motioned to some men in the hallway to come in and begin work. In they trooped with their cameras and tapes and black bags. Another officer stepped up to him and spoke in his ear.

"Mr. Fields, my men are relieving your force. We've closed the access road. We'll be checking the surrounding woods. I'll want you come with me and explain to your guests that I need them to remain and cooperate with my men."

"Matheson, they don't even know what's happened. The press is here. That's what this is, you know, one big press party."

"I understand that, Mr. Fields. Now you please understand, I have a job to do. We'll deal with the reporters." He started to turn away, then turned back. "By the way, I wouldn't count on business opening up tomorrow."

"Right." Jason's voice held a bleak note of cooperation. "All right, I'll be right with you."

"Actually, first I think I'd rather use one of these empty rooms and interview you and Dr. Wilder. Separately." He watched as Jason and Mackenzie glanced at each other. "You're becoming familiar with procedure these days" - a reference to Mackenzie's relationship with Lt. Bryan Jamison of Albany Homicide - "so you'll understand why I want to ask each of you about what happened. I'll admit I'm curious. Are you trying to add another body to your collection, Doc?" The question sounded far more amused than his steel gray eyes looked. He turned to Jason. "And why is the man responsible for your not writing any more country songs in your building, late at night, dead?"

"I'd like to know the answer to that as well, Matheson. I haven't seen Tyler McCloud in almost eight years. He's still one of my favorite country singers. I even have tickets for his show this weekend. But I've no idea why he'd be here, tonight. I certainly don't know how he wound up - like that. It's terrible. You've got to understand; he was a friend."

"Look, Officer Ma - oh, come on, Ted We all know each other. Surely you don't think Jason is involved in this! I thought we were all friends."

"Mackenzie, Dr. Wilder, you know how this goes. I don't know what I think until I hear all you have to say. Now, please."

He ushered them to the door, through the corridor and into another conference room an officer had already prepared with recorder and legal pad.

"Dr. Wilder, if you'll go next door with Officer Gates and make yourself comfortable until I join you? Mr. Fields, you and I will talk in here."

He closed the door on Mackenzie, and the officer referred to as Gates escorted her to the other room. He saw her in with silence, then deserted her for other duties. She paced the room, pondering options, wondering how and when she was going to explain the evening's highlights to Bryan.

Long about now you're wondering who Tyler McCloud was to me. Well, Tyler was my brother. He was my only brother, and we performed together with our band. Like Jason said, we had a concert scheduled at Albany's Pepsi Arena. We'd been in rehearsal for a couple days, a little longer stay than usual. That had been okay by me. I had plans for the extra days. I didn't know Tyler'd gone out that night, and I surely didn't know he'd taken himself out to crash Jason's grand opening.

If I had, I might have gone with him. He wasn't the only one who knew Jason Fields from way back. Maybe then he wouldn't have been in that conference room.

Mackenzie Wilder and Bryan Jamison also have a history worth knowin' about. They grew up together in Kings Hill. There was a gap in their relationship, lots longer than the gap in Jason's and mine. They've even been married to other people. When Mackenzie came back to Kings Hill and started up her medical practice, they found each other again. And, like the best country songs written, they took up where they left off, only better.

I might have mentioned earlier that Jason was a little sweet on Mackenzie? Well, that didn't set too well with Mr. Lieutenant Bryan Jamison. Mackenzie being Jason's company doctor didn't help. As Mackenzie told it, this night's events were just goin' to make matters worse. Right then, though, to give Mackenzie all the credit she's due, she was more worried about my brother and Jason, and their relationship.

She paced around the conference table in the empty, new-smelling room. Jason would never harm a soul. She thought she knew that, but things did not look very good.

How much of the evening had she spent in Jason's company? Could she give him an alibi? Or would the State Troopers of New York, in their infinitely silent wisdom, merely add her guilt to Jason's?

She almost wished she smoked, she felt so agitated. Certain she'd never find an ashtray in any of Jason's conference rooms, she looked around anyway. The surface of the table was unmarred by anything so hazardous as an ashtray. Instead a bell-shaped jar held shiny pebbles of varied hues. She popped a handful of them into her mouth. Chocolate had it all over tobacco anyway.

Mackenzie reviewed everything she could think of about how they'd spent the evening. Had they been together long enough to prove Jason couldn't have killed this man? He'd been with her the whole time. She hadn't examined the body long enough to know when Tyler died, yet it had to have been while she and Jason toured the building. Which, naturally, meant the murderer was loose somewhere nearby.

She shivered, wishing Matheson were interviewing her first. At least then she wouldn't be alone. She gulped some more candies and went back to pacing around the table. Every lap brought another thought.

What had Jason meant when he said Tyler was the reason he'd stopped writing country songs? He'd only written a couple songs ever, but Mackenzie had put that down to him being easily distracted.

Jason Fields, the quintessential Renaissance Man. This venture in applied computer technology was only the most recent in a lifetime of innovative undertakings by a brilliant man. Jason held Ph.D.s in Philosophy and Criminology and a law degree as well. He'd written two texts on criminal justice and six mystery novels. He was an inventor with seventeen diverse patents, including some in chemistry and engineering.

His more artistic accomplishments included - besides his country tunes - a couple commercial jingles and several better-than-average oil paintings and watercolors. He flitted from project to project as easily as any butterfly. So the idea that he'd never written more than a couple country tunes had not seemed illogical to Mackenzie. Apparently there was more to it.

These thoughts created empty circles in Mackenzie's mind. She wouldn't have any answers until she spoke to Jason, and she wouldn't be able to do that until the State Troopers were done with them both. About the time she reached that discouraging realization, Trooper Matheson stepped into the room.

The interview did not go well.

"What time did you and Fields find the body?"

"Shortly before you and your men got here."

"Dr. Wilder. Time, please?"

"Seriously, I'm not sure what time it was, but it was probably fifteen minutes before you arrived."

"I'm surprised you didn't check the time on your watch. Isn't that standard?"

"Ordinarily, but this isn't an ordinary occasion, and I neglected to put on a watch when I dressed."

"Couldn't you have asked Fields? Or checked the clock in the room?"

"There was one in the room?"

"Yes. There's one in each of these conference rooms, like that one over there." He indicated a small electronic message screen built into the wall. In one corner a colon flashed, marking the center of a time display.

"Oh. Well. I hadn't realized it was there. I suppose I was too shocked to notice."

"I'm surprised Fields didn't point that screen out to you during your tour. Apparently it's one of his pride-and-joys in this fancy building."

Well, Mackenzie got her feathers ruffled over this. I would have, too.

"Jason has many 'pride-and-joys' in this building, Officer Matheson. He probably did point one of those screens out to me someplace along the way. I didn't think about it right then. I was too busy trying to deal with the shock - Jason's *and* mine."

"What were you doing prior to discovering the body, Dr. Wilder?"

"Touring the building, as you've obviously already noted."

He ignored the jab, which only irritated Mackenzie more. Ted Matheson knew both Mackenzie and Jason. That he could think they had anything to do with this was just plain silly. Although I think Mackenzie called it ludicrously unfair.

"Why exactly was Fields giving you a private tour?"

"Look, Officer - Ted - oh, this is ridiculous. You know Jason and I are friends. *We're* friends! You, me, Jason. Why are you being like this?"

"Mackenzie, I have to ask questions like this. You know that."

That set her down for a minute. She closed her eyes and counted. "All right. I'm also Jason's business associate. I helped him select this site for the complex. I agreed to be physician to his employees, so I need to know the building's layout. Besides, this was the completion of a project Jason shared with me when we first met. The private tour was his way of showing it off."

Matheson played with corner of the tablet he was taking notes on. "RFD - What exactly goes on here?"

"RFD is Jason's research and design company working in the field of applied computer technology. Programming, solutions research, product modification, software and hardware development. Everything short of robotics. They're going to partner with local schools to improve student-computer interaction, taking it beyond Facebook and gaming and Hulu and introducing them to web development and science business models. That's why the Board of Education was invited tonight."

"Where does the name come from?"

"RFD? It's just based on the way the company logo was drawn. The name is actually Fields Research and Design. But, look, why ask me? You just interviewed Jason."

"Wanted to see how close you were to the project, and to Fields. You seem to know a lot about his business."

He tapped his pencil on the tabletop. Then he leaned back, lacing his fingers behind his neck.

"Had you ever seen this Tyler McCloud before?"

"No. I mean, I've probably seen his face on billboards or on TV or something. I've never seen him in person."

"Did you know Fields knew him? Ever mention him to you?"

"No."

"He never said anything at all about knowing Tyler McCloud, or having had some kind of problem with him?"

"No, he did not."

"Dr. Wilder, how was Mr. Fields acting immediately prior to finding the body? I mean, what was his demeanor?"

Mackenzie stood up to walk around the room, taking her time with her answer, deliberately turnin' her back on the trooper so he wouldn't see her face. What she said now could be so important. Matheson sounded as if he was trying to point the finger right at Jason! She knew if she said the wrong thing, it could sound like she was supporting his theory. She pushed at her temples with both hands, like she was tryin' to feel the thoughts inside her head, when really she was trying to hold herself together.

"His manner? Normal, I'd call it. He was excited about the opening, enthusiastic about giving me the tour. Energetic. His usual self."

"What about during the rest of the tour?"

"The same. Jason was the same as always."

"Dr. Wilder, this next question is important. Did Mr. Fields leave you at any point in the tour? Were you alone at any time after the two of you started the tour of the facility?"

She stared at him. "No. No, Officer Matheson. Jason Fields and I were together the entire time, from start to finish. Can I go now? I think I'd better call Bryan before he gets wind of this through his department, or the news."

Matheson nodded. "Don't leave the premises yet. In fact, it will probably be a while before you can go. If you want to have Jamison here, I don't care, but don't let him step on any toes." He began shuffling his papers together.

Mackenzie turned to go out, not about to use the telephone, or even her cell phone, in the same room with this man who so clearly put his job sense above common sense.

"Dr. Wilder?" Matheson picked up the recorder, checking to make sure it was off. He grabbed the notebook with his other hand and stood up to loom over Mackenzie's five-foot-two-inches. I knew how intimidatin' that must have felt.

"Yes?"

"Where did your tour start? What part of the building?"

"Jason and I met in the main lounge, but I suppose you'd say the tour actually began in his office."

"By main lounge, you mean the large room at the end of this hallway, the entrance area?"

"Yes."

He nodded. "I have down here that you did the top floors of each wing, then moved to the main floor. Is that accurate?"

"Yes. Why?"

He didn't answer. Mackenzie hates that sort of thing. So do I. But then he asked, "What time did your tour start?"

"I think it was about five after nine. Why?"

Matheson sort of shrugged. "Wanted to nail down the time. One of those detail kind of things. Go ahead and call Jamison. We're done for the moment."

Matheson stepped out of the room, the door clicking shut behind him.

Well, if *he* was leaving, Mackenzie was staying. Let him put the distance between him. She just wanted to be alone - to think, to call Bryan, to pull herself together so she could help Jason.

She found the phone near the communication screen and dialed Bryan's home number. Her cell phone was unreliable inside these buildings. As she listened to the phone ring, it occurred to her to wonder not only why, but exactly how Tyler McCloud had gotten into the complex. Not that it was all that important now. The young man was dead. Who cared whether he'd sneaked in an open door or slid in behind a reporter? Still, knowing it could be useful. It was one of those detail kinds of things.

·C·H·A·P·T·E·R· *3*

·T·O·R·Y·

"If only we could see..."

- from "Simple Song" by Tory McCloud and Jason Fields

Mackenzie's Bryan didn't step on any toes, but he did lean on his position as an Albany Homicide Lieutenant and Police Academy instructor to get Matheson to let Mackenzie leave. Only for her to find her beloved grillin' her for himself.

It began on the drive home. He took her back along the River Road, a trip of about eight minutes. Instead of turning left into her driveway, he turned right, into her office parking lot. They pulled 'round back to sit facin' the Hudson River where it runs behind the building. Her boat bobbed at its dock, the butterscotch finish reflecting the halogen docklight.

"Mackenzie, you all right?" Bryan asked.

"I think so. I feel badly for Jason. When I told him we were leaving he was fending off the press. This wasn't the kind of evening he had planned." She kept staring at the boat. Something didn't look right.

"The press probably didn't mind."

"No, I'm sure they liked this story better than what they would have had otherwise. What a way to end his open house!"

"Not too great a way to end a life either. What was Tyler McCloud doing at the open house?"

"I have no idea. Bryan, hang on." She got out of the car and hurried to the dock. Her heels weren't fit for running.

Bryan came after her. "Mackenzie, where are you going?"

"The dock! My boat's out!" She scrambled over the gravel and onto the dock.

"Well, it's not like it's a horse. It'll be all right. You don't want to turn your - ankle," he finished, watching her trip over the boards.

She caught herself and kept moving. She expected to see some kind of damage or signs of vandalism; after all, she hadn't left it here or told anyone they could use it. No tellin' how it might have been mishandled!

She lunged the last few feet on her knees, but for all her hurry, there it was, tied up, prim and proper. As Bryan sauntered up, she stood, rubbing her knee where her hose had torn. There were no scrapes or dings or gouges on the antique wooden boat that was one of her treasures. It was simply moored outside instead of in.

"See? Safe and sound. You must have forgotten you left it out. I can understand it, after all you've been through tonight," said Bryan. He gestured toward the sky. "It doesn't look like rain. It'll be fine. You've left it out before."

Mackenzie couldn't believe what she was hearing. *'All she'd been through'? 'Forgotten'?*

"I haven't left the boats out once since that boathouse was built, Bryan. That boat was secured inside when I left for the evening. Now it's out here."

Bryan was shaking his head, a condescending move so far as Mackenzie was concerned. She pointed at the line holding the boat fast to the pier. "And I don't recognize that rope. It isn't mine."

"Huh?"

"It's not my rope, Bryan. Someone's been messing with my boat. And I don't like it." She picked her way along the floating dock that ended at the boathouse.

"Wait, Mackie, let me."

She let her appreciation of his concern outweigh her irritation at his chauvinism. Plus he was a cop, after all. He brushed by her and came up to the boathouse at an angle. He peered carefully in the window, and motioned her to come closer. Then he took her hand.

"The outer doors are still open," he said. "They look like they're fastened back. That make sense?"

"Well, it would if someone took the boat out. Did someone go joy-riding in my boat tonight?"

"I don't know. Can you tell if it's been taken out?"

"I could check the gas level, but not in these clothes. I can check it in the morning, I guess. I mean, it's here, and it's not damaged any. No harm, I guess." The evening was wearing on Mackenzie, but she wasn't going to come out and say it. Bryan should have been able to tell. It wasn't like her to trip over things or put off something until the next day. He didn't even notice her sighs or that she kept rubbing her hands across her face.

"Wait here," he said. He trod the boathouse's wooden walkway to the side of the building nearest the parking lot, disappearing from view for a minute then returning, shaking his head and continuing past Mackenzie to the other side. "Mackenzie! Come around here."

She followed his command, recognizing urgency in his voice.

"Was this like this before?" He pointed to a large tear in the outer screen that matched a hole in the interior window.

She kept the inside windows shut at night, to keep out damaging pollen and any pollutant-bearing rains that might offend the brilliant glazed decks of her boats. She started shaking her head. "No, Bryan, that was definitely not there."

"Then I'm afraid you've had an actual break-in. Maybe it was just someone joy-riding. Maybe someone so taken with your boat they couldn't hold off anymore."

"You sound awfully complacent about this, Bryan. Someone broke in on my boat! The same damn night Tyler McCloud gets killed at Jason's. God, you don't think they're related, do you?"

"I don't think - " he paused and looked at the window. "I can't see how they could be, but it is odd. Even for a coincidence."

"Look, I need to check the other boat, and I need to get this one under cover. Come on, help me."

"You know I don't like the water."

"Would you rather I do it myself?" she asked, moving to do just that.

"No, of course not. What do I do?"

"I'll get in and use the pole. Hey, it's wet. Just like somebody used it! Do you think they poled the boat out here? But that's weird. Why would they do that?" She was rambling on, half muttering. "Unless they wanted to move it without making noise, so they pushed it out here with the pole. I can't tell if they took it anyplace or just moved it to the dock."

"We'll check the gas tomorrow, and I'll have someone come check for prints, although it's unlikely it'll do any good. Let's get this thing in there."

"Okay. Untie her and hold onto the line. I'll pole it around the boathouse. You walk with me around the side. Okay. Give me enough line to get in front of the door and head in. Right."

Bryan might not have liked boats, but he could follow directions. They tied up the boat, checked the other one, which appeared to have been untouched, and closed the boathouse doors. Since the intruder opened them from the inside, there was no damage on them. Mackenzie keyed the sophisticated lock Jason had had installed for her and headed back to the car.

"You would have been better off with a simple lock-bolt on that thing. It would have stopped anyone without the key." Bryan sounded grumpy, and his words brought them right back to Jason and the night's other disturbing events.

"Assuming they didn't have bolt cutters," said Mackenzie. "If they were serious, they would've used bolt cutters or used the window anyway."

Bryan didn't reply.

Back in the car, he made a move to turn the ignition. He hesitated. "Did you say you knew what McCloud was doing at the open house?"

"No. I said I had no idea. Please let's go up to the house. I'm cold and I'm tired."

Bryan's voice was low, hesitant coming out of the car's darkness. "Are you sure Fields didn't invite him?"

"He said he hadn't heard from him in eight years."

"What was that all about anyway, that business?"

"All I know is that Jason told me Tyler was the reason he didn't write country music any more. I don't have any idea what it meant."

Bryan grunted, stretching. "That doesn't sound good."

"I got that from Matheson, too, but he ought to know better. And so should you."

Bryan shrugged. "You've got to admit it looks bad. Some guy who keeps Fields from pursuing something he enjoys - something that might be profitable, remember - shows up supposedly uninvited and murdered at Fields' open house. Bad coincidence."

"And police don't like coincidences," Mackenzie sing-songed. "Bryan, sometimes a coincidence is just a coincidence. Like this boat thing happening tonight. A coincidence." Mackenzie wasn't even sure she bought her own words. Mostly she wanted to stop talking about it altogether.

But he kept throwing questions at her.

"What time did you and Fields start that tour? Did you say you started from his office or the lobby?"

"Bryan! That is the third time you've asked! Nine-oh-five; his office. Now, can we drop it? Please? A terrible thing has happened, and I'm tired. Trust me, my answers will still be here in the morning."

"Okay, okay." He reached over and took her hand. "You're cold, aren't you? Here, give me your other hand, too." He began chafing them, rubbing them to warm them up.

Mackenzie appreciated that. She told me she wasn't sure if it was from the water or from everything; her hands always seem to get cold when she's under stress. In the moment, it seemed such a sweet thing for Bryan to do. Then he opened his mouth again.

"How bad was it?"

"What do you think? He was strangled! I tried to focus on Jason. He really didn't take it well. He's not used to seeing things like this. Not that I am." She stopped. It was black outside. Too black. Too cold. "Bryan, take me up to the house. Now. Please."

In no time they'd circled round, shot across the road and up the sloping drive to Mackenzie's house. He escorted her inside, and she went upstairs to change into sweats and thick socks. There is something chilling about violent death as opposed to the deaths a doctor sees in the course of her practice. Mackenzie needed warmth. She returned downstairs to a table set with mug and spoon, tea bags and her blue sugar bowl. Bryan brought over the whistling kettle and poured for her.

"Thank you." She dunked two bags into the water, in too much of a hurry to wait for just one to steep. She added in spoonfuls of sugar. Sinful to purists, but she wasn't fond of feeling shock-y.

She sipped at the tea. Earl Grey and Bryan, good for what ailed her any time. Then she addressed the last question he'd asked.

"It wasn't easy. That business on the farm last year...that was skeletons. This was a person who'd just, literally just been murdered. And horribly. I've never seen anything so ugly."

They were at her kitchen table, seated in maple captain's chairs drawn close together. Bryan placed his arm around her, leaning in so that he could look directly into her face. That curling lock of hair that insisted on dropping forward onto his face had done it again. She reached up and tucked it aside.

"You're probably more used to scenes like that than I am. I don't envy Betty having to deal with that kind of mess," she said, referring to the County Medical Examiner. "But what worries me most, Bryan, is the way this looks for Jason. I mean, I know he didn't kill Tyler McCloud but even you're questioning it! And what was Tyler McCloud doing there anyway?"

"That's just it, Mackenzie. If Tyler McCloud had gotten himself killed somewhere else, or even if it were someone else killed on Fields's property, someone he didn't know, this wouldn't look so bad. Not only did Fields know him, he had reason to have a grudge against him. That looks bad to a cop, even a sympathetic one like Matheson."

Now, when Mackenzie told me this, I got caught on those words. "Got himself killed." Words have power. I wouldn't be a songwriter if I didn't believe that. What had my brother done to get himself killed? Did it involve Jason? Wasn't whoever killed Tyler responsible for his own actions? Actually, the answer to that question didn't really matter. I'd make sure they were.

Mackenzie asked Bryan if he was sympathetic to the fix Jason was in.

"I'm not sympathetic to him getting you mixed up in murder again, that's for sure."

"Bryan!"

"Well, if you weren't doing this for him, you wouldn't be caught up in an investigation again, would you?"

"You know why I'm working for him."

"Why?"

"Because I believe in how he treats his employees."

"No, I mean, why you, not some other doctor?"

"Because I'm the only one he knew!" Mackenzie snapped, ignoring that she knew there were personal feelings at work in Jason's selection.

"Look, I'll drop it, okay? I'm just saying that Jason Fields is in a tight spot right now. Some of his troubles might rub off on you. You don't need that following so fast on last spring."

"Maybe, but I can't desert a friend in trouble. Jason didn't kill Tyler McCloud!"

"Maybe," echoed Bryan, "but it isn't up to you to prove it!"

"No, but - " she paused, frustrated, "it isn't up to me to help prove he did do it, either!"

Bryan eyed her. "Don't do it, Mackenzie. This isn't like last time. If you know something, you can't hold it back."

"I wouldn't do that!"

"You would and you did, but it's different this time. This isn't about protecting family memories." He quelled her protest with a look. "This is about protecting you. There is a very real killer out there. Give the State Police any information you have and then stay out of it."

"But Bryan, I have an obligation - "

"You have an obligation to tell the truth. I know you work for him, although I wish you didn't. I get it that you want to stand by your friend - "

"You'd probably rather he wasn't my friend either."

"Hey, I like Fields well enough. He's a talented guy. I was grateful for his help last spring, and I'm even glad he's giving you a job, sort of. I just don't want you mixed up in another murder case. They're dangerous. I should know." Bryan took her mug and spoon and deposited them in the sink. "I can wash up here and let myself out. You go on up to bed. We'll talk about it tomorrow, when you feel better. This has been a tough experience for you."

Mackenzie stared at him. *He really said that.*

"Maybe you could take tomorrow off or something," he urged.

"Bryan, I think it might be a good idea if you left now." The words were clipped, her tone was flat, but he didn't seem to notice that, either.

"Sure, just let me - "

"No. I know what I need to do. I don't need all this fuss tonight. Come on, good night." She walked him to the door. He frowned as he turned away from the closing door, sure something wasn't right, but totally clueless it might be him.

She'd planned to fall asleep right away, but Bryan's behavior had done more than ruffle her feathers. It set her thinking. No one knew better than she what she needed. She needed to see Jason as soon as possible.

Men! Here was Mackenzie, concerned for Jason, wanting justice for the person who was killed, and brave enough to stand up for both of them. All Bryan seemed to think about was how she was his little lady and needed protection. Good for her for standing up to him. Good for her for carin' enough about the men in my life to take up for them.

·C·H·A·P·T·E·R· *4*

·M·A·C·K·E·N·Z·I·E·

"The second one will follow"

- from "Simple Song" by Tory McCloud and Jason Fields

I heard from Jason the next day, but not until I'd seen the newspaper.

MUSICIAN McCLOUD MURDERED.

I groaned, scanning the article for details. It didn't say anything about Jason being a suspect, just named the RFD center as the place the body was found. By us. It didn't mention the ties between him and Tyler, either. It wouldn't be long before some reporter nosed it out.

Here we go again.

I tried to focus on the comics and the Living section for the next half hour, but my brain wasn't cooperating. I went on to work, as I'd told Bryan I would. It was the best medicine under the circumstances.

Jason's call came in around ten-thirty.

"Mackenzie. I wanted to call you. Needn't worry. Do you have - I need Lloyd Kerns's office number. Do you have it?"

"Not handy. Can you get it from Brooke?"

"Brooke?" He sounded disjointed.

"Yes. Brooke. Bryan's sister. Lloyd's wife. You probably still have her number on your computer or Rolodex or something."

"Oh, Brooke. Yes." There was silence.

"Jason?"

"Uh, yes. Mackenzie! Fine, how are you?"

That did it. "Jason, where are you?"

"I'm at my office. Although it's rather lonely here."

"I'm coming over. Stay there. All right? Do you hear me? Stay there. Look in the phone book or online for Lloyd's number, okay? But stay there. Have you eaten today?"

"Of course I have. Well, I think so."

"I'm bringing you food. Stay put, okay?"

"Sure, Mackenzie." He hung up.

I hustled out the door, stopping once at my house to pick up some of my housekeeper's homemade bread, flinging ham and cheese between two thick slices. I grabbed an added bonus: Jean's to-die-for best-in-three-counties buttercream-frosted chocolate cake. Armed with this down-home fare, I hopped in my Subaru and headed for Jason's office.

I sped to the complex, retracing last night's route. Up the River Road to the winding access road that climbed up to RFD. There were more cars on the River Road than in Jason's parking lot, and that wasn't good. Inside was near deserted. Security waved me on, although the State Trooper nearby scrutinized me thoroughly. Riding up in the elevator, I kept bouncing on my heels as if I could make the thing hurry. All I wanted to do was get to Jason and make sure he was all right. The secretary's desk was unoccupied. Where was Bonnie? Was everybody out? I kept on moving down the hallway to Jason's office.

Bump. Jason's office door bounced back toward me in a sickening imitation of last night. I had to make myself peer around the edge of the door. Jason lay stretched out on the floor in nearly the exact same position as the body in the conference room last night.

"Jason?"

He turned his head toward me and rolled over onto his back. Immediately he was on his feet, catching the food as it tried to slip out of my hands

"Jason! You scared me! What are you doing?"

"Well, you see, I rather thought I'd try to figure out what happened last night. So I was sort of re-enacting it. I mean, the way I thought it might have been."

"You took Tyler's place?" I started setting the food out on his desk.

"I wanted to see if that prompted any ideas." He shook his head. "It didn't. Except it made me wonder about why he was in the conference room with his back to the door. Why do you suppose he went in there?"

"Jason, I don't even know why he was *here*!" I pushed him into his leather chair and put the sandwich in his hand. "Do you?"

He put down the sandwich with a sigh. "No. I don't. It's been five years since I saw him."

"Five? I thought you said what, seven or eight years?"

"Well, actually, I suppose it's been more like five. The lawsuit was eight years ago."

"Lawsuit? - Here, eat." I handed him the sandwich again.

He stared at it as if not quite sure what it was.

"Jason. How long have you been here?"

"How long - you know how long. About the same length of time you have: five months."

"No, Jason, I meant today. Here, I'm going to examine you." I pulled a blood pressure cuff out of my bag. After getting his blood pressure and checking his heart and eyes, I repeated my question.

"How long have you been here in the office this morning?"

"Oh, well. All night, actually. Do you know your thermometer tastes horrible? Can't you get flavored ones?"

"Jason! Eat. Now! You're exhausted, and I'm sure your blood sugar is off. If you don't start eating right now, I'll do a finger stick to test it. Now eat!"

"Oh. All right." At last he began eating the sandwich and other food I'd brought. I rustled around in a credenza against the wall opposite his desk and found some Chinese blend tea. Not Earl Grey, but maybe even better.

I watched as he chewed. So closely that he exaggerated a couple mouthfuls to get back at me. His green eyes had lost some of their glitter, and they seemed to have sunk a little. Surely he wore a haunted look, although his pallor was beginning to go away. His movements were smoother, stronger. There was an overall lightening of the tension about the neck and shoulders.

I pushed the cake at him. "Tell me about this history you have with Tyler."

"Um, what?"

"What was the lawsuit about?"

He sat hunched over the plate, his curly hair awry, as if he'd run his fingers through it two times too many. "I told you. Tyler was the reason I quit writing country music. I'd only written a few songs. It was fun. It appealed to my liking for word play, all those puns and metaphors about life. It was just a small part of my life then, but I enjoyed it so much. I considered doing a lot more with it. Can't you just see it now? The cowboy hat?" He paused to stare at the quiet backwater area of the Hudson River out the window behind me. His mind was tracing its own river of time twixt past and future.

"I wonder what I would have written. Ever wonder about things like that? How they might have been? Somebody did a country song about that."

"I've wondered that all too often," I said, remembering the husband I'd lost and the children we'd never had. "What went wrong, Jason?"

"It's a bit of a story. I sort of stumbled into country music through people I knew in Nashville. I met the McClouds one night at a CMA - Country Music Association - function. Friendly Southern people. First thing they did was invite me over for dinner. It became routine, Sunday dinner at the McCloud's. Chicken and ham, biscuits, gravy, macaroni and cheese, okra, peach pie. You know, the kind of meal you think doesn't exist anymore. We'd sit around sipping sweet tea - I need to show you the Southern way to make that, by the way - and telling stories. Dan McCloud, their dad, was a natural storyteller. Tyler and his sister and I would listen to him for hours. One day, I wrote a song based on a story he told us."

"Was he okay with that?"

"Oh, sure. He always said it was fine with him. Dan liked the stuff I wrote." Jason sort of chuffed. "He gave me a nickname. Said I wrote so many puns into my songs I was just full of corn. He started calling me 'Corn Fields'."

His eyes were hazy with remembrance as he slumped down in his desk chair.

"Tyler started writing songs when he was twelve," Jason said. "When I got to know him he was about nineteen. He hadn't written anything notable yet, but you could see the talent in everything he wrote. It was only a matter of time. He was already performing locally. He was going to be a star. Anyway, without knowing it, Tyler and I both wrote songs based on Dan's stories. That shouldn't have been a problem. If I'd realized it, I'd have talked to him, made sure we were okay over it. But, I didn't even know."

"What happened?"

"I'd had those first few tunes published and recorded. The one based on Dan's story was called 'Don't Lock the Door 'til it Stops Swingin'. Tyler had written his a couple years earlier. Then Dan died. We didn't have the same connection anymore, even though..." his voice trailed off.

"Jason?"

"Oh. The song did pretty well. Got recorded a couple of times. I was starting to think I could really enjoy making money this way. I didn't see Tyler so much by then; I was finishing up law school and working on a book and one of my patents. He and Tory were playing and touring a lot, getting started with their band. I saw Tory now and then. Less so Tyler. Then a couple of years after 'Don't Lock the Door 'til it Stops Swingin' came out, I got hit with a lawsuit."

"Tyler?"

"Tyler and his manager. They claimed copyright infringement."

"Copyright infringement? How? It was your song, right?"

"Absolutely. I couldn't understand why Tyler was doing this. Especially now, er - then. We were still sort of close when my song came out. If there'd been any question over copyright, it should have come out then. It was as if suing me had just occurred to him."

"So, how could they sue? What did you do?" I felt like an idiot, rhyming. Maybe it was the subconscious influence of discussing songwriting.

"Well, I decided to go to court to fight it, of course. Law degrees do come in handy. I was hurt. I was angry. I knew I hadn't done anything underhanded. Then, before anything got to court, his manager showed me their evidence."

"Which was?"

"Tyler had written a song when he was seventeen that was remarkably similar to what I'd written. He called it 'Waitin' 'til I'm Good and Gone'. He'd kept his notes and everything. Including some papers that helped date when he'd written it."

"So?"

"So, I could tell from the notes and the date; Tyler had truly written this song before I wrote mine. It was clear it was based on the same story of Dan's that mine was. Dan didn't tell that story too often - not the way he repeated some of them - but I remembered hearing it on at least three different occasions in the few years I knew him."

"But, that doesn't mean anything, does it? Who recorded their song first?"

"Tyler never recorded his, but it was copyrighted, and it pre-dated mine. We'd been close. Even though I was confident I could argue it successfully in court, there would always be people who thought I'd taken advantage of Tyler. It would get really messy, and I didn't want that for people I still considered friends. The whole issue was becoming distasteful. So I conceded."

"You what?"

Jason faced me, his darting green eyes belying a toothy smile below. "How can I explain it? Country music is like family. When people start getting mad and attacking each other, it takes all the fun out of things. I didn't want to make things worse. I had no quarrel with Tyler or Tory, and I wanted them to succeed. Other projects were coming along that I wanted to try my hand at, so I just let go. Problem was, it ruined songwriting for me."

"Did you try to write other songs?'

"Oh, yes. Let me tell you, it was quite a shock the first time I sat down and expected to knock one out. I'd always been rather quick at it, but this time I came up empty. Same thing happened the next time I tried, and the next, until I realized it just wasn't the same. Country music and I didn't travel the same road anymore."

"Wow."

I asked him about the notice in the paper, the one about the concert. "They're saying they're only closing the show down for one night. Isn't that a little extreme, especially for country music people?"

Jason smiled and shook his head, shutting his eyes in amusement. "That's Tory. She always did have a different way of doing things. Say!" His eyes flew open. "Why don't we go to that show? You can bring Bryan!"

"I don't think we'll be showing up there. You probably shouldn't either!"

"Really? Why not?"

"Jason, somehow I don't think Ted Matheson would think it looked right. You know?"

"Oh."

I stood up and started putting up the food things. "As your doctor, I'm telling you to go home and get some rest. Go - "

The phone rang. Jason reached for it.

"Let your secretary get it."

"I gave Bonnie the day off."

"Then I'll get it! Hello? This is his doctor. Mr. Fields is not available right now, he's tired after the open house last night - what? Can you give me any details? I'll pass them on to Mr. - "

He took the phone from my hand.

"This is Jason Fields. Tony, what is it? Slow down. He what? Is he - oh no. How terrible! Have you contacted his family? Okay, well, when you reach someone, let me know. Tell them I'll call, too. Thank you for letting me know." He hung up the phone, staring into space.

"Jason?"

"He told you?"

"Some of it. One of your test drivers. Killed in on-track testing, right?"

Jason nodded. "Yes. J.D. came to me for a job a couple years back. Talented mechanic and interested in getting into driving. I never mentioned my race car, did I?"

"You might have. You own one, right?"

"A team, really. It's a partnership; eight of us got together and bought shares. We use one of my testing facilities, though, and I hold the majority of stock." He sat back in his chair, staring at the desk blotter, fiddling with its alignment to his desk. "Mackenzie."

"Yes?"

The phone rang again, and this time Jason reached for it automatically.

"Yes? Oh. Hello. Yes, that's correct. Yes, you heard correctly. Oh. All right. I'll expect to hear from you then. Right. Good-bye." He hung up slowly, sinking back in his chair.

"What is it?"

"That was Matheson. He wanted to make sure he got..." he sighed and fell silent.

"Jason? What?"

He licked his lips. "You see, J.D. came to me for a job because he knew me from some old associations. He was into country music, too. Fact is, I picked up NASCAR the same time I picked up country music. They really do go together, you know. He'd been fired from his job, and he knew we had similar interests, so he came to me. I hired him." He paused, tapping his desk with a pencil. "And now he's dead. There will be a track investigation, of course. That second call was Matheson telling me he'd heard, and that he'd be requesting a report from them."

"What on earth? Why?"

"J.D. was one of Tyler's roadies. That was the job he was fired from before he came to me. Quite the coincidence, isn't it?"

·C·H·A·P·T·E·R· 5

·M·A·C·K·E·N·Z·I·E·

"You have to ask the question: where have we come and how?"

- from "The End's in the Beginning" by Tyler McCloud

Thursday, I checked in with Andrea and ran the gauntlet of allergy shots and questions from my Seniors group. This time the focus was on when the waiting room was going to be re-done. After that brief encounter, I headed back out to RFD.

Jason was missing from his office. I tried calling his condo, but there was no answer. Not even his machine.

His secretary wasn't worried. She had instructions for me. Jason wanted baseline physicals on all his employees. With a new facility of this size, the task promised to be huge and time-consuming. However, Bonnie helped me schedule sessions that would streamline the whole process - at least so long as I stayed on top of things. With her blessing I arranged for a part-time LPN to help me with the exams and subsequent documentation. We made a pretty good dent in the list of names we had, with plans to continue the next week.

I left around eleven and raced back to the office in time to catch Andrea rearranging her hair into a precariously balanced topknot.

"Isn't that the third hairdo this week?"

"Umm, maybe. It might be the fourth. You didn't see how I had it last night. Hey, I just got a call. Dave Simpson is coming in with his broken leg."

"I told him there was nothing I could do until they took the cast off. I told him to follow Fortescue's instructions."

"He said his leg really itches and that he wants you to see if there is a way you can work out for him to scratch inside the cast." She grinned at me.

"I don't suppose he could figure out something for himself."

"I think he's got a thing for you, Doc," Andrea said.

I groaned. "What else is there?"

"Couple soccer players coming in for their physicals. Coach Green said he wasn't going to bring the team in all at once. Some of them got physicals last spring and don't need another one yet."

"I'd rather see them. Maybe I should give the coach a call."

Andrea nodded. "He said you could call him. Then there's the cheerleaders."

"Cheerleaders?"

"Oh, yes," she said, her pencil poised over her list. "Cheerleaders are athletes, too, and the high school is sending over the whole squad for physicals before Empire State Cheerleading Camp next week. Ms. Wygant said she wanted her squad in competition condition."

"They compete?"

"Sure! Missy Schoonbeck has a cousin who choreographed her squad's whole routine, and they took first at regionals last year. It's big stuff!"

"If you say so." I heard a car pull into a space outside the window. "Looks like we're starting up."

Things passed quickly. My soccer players were early, and all three were in great condition. I sent them out with a warning not to land on their heads. Andrea and I snatched sandwiches from the back just as the cheerleaders burst into the waiting room, bubbling over about some flip they'd mastered. They wanted to come in together. Felt there was safety in numbers, I guess. They were all abominably healthy. I overheard one of them refer to Caitlin Cooper as captain of the junior cheering squad. It seemed so odd to think of my friend's daughter being old enough to cheer at football and basketball games. An hour and a half later they left with as much noise as they'd arrived.

"Watch where you're goin'!" Dave Simpson snapped at them as he maneuvered his walker through the door. He claimed crutches felt like he'd fall down any minute and that they hurt his armpits. His cast, pristine, snowy white, ran from open toe to mid-thigh. A man whose preference for the shortened version of his name seemed at odds with his demeanor, Dave was sixty-seven. He was a mild-appearing retired insurance man turned tour boat captain whose first tour had resulted in an angry vacationer shoving him off the dock. It had happened near the launch ramp where the water was too shallow to break his fall, so he'd broken his leg instead. Now his Kings Hill Hudson River Day Boat Tours and Fishing Expeditions was in dry dock until its captain's leg fracture healed. Frustration did not rest well on Captain Dave. Although the behavior it generated did lend credence to his preferred nickname.

"Don't try to help me, young lady!" he snapped again as Andrea reached for his elbow. I understood why his driver always chose to wait in the car. "Dr. Wilder, you need to help me. This itching is driving me crazy."

"Come on in, Mr. Simpson. Let me see what I can do. Here, can you get up here? Try lying down."

With him settled on the table, I could get a better idea if there was a way to reach this itch he complained of. The skin was clean and a healthy color. It seemed a little dry and abraded, not surprising considering its exposure to the plaster and open air. I put on gloves and pulled out a moisturizing lotion.

"Don't put too much of that on me. I'll smell like one of those body perfume shops in the mall! And it doesn't do anything for the itch either. It itches *here*!" He reached past my arm to thump his leg below the knee. "Ow!"

"I could have warned you that would hurt. Relax, Mr. Simpson, please. Lie back. Let's get this on the leg, then I'll see what else we can do."

"Dammit, that stuff is cold, too. And now you've got it drippin' down my leg. Doc, this is a mess!"

I gave up on the lotion, several uncomplimentary words flowing through my brain in Mr. Simpson's direction. *How can I get him out of here?*

While I pondered the problem, my patient busied himself with studying the examining room.

"Maude Davenport tells me you're going to spruce things up in here, Dr. Wilder."

"We're redoing the waiting room."

"Might want to give some thought to doing some work in here, too. This room is drab-looking."

I let him run on without comment while I searched for an appropriate device to fix his itch.

Fix his wagon is more like it!

Prowling into the back of my office closet, I found something I could use.

"What's that?"

"Your new leg scratcher."

"Looks like a bent coat hanger."

"Not far off. Actually it was a fork for toasting marshmallows. I untwisted it to make it longer." I rustled around my desk drawer for pliers.

"Why'd you undo it?"

"So I could reach under things better. Helps me reach high stuff, too."

"What can you reach with that thing?"

"Papers, mostly, when they slip behind shelves." I struggled with the pliers and the former fork to curl the ends under. "I can scoot stuff forward so I can take it down, too."

"You're not very tall, are you? Is that thing clean?"

"Yes, it is, Mr. Simpson. Now, see? I've hooked each tip under so you won't scratch your skin too hard. Slide it along inside your cast like this."

Simpson frowned as I started to pass the heavy gauge wire through the space between his leg and cast. Then he flinched and started twisting about, emitting a high-pitched squeak each time he thrashed from one side to the other. He was laughing!

"Mr. Simpson? Are you all right?"

Some devil in me made me keep tweaking the 'scratcher'. I grinned at him.

"Hee. Hee. Hee," he squeaked. "Yes, dammit! Give me that thing!" He grabbed it from my hand much more gingerly than I had and began to move it about. There were a few more wiggles and squeaks, then he found the spot.

"Aah," he sighed, a blissful expression coming over his face.

While he finished giving things a thorough scratch, I finished paperwork. I heard him touch down on the floor with his good leg. He reached for his walker, clutching the wire like an overgrown riding crop.

"Thank you, Dr. Wilder, for your time. I knew I could rely on you." He began his trek toward the waiting room.

"Glad to be of help, Mr. Simpson."

"Well, you shouldn't see me back here until after Fortescue's taken this thing off. Come by the boat sometime and I'll give you a discount on a day trip. Heck, you can have one for free. And, call me Dave, why don't you?"

He shuffled out the door and across the waiting room. "Good day, young lady," he told Andrea with a wink.

She stared at him, then me.

"Hey, I just solved his itching problem, that's all."

"Wow. It's like he had a personality transplant! I think that's it for today, unless something else comes up."

Which, of course, it did, almost immediately.

"Doctor Wilder? I need to see you."

Ted Matheson spoke to me across Andrea's desk. He stood tall in front of my short, seated nurse, who raised eyes and eyebrows as she craned her neck to see his face.

"Dr. Wilder is still in office hours, Mr. - er, Trooper," Andrea floundered.

"Matheson, ma'am. Ted Matheson. If you'll excuse me, ma'am, I don't see anyone here in your waiting room. Anyone in your office, Doc?"

"It's all right, Andrea, really. I know you'll tell me if any patients come by. And I assure you, Ted will step aside to let me see them."

"Absolutely, ma'am!"

He held his hat in his hands like a small boy, and his quick response softened Andrea's expression. "All right, then, Trooper Matheson. You may see Dr. Wilder."

I caught the twinkle in her eye and turned away before I could laugh.

"What's with all the 'ma'am's out there, Ted? You sounded like you were up before the school principal."

He set his hat on my desk and took a chair, casting a glance over his shoulder in the direction of the waiting room.

"Ted?"

"Sorry, Mackenzie. Guess I'm a little distracted. It's been a long week."

"I know. Has there been any more news?"

"We haven't gotten much more than you already know about. We're still waiting on a complete report from the racetrack." He hesitated. Then he pulled a sheet of paper from his pocket, standard copy paper folded over a couple times. "I'd like your opinion on this."

"You're asking for my help? I'm flattered, if a bit confused."

"You know I think you're intelligent, Mackenzie. I'd like you to look at something and tell me what you think. Then I'll tell you what I think." He handed me the paper. "This is a copy of a paper that was in Tyler McCloud's blazer pocket the night he died. No one knows about it except my team. I haven't even told Bryan about it yet. I'll be talking to him later today, and I'll tell him then."

I unfolded the page and flattened it on my desk. "Looks like a form?"

He nodded and gestured toward the paper. "The original actually is a duplicate form, first page white, second page yellow. I couldn't bring that with me, but if necessary I can let you see the original. You can see there's a heading with a logo on it."

"What is that? A club or something?"

"It seems to be."

"And this is - what? A press release?" I was looking at the style of the fax-like form. The words "For Immediate Release" followed by a date led my thinking that way. I'd never seen a form like this, but I had seen a few press releases over the years.

Ted settled back in his chair. "Read it, Doc. Carefully."

I did, wondering what he was expecting me to find.

FOR IMMEDIATE RELEASE: September 4, 2008

This month marks the 8th anniversary of the liftoff to fame for Tyler McCloud. It was eight years ago that he succeeded in laying claim to the popular country song "Don't Lock the Door 'til it Stops Swingin'", a legal victory that drew attention to the fledgling artist. With a high court's affirmation that the song was indeed legally his, a widening spotlight brought attention to his talent. Tyler was picked up by Roundhouse Records, which parlayed into a smashing career with Epic after his third hit, "Caterwaulin' Cate".

The dispute over "Don't Lock the Door...." was with Jason Fields who originally published the song under his own name. Tyler brought suit against Fields with the counsel of his attorney/promoter Peter Himes who pointed out the substantial similarities between the lyrics to Fields' "Don't Lock the Door...." and an unpublished song of McCloud's written when he was seventeen, "Waitin' 'til I'm Good and Gone Before You Close the Door". Despite high-powered attorneys, and amid disclaimers of never having copied McCloud's song, Fields staged a last-minute capitulation and acknowledged legitimacy of Tyler's claim. More important than any monetary award was the public avowal that Tyler McCloud had the talent necessary to make a hit. Jason Fields disappeared from the country music scene, a temporary talent who'd committed an unforgivable sin.

Today, Tyler McCloud is a country music star - our most favorite star - and Jason Fields is famous in his own right as writer, inventor, and entrepreneur. Would Mr. Fields want to be reminded of his past transgression? Probably not; especially if the public were to learn.....

I frowned at the page. "It's a little hard to tell anything, this being a photocopy. I know, you couldn't bring the original. I'm just saying the copying process flattens some things out. Like this for instance. See where these quote marks were added? And these capital letters? Were they done in a different color?"

"Yeah. Red pen."

"I thought so. The copy looks like it's in grayscale, and that makes it show up differently than if it had actually been in black and white. I wasn't sure, though." I bit my lip in concentration.

"That could actually be significant in this case."

"Oh?"

"We think this might have been a rough draft, Mackenzie. It's postdated for one thing - "

"A lot of press releases are." I put in, "This one's written on the form though. Kind of unusual for a rough draft."

"True, most of them are issued as fresh copy, not with handwritten corrections. It looks like someone decided to make some changes."

"Mhmm. It does. I don't see how that means any - Oh!" *That looks odd.*

"What is it?" He leaned forward.

"Well, I can't tell for sure, but it looks like these two changes were made with a different pen, or maybe pencil? See where they inserted the word 'public'? and then there's this 't' over here." I leaned across the desk, pushing the paper ahead of me. "The writing is chunkier, fuzzier, as if done in pencil. Don't you think?"

"Those two changes *were* done in pencil, and they're the only ones that were." He stopped there, his eyes watching me, never wavering.

I looked back at the paper. He seemed to be awaiting my verdict. I studied each correction in depth, seeing if it would have made a substantial difference if it had stood uncorrected. Nothing to be said for the commas, or the spelling or capitalization changes. But the insertion of that word, 'public'. If you left it out, what did you have?

'Probably not; especially if the were to learn....' That didn't make any sense. Probably someone had just left - wait, I was forgetting something. Ted said that the other change was also made in pencil. So the same person probably made both changes, and they go together. Someone had inserted the 't' in the word 'the' before public. You almost couldn't see it, but again, the letter had the fuzzy look of graphite. So, if the changes were taken out, the sentence would read 'Probably not; especially if he were to learn....'

"Ted!"

"Yes?"

"Did you read this? I mean, did you read this without those changes?"

"Which ones?"

"These! These two here, the penciled ones."

"Read it out loud to me."

"Wait, I'll back up a sentence. 'Would Mr. Fields want to be reminded of his past transgression? Probably not; especially if he were to learn....' Ted, that not only makes sense, it turns the implications of the sentence completely on its head!"

Ted leaned back in his chair in apparent satisfaction. "That's what I thought. Read without those penciled changes, it's definitely less damaging to Fields. Not only that, it makes it sound like there was something big to be known that might displease *Jason*, not something he was worried would displease the public. It's still possible that whatever this is talking about could have made Jason murderously mad, but I'm convinced someone made those changes after the fact in order to change the whole tenor of this release."

"Maybe it's information someone else didn't want released because it would make Jason mad at him. So the Press Release was altered so no one would know. But why would Tyler have this with him? Unless, unless he was taking it with him to *show* Jason." I was getting excited. This opened up all kinds of alternatives.

Ted was holding up his hand again in that annoying way of his. "Hold on. He could have been showing it to Jason in order to threaten him, too. This isn't clear-cut yet, Mackenzie."

"You said 'yet'."

"Well. Yeah. I did. I agree this was altered. I think the red pen editing is just standard stuff. I think this other was done in pencil so it wouldn't stand out. And if - *if* we are right about Jason's innocence, I think it was left behind on purpose in an attempt to implicate him in the murder."

I slapped my hands against the desk. "'We', you said 'we', you *do* believe Jason's innocent!"

He shook his head in defeat. I'd caught him again. "I give up. Yes, based on what I know about Jason Fields, and the timetable, as well as my interpretation of this evidence, I'd have to say it wasn't him."

"Well, then!"

"But we're not telling anyone that. Not even Jason."

"What! You can't do that. If you don't think he's guilty, you can't hold him."

"True. And we're not holding him, remember? We've told him to stay in town is all. So far as he and the public are to know, we do suspect him. It's for his protection. And so is this. You, and Bryan, and Jason (when we tell him) cannot talk to anyone about this press release. It does not exist. Same as you cannot tell anyone what the weapon was."

"That's easy; I don't really know what that wire was," I told him, shuddering just a little.

"You didn't recognize it?" he asked.

"Recognize it? Should I have?" I squeaked.

"Maybe not. It was a guitar string. An E-string, to be specific. Either Tyler had it on him, or the murderer carried it in. If he carried it in, it probably wasn't Jason. There's no good reason for him to be carrying one around, and if he were planning to kill Tyler, it's an unlikely weapon, excepting the possibility he was trying to throw us off. It's not likely Tyler was carrying it, because how would Jason have gotten it off him and gotten behind him to use it?"

"So, you don't know," I said, rubbing chills from my arms.

"No, same as we don't know if Tyler walked in there with the press release in his pocket, or if it was planted there. Those are details we probably won't know until this case is solved."

I thought for a few moments. "Does Jason know about the guitar string?"

Ted shook his head. "Not unless he recognized it for what it was, or actually is the one who killed Tyler. We don't want to give him or anyone else too many details. We're playing this pretty fine as it is, trying to protect him from himself. If someone has tried to set him up as a murderer, they don't like him very much. They may change their minds and try to kill him, too. We want everyone, even Jason, to think he's still under suspicion."

This was not going to be easy. I don't normally hide things from people, especially people I care about, and especially if I have information that will alleviate their distress. I understood the logic of what Ted was saying, about protecting Jason, and Lord knew I didn't want him killed. It just wasn't going to be easy.

"Ted, I appreciate you taking me into your confidence."

He stood. "I'll be telling Bryan all this when I talk to him, too."

"Good. I still wonder why, though." I raised my eyebrows.

He turned his hat over in his hands. "Bryan's a good cop, but this isn't in his jurisdiction, same as last year, so I can't officially ask for him to participate in the investigation. And I have to admit, I don't think you're involved in this, and generally you have a level head. I need someone who can keep an eye on things, and maybe pick up some background information that I wouldn't get by questioning. I think that between the two of you, you can do that. Bryan is the professional. I can count on him to run the investigative part the right way. We don't want to alert anyone to our suspicions or put anyone in danger. Or turn up things we can't use in court," he added sternly. "You're closer to the whole situation. You're friends with Fields, and he might confide in you."

"But if he's not actually under suspicion? That means there's nothing for him to confide."

"Not necessarily. He still may have background information that will be helpful. Information that might, if it came out in some public way or through regular questioning, seem threatening to our real murderer. That's why we are keeping this as quiet as we can. You might pick up on something just being around him, something he doesn't even see himself. In which case, I want to hear about it right away. You and Bryan both report directly to me." He paused and straightened the band on his hat. "Which brings me to my other point."

Andrea approached the door to my office, finger pointing to her watch. It was time to close up.

"What is it, Ted?"

"Look, I know I can trust Bryan. He's a cop. But you're a civilian, and civilians, especially you, Doc, don't think like cops. You can't tell anybody, and I mean *anybody* anything about this investigation. I don't care how innocent you think Jason is, or how strongly you feel about transparency, you can't discuss this with anyone. No one can know you're helping me. No one - "

He caught sight of Andrea. "No one. Oh, all right. If she's heard this much, I guess it's too late where she's concerned. But you can't tell anyone anything either, ma'am."

Andrea stomped into my office, eyes narrowed, voice stern. "What do you mean, talking to Dr. Wilder that way? She's a professional. Do you really think she doesn't understand confidentiality? Or professionalism? Of course she understands. If she's helping the police, of *course* she knows not to tell anyone. And I always, *always* follow her instructions. *Her* instructions. Dr. Wilder, I don't need to know anything about what this might be, and I certainly won't tell anyone what I do know, if that's what *you* say."

She folded her arms and planted her feet. "Trooper Matheson, you should be ashamed of yourself! Dr. Wilder would never dream of betraying a confidence. If you told her not to say anything about something, she wouldn't say something about anything, no matter if somebody did something to her like - like - well, like anything! I know you've worked with her before, so you know all about her, and you should know what kind of person she is, and after all she did last year, you of all people should know that she wouldn't do anything wrong!"

Her vehemence threatened to topple her hairdo. Matheson looked down at her in bemusement. I was ready to take offense for her, when he broke into a type of grin I'd never seen on him before.

"You're certainly loyal, Miss - uh Ms. - "

"Kinney, Andrea Kinney. Yes, I am loyal. I have reason to be. Dr. Wilder is one of the finest doctors, one of the finest people I know. Why I - "

"Please, Ms. Kinney. I surrender to your superior knowledge of Dr. Wilder. Really, Mackenzie, I'm sorry if I was out of line, but as Miss Kinney says, you do know the importance of discretion. In my profession, leaks can lose a case faster than water running through a bucket with a hole in it. I know I can trust you, but you've also got to be vigilant about what you talk about and who to. And now you too, Ms. Kinney. I'll take it at face value that if Dr. Wilder hired you, you must be good at what you do. Now I need to be able to depend on you for discretion as well. Nothing about my visits here - not even that I stopped in - can be talked about. Is that clear?"

"You'll see how clear that is." Andrea turned to me, but her attention never really left handsome Trooper Ted Matheson. "Dr.

Wilder, I was getting ready to close up, but I noticed that we have some of Ms. Hesford's cake left in the back. Would it be all right if we split it?" She eyed Ted. "Amongst the three of us?"

"Is that Jean Hesford's chocolate cake you're referring to?"

"You bet. Let me take that and you follow me." She reached for his hat and, holding it hostage, led him to our tiny backroom kitchen.

I closed up my desk, confused by the ending to the conversation, and concerned myself over how well I could follow Ted's instructions. This kind of discretion was never my strong suit. Ted was right, I didn't think like a cop.

I followed them out to the kitchen, and the three of us finished off Jean's cake. Then I trailed them back to the waiting room to show Ted out. He was holding the door for Andrea when my phone rang.

"Let it ring, Doc," Andrea warned.

"No, I think I know who it is. You go on." I grabbed the phone at Andrea's desk. "Brooke, I am so glad it's you! .... I know, we never get to talk. It's like there's never time."

I sank down into Andrea's chair. I needed a good long talk with Bryan's twin. I didn't have to be as discreet with her as with some others. I stuck my tongue out at the door Ted Matheson had closed behind himself and Andrea.

Brooke went right to her point. "What's this I hear about you and Bryan working together to clear Jason? Or rather, you wanting him to?"

"What? Who told you that?" I sat straight up. *I swear, Ted, I didn't tell Brooklynne anything!* Excuses were already playing in my head. *Wait a minute, I really didn't tell her anything yet anyway. So, okay, I won't.*

"Bryan, of course. He's not exactly thrilled with the idea. It kind of worries him that you were there when the body was found. Then you were so insistent on the two of you standing up for Jason. Kind of have to wonder about how close you are to him."

So that's what this was about.

"Why do you and Bryan always suspect my feelings for Jason? He's my friend, nothing more."

"I know he's your friend, but the two of you got close last spring. He helped you and Bryan catch Lamberson. I know you're grateful. But you know he's always been interested in you, and now this incident. It's the kind of thing that brings people close. Are you sure he knows he's just a friend?"

"He knows it. It's Bryan that doesn't seem to know it." I grumbled. "Look, if Jason hadn't been there last year, Bryan and I and who knows who else wouldn't be here now. You and I surely wouldn't be having this conversation. I think a certain closeness is understandable. Bryan doesn't know how to be grateful."

"Bryan doesn't like competition."

"Hmph. We'll see."

"That doesn't sound promising."

"Sorry. Look, I know I said it would be great to talk, but I've got to run."

"Sure. Sure. We'll talk soon."

We would. It wouldn't be about Jason, thanks to Ted. But it wouldn't be about Bryan, either. She might be his twin, but there was a limit to how much loyalty I could face. Bryan was not right in his attitude about some things. I wasn't going to back down in this. He needed to respect me and my judgment, and above all he needed to trust me. As did Ted.

I growled in aggravation and left.

·C·H·A·P·T·E·R· 6

·T·O·R·Y·

"If you become a part of me,"
- from "The End's in the Beginning" by Tyler McCloud

Having thought it over a couple days, Mackenzie finally decided going to the concert might be a good idea. She didn't think Jason should go; she would. It turned out Bryan was eager to go with her. In fact, he tugged on a couple of city strings to get floor tickets to our sold-out show.

Country music is one of those things Mackenzie is not too sure about. She'd always thought of it as twangy bluegrass or rockabilly so close to crossing over that it didn't matter. She has no use for vine-swinging guitar players on a regular basis. Well, neither do I. That's not country music, that's just showmanship, or maybe show-offmanship.

She does like songs that tell a story or use wordplay. As she told me later, kind of red-faced, she is not usually fond of female country artists at all. Too sexy and too innocent-actin' all at once she said. Now I ask you, is that a bad thing?

But, there she was, talking with Bryan, and him hummin' a tune she'd heard from the commercials for my concert. Probably my latest hit, that's usually what they run with concert promos.

"I didn't know you knew her music," she said to him.

"Oh, sure. I have a couple country CDs in the car. One's hers."

"You always seemed more like classical and jazz to me."

"Then it's time for me to take you out line dancing." He pulled her over to him and twirled her around.

"Hey! I don't line dance."

"Rachel can teach you some beginning steps. You'll get it. Then we can go out. There's a great place in Sand Lake, just like an old road house."

He hadn't ever offered to take her out dancing before. She'd assumed it was his job keeping him busy. Now she realized they hadn't been frequenting his type of place.

"I don't want to impose on Rachel. We don't know when we'll get a chance to go - um, dancing. So don't worry her over it, okay?"

He shrugged, but she could tell he was disappointed. She moved on.

"Do you suppose we should try to see Tory backstage tonight? I mean, are you going to question her or anything?"

"Mackie, you know this isn't my jurisdiction. Matheson's already talked with her at least once. She might not understand or appreciate someone else talking with her."

"She wouldn't know you weren't an investigating officer."

"You know that's not how it works. I wouldn't question anyone under false pretense. Ted asked for our *unofficial* help, not for me to butt in."

"That's not what I intended. I want to see what she thinks about who might have wanted Tyler dead. We know Jason didn't do it."

"Do we? I know, I know, you and Ted do. Maybe I do, too, but lawsuits have prompted murder before. Besides, I understand she's a very emotional person. If she's feeling anger at Jason or anyone for Tyler's death, it'll show. We should just observe tonight. Relax and enjoy the concert."

She thought about this for a minute. She let herself nod, as if in agreement, but a stubborn part of her held out for trying to talk to me.

Bryan wrapped his arms around her again. "I'm going to be glad to get you out for once. Even if you're doing this for Jason, at least he won't be around. You'll be with me."

The Pepsi Arena, located in the middle of Albany's South End, was packed. I could tell that from backstage, and Mackenzie was caught in the mess out front.

The venue had been called the Knickerbocker Arena for some years, until the 'other cola' bought the rights to name it. Parking was a bear, despite satellite lots. Mackenzie said she always thought the arena looked like a spaceship cramming itself into a landing space amongst older, traditional architecture. Capacity was around fifteen thousand and tonight the Pepsi Arena hit it. Seats were full, concessions crowded, and music lovers milled about the concourse.

Country music lovers. I could hear them from backstage. The best kind of fan, enthusiastic but courteous, ready with a rebel yell, a 'yes ma'am', and a tip of the hat.

Mackenzie was surprised at how popular country music was here in upstate New York, but I told her country music fans are everywhere, even in New York City. There's something about the mix of down-home music and country ideals that ties itself to the American vision and appeals to people all over.

The stage was set up at one end of the arena. Seats on the floor around it were mostly reserved for pass-holders, contest-winners, and friends. Bryan's tickets paid off, and they used his badge to get down close to the edge of the stage. As they pressed by some young men and women who were clearly my roadies (black jackets with white letters identifying them as McCloud's Maniacs), a curly head of brown hair rose above theirs. *Oops.*

Bryan glanced down at Mackenzie.

"He wasn't supposed to be here!" she protested. "I told him not to come."

As they moved up alongside him, Bryan spoke from the side of his mouth, not looking directly at him.

"I might've expected you'd get in here, Fields. I'm surprised they're going on with this." He nodded toward the stage.

"You know the old adage, Jamison." Jason grinned in response to Bryan's hostile manner. He turned back towards the stage, gazing at it with an intensity that intrigued Mackenzie.

"Yeah, I know," said Bryan. "Still, I thought country music people were supposed to have more heart."

"Just watch," said Jason, sounding mysterious. He seemed to know something the others did not. Well, sure. Me.

I had come out on stage. It was the hardest thing I'd ever done. Tyler and I were only a year apart. He was the brother I adored, and he was not only gone, but someone had taken him out. I didn't know whether I was more angry or more broken-hearted. I knew one thing, this was gonna be for him. I had to sing for him. I had to speak to the fans he loved who loved him.

I came forward, mic in hand, head bent, trying to gather my strength. Jason said later that I looked like an essence of myself, the image of what he'd always known I'd become. Coppery feathers of my hair catching the brilliance off the lights. Barely five feet tall. 'No bigger'n a minute', Daddy used to say. I was wearing a white and blue embroidered satin shirt that Tyler always liked over black leggings and shiny black cowboy boots. I spoke to Tommy, my lead guitarist, telling him what I had in mind to do. He nodded and fiddled with tuning keys, then conferred with the drummer. I headed to the apron of the stage. The tears were coming, and they slowed me down. My lips were trembling, too.

"Ladies and gentlemen, country music fans, tonight I want to pay tribute to my brother, Tyler McCloud. He loved to sing. He especially loved to sing for all of you, his fans. The songs he wrote were for you all, about the lives we live, the things we see, the events we live and love our way through. I love my brother deeply. I can't think of any better way to honor him than to come onstage and sing his songs."

I waited for the applause to subside, scanning the audience like usual. That's when I saw him. The shock made me drop my head again. I knew what I had to do. I raised my hand to signal Tommy.

"Just a minute." I waited for their full attention. "Tyler started writing songs when we were teenagers. Some of them weren't real good, but they always had heart. Sometimes he'd listen to our daddy tell stories, and those stories would wind up in his songs. It helped him figure out things he was too young to understand. One song like that was one he never published, 'Waitin' 'til I'm Good and Gone.' Even though it was never recorded, that song helped make Tyler famous."

I sneaked a look at Jason. He was frowning, his arms folded tightly across his chest. There was a woman next to him who seemed to have noticed I was watching them. That was Mackenzie, and even though I hadn't met her yet, from the scowl on her face, I could tell she was worried about what was going to happen.

Ty, I thought, *I'm doin' this for you, baby.*

"Another version of that song *was* recorded, and it created a legal stir, because it was written by another man. All the fuss brought Tyler's name into the public eye, and people started listening close to what he was writin' and singin'. In a way, even though he didn't write it, that was the song that started it all for Tyler. I'd like to sing it."

I ducked my head down like I always do at the start of a song, and the band started playing the tune, a sort of mid-range, old-school rockabilly type tune. Then I lifted my face to meet the mic and belted out the song I remembered so well. For a pint-sized sort of person, I pack a lot of wallop, if I do say so myself.

> You've gone and sent me packin'
> Don't you worry none, I'll leave.
> But if you want me back in,
> Darlin', you're gonna grieve.
>
> Don't lock the door 'til it stops swingin'
> Or it'll stick ajar.

Sweet Corn, Fields, Forever

You don't know when I might sneak in,
Like some stranger from afar.
If you really want me long gone,
This time I'm gonna stay.
Don't lock the door 'til it stops swingin',
No more games we're gonna play.

You've told me you don't want me -
Not to come around again.
That's the same thing you done told me
When this first happened way back when.

But then you let me back in;
Tho' you swore you never would.
This time I swear I'm leavin',
And it'll be for good.

Don't lock the door 'til it stops swingin'
Or it'll stick ajar.
You don't know when I might sneak in,
Like some stranger from afar.
If you really want me long gone,
This time I'm gonna stay.
Don't lock the door 'til it stops swingin',
No more games we're gonna play.

'Cause I can't take this any more -
I love you more than my own good.
If you can't close up that dang door,
Guess I'll be in the neighborhood.

I repeated the chorus an extra time, walking over to the side of the stage as I crooned that last note.

"Jason. Jason Fields, come on over here. Boys, swing that light over here."

A spotlight out of nowhere illuminated them. Jason's eyes glittered, a smile not quite settling on his lips.

"Ladies and gentlemen, this is Jason Fields. Jason wrote 'Don't Lock the Door.' Wrote it about two years after Tyler wrote his song. Made a little money off it, too, 'fore he graciously honored Tyler's claim."

I smiled at Jason like I might at a child. I didn't want to scare him, really. I spoke directly to him. "Don't worry none, I know you made it up to us. Now, folks, there's been some talk goin' 'round, because Ty - " I choked over his name, but I kept going. "Tyler was found at Jason's company the other night."

I could read the shock on Mackenzie's face plain as day in the spill of the stagelights. She went white and shook her head as if to make sense of my saying those words in this place.

Jason stared back at me, but he looked more interested than alarmed. Good.

The guy beside Jason's woman friend frowned at me and put his hand to his hip as if to pull something from his pocket.

"There's been a lot of talk goin' 'round, but I want to put a stop to it. We're just going to settle this right now." I looked straight at Jason and fired it off. "You didn't kill my brother, now did you, hon?"

A quick downstroke of my hand and the spotlight on Jason blacked out. I relaxed and swung into one of the foot-stompers our band is so famous for. I raised my fist in the air, same way Tyler would have if he'd been here. The amps throbbed and the sound erupted around us as the audience applauded and whistled.

This is for you, Ty. Ty, I'm so sorry. But you know, I can't let people think Jason killed you. Whatever may have happened, it wasn't that. And we'll find out who did it. I love you, Ty.

I stole a glance at Jason. My words had the desired effect. Bystanders were slapping him on the back. My fans knew me, knew my straight-shootin' way. If Tory McCloud said Jason Fields didn't kill her brother, then it must be so. Jason had my entire fan-base on his side. Let the police deal with that!

·C·H·A·P·T·E·R· 7

·M·A·C·K·E·N·Z·I·E·

"and I stay at your side."

- from "The End's in the Beginning" by Tyler McCloud

I didn't believe it. I didn't understand it, and I didn't believe it. Bryan wasted no time getting us backstage. He flashed his ID at one roadie as another moved in to pump Jason's hand. We slipped behind the curtains. Everything was black at first, except for the diamond brightness of the stage lights. A young woman in black wearing a headset with the mouthpiece turned up motioned for us to follow. We trailed down a labyrinth of dimly lit curtained corridors. The black rubberized flooring gave way to concrete, then tile, then carpet as we entered the civilized part of the Pepsi Arena's backstage. A gray door with a blue star stood open. Below the star was stuck a card with Tory's name hand-printed on it.

Concert tours mean fleeting fame where dressing rooms are concerned.

"Tory said for you to wait here," said our guide.

"Thank you," said Jason, flashing his toothy grin, receiving a shy smile in return.

Bryan glanced about the room then turned to face Jason.

"Why are you here, Fields?"

"Tory asked me, actually," Jason straddled a metal chair then leaned back against the gray wall. Light reflected off the black marble tile countertop covered with post-makeup litter. One of the bulbs around the mirror was out. An overhead speaker broadcast sound from on stage. Tory was still singing.

"Did you know what she was going to do?" I asked, my tone bordering on accusing.

"No." He grinned. "Wasn't she great?"

"She was great, Fields, but I don't know what Matheson will make of it," Bryan warned.

"I do. He'll think Jason came here on purpose and found some way to make Tory say that."

Bryan's narrowed his eyes. "What could Jason use to make her say anything?"

"Jason, you tell him."

"I think Mackenzie is referring to the fact that I knew Tory at the same time as I knew Tyler. However, it wouldn't necessarily follow that I could use that to manipulate her. Or is that the way police minds work nowadays?"

A youngish-looking man appeared in the doorway. He was stocky, with dark hair styled so carefully you wondered if it moved even when he combed it. He wore a black suit with a perfect fit and red piping on the lapels. A red handkerchief peeked primly from his pocket.

"You folks all right in here? You waiting on Tory?"

I nodded, assuming Jason would clarify, but Jason wasn't saying anything. His arms dangled loosely down the back of the chair. His right foot twitched, as if it wanted to stand him up, but he wasn't letting it. His eyes were on the man in the doorway, his expression one of the dead.

"Mr. Himes. Still with Tory, I see."

The man stepped into the dressing room. He offered his hand to Bryan, not quite looking at Jason. "I'm Peter Himes. Nice to meet you. You all know Tory?" He gestured at Jason with a nod of his head. "Jason does, of course. I'm her manager." He looked hard at Jason. "And friend. How are you, Fields?"

"These are friends of mine. We came here tonight to see Tory, and she invited us to come backstage. We're waiting for her." He didn't actually introduce anyone.

His story wasn't exactly accurate, either. Bryan brought us back here. Unless - I regarded my friend. *Had* Tory issued such an invitation?

Not to be outclassed, Himes glossed over any impoliteness. "I'm glad her friends are being supportive. She's not in need, of course. I make sure of that, but it's nice for us to know you all are there for her." His voice dropped, deep, confidential. "I told her it wasn't necessary for her to go on tonight. I don't think it's good for her. The kids had a tough schedule this tour as it is. Now this. I'm afraid it's going to be more than she can take."

I contradicted him. "She seemed all right on stage. She even gave Jason a vote of confidence; told everyone there was no way he could have killed Tyler."

"She did that?"

"Yes, she did. Very generous under the circumstances," Bryan added.

"That's my Tory, generous to a fault. Not - " he turned to Jason, "that you don't deserve the vote of confidence. We know you wouldn't have killed Ty. Not now."

He paused to light a cigarette. "I told the police that, too, Jason. Despite the lawsuit, you never held a grudge."

"Against Tyler, no," Jason said, his eyes glittering.

"Mr. Himes, I'm Lieutenant Bryan Jamison of Albany's Homicide Division." Bryan forestalled Peter's response with an upraised hand. "I'm not working this case, but Jason and Mackenzie are friends of mine. Mackenzie was with Jason when he found the body. I wonder if you'd tell us some of what you told the State police. If you're comfortable with that. If not, I can request a transcript of the deposition."

Peter drew on his cigarette and cocked an ear towards the ceiling. Tory had slipped into an old country ballad.

"She's got two more numbers after this one." Peter spoke abruptly. "I can give you about five minutes. What do you want to know?"

Jason settled back against the wall. He looked relaxed. Only his head, set at an angle and very, very still betrayed how intent he was on what was being said.

I watched in silence, knowing better than to interfere with Bryan's work. There was no rule against my observing. In fact, both Ted and Bryan would want me to do exactly that.

Bryan spoke. "What exactly did you tell the police, Mr. Himes?"

"I told them Jason couldn't have done it, of course. He and Tyler were old friends. Jason do something like that to Ty? Ridiculous!"

"The body was found in his company building."

"Doesn't matter." Peter waved the thought aside. "Jason wouldn't have done it."

"What about that copyright business?"

"Oh, that." His expression made it seem that the memory was painful. "That was just business. Right, Jason? It's long over with. If he were going to do something about it, like killing Tyler, he'd have done it then. Right?"

"If I were that sort of person. Actually, Himes, if I were that sort of person, I'd have killed you." Jason said, a glittery grin pretending to belie his words.

"Hey, I was just tending to Tyler's interests. That was my job. Like now; I look out for Tory."

It wasn't just Himes's cigarette smoke that hung thick in the air. My eyes started playing ping pong between Himes's face and Jason's.

"Do you know of anyone who might want Tyler McCloud dead?" asked Bryan. "As his manager, it seems you ought to have a good idea of who his contacts and enemies were."

"No one wanted Tyler dead. The kid was a nice guy, easy-going, talented. Not that there weren't conflicts. You don't get to be a Tyler McCloud without steppin' on some toes, but no one would seriously want to kill Tyler."

"Someone did," said Bryan.

"Well, yeah. Probably some roadie or something who got pissed off. Those guys are unreliable. We usually fire about ten a year. You all should check them out."

"Funny you should mention roadies, Mr. Himes. A former roadie of Tyler's was killed this week, too. Same day as McCloud, in fact." Bryan informed him.

"Really? It wasn't murder too, was it?"

"Probably not, but the track officials are investigating."

"Track officials?" asked Himes, tapping ashes off his cigarette. "I thought you said he was a roadie."

"Was. As in used to be. He switched. He was working on a race track, testing cars."

Jason cleared his throat, but Bryan ignored the warning.

"Actually, Jason, have you heard back anything yet about Lazenbee's death?" Bryan caught Himes looking at Jason in confusion. "J.D. Lazenbee, a former roadie for your people, was killed testing a racecar at a track belonging to Jason."

"He worked for you?" Himes asked. "Sounds like you've got some bad shit building around you this time, Fields."

Once again Jason ignored Himes and answered Bryan's original question. "No one's gotten back to me yet, Jamison."

Himes glanced at his watch. "Some coincidence, two people getting killed at two places you run. Doesn't look good, now does it?"

Bryan intervened with another question. "Did Tyler have any habits - gambling, drugs, alcohol?"

Himes shook his head at each one. "Nothing like that. He was as clean-cut as they come in this business. Ask Tory. She was mad at him last week for getting on her about some party we'd gone to. Something about the 'appearance of evil' I think he said. Tory got really hot about that one.

"Not that she would've done anything. It wasn't like that. There never were two closer kids. Peas in a pod. No. I meant how moral Tyler was. I can't think of anyone who'd want him dead. He didn't have contact with 'bad guys', you know? Unless there were record pirates involved, or something like that. Jason, you don't know any record pirates who might have had it in for Tyler, do you?"

Jason closed and opened his eyes one time. "No" was all he said, but his opinion of Himes for asking the question was clear.

Himes shrugged. "Might have been a deranged fan. Even country music has a few of those."

There was a thunderclap of applause from the speaker before it cut out.

"Concert's done. Sorry I can't tell you more." Himes stubbed out his cigarette.

Bryan nodded, but he asked one more question anyway.

"Do you have any idea why Tyler McCloud was at the RFD complex Wednesday night?"

Himes was almost out the door. He paused with his right hand on the doorjamb. "No, no, I haven't a clue as to why Tyler was out there. Unless it was to see Jason. Excuse me." he slapped the jamb with his hand and disappeared down the corridor.

I hugged Bryan. "Thank you. I know you didn't really want to get into this tonight."

"Yes, thank you, Jamison. I can't say I mind seeing Mr. Peter Himes uncomfortable. Although I could have done without the reference to J.D. It's none of Peter Himes's business."

"You don't like the guy, do you?" Bryan actually smiled at him. Then his smile faded. "You know, if I were Matheson listening to some of what that guy said I wouldn't be any less suspicious of you."

"Bryan!"

"He's right, Mackenzie. Himes has a real way with words. There's no love lost between us, Bryan. I'm sure he feels enormous satisfaction at my rather uncomfortable situation."

"How'd you piss the guy off?"

"I've never really understood. All I know is he really enjoyed coming after me when Tyler sued me. I've loathed the man ever since."

A commotion in the hallway.

Tory burst through the door full tilt.

"Jason!" she cried, and flew across the room to throw herself into his arms like a long-lost child come home.

I gaped at them, but then Peter came back into the room. The expression on his face when he saw Tory McCloud in Jason's arms made it plain. There was at least one reason Peter Himes disliked Jason Fields.

·C·H·A·P·T·E·R· 8

·T·O·R·Y·

"- stories, lies, and misconceptions - "

- from "The End's in the Beginning" by Tyler McCloud

F or the first few days after the concert, no one knew where Jason was. Well, almost no one.

It had been five years, after all. You couldn't expect us to meet up and then separate again right away.

I didn't pay much attention to the others in the dressing room after my concert. I caught their names, and I know we made some small talk, but I was so glad to see Jason again, it all sort of floated by me. After that we left for Jason's, and we hadn't gone anywhere since.

We kind of worried the people at his office. I mean, his cell phone was on, but he was screening all his calls. Only his most private secretary could reach us - well, him. That Ms. Greenwood has a healthy respect for privacy.

Finally, after watchin' the same number appear on the caller ID three days in a row, I took matters into my own hands.

Half past ten Wednesday morning, I called Mackenzie's office. I put on my sweetest voice and began, "Is this Doctor Mackenzie Wilder, the Dr. Mackenzie Wilder who's a friend to Jason Fields?"

"Yes."

She managed to make that one syllable say how busy and professional she was. Or maybe my nerves made me read more into it.

"Dr. Wilder, I'm Tory McCloud. We met the other night?" I turned on my honey-coated Southern politeness.

"Yes, of course, Ms. McCloud. How can I help you?"

"I wanted to thank you again for your kindness about my brother Tyler. Jason told me you were eager to help Tyler when you and Jason... found him. It means a lot to me that you tried."

"Ms. McCloud, of course I tried. I'm only sorry we were too late. I'm sorry anyone wanted to kill your brother at all."

"Thank you, ma'am." *Oops. There I go with those auto-ma'ams. That was always getting me in trouble with Northerners. Was she mad?*

"Um, Ms. McCloud - "

"Call me Tory, please."

"Okay then, Tory. Is there anything else I can do for you?"

"I don't know if anyone has told you, but - " I felt myself holdin' my breath over this one, which is not easy to do if you're tryin' to hold a conversation at the time. I rushed my next words. "I'm staying here in Kings Hill for a while, with Jason."

She spoke slowly, as if considerin' this from all the angles. "I think it will probably be good for both of you. I understand from Jason that you were friends with him in Nashville, same as Tyler."

"Well, not exactly the same as Tyler." I stifled a giggle, then paused. *Tyler.* "Dr. Wilder, may I ask you something?"

"Sure."

"How - how close are you to Jason Fields?"

"Well," she said, drawing the word out as long as I had. "I'm working for him as his company physician. Shortly after we met last spring, I helped him pick out the site for his RFD complex. He also helped save my life last spring. We're friends, close friends, I think."

"Oh." Maybe this was going to be trickier than I thought.

"Actually, Tory, we're close enough friends that it keeps my boyfriend on edge. He was the other man Saturday night? Lieutenant Bryan Jamison." Her voice was warmer now, and I thought I caught a teasing tone in it.

"You mean that tall handsome blond man? Looks a little like Roy Rogers? I liked him! You all engaged or something? You make a lovely couple!" I felt lighter already.

"No, no we're not engaged." There was another pause. "What about you and Jason? He never told me about you before, but you two seem awfully close."

Now I can recognize someone seizing an opportunity to snoop quick as they can seize it. You get good at that when you've got rag reporters trying to get the dirt on you to stir things up. In this case, I didn't mind. It might even work for me.

"It's wonderful to see Jason. It's been a long time. I can't tell you how glad I am to be here. We were real close once. Dr. Wilder?"

"Please, Tory, call me Mackenzie."

"Thank you. It's just, Jason and I were so close once that - Mackenzie, can you come up here and see me? I don't mean today necessarily, but could you get away sometime? Or, I could come there? I really want to talk to you about Jason and me."

"Tell you what. Have you ever been out on a wooden boat?"

"No. Why?"

"If you like, you can come by the office here this afternoon, and I'll take you out on the river in one of my antique boats. We can talk. Would that work?"

Now, I'm always up to try something new, and this sounded like fun. *Antique boat, huh? I bet that would be just as private as I needed.*

"What time should I show up?"

"Come by around three-thirty. I'll be close to done then. Jason can tell you how to get here."

"Thanks, Mackenzie." I hoped this would help us become friends. My mama always said that one good way to develop a friendship was to let someone do something for you.

Neither of us knew what we were in for.

I got there around two-forty-five. Drivin' around here was new to me, and I never like to be late, even if it's because I got lost. I walked into Mackenzie's office to find a feud abrewin'. Leastways it seemed that way.

A young woman, maybe twenty-five, sat at the reception desk looking through a catalogue, a pen stuck in her 1980's big hairstyle. An older man and woman stood in front of her desk, pointin' to different things in the catalogue. They were arguing with another man sitting in front of the desk. Two women about my age were talkin' in a corner seat. One of them looked deathly pale, but I knew that look from my Aunt Kitty who had seven children. This lady was pregnant.

Mackenzie was leaning over the shoulder of the receptionist, makin' comments on the things she pointed out. She glanced up when I closed the door.

"Tory. Glad you found me. But - you're early. I have a couple more exams to give."

"That's all right. I don't mind waitin'."

"Is that Tory McCloud, the country singer?" exclaimed the old woman. She wore a visor atop her head, and her arms looked athletic, even at her age.

"Who's that?" asked her companion.

"Merton Carr!" exclaimed the woman. "Don't you recognize a talented country singer when you see one? She's pretty, too. Hi, honey, I'm Maude Davenport. You are a wonderful performer, and I am so sorry about your brother. Are you here to ask Mackenzie to find the person who killed him?"

"Maude!" Merton and Mackenzie made a chorus of it.

I smiled at Maude and gave her a good old-fashioned respectful Southern hug.

"Ma'am, if Mackenzie - Dr. Wilder - can help me find out who killed my brother, I will be eternally grateful. Maybe I'll even do a little concert for you all when she does."

"Um, Tory, I can't - " Mackenzie looked real uncomfortable. "I don't solve crimes. Not even as a hobby."

"Nonsense," said Maude. "You've got that nice Lieutenant Jamison at your disposal, and everyone in Kings Hill knows how you turned history around when you found the man who murdered your father and Jake Terry. Why, people didn't even know they'd been murdered, let alone who was responsible, until you started poking around in things."

"Maude, that was just something that happened. I didn't want my father to be blamed for something he didn't do. Uncovering all that other stuff was completely accidental. I'm a doctor, not an investigator!"

"Mackenzie, I get it. I did think we could talk about my brother and all, but really, I'm here to get to know you a little better. And - and to talk about Jason." I met her eyes shyly. I didn't know what her reaction to that might be. To my surprise, she was grinning.

"I'll be happy to talk about Jason."

I felt myself blush.

The man who'd been looking over the catalogue with them pawed at Maude's hand.

"Now look, look here, that's what I meant. We need a comfortable couch or two in here. When my leg's actin' up, I need to be able to stretch it out and rest it. And that red is real spiffy! Don't you think so, Miss?" he turned his face with its wrinkles and age spots and careworn lines towards me in an appeal for support.

"Well, I always have liked red. What all are you doin'? Picking out furniture for the waiting room?" I glanced at Mackenzie who rolled her eyes ceilingward, shut them once and smiled.

I liked that she didn't say a word against them.

"Excuse me while I see my last patient, won't you?" Mackenzie beckoned in the direction of the corner, and the two young women rose together and came towards us. They smiled at me, friendly-like, as they followed Mackenzie into the back.

I hunkered down for a closer look at the catalogue. The receptionist, whose nametag read Andrea, pushed it toward me.

"These are our Seniors, Ms. McCloud," she said. "It's a special group of older folks - "

Maude hmphed.

" - who come in every week for their check-ups and shots and stuff. Since they're here so much, I asked them to help pick out the new furniture Doc is getting."

"You mean she's getting new furniture because we kept complaining about it, and so you're making us help!" Maude corrected.

Andrea grinned. "Right as always, Ms. Davenport."

I looked at the catalogue. "I do like the red couch, but it seems a mite big for in here. Here's a smaller style. It doesn't come in red, but there's a cheerful-lookin' green stripe. And there's armchairs in a matching solid green."

Maude peered at it. "Nice pattern. And a durable fabric."

"There's even a coordinating set of wing chairs, and a solid color sofa. We need two sofas," Andrea explained, "because some prefer a soft-cushioned sofa, while others like a firmer one."

"Looks like you picked us a good one," cackled the old man. Merton just looked on and nodded.

Maude was eyeing me with speculation. Somehow I just knew what was comin'.

"So, you announced the other night that you didn't think Jason Fields killed your brother. Right?"

"Yes, ma'am. That is what I said."

"Did you mean it?"

"Yes, ma'am. I did. Jason Fields could no more have killed my brother than - than Dr. Wilder there could turn down a new patient comin' in here with a broke leg!"

"You say that with a lot of confidence for not knowing our Doc," Andrea chimed in. "You're right, of course. Dr. Wilder never turns down anyone!"

Miss Maude continued to assure me. "Dr. Wilder is one very intelligent woman. Not only is she a wonderful doctor, but very little gets by her. I wasn't kidding when I talked about her finding your brother's killer. She's smart, she's got a boyfriend in Homicide, and she's very, very lucky."

"Thank you, ma'am, I'll remember that."

Merton leaned past Maude to say, "You are the politest young woman I have ever met."

"All that Southern raising," said the old man with the chronic leg trouble. "My name's Charlie Osterhout. I watched Mackenzie grow up in the Methodist Church down Main Street here. Head Usher for forty years, 'til my leg started acting up. It's gotten a lot better since Mackenzie's been treating it."

"How do you do, Mr. Osterhout. It's nice to hear such good things about Mackenzie, um - Dr. Wilder. Makes me feel I can count on bein' friends with her."

"You can that, and you can count on her skills as a doctor, too." The two women had returned. The one I thought was pregnant looked far more relaxed than when she went in. The other one was smiling.

Andrea ceremoniously clapped the catalogue shut. "All right, everyone! Doc's hours are over, and while I know how exciting it is for you to meet Ms. McCloud, it is time to close up. You'll have to get to know her another time."

"Just a minute, Ms. McCloud, Tory McCloud? Tyler McCloud's sister?"

"Yes, ma'am." It was the pregnant lady again. She no longer looked relaxed. But she did look familiar. Where could I possibly know her from?

"It was your brother's fault! It was all his fault!" She came at me stiff-limbed, and shouting.

I backed up, holding out my hands, not sure what to do. I looked to Mackenzie for help. I didn't want to fight with a pregnant woman, or a sick woman, or whatever. Now she was directly in front of me, towering over me and ranting, spitting a little with her words.

"Tyler McCloud! The famous Tyler McCloud! My brother worshiped him! You probably don't even know, but my brother worked for yours two years ago. Tyler became his pal, his buddy! They went everywhere together. The letters we used to get, the postcards! Braeden thought Tyler McCloud hung the moon."

"Braeden. Braeden. Braeden Snyder? I remember him sort of. Didn't he work with our manager? I didn't realize he and Tyler buddied around a whole lot. I know he was learnin' a little guitar from Tyler, but what happened?"

"You mean you don't even know? I guess Tyler didn't think it was important enough to share." The woman's face was getting red, and her breath was coming short.

Mackenzie looked alarmed and came up behind her. Her friend spoke.

"Naomi. Calm down. So she doesn't know. Getting upset isn't good for you or the baby."

So I was right on that score, but it didn't mean much.

"Look, I'm sorry if somethin' bad happened, but I don't know what you're talking about. I can't imagine Tyler havin' a part in somethin' so awful it makes you this upset."

"You can't? You can't imagine that your brother would get someone so hooked on gambling that they lost everything and then killed themselves?"

The screech of her voice echoed across the room, and everything sort of hung there, then started to swirl.

·C·H·A·P·T·E·R· *9*

·T·O·R·Y·

"The truth might have its root in lies."
- from "The End's in the Beginning" by Tyler McCloud

My knees buckled, but I caught myself on the back of Maude's chair. In a minute, Andrea was at my side, checking my pulse and my eyes while Mackenzie's hand was on Naomi's arm, tugging her towards the examination room.

Maude stood up and shooed the men out of the room. "Andrea, I'll call if we've forgotten anything. Come along, Merton. Lend a hand here."

Naomi's friend remained with us. She twisted her hands and kept glancing back after Naomi.

"Hey. Look, I'm sorry Naomi came at you like that. She's never gotten over her brother's death."

"I know how she feels, okay?"

"I - of course you do. I'm sorry. It's just, Naomi's my sister-in-law. It was her, her dad, and Braeden when they were growing up out in New Mexico. She was so excited when he started working for you and Tyler. Then when Braeden started gambling, Naomi started worrying. Their dad had a gambling problem, see, and it looked like Braeden would, too. He did. He lost everything, and when he had more debt than he could pay, he killed himself."

"And you say he worked for us?"

Naomi's sister-in-law registered surprise.

"Like you said, he worked for your manager. Braeden was an accountant, with dreams of being a songwriter. That's why he was so happy Tyler befriended him. I've got to ask, you're part of the group, you're Tyler's sister, why don't you know about this?"

The light-headedness came back for a minute. I was embarrassed to admit there were things about our operations I didn't know.

"Our manager takes care of a lot of these things. He reported mostly to Tyler. Close as we were, Tyler and I didn't always hang out together. I never did like gambling, so I never went with him. I sort of recollect Braeden, but we didn't talk much. Peter must have hired him. Peter Himes, our manager."

She nodded. "Naomi mentioned a Mr. Himes contacting her about Braeden. She said he was very friendly and helpful. He even found some insurance policy you kept on Braeden that covered the gambling debts and the cost of the funeral."

"Yeah, Peter's like that. He always looks after the details, making sure everyone is taken care of. Look, I'm sorry about your sister-in-law. I hope she's okay. I heard you mention a baby?"

She nodded. "Naomi will be all right, eventually. This is her fifth. I'm Sandy, by the way, Sandy Fletcher. Naomi is married to my brother Bob Cooper. Once I explain to her, I'm sure she'll under - "

"Don't make promises you can't keep, Sandy." Naomi had returned, Mackenzie trailing her watchfully. "It'll be a cold day in hell before I forgive Tyler McCloud and what he did to my family!"

"Naomi," cautioned Mackenzie.

"Naomi, Tory says she didn't even know Braeden or anything about the gambling."

"Of course she says that. Why should I believe her?"

I stood up. "Naomi, Ms. Cooper," I corrected hastily. "There is no reason you should trust me right now. And, truthfully, there is no reason I should trust you either. You've said some pretty damning things 'bout my brother. I need to think about this some, and ask some people some questions. If Tyler was at all responsible for your brother's actions, I sincerely apologize. I can only guess he didn't expect what happened. Tyler never, ever, purposely hurt anyone in his life."

Naomi stared at me, her mouth twitching. Then she pushed past me, towards the door, Sandy in her wake. Naomi paused before the door, turning back to face me.

"I'll accept your apology, for now. But, if your brother never purposely hurt anyone, then why did someone kill him?"

I sat back down as the she and Sandy left the building.

"Oh, wow," said Andrea, her voice as soft as the air let out of a balloon.

Mackenzie sat beside me. "Tory, are you sure you're all right? We don't need to go out on the boat today. We can talk right here, or go over to my house. It's right across the street."

"No. I'm all right. Fact is, I could use the fresh air. I've never even seen an antique boat, a classic boat? Isn't that what you called it?"

"Yes, it is. If you're sure, I'd love to take you out. Andrea will lock up, right?"

"Sure, Doc. I'll lock up; I always lock up."

"Andrea!"

"Just kidding. You two go ahead. It'll be good for both of you after all that." She waved us away.

Mackenzie took a minute to change and then led us through a small kitchenette and out a back door. The Hudson River flowed by on the other side of a narrow parking lot. The lot turned to grass, and then a boardwalk took over, angling out to a floating dock and boathouse. I'd been on plenty of boats before, on Old Hickory Lake back home in Tennessee, and at Lake Mead out near Vegas. But I'd never been on a river before, and surely not in some little old wooden boat.

"Tory, wait here, I'll bring the boat around. Okay?"

"Sure." I faced the breeze blowing in off the water, letting it boost my spirits and blow away all the awful things Naomi said. How did this all happen? One day Tyler and I are coming into town to do a concert, me hoping I can meet up with Jason again, and a few days later Tyler is dead, Jason's a suspect, and some stranger is accusing Tyler of making her brother commit suicide!

I never did like it when things happened too fast. I liked to think about things more, move a little slow. Tyler was the one who liked the fast lane, liked to make things happen and have the glitz and glamor. Only thing I ever wanted to happen fast was for Jason Fields to fall in love with me. For good. Which brought me to the little 'fessin' up I was gonna have to do on this boat ride.

Mackenzie was done knocking around the boathouse. Now I heard the slow, throaty swish of a boat sliding through the water. Sure enough, here she came, pole in hand.

The boat was long, maybe twenty-one feet. The seating compartment was completely open, with a three-quarter wooden seat fore and a full-width one aft. The engine was housed in a wooden box that occupied a central position behind the front seat. A shelf-like board attached to the back of it made a sort of jump seat. All I could see up front was a steering wheel, none of those fancy gauges and read-outs that crowd the dashboards of modern boats.

Mackenzie sidled it up to the dock and grabbed one of the dock cleats to hold it steady. I took the pole from her and laid it along the topside of the deck, then stepped down into the boat. She grinned at me.

"You've done this before!"

"Not with a boat like this one. It's gorgeous! This wood is as nice as the wood on my guitar. What is it?"

"Mahogany, mostly. Chrome trim. A Volvo engine. Leather seats - your favorite red."

I ran my hand along the deck, fascinated by the finish that seemed to be an inch thick, looking like butterscotch poured on and turned solid in place. The boat rocked with the river's waves, rocked a little more as Mackenzie pushed it off the dock. She took ahold of the steering wheel and flipped the starter switch. The engine didn't so much roar as it popped; large, explosive pops that came faster and faster until there was a rhythm and a continuous flow of noise as the engine got fully underway and became a proper source of propulsion.

Mackenzie stood at the wheel, not as short as me but still too short to comfortably sit and steer. She pulled the throttle back for a more even gas flow, and we moved out just fast enough to keep control over the current and determine our own direction. We moved away from the dock, away from shore, around the side of the boathouse, and out into the open river. She aligned the boat parallel to the shore, and opened the throttle. The engine roared and we shot forward, the hull lifting slightly, wind and spray shooting over the windscreen and misting our hair and faces. Mackenzie's hair blew all over in tangling curls, and I could feel mine flying out in tendrils and wisps. Keep this up and it would look more like straws and sticks, but I didn't care. It felt wonderful!

For a long time we didn't say anything. We were motoring upstream, and that made the water flowing by do double time. I watched as branches drifted by, and small pollutants like fast food containers and random plastic auto parts. Once I thought I saw a fish break the water, and a small flock of seagulls formed a flotilla to our right.

I closed my eyes, and it made me feel the way I did sometimes when I went to the Ryman Auditorium where the Grand Ole Opry began. The vintage, old-timey feel of the boat was just like the Ryman. How many years had each of them seen? How many people had sat here, sat there, workin' out the ways of their lives? How much of each one's soul had seeped into the wood of this hull or the wood of the pews at the Ryman? I felt connected to these people. None-the-less connected for what was happening in my life. The stark thought recaptured my brain, and I knew I was ready to talk to Mackenzie. I motioned to her to slow down and let the engine run quiet.

"You ready?"

"Thanks, I think I am."

"I'm sorry about Naomi. We just confirmed her pregnancy today, and it seems to be taking a lot out of her at this stage. It really hit her hard when Braeden died, and I don't think she's past it yet."

"It's okay. I mean, I feel the same about Tyler. Whoever took him out don't know who they're dealin' with. I aim to make 'em pay."

"So, you really are convinced Jason had nothing to do with it?"

I smiled. "Jason Fields would never hurt anyone, and he surely wouldn't have hurt Tyler."

"So they were that close?"

"No, *we* were that close. Are that close." I smiled.

"Uh-huh. So that hug was for real, huh?" She looked at me real hard, like a symptom she was trying to diagnose. "Are you sure this isn't just a reaction to not having seen him in so long and liking him so much?"

"Well, that certainly has somethin' to do with it! Look, Mackenzie - Doctor Wilder, I thought you were on Jason's side!"

"I am, Tory, but I want to be absolutely certain about how you feel. Jason is my friend, and I know he's innocent. I don't know anything about the years in Nashville except what you and he tell me, and I don't want to find out that maybe because he didn't stay in Nashville with you, maybe you don't trust him as far as you think you do, and that maybe, after the shine has worn off this reunion, you'll decide he could have murdered Tyler after all!"

·C·H·A·P·T·E·R· 10

·T·O·R·Y·

"Life is all based on perception."
- from "the End's in the Beginning" by Tyler McCloud

H ow dare you! How dare you!" I'd have jumped to my feet, but the boat threw me back. I grabbed ahold of the edge of the engine compartment and leaned forward. "You know what a good man Jason Fields is! You know how creative and talented he is. Did you know most of his patents are for inventions to help disabled children? Look at the way he set up his new computer business, workin' with the schools. He's a good man, worth lovin' in the worst way!" I started shaking and mixing up my words.

Mackenzie twisted around to look at me, keeping one hand on the throttle.

"I have spent the last eight years waitin' for the right moment to come back to him, to get him to come back to me! Jason was the reason we booked the arena. Peter thought it was his idea, but it was me who pushed for the gig."

A wave rocked the boat, pushing me back into my seat. "I just had to see Jason, I love him so much. I had to see him."

"Apparently Tyler had a similar idea. Did you know about that?"

"No. I had no idea he was going to see Jason." I grabbed at the side of the boat as another wave rolled by. "I thought this was a small river. I mean, I like your boat and all, but..."

Mackenzie looked amused. "Bryan isn't fond of the water either. I haven't gotten him out in this thing yet. Or Jason for that matter. I'd like to show what she can do. Although my Hacker Craft is faster. And more sleek."

"How many boats do you have?" I asked, looking around at the stark interior of the boat. I liked it, but I couldn't imagine having more than one.

"Only two. I've been thinking of getting a couple more, different than these. I 'd love to locate another barrelback like the one I lost last spring."

"Barrelback?"

"A 1941 Chris Craft barrelback. Newer than this Smith launch, and much, much faster."

"How old is the launch?"

"It was built in 1910," she said with evident pride. "That's why I was so upset the other night when we found it outside the boathouse - oh! I haven't told you. No reason I should have, really, but I feel like we've known each other longer than we have."

"Mackenzie, what are you rattlin' on 'bout?"

"Sorry. The night Ty - the night your brother was killed, someone broke into my boathouse and took this boat out and tied it up to the dock. Outside."

"Why would they do that?"

"I don't know. I thought maybe someone had taken it for a joyride and then left it out, but there wasn't any gas used up. They just left it outside."

"Huh." An idea floated by me, not much different from the leaves floatin' by on the river. "Could it have anything to do with Tyler's death? I mean, could there be some kind of criminals runnin' around Kings Hill? - Or, could the murderer have used it?"

Mackenzie frowned and shook her head. "Bryan and I talked about that, but we didn't come up with anything that put Jason's complex and my boathouse together in any kind of crime ring. But now that you say that...." her voice trailed off. "I don't know."

"Maybe that Bryan of yours should look into it".

"I'm sure he will." Her reply was a little stiff.

"I reckon this means you've been thinkin' about it. Workin' on it, like Miss Maude said."

"Oh, no you don't. I'll help support Jason. I know he didn't do it. But I can't help find the person who did it. I'm a doctor, not a detective."

"I'm sure you can't help havin' ideas about what the police turn up."

Mackenzie grimaced. "That's what usually gets me in trouble."

"We have to help clear Jason. You want to! You said as much."

She sighed, looking out at the river over the windscreen. "Come on."

She pushed on the throttle and steered further out into the river. Then she pushed the throttle as far forward as it could go. The boat rattled a little, plowing upstream and thumping on waves. I knew fiberglass boats could take this kind of beating; I'd watched them plenty of times. Could a wooden boat?

Mackenzie eased the throttle back a hair and maneuvered the boat around so it didn't bounce on the waves. Still, we kept going forward, and there was no way to talk. The wind still felt good, but I was no longer so sure about this little 'chat' we were havin'. I didn't know if she could help, and here I'd trusted her with the details of my own personal love story. Dang, why didn't I just keep my words in my songs! Peter would have a fit if he found out I'd poured out my soul to a stranger.

"Never let a stranger know too much about you. They'll find some way to hold it over you," he said. "You need to share a confidence, bring it to me. Or put it in a song, where people can wonder about it but never know for sure if it's real."

Peter had looked out for Ty and me for years. That was one reason he didn't like Jason. After that whole songwritin' thing, he didn't trust him. He meant well. Everybody has their blind spots.

Mackenzie was slowin' down. We were approaching an island, a breast-shaped hump of an island covered with scrub oak and pine. She ignored that and gestured toward the shore.

"Look up there, Tory. That's Jason's RFD complex."

She didn't say it, but the words were there. That was where Tyler died.

"Funny. It's like I think there ought to be a sign, or a giant red stain, something to tell the world my brother died there."

"I know. Whenever someone we love dies, especially if it's violent, we think the world should pay attention. And they should. I've had a rethink, Tory. I don't know if I can help, but I'll try. What about Braeden?"

"What?"

"Tell me what you know about Braeden."

"Well, it's - it's like I told Naomi in there. Braeden was around, but mostly he hung out with Tyler. I saw him when they were going out someplace, or when he came in to talk to Peter. *He* couldn't have anything to do with Tyler's death. Unless - you can't mean Naomi!"

"No. It would kill me if I did. She's married to a good friend of mine. No, I was just trying to make connections. If you didn't know much about Braeden, what about J.D.?"

"Who?"

"J.D. Lazenbee. The test driver out at Jason's track that was killed. The one who was a roadie for you and Tyler."

"Oh! J.D." I tried to keep the guilt off my face. I knew J.D. all right. Too well. I shrugged. "He was mostly muscle. He liked my Dad a lot. He used to hang out with Tyler and me, and I think he knew Jason back when we were all together." I studied the front of Jason's building, still closed, seeming almost abandoned when it was supposed to be bustling over with nerds and geeks and techies and high school kids messin' with the latest software.

"Tory."

"Hmm?"

"What else about J.D.?" Mackenzie was watching me.

"What else about J.D.?" I stalled.

"What else is there about J.D. that you can tell me? What else was going on back then?"

I stared at her. "How did - ? You are good! Okay. I didn't want to tell you this, but J.D.used to bother me, pesterin' me for dates and such. He didn't exactly give me the creeps, but he didn't like hearin' the word 'no'. Jason warned him away from me, and Peter would never even leave me in the same room alone with him. Tyler figured I could take care of myself, but I needed the extra back-up Jason and Peter gave me. How did you know that?"

"Did I mention I was a psychiatric social worker before I became a doctor? I don't miss much. One other thing. You said Peter stood up for you, too. He doesn't like Jason. Are you - or were you - dating him? In a relationship?"

I squirmed. Then I waggled my hand at her. "You know how it is. Sometimes things are just - convenient. Peter is always around, and he's a handy escort. We're together a lot; we've dated some. But, he's kind of old for me to take seriously. It's like having another brother."

"Not any older than Jason, is he?"

"I don't suppose so. Maybe it's not exactly the age, but...I don't know. I think if I hadn't found Jason again, if he didn't mean so much to me, I might have settled on Peter. He really does care about me."

"Is it fair to him?"

"Is what fair to him?"

"This - well, leading him on. Have you told him how you feel about Jason?"

"I - no, not yet. I will. It's not going to be easy. He and Tyler were buddies, and he's been stayin' right close to me - or tryin' to. I sort of haven't been around the last few days, you know?"

"I know that Jason hasn't either. That wouldn't be a coincidence, would it?" Mackenzie raised an eyebrow at me.

"Not if coincidences happen on purpose." I grinned at her. Sappy as it was, thinking about Jason made me grin.

She shook her head and started easing the boat around, heading us back downriver.

"If Matheson will talk to me, I'll see what I can figure out. And we can ask about the boat thing. That's probably about it. I'll do some mental work on whatever gets turned up." She pushed the throttle forward again. "Don't think they'll get mad at me over that."

It didn't take any time to get back to her boathouse. She dropped me at the dock and put the boat away.

"Would you like to come see my house?" she asked as she joined me.

"Sure, but how do we get there?" I knew I hadn't seen a car in the lot.

"I live across the street. Come on."

We cut around her building and across the road. Directly across was a metal staircase that climbed the steep hillside, clambering its way past vines and a meandering stream.

"It's a great convenience, being able to walk to work. This was all part of the package when I bought out the previous doctor's practice. The house was built in 1850. It even has a tunnel from the garage down through this hill to a cave by the river. They say it was part of the Underground Railroad."

I stepped around her as we topped the stairs. The 1850 house was a clapboard-sided mansion painted the color of buttercream icing. There was an attached portico at the main door, which faced the driveway, not the road. A windowed gallery ran along the front, and atop it was the kind of balcony they call a widow's walk. The house was solid and dignified, like the gemstone necklace of a Southern debutante's sponsor.

"Mackie, this is beautiful! Down home it would probably be all brick, but I love this gorgeous yellow siding!"

"Thank you. I've felt tremendously lucky. Wait 'til you meet Jean. She's my housekeeper, also inherited from Dr. Kesselman. She keeps this house in shape and keeps an eye on the men renovating my old homestead. We do some of the work ourselves, but mostly our part is kept to decision-making and fuss-raising when things aren't done right."

As she opened the door, it appeared one of those fusses was going to be directed at Mackenzie herself.

"You're doing it to me again, Doc!" A woman with steel gray hair capping her head stood in a short foyer, hands on her hips, a dishtowel in her hands. "Who is this?"

"Jean, this is Tory McCloud. She - "

"She the wife of the young man whose body you found?"

Mackenzie threw an apologetic look over her shoulder. "She's his sister, and what exactly is it I'm doing to you again?"

"You've set that State Trooper Matheson on me. You know I can't get anything decent out of those workmen with him around." She turned and headed into the kitchen to rescue a screaming teakettle.

"Matheson was out at the farm? Tory, please go ahead and have a seat. Jean, you calm down, please. I think you're frightening our guest."

"Mackenzie, it's okay. I - "

"See, she understands. My goodness, you sure are tiny," were Jean's only words to me, then she lit back into Mackenzie, who'd started putting a plate of crackers and cheese together. "Did I not just say he was out there? He said he was looking for you. I told him all he needed to do was to check your office. Nine times out of ten, that's where you are. Hand me the lettuce, please. I'm fixing a sandwich."

"Shouldn't I be? At my office, I mean. It is where I work."

"Of course you should be there, Doc." Jean's voice was muffled by the open cabinet door as she pulled out cups. "It's just that sometimes you work too hard. You expect too much of yourself. Like this business with Mr. Fields."

Mackenzie frowned. "What do you mean?" she said.

Jean brought over cups of tea. I found myself wishing for ice and tablespoons of sugar. I never did get to likin' hot tea. Part of me wished I wasn't even here. Mama always had a thing for keepin' family disputes to home, and not in front of company. I'd learned that one real well.

Sweet Corn, Fields, Forever

"Cheese?" Mackenzie offered, setting the plate at the center of the table. We both helped ourselves, Jean adding hers to her sandwich. She was not to be deterred from her subject.

"Look, here you are, a busy doctor. You've just got your practice set up. You're rebuilding that barn and house out there. You're taking on patients right and left. Now Mr. Fields gets himself in this fix, and all you can think about is how to solve this mystery like before. And I know without you tellin' me that that's where Matheson's stop fits in. He wants to see you about that murdered singer. Hmph. Don't you have enough to do?"

"Jean! His sister is sitting right here! I can't desert my friends; you know that. Besides, stumbling over the body - sorry, Tory, - gives me a stake in it."

"I fail to see how. It's not like you knew the fella. Sorry." Jean threw the word my way as she bit into the turkey-lettuce-tomato sandwich she'd made herself.

I lifted a cracker from the plate. "Jean, I understand you're tryin' to protect your employer. I got a manager who's just like that. But, Mackenzie has a point, and I'd say this even if Tyler weren't my brother and I knew Mackenzie better. She and Jason found Tyler together. If the police have suspicions of Jason, then they have suspicions of Mackenzie, too. I don't see how she could ignore something like this."

Mackenzie smiled and patted Jean's arm. "You know, right now you seem more like a squawking goose than the mother hen that I know you are. As far as the police are concerned, Ted's friendship notwithstanding, why couldn't it have been me?"

"You didn't lose a lawsuit to him eight years ago like Jason Fields did!"

Mackenzie drew a cube of cheese away from her lips. "Now how do you know about that?"

"It was in the papers. All about how Tyler McCloud sued Mr. Fields for stealing his song."

"It wasn't like that!"

"Yes, it was," I said.

Mackenzie stared at me.

"That's what they said!" Jean asserted.

"But - but, Tory, that isn't the whole story, is it? Jason explained it to me. He didn't steal from anybody!" Mackenzie protested. "Tory, you said that last night!"

"Then why did they rule against him?" Jean demanded.

"I didn't say that last night, Mackenzie. I said Jason hadn't meant any harm. The judge ruled against Jason because my brother and our manager proved their case."

"No, they didn't! I mean, well, Jason said they had proof of the timing, that Tyler wrote his song first - "

"See? That's what I mean."

"But Jason conceded without there being a ruling. He didn't want a big public discussion of something that's fairly complicated. He and Tyler wrote songs based on an old story of your dad's, right, Tory? So the songs were connected, and Tyler's was written first. Jason didn't want a huge mess made, so he settled!"

That wasn't how I remembered it. But this was Mackenzie's house, and you don't have a disagreement with your hostess the very first time you're there. I decided to wait until I could talk with Jason. He needed to straighten this out with her before Mackenzie based too much of her investigation on the wrong information.

"Who wrote that story anyway?" she was asking. "Where do they get their so-called facts?"

"Paper referred to 'a confidential source'," said Jean.

"There you are. You should almost never believe anything called a 'confidential source'!"

"Hmph. I guess. How would they get that story if it wasn't true?"

"I don't know. Probably someone who likes dumping on celebrities when they're down. Because of how he settled in the case, a lot of people don't really know the facts." She threw me a puzzled look before going on to say, "I get the feeling there's going to be a lot of confusion before this thing is resolved." She licked her lips. "Tory, maybe you'd better ask Jason for his version of the story. I don't know if it will make a difference to you or not, but it seems to me it's something you'll want to know."

"I reckon we both better get the story straight," I told her. "This isn't the kind of misunderstandin' we all need to start out with."

"Regardless, we both know Jason didn't kill your brother. That's one thing we *can* start with."

"You don't need to start out with anything," insisted Jean. "Let that crew of lawyers he's got solve this thing for him. You've got other things to do. Like answering that."

Mackenzie's cell phone was ringing. No sooner had she pressed the answer button than my phone started in ringing, too.

"Hello?" I said. It was Jason.

"Tory? Where are you? Can you come home? There's been something more. They found some papers on Tyler. They're not going to help my case any. We need to talk."

"I'll be right there." I closed my phone as Mackenzie was closing hers. "That was Jason. I have to run."

"Oh. All right." Mackenzie looked at her phone in her hand. "I'll see you out. Tory, maybe you can get that stuff straightened out with Jason. I'll find out what Matheson wanted."

"Was that him on the phone?" Maybe there was some sort of break, some good news I could bring to Jason.

"No - no, it was Bryan."

Mackenzie still seemed distracted, but I didn't have time to wonder about her troubles. Jason's were enough for me to take on. Even if there was some confusion as to the history of it all, I certainly wasn't confused as to the present. Jason needed me.

·C·H·A·P·T·E·R· *11*

·M·A·C·K·E·N·Z·I·E·

"No more games we're gonna play."

- from "Don't Lock the Door 'til it Stops Swingin'" by Jason Fields

I t was pure luck that Tory got a phone call from Jason just then. With Jean having been so close to outright rude, I hadn't wanted to ask Tory to leave.

Bryan was coming over, though, and I didn't think Tory was going to want to hear what he had to tell me, nor did I think she needed to hear it from us. Matheson had shared with him some news that wasn't going to be made public, but it was damning, very damning to Jason. Or at least, it appeared to be. I needed to figure out some way to neutralize it.

"Hey," he said when I answered the door.

I led him into the living room with its arches and gallery of windows to the out-of-doors.

"Okay, what have we got?" I asked, right into the space he was leaning to kiss me.

"O - kay," he said, pulling back.

"Sorry, it's been a long day." I planted a perfunctory peck on his cheek.

He tilted his head to one side, his sapphire blue eyes dark. "I knew bringing Fields along tonight was a mistake."

"Jason? Where?" I looked around, startled.

"In here," he said, tapping the side of my head. "We're going to be spending our time talking about him again this evening, aren't we?"

"I - well, we - oh, I suppose so. How about I promise that it won't be the whole evening? Just a little bit at the start? Is that fair?"

"That might work, if there's some time spent talking about us to back it up."

He put his arms around my waist. I slid mine up to his shoulders. He was so much taller than me. I kissed him once, once again lightly. Then I stepped back.

"Okay. Let's get this discussion over with. What is this that Matheson found and why is it so damning for Jason?"

He held up a finger. "First, I need to tell you that my men didn't find any fingerprints on the boat."

"So, no one took it out?"

"Not exactly. When I say they didn't find any, it was almost that. Aside from our prints from when we moved it back in the boathouse, there were no prints on the boat at all. While I know how obsessive you are about the finish on that thing, even you don't wipe it off every time you handle it."

I bristled at the term 'obsessive' but he was right enough. "So, somebody handled it, and then wiped it off. It wasn't down a significant amount of gas. I checked that myself. That is so weird. I don't know who would do such a thing."

"Neither do I. I thought you pretty much won over everyone who objected to your coming here. Who would still be out to cause you trouble?"

"No one that I know of. I thought I'd won them all over, too." I said, picking up my purse as I caught Bryan checking his watch. "Reservations?"

He nodded and we made our way back through the house to the door to the portico.

"So, if there's nothing more about the boat, what about Jason?"

He sighed, swaggering a little towards his semi-customized, purposely nondescript Ford. "You spoke with Ted about that press release they found on Tyler, right?"

"You know I did."

"Didn't you tell me that he warned you - here."

He broke off to open my door. I slid over and pulled the handle on his. I meant it as a gesture of courtesy, really, I did, but he was frowning as he sank behind the wheel and started the engine. Checking over his shoulder for traffic, he resumed his questioning.

"Didn't you tell me Ted warned you about saying anything to anyone?"

"Yes, I did. I mean, I told you Ted warned me about talking about the press release."

"Did you?"

"Did I what? Yes, I told you about what he said."

"No, I mean did you tell anyone?"

"No, I didn't. I told both you *and* Ted I wouldn't do that, and *I didn't.*"

"Not Andrea? Or Jean? Or Brooke?"

Okay, so he knows you well enough to name the three people you might spill the beans to. You can't let him get away with it, though.

"I didn't tell anyone. Not them, and not Jason either, before you ask. What is this about?"

Bryan grunted. "Today's paper."

"Today's paper? Oh!"

"You saw it then?"

"Jean told us about it. I don't understand what the fuss is. It doesn't mention the press release. It talks about the lawsuit is all, and it creates a bad impression, because it's inaccurate. It doesn't mention the press release at all. So what's the deal?"

"Ted wouldn't tell me all the details. He said he'd catch up with me later. But he's concerned about even that information getting to the papers. He's afraid perhaps you said something - out of loyalty to Jason, and that you might say more. You sure you - ?"

"Bryan, I said absolutely nothing. And I'm getting a little tired of having to repeat that to Ted - and you!"

"Okay, okay. It's just that, look, we can't have that press release made public. If Tyler was carrying it, probably he was going to talk to Jason about it. Which goes to motive." He turned the car right. "We're going to the Spaghetti House, right?"

"Yes, I'm dying for some good Italian food. I plan on their lasagna platter."

"Where do you put all the food you eat? You never gain an ounce!"

I smiled at the compliment, but I brought him back on track. "Don't change the subject. They're trying to say Jason would kill Tyler, an old friend, just to squash a Press Release? What kind of information was it going to let out? That he was an alien or something? Seriously!"

I watched the traffic go by. I know that the police have to operate on evidence, but even they have gut feelings and read people. How bright did you have to be to know that Jason Fields wouldn't operate that way?

"Besides, Ted and I talked about all that. It was more about how the press release was altered, wasn't it? I thought they were thinking Tyler wanted to show the alterations to Jason?"

"That was one line of thinking, but even so, if those alterations were actually legit, then we're right back to Jason again. They don't want anyone to know about that release."

"They won't find out from me," I said. "Are they telling Jason yet?"

"Not so far as I know."

I thought of the simultaneous phone call Tory'd received from Jason.

"Wait a minute," I said. "Why did Matheson tell you all this? He knew you'd tell me."

"Yes, he did. Look, Ted knows us, and he knows Jason. I'm pretty sure he's not happy with the idea of Jason as a suspect. He knows you didn't do it. That's why he asked for your input on the release. He told you that."

"I knew he knew better than to think Jason was guilty!"

"*But* we're not going to do anything until we hear from him and see what our parameters are, right? Right?"

He was doing it again; without even knowing it. I had to resist sliding into the expected response. I really did want to pout as if he were spoiling all my fun. This was far more serious, however. Both Jason's situation and the fact that Bryan was treating me like a child. It had to stop.

"Bryan, if it's not the right time to act, I won't act. How soon can we talk to Matheson? I'm worried about Jason and what this will do to him publicly. Remember how Tory turned the crowd to his side Saturday?" I went on at his nod. "It seemed like everything was okay. She was so glad to see him."

"I'll say. That hug she gave him looked like it was for life!" he exclaimed.

"Exactly. She came by today, verifying that. Then Jean told us about the story on the lawsuit thing. You know it made it sound like a judge ruled against him! That's what Tory thinks, too."

Bryan jerked his head back. "What? What about what she said at the concert?"

"Oh, she thinks he didn't mean any harm, but she still thinks a judge ruled him guilty. You heard how he explained it. It's not something he'd lie about; it would be too easy to check on."

"You're right. So, why wouldn't Tory know what actually happened?" His brow knit together as he negotiated a tight turn through traffic into the parking area. "Who ran the story? I mean, who wrote it?"

"It cited 'confidential sources'. You see how that all sounds, though, right? No doubt that's why Ted thought I did it."

He helped me out of the car, unnecessary, but tolerable. As we walked toward the restaurant, he said, "You know, some of this stuff is coming out just a little too pat. It doesn't feel natural."

I paused. "Is there more, or is this a gut feeling?"

"Right now it's a gut feeling; I'll have to see if there's more to it."

Candles flickered at our table and all around the room. The Risetti's had built their restaurant with a total retro Italian restaurant look: red-

and-white checked tablecloths, Chianti bottle with requisite candle, bentwood chairs, and red and black decor. Mrs. Risetti worked the cash register, Papa Risetti (as he insisted he be called) worked the kitchen, and their daughters and their friends waitressed.

"Bryan, I don't get it. What is that Press Release all about?"

"Uh, bring us the linguine," he told the youngest Risetti daughter. "Thank you. Mackie, I don't think we can second-guess this. We may not know until everything is solved."

"Miss? I'd rather have the lasagna platter. Not the linguine. And could we have another basket of bread and cheese sticks?" I swear I heard him sigh again. "Bryan, I'm worried about Jason. We need to do something about this."

"There isn't anything you can do about it tonight. Why don't we try to relax, recharge? I can call Matheson after court tomorrow, if you want. I think Jason has used up his quota of attention for the evening."

A remark I would have resented if I hadn't agreed with him. "All right. Thank you. You really think Matheson will level with you?"

"Yeah. Things have gotten pretty smooth between us. Especially if I tell him about Saturday."

"What do you mean?"

"I can fill in the details about our little backstage chat with Peter Himes, and show him the man might have his own reasons for wanting to implicate Jason Fields."

"Why would he kill Tyler?"

"I don't know that he would. It just gives them something else - someone else to look at."

I shook my head over his inconsistencies. "I thought you didn't want Matheson knowing you talked to anyone."

"I'll work around it. I'm declaring a moratorium on the topic for tonight. Tell me about your day." He drank from his wineglass, the red of it glowing back against his hand. Such reliable hands.

"It was pretty hectic actually. A bunch of colds and viruses in the morning. Plus the Seniors were in, to pick out the furnishings for my new waiting room as much as get their shots. Tory showed up while they were there."

"Tory?"

"You know she's really sweet? And then something strange happened. Naomi Cooper was in to get checked out. Nothing's wrong; you'll hear soon enough that she and Bob are expecting again."

"Number five?" Bryan smiled.

"Mhmm. That wasn't the strange part. When she found out who Tory was, she nearly blew a gasket."

"Why?"

"Turns out her brother Braeden - you remember about him - worked for Tyler the year he committed suicide. Naomi blames Tyler, and now Tory, for his death."

"Why would she blame either of them?"

"It seems Braeden had a gambling problem. According to Naomi, Tyler encouraged it, and therefore is responsible in part for the losses that drove him to kill himself. Ergo, Naomi blames Tyler for Braeden's death. I thought she was going to have a stroke, she was so angry at Tory."

"What did Tory have to say?"

"She barely knew Braeden. She recognized his name, but that was it. He actually worked in accounting with the manager."

"Wow. I know the world is getting smaller, but that is a weird one. We should let Ted know about this connection. Maybe I'll call out there for some more information first." He pulled out his notebook - he still hadn't made up his mind to use his smart phone for this stuff - and made a note to himself.

Just then the waitress brought our order. My lasagna platter was a sampling of three different lasagnas. Classic meat, a meatless version titled Vegetarian Delight, and a lobster lasagna with Bechamel sauce and lobster mushrooms, with three buttered oysters laid precisely on top. Bryan's linguine helping was a huge one blanketed with Alfredo sauce and extra cheese. We both received sides of home-baked focaccia bread and salads with a small crockery pitcher of their house dressing. The food covered the table, crowding aside our Chianti-container candle. Bryan looked bemusedly from my plate to his, opening his mouth to speak, then shrugging it off.

I started eating my salad, but soon switched to the lobster lasagna. I wanted that while it was fresh and hot. Reveling in its savory smoothness, I continued.

"Brooke called me today, too. We didn't get much of a chance to talk, but she told me Dr. Green has taken care of the adhesions problem, and chances are she'll get pregnant soon. I wish she'd relax about it, though."

"Relaxing about that sort of thing isn't easy. Sometimes I think nothing about kids ever is."

"I guess I wouldn't know."

Bryan's eyes turned a deeper blue. "Mackenzie - "

"It's okay. I can't get down every time someone talks about children. It's just - sometimes I feel - well, not exactly left out, but like - like I have no right advising my pregnant patients, or even young parents, because I haven't a clue as to what it's like to be pregnant or a mother."

"You know Rachel thinks you're terrific. You can borrow her any time you want." He smiled at me.

Rachel was his nine - excuse me, ten-year-old daughter. We'd met for the first time last year, when I returned to Kings Hill. When her mother was killed, I helped her as best I could, not trying to step in, but by just being there. We became fast friends, and she had no reservations about Bryan and me dating. If that was any kind of reference, I guess I was doing okay in the kids department.

"Besides," he continued, "you don't know what it's like to be old, either, yet I've seen you give great advice and care to that Seniors group of yours."

"Well, yeah, but that's different. I don't want to be old yet." *Oops.*

He grinned, his eyes twinkling. "You want to be pregnant?"

"You know what I mean! I do want to have children someday. Only, like Brooke, I don't know how many 'somedays' I have left." *This could turn into another oops, you know*, said that little voice I carried in my head.

"Maybe that's a factor we should take into consideration in our own plans," Bryan quietly, a purposeful gleam in his eye. Or was it just the candle flame?

"Well," I said with care, "maybe when we make plans, we should."

The gleam in his eye faded. Disappointment? He bent his head over his food, and so did I.

Where were Bryan and I going? I always admired him, right from when we were growing up. He was the one person who could tease me and still treat me like an equal. He'd been my hero in make-believe games of cowboys and Indians, cops and robbers, and rescuing the damsel in distress. Last spring he'd saved my life for real. I'd had a hand in saving his, too. We'd grown incredibly close.

Lately, though, I wasn't sure what was going on. We seemed too comfortable, and yet, we both seemed to feel insecure. Was there really anything to 'us'? Maybe it was just the newness of my return that had prompted his interest. Maybe the newness was wearing off.

Or maybe you aren't so thrilled being bound to another person who's as independent as you are. My little voice was back with a vengeance. *You seem to have forgotten what Bryan feels for you, how passionately he cares for you. Why do you think he acts jealous anyway?*

"What is it?" Bryan asked, looking concerned.

I felt the expression of surprise on my face. It's a wonder he didn't hear my thoughts that little voice had been scolding so loud. "Bryan, tell me something. Whenever Jason's name comes up - "

"I thought we were done with this subject."

"No, this isn't about that. Whenever Jason's name comes up, you get all bristly and annoyed. You act jealous."

"I do not," he protested, a flush creeping up the long plane of his cheeks. Could a man look indignant and guilty at the same time?

"Yes, you do. Your sister does, too. Well, on your behalf, I mean. I don't understand it. Jason's my friend. I turned down his attentions last spring, and I showed him very publicly how I feel about you. Why do your react whenever he's mentioned?" I attacked my food now with the same vigor I was attacking the subject.

Bryan waved his fork around in the air aimlessly, then set it down, frowning. "You think your feelings for me are public, huh?"

The waitress appeared at our table. "Can I help you, sir?" she asked.

He looked bewildered. I rescued him. "Could you bring us some iced tea, please?"

She threw me a funny look, then said "Certainly," and whisked away. In a second she was back, glasses in hand.

Bryan spent the time studying his plate. His napkin. The oil painting of a Sicilian harbor on the wall. The used Chianti bottle with the candle stuck in it. When she left, he spoke quietly.

"Mackenzie, you know I was burned in my first marriage. Deb was a big disappointment to me." He hesitated.

"I know."

"When you came back to Kings Hill, and we started seeing each other, it was like a new beginning. It was wonderful."

"Was?"

"Mackenzie, it *is* wonderful. I'm so glad to have found you, sometimes I find myself whistling when I'm locking somebody up just because I'm so happy for myself."

"I'll bet that scares them."

"Yeah, sometimes. Mostly it just ticks them off. My point is, I'm happier than I've ever been. Rachel is happier than she's ever been, too. We are both so lucky to have you in our lives. I think that's it. It seems like luck. Luck runs out. When you talk about Jason Fields, and I know you admire him, it worries me. It worries me that someday you'll see him as the man you want in your life, not me."

"And that makes you cranky?" I said lightly.

"Yeah, that makes me cranky," he said, bristling again.

See, he's not trying to be annoying; he's scared.

I reached across the table and took his hand. "Look, I'm not used to all this. I can't believe that something that started back when we were kids flourished once I moved back here. Sometimes it seems so unreal that I think it *can't* be real. Bryan, my feelings for you are rock-solid. I admire Jason, sure. He's fun to be around, exciting even, when he's off on some new idea of his. But..." I licked my lips. I wasn't sure I wanted to make myself this vulnerable, but Bryan seemed to need this.

"Bryan, last year, the night Deb was killed, do you remember when you first spotted me and Jason at the Black carriage? Do you remember how you reacted?"

"I remember all right." His voice was tight.

"I looked over my shoulder and saw the two of you together. I had just realized that I was in love with you, just realized that I wished I'd kept our date and that I was dining with you, even though right then that would have complicated things for me."

He looked questioningly at me.

"Because I was hiding information about the skeletons from you and my feelings for you were making me want to tell you stuff I wasn't ready to." He nodded, and I continued. "When you and Deb stood up to leave, you looked over at me, that cold, angry, banishing expression on your face. I was devastated. I thought you'd decided Deb was the one you wanted, not only for a dinner date, but for everything. I thought you were getting back together. Then, when she was killed, it was worse. I was sure you'd be so locked up in memories of your marriage that you'd never turn to me."

"You were wrong."

"I know I was. You let me know right away. I learned from what I felt even in those few moments. I was so in love with you, Bryan, so quickly and completely, that the thought of you not returning my love just turned my whole world black."

He stared at me. Neither of us touched the table, our plates, anything.

"Bryan, that was then, when I'd only discovered how I felt. Now, now if something were to happen to break us apart, it would be as bad as when my first husband died."

He cleared his throat, but no voice returned.

"Bryan, I love you. Don't ever doubt that. Please."

"Mackenzie," he said, his voice dropping so only I could hear. "You need to know I love you, too."

It was his look that did it. I felt my hands uncramp from where they'd been clenching my napkin in my lap. My feet were cold, and everything in the room seemed very far away.

He stood up then, taking my napkin from my hands, casting a tip upon the table, handing me my purse. He guided me past a bewildered Risetti family, out the door, into the car.

As we swung out of the lot and headed toward Kings Hill, he said, "Rachel's spending tonight at Amanda Cooper's."

I knew where Rachel's dad was spending his night.

·C·H·A·P·T·E·R· 12

·T·O·R·Y·

"Look at Jack and little Jill"

- from "Simple Song" by Tory McCloud and Jason Fields

F unny how some lives run parallel at times. It's an idea worthy of a country song in itself. There was something kindred between Mackenzie's life and mine. Our lives were intertwined, for good or bad or whatever it would mean.

I raced over to Jason's as fast as I could. I made pretty good time, takin' into account I had been in the area barely a week. A week, I now realized, during which I hadn't seen or talked to my manager for more than ten minutes. I was going to have to do some fancy footwork to get back in Peter's good graces. I had no idea how he would react to my takin' up with Jason.

For that was what I had done. I told Mackenzie I was stayin' with Jason. Fact of the matter was, I'd moved right in. With no plans to leave.

I came through the door of the condo and headed straight for his arms. It was becoming a habit, one I enjoyed, except not so much when I was hugging him out of concern like I was now.

After an embrace that squeezed the breath out of me, he eased back, took me by the hand and settled us on the couch together. I didn't move away from his side. He seemed to need to be touching me, too, for he held my hand and stroked it, each stroke moving him closer to whatever he had to say.

"God, I'm glad you're here, Tory. Not, of course, glad about how it's connected to Tyler's death. But, it is so good to have you back again."

"Good, 'cause I don't aim to leave."

He smiled a smile that was way smaller than the usual Jason Fields smile. "I have to tell you something. They found some papers on Tyler's body that imply I had a reason to kill him."

"You didn't have any reason to kill Tyler! You didn't kill him! Jason - !"

"Hush, hush. I know. Tory, I promise you, I did not, would not, ever harm your brother. He was your brother, and he was dear to me for that reason, but also he was special in his own right."

"What do these papers say?"

"It's a press release, and the police are saying that if it had gone out, it would have made serious trouble for me."

"They think you killed Tyler because of this? They really don't know you very well, do they?"

His smile faded even more. "I think that's what worries me the most. Ted Matheson does know me pretty well, but he still thinks the evidence is firm against me."

"I reckon that story in the newspaper today didn't help."

"What story?"

"I - I hope you won't mind. I went to see Mackenzie today. I wanted to meet her. She's real nice, Jason. She said she doesn't feel about you like I do."

"Thank goodness for that!" he mocked.

I always did admire how he could see the funny bit in anything. I pushed at his arm.

"You know what I mean. Anyway, we had a nice talk. She took me out on her boat, too. It's beautiful. Jason, she agreed to help us prove you're innocent! When we got back, she took me over to her house., and her housekeeper Jean said there was a story run in the paper talkin' about the lawsuit Tyler won against you. That was the very reason I made sure to say what I did the other night, you know that."

"Yes, and you know how much I appreciate it." He squeezed my hand.

"The way Jean read it, it made it seem like you could have killed him out of anger over how he won the lawsuit. With all the other success you've had, why would you? I know how much country music meant to you, but you weren't homicidal about it." I snuck a look at his face, drew a breath and went on "Mackenzie - she sure is loyal to you. She argued with Jean over it."

"Over what?"

"That news story. Told Jean you couldn't trust 'confidential sources' 'cause mostly that's when the newspapers are making it all up."

Jason laughed. "Mackenzie would say something like that."

"She also said you told her that you conceded the lawsuit before the judge could rule against you. Did you tell her that?"

"I told her I didn't want the lawsuit to turn ugly. I liked Tyler too much, and there was you - "

"Somehow she got the idea that you didn't fight it."

Jason shrugged. "Well, I didn't, really."

"I thought Peter went up against you in court. That's what he always told me."

"He always tries to make himself look good, our Mr. Himes."

If what I was saying to him was much different from what Jason told Mackenzie, he sure wasn't showing it. He didn't even seem to mind. "So, it's not important that the newspaper ran this story? It won't hurt you?"

"I don't know if it will hurt me or not. Publicity-wise, it's not good, but it won't affect how the police think. Bad publicity fades, despite what people say. What will be important is whether or not I'm convicted. Thankfully, I'm not even arrested yet." He settled back into the couch, pulling me into him.

"Look, if I can know you wouldn't kill him, why can't they? I'm the - the victim's sister!"

"Shh, shh, I know. So do they, actually. I think it's one reason Matheson isn't here with handcuffs right now. Thank you for standing by me."

"It's kind of a tradition in country music, you know."

"It is, isn't it?"

I could tell he wanted to just sit there, be together, but I was too bothered by the other things that had happened earlier. I wiggled out of his arms and faced him.

"Jason, hon, there was some other stuff."

He raised an eyebrow at me. Jason Fields has this way of raising one eyebrow about three inches higher than the other. It's like a facial question mark. With his Roman-type nose, it makes you feel like you're being called to judgment.

"First of all, have you heard anything about J.D. yet?"

"No. Well, not actually. My senior crew chief generally reports in once a week. He's feeling harassed, because the police are calling him every day wanting to know if they've found anything wrong with the car."

"Have they?"

He grimaced. "Aaron says there was so much damage, it's going to be hard to sort it out. The only unusual thing, he said, was that J.D. had seemed a little anxious that morning. Like he had somewhere else he needed to be. He's going to get back to me if there's anything more. He'll know by the end of the week."

Jason heaved a sigh as he wound it up. "He fussed at me a little over asking the drivers for direct reports. I like hearing what the man in the seat has to say. He grumbled some about extra paperwork and hung up." He shrugged. "That was it."

"Did you talk to J.D.'s family?"

"I don't think J.D. had much family. Did he?"

"I think I remember a little brother is all. I can ask Peter."

"Do you think he'll remember if one of your roadies had family?" he asked dryly.

"He might. Besides, he's got records on everybody. Which means - huh."

"Huh?'

"Yeah - huh. Something else that came up at Mackenzie's office today." I outlined the meeting and conversation with Mackie's friend Naomi about her brother. "I wonder if Peter has records on him."

He'd stood up, running his hands through his curls, and started pacing. "I was afraid something like this would happen."

"You were afraid Tyler would make someone kill himself!?"

"No, I was afraid his gambling would cause someone trouble. Not like this though. I thought I'd talked him into getting help."

"Jason, what on earth are you talkin' about? What gambling problem?"

"Tory, sweetheart, Tyler gambled. A lot. He always did, even when you were kids. He used to tell me about the bets he'd make on the minor league baseball team there in Nashville. By the time I got to know you, he had some regular accounts with legitimate betting agents, and quite a few with the less than legal ones. Nothing unsavory, mind you, and your brother was always quite good about paying his debts."

"Now wait a minute! You mean to tell me that my brother, my brother had a gambling *problem*? Tyler didn't even like state lotteries!"

"Only because he never won anything. I'm sorry, Tory. I tried to keep it secret. Tyler never wanted you to know."

"Why? I mean, we knew a lot of people who gambled. Daddy wouldn'ta liked it, of course, but - we played Vegas all the time! People gamble!"

"You know how Himes always liked to keep your image clean. It wouldn't have looked good for the country boy next door."

"What did Peter have to do with this? It was Tyler who was always fussin' about how things looked. Why, the other night he was gittin' on to me about some of my costumes lookin' - " I started to shake. "Much as he liked all the glitz, he wanted to keep it clean. And - and you know?

He started a new song, well, we started it. I reckon it won't be finished now he's gone." I hiccuped. "Gone."

I shook my head to clear the tears, but now I was bent over double, like I'd been punched but hadn't felt it. Jason caught me before my legs gave way completely.

"He's gone," I whispered, and hid my head in Jason's chest. Then my heart ripped open, and all the grief I'd been ignoring poured out.

It must have been an hour before I could speak.

"Jason, do you know anything about Braeden?" I asked in a small voice.

He stroked my hair. "No, not Braeden. His sister was upset?"

"So upset I was afraid she'd lose the baby. Mackenzie just told her she was pregnant. Who am I to blame her for missin' her brother and hatin' the person she thought was responsible? Here, Tyler's dead, and I find out he was involved in somebody else's death, and I still mostly wish Tyler were here. I'd probably try to beat him up, I'm so mad at him, but at least he'd be here." I started to hiccup again, but it subsided. "Do you suppose Tyler was involved with something or someone because of the gambling and they killed him?"

"It's possible."

"I wish I'd known. I wish I'd known. I might have been able to help him." I'd gone from upset to calm, and now I was pushin' angry.

"Why do all the men I know keep tryin' to protect me from stuff that goes on? I didn't need to be kept in the dark about Tyler gamblin'. How could I help him if I didn't know? You and Peter, and even Tyler! Did you all think knowin' that would break me or somethin'? Don't you know I'm stronger'n that?" My accent always comes back when I get emotional.

"If you all would just let me help instead of thinkin' I need to be protected from the big bad boogie men out there. Jest exactly what do you think I'm made of? China?"

"Tory, look, we - I know you're strong. It takes a strong woman to get where you are. Look at what you did the other night. Going out on stage to support me and give a show right after your brother's been murdered."

The word still made me jump, but I motioned Jason to continue.

"It was never that I thought you couldn't handle the idea of Tyler gambling. I wanted to tell you. Tyler asked me not to. He didn't want to lose your good opinion. I kept quiet against my better judgment. I hoped he had it under control. Once the lawsuit came up, I didn't think it mattered anymore. I didn't know if I would ever matter to you again."

"You dummy. All those years of me thinkin' I wasn't woman enough to keep you interested."

"You! Not woman enough! Tory, you are the strongest woman I've ever known. You are talented, and beautiful, and you have more passion and strength in that little body of yours than women twice your size. I couldn't love a woman who wasn't strong."

"What about Mackenzie?" I was only half-teasing.

"Even Mackenzie Wilder is only a runner-up where you're concerned. I promise you, no more protecting you, or even seeming to. You and I are equals. A team."

Dinner was forgotten. We sat there forever it seemed, snuggled together. I was numb. Everything from the day was runnin' round in my head like wild animals. Bein' there with Jason calmed me. I could be strong for him; we'd get him out of this mess. We could be together.

With my head clearing and my spirit calming, I started getting squirmy. It takes a lot of energy to do what I do, and I'm used to always being busy. Sittin' around don't set right with me. I'd always thought Jason was like that, too, but the last couple days we'd spent sort of hidin' out, not doing much except being together. And here we were again.

"Tory?" said Jason in a voice so quiet I thought he was near asleep.

"Yes?" I said, tilting my head up. Sure enough, his eyes were closed.

"Is that your answer?"

"Is what my answer?"

"Is 'yes' your answer to my question?"

"Sure. Yes." I smiled up at him.

"Good." He smiled a satisfied smile and settled his chin against my head.

"Jason."

"Mmmm?"

"What's your question?"

He lifted his head and we faced each other, him frowning and me expecting him to respond.

"What do you mean, what's my question? You just said your answer was 'yes'."

" 'Yes' was my answer to you saying my name. You said my name like a question. What's your other question?"

He studied my face. His expression was all caution now. The green of his eyes sparkled less as they wandered my face. "It was more of a suggestion, really."

I wriggled around to face him, bracing myself for something I wouldn't like, hiding behind a false cheer. "Okay, what is your suggestion then?"

"Let's get married."

I stared at him. I sort of expected he'd continue, go into all the reasons he wanted to marry me, why it was a good idea to all of a sudden rush into marriage when we hadn't been together in years and the police suspected him of killing Tyler. I expected him to say something about loving me. Instead he sat there, facing me on the couch, his head dipped down, his eyes meeting mine, holding them to his own with a seriousness and a wistfulness that was irresistible.

He wouldn't explain. He wouldn't implore. It was all very simple. The idea was right, or he wouldn't suggest it. If I didn't agree, then I didn't agree, and that would be that.

I never think long about anything. That's just lost time. I threw myself at him once again.

"Yes! Yes is still the answer!"

Some minutes later I disentangled myself from him and headed to the kitchen to make us a salad dinner. Jason was still not eating with his usual appetite. "When shall we get married? And where?" I asked. Tyler was the only family I'd had, and Jason knew that.

"How about Friday? We can fly out to Vegas and get married out there. I keep a suite at the Bellagio, and we can go to one of the better chapels there." He pulled orange juice from the fridge and poured a long drink.

"Hmm. A Vegas weddin'. I might like that. I know some people out there, too. Will Matheson let you leave town? I thought suspects always had to stay put."

"I think he'll let us go if we arrange to have Bryan and Mackenzie come along."

"Oooh, we could make it a double weddin', couldn't we?"

Jason grinned. "We could, but I don't think they're ready."

"Do you think we should call them tonight?" I asked.

Jason set the glass down on the counter and scooped me up beside it. "No. I think we - you and I - should celebrate this evening. We'll call them tomorrow, or the next day." He nuzzled my hair

"Or whenever," I murmured, looping my arms around his neck. "Good enough for me."

·C·H·A·P·T·E·R· *13*

·T·O·R·Y·

"Time pursues its ceaseless prize,"

- from "The End's in the Beginning" by Tyler McCloud

Jason didn't answer on the first ring. Or the second. Or even the third, although whoever it was certainly held the button down long enough.

Finally, he swung the door open and leaned his curly-topped head around it.

"Mackenzie! Bryan! What a wonderful surprise! What are you doing here?" He did not open the door farther.

"You called us, remember? Or asked us to call. We decided to stop by instead."

Shoot! I tiptoed up behind Jason to listen. He motioned me to stay back, so I took a step backwards.

"Aah. You must have been worried. Yes, well. You know, Tory's here, now, with me." I leaned to take a step towards him, but he waved me back, again. "She's sort of - I mean, she's looking out for me."

Mackenzie hesitated, and she spoke as if she were puzzled. "Actually, we did know. She came to see me the other day. Did she tell you about our boat ride?"

"She did, I think. Lovely girl, isn't she? Always been one of my favorite people." He glanced at me over his shoulder, and waved me back again.

I slid my left foot backwards. I didn't want to make any noise. I also didn't know how far back I could go and not run into the wall. That wouldn't be a great idea, either. I slid my right foot back.

"Shee-it!" So much for 'lovely girl'. I'd backed up too far, right into a cactus he had potted in the foyer. Two-inch long needles, seven of them, stuck in my right calf. "Dammit, Jason. Let Mackenzie in here. I need a doctor!"

"What on earth?" Mackenzie brushed past Jason. Bryan followed her. "Tory?"

I pointed to the cactus and then my leg. Mackenzie dropped down on one knee to look. She was real polite about not noticing how my hair was mussed or that I was wearing mostly a long tight tee shirt. I did have dance trunks on underneath.

"I've got tweezers in my purse. Jason, got any ice?"

Bryan was real polite, too, but I noticed he couldn't help but check out my legs. Jason grinned like a wolf.

"Sorry to come by without calling," said Bryan. "Mackie kind of insisted. She was worried about you...." His voice trailed off. "Anyway, I thought maybe we needed to talk about the press release and everything."

Mackenzie grunted. "Yeah, the press release."

"Press release?" Jason caught my eye as he spoke.

Bryan nodded.

"Y'all, when Mackenzie's done with my leg, I'll get us some drinks. Jason, honey, I got the bags all ready upstairs."

"Bags?" Bryan asked.

"I'll explain in a few minutes," said Jason. "Let's sit down. Let me guess, you're referring to the press release Tyler was carrying the night he died."

Bryan nodded, saying, "So they told you?"

"I got a call yesterday."

Mackenzie shifted position and re-applied her tweezers, squinting to find the tiniest needle. "Matheson came by to see me before the concert - and he talked with Bryan, too. Sorry, Tory," she added as I winced.

Bryan nodded again. "You tell him."

"He came in saying he wanted to show me something they'd found on - " Mackenzie glanced at me, tweezers poised in mid-air " - in Tyler's pocket. It was the press release, which I take it you've heard about. He also said he wanted us to keep an eye on you."

"He has you watching me?" Jason looked amused.

"No, but .... " Bryan seemed hesitant to elaborate. Not Mackenzie.

"He wants us to see if there's anything else you remember about Tyler and your relationship, or anything else, that might have something to do with Tyler getting killed." Mackenzie avoided my eyes as she finished with my leg. She gave an exasperated sigh as she stood up. "Bryan, I can't spy on Jason - or Tory. We have to be straight with them. I'd really prefer to tell them everything."

Now Bryan looked uncomfortable.

"I'll get those drinks," I said and headed for the kitchen. I wasn't sure how we were going to get to Vegas at this rate, or even if! When I came back in with hard lemonade coolers, there were serious looks all around. Bryan and Mackenzie had taken the two wing chairs, and Jason had the couch.

"Okay, y'all. What's up?" I asked as I sat next to Jason. "Is it that bad?"

"Actually, some of it's good news," began Mackenzie. "That Ted is sharing this information with us at all is a good sign."

Bryan said, "He's feeling a little frustrated, and he trusts us, so he's letting us know a few things the general public does not. However, we're not free to share everything he's told us. That's what Mackenzie's so unhappy about. None of us like it."

"Well, seein' as how you're Jason's friends, don't you think you can bend the rules a little bit?" I asked, grabbing onto Jason's hand.

Bryan picked up two of the drinks and passed one to Mackenzie. "I can't."

I looked at Mackenzie, hard. At last she spoke.

"I might have a little more leeway, but if I'm too indiscreet, Ted will have my head. I've had experience with that before."

"What is this all about?"

"Did you see the paper?"

I slid my eyes towards Jason. "Not really. We - I was kind of busy yesterday. Wait, there was another article?"

"Mhm - they carried a story, sort of a speculative one - on the murder and arrest. Do you have the paper? It might be easier if you read it."

It was only easier if you were referring to the physical act of reading the paper. What it said was hard to swallow. It was the front page of the Entertainment section this time. To the average eye it seemed like reporting as usual; from an investigative standpoint, it was devastating.

Sources today revealed further evidence in the murder of country music star Tyler McCloud. McCloud, whose body was discovered at the open house of the new Fields' Research and Design facility just south of Rensselaer, was apparently carrying an official press release from his fan club. The release referred to McCloud's unusual start in country music in which his career was cast into the spotlight by a lawsuit over copyright infringement, which he won. The lawsuit was brought by McCloud against one Jason Fields over a song titled, "Don't Lock the Door 'til It Stops Swingin'". Jason Fields, the losing litigant referred to in the press release, is the same Jason Fields of Fields Research and Design, where McCloud's body was discovered by Fields and his physician on Wednesday, September 7th. The press release, dated for release September 9 (two days after his death), was reported to have referred to information Mr. Fields might not want the public to know.

Mr. Fields's life has been further clouded by the death of an employee testing a racecar owned by a consortium Mr. Fields heads. The crash took place at a test track owned by Jason Fields.

I passed the paper to Jason. *Why would Tyler be carrying a press release? He never worked on those. We had a staff who turned those out.*

"Damn! There's still no real indication here of what that release said," complained Jason. "Mackenzie, why would this article land you in trouble with Matheson?"

"We-l-l, it's like this. When Ted stopped by the office to see me, he brought a copy of the press release with him so I could look at it. He also warned me not to speak to anybody about his visit or what he said. He got pretty vehement about warning me. They're trying to keep some of the details away from the public."

"Mackenzie," Bryan warned.

"Let me do this my way. I can handle Ted if I have to."

"Yeah, I know," said Bryan, the corner of his mouth twitching.

Wait, what's going on here? I may not know these folks real well, but that's the most comfortable together I've ever seen them!

"Jason, Ted let me examine the press release. Actually he asked me to. There's two ways to interpret it. One way is the way this story presents it. What it doesn't say, couldn't say, is that the press release may have been altered."

"Altered? Edited? So?"

"Well, see, there's a slight difference in those words - " she began.

"One means corrected or revised, supposedly by someone who has the authority to make the change, so that it says what was intended. The other implies that maybe someone without that authority changed it to say something different," I put in. *It always comes down to words and how the story is told!*

"Someone else? What difference did the change make?" Jason asked.

"It's subtle. Here, I wrote out the important part."

We huddled together over her piece of paper.

"It starts out referring to the lawsuit - sorry, Jason," Mackenzie apologized, but he was already shrugging it off.

More important than any monetary award was the public avowal that Tyler McCloud had the talent necessary to make a hit. Jason Fields disappeared from the country music scene, a temporary talent who'd committed an unforgivable sin.

That was eight years ago. Today, Tyler McCloud is a country music star - our most favorite star - and Jason Fields is famous in his own right as writer, inventor, and entrepreneur. Would Mr. Fields want to be reminded of his past transgression? Probably not - especially if the public were to learn....

"See, that's where it trailed off, as if it had been printed out prematurely, or with a page missing. And it had changes marked on it. The changes are what Ted asked me about. It looked to me like most of the changes were plain old edits. A comma here and there, a capital letter in the song title. Those were all done in red pen. But this one at the bottom, somebody had taken a pencil and inserted the word 'public' in the last line. It was kind of smudgy, so you didn't notice at first that another change was made. Right here, where the word 'the' is before 'public', that 't' was added in. Originally it read, 'especially if he were to learn....' That's a significant change!"

I searched out Bryan. "Is that what you think, too?"

He nodded, leaning forward to set down his drink. "I agree with Mackenzie. For that matter, so does Ted. Problem is, we don't know who changed it, or why, or who wrote it to begin with."

"It says it came from some Fan Club," said Mackenzie.

"Our Fan Club?"

"Maybe. Does your fan club have a logo that looks like an 'M' on top of a cloud with music notes in it?"

I blushed. "Actually it's 'Mc' over the cloud. A little silly, but they're enthusiastic, and we need 'em. I know the president. We went to school together. She had the biggest crush on Tyler. When we started performing, she started up the Fan Club. It's got a web page and everything. I've been sort of wondering why she hasn't contacted me."

"You've been kind of out-of-pocket since this happened. Maybe she's tried to reach you but hasn't been able to," said Bryan, working his mouth to hide a grin.

"That would explain my phone call from Peter Himes this afternoon," said Mackenzie.

"Peter? He called you?"

"He asked if I knew where you were. I kind of assumed that meant you hadn't talked to him yet, and I wasn't going to be the one to explain, so I said I didn't know. Maybe he's heard from this person."

Jason was stroking his chin. "Tory, I'm sure she must have called to express condolences. If she had a crush on Tyler - "

I pursed my lips, thinking. "She's married now, but she does still run the Fan Club."

"She has a lot to do to deal with the fans, then. But, if she knows about this press release, surely she'd be contacting the police." Jason looked at Bryan expectantly. "So - "

"No one knows the details of the release except the police and us. And Jason, you can't let the police know that you know. Ted told me specifically that they didn't want even you to know about it. As it is, I'm waiting for him to blame me for the story in the paper. So you can't say anything."

"Wait a minute," I spoke up. "Even though the details aren't public, if the McCloud Fan Club wrote the release, and the paper is referring to a press release, it wouldn't take much for Janie, that's the president, to assume theirs was the one in his pocket. Especially if it's as damning as it seems."

Mackenzie stood up to face us. "Bryan?"

"Not a bad thought. Tory, you say this Janie is a friend. How sharp is she really? You think she'd realize this might refer to their press release?"

"I think so. An awful lot of press releases get put out by different fan clubs. By our staff as well. With the news story about it, if it was hers, she'd recognize it. But I don't know if her paper is carrying the story."

"We'll check," Bryan said. "I might need you to contact her.

I nodded. *I should be contacting Janie anyway.* "What if it's not hers?"

Bryan answered, thinking as he spoke, "I suppose it could still be from another fan club, although I don't exactly see what good a release like this would do. I would think they'd spend more time honoring Tyler than spreading stuff about Jason."

"Some fan clubs will latch onto any news about their hero," I said. "They develop a personal stake in them. Some fans will be out there tryin' to catch the killer, or, if they think it's Jason, to make his life miserable. They might not quit until there's a trial."

Bryan was waving his hands. "Wait, you're forgetting. This news story is post-murder. The press release was written before Tyler was killed."

"Which was partly why the police didn't want anything published about it. Ted and I talked about it, and we came up with something." Mackenzie glanced at Jason. "I have to tell him."

Bryan nodded, and sighed.

"Jason, Matheson doesn't really suspect you."

"What?"

"He doesn't really think you killed Tyler. He hasn't said anything, because he thinks it improves the chances of finding the real killer. It also might keep you safe. So that information does not leave this room." She swung to look at me. "Okay, Tory?"

"Sure." My feathers ruffled at being singled out, but I was the only 'outsider' in the room. I suppose I might be the most likely to say something to the wrong person. I shivered at the thought.

Bryan was explaining to Jason. "The department doesn't want the public to know you aren't a real suspect. They want everyone to think you're guilty. That's to protect you."

"Why exactly was Matheson mad at you? He thought you - ?" Jason focused his eyes on Mackenzie.

"He thought I might be tempted to take the story to the press, out of some misguided idea fed by my loyalty to you. He figured I couldn't stand that the world thinks you might be a murderer. Heck, I know you're big enough to stand the heat for a while. I still thought he should tell you what was going on. Fact is, I wouldn't go against Ted's instructions - "

"Mackenzie?" Bryan said. Even Jason raised an eyebrow.

"Oh, well, yeah, I am now, but for good reason. Anyway, I *didn't* leak the story. The only other possibility is someone from Matheson's department - which he certainly doesn't want it to be. We think there's two reasons to make Jason look guilty: one, to protect him, the way Ted's doing. The second is to make everyone - including the police - think he actually did it. Leaking the press release this way increases the perception of guilt. The only person who'd want to do that - " She paused.

"Is the killer?" I finished, a shiver spinning along my spine.

"Exactly," said Bryan. "Someone miscalculated. They must have either gotten impatient or thought the information was already out there. Someone leaked information to the press about that release. Not us. Not the police. Only the real killer would have a reason to do that. That action indicates he - or she - exists."

Mackenzie let that sink in for a moment. Her eyes landed on me even as she seemed to speak to Bryan. "Remember what Matheson said? I confirmed it with Betty McBride."

"About the murder weapon?" asked Bryan.

She nodded.

Silence. Then a small voice - mine - asked, "What exactly was the murder weapon?"

"It was a guitar string. An E string, thick enough and strong enough to do the job. Although Betty made it clear it could have been a strong, hefty woman, chances are strongest that a man strangled Tyler with that E string."

Jason placed an arm around me. I felt cold inside. No matter how wonderful my life might become, no matter how solid and firm and secure I knew Jason's love to be, the emptiness where Tyler had occupied my heart would never go away. It's how it is in life. I filed the thought, and the feeling, away. Tyler would understand when it showed up later in a song.

I sighed. *Is this what it's like to say goodbye, Tyler?*

Jason rubbed my arms, looking down at me, a slight question in his eyes.

"Mackenzie, is that the last bit of news you have for us?

"I think so. Matheson is checking with the paper to see who called the reporter who wrote those stories. I mean, we're assuming someone called. Maybe they were sent in or something. At any rate, he hopes to get a lead from the writer."

"Meantime, Mackenzie and I are supposed to help keep an eye on you." Bryan downed his drink.

"If I'm not a suspect, why is it you and Mackenzie are supposed to keep an eye on me?" asked Jason, a frown line settling between his brows.

"It's partly to pick your brain, but also - " Mackenzie stopped.

"To keep you safe," said Bryan.

Mackenzie turned her head away.

"Keep me safe?"

I grabbed Jason's hand tighter. *Oh, sweet Jesus!*

Bryan spoke calmly, "Matheson thinks this is as much about you as Tyler. Someone is working very hard to implicate you. More people around you besides Tyler are dead. There's J.D. And now we hear about this Braeden guy."

"That was someone Tyler knew, not me," Jason protested. "I wasn't involved with that at all!"

" Tyler was. He's the connection," said Mackenzie, leaning forward.

"He's one, anyway," said Bryan. "Someone killed Tyler, and it had something to do with you. Someone else you and Tyler are tied to is dead, and someone else tied just to Tyler is dead. You could easily be in danger. There has to be something, some other thing you all had in common, Jason. Something else that must be important."

"There's me," I said.

Mackenzie stared, but Bryan responded. "I've thought of that, Tory. I'm still thinking about it. You could be the key, but I don't know how. At any rate, until we discover what it is, and who the killer is, Jason and you are going to be seeing a lot of us."

"Perhaps more than you think," said Jason. "Tory?"

I looked at him. I couldn't switch gears as fast as he did, but I realized he was right. We needed to go on with our plans. Which included them.

Jason and I stood, he reached out his hand for mine; I took it.

"Mackie," Jason began, "are you and Bryan busy tonight?"

"I don't think so. Why? Did you want to go out? Dinner?"

"Sort of. See, I - that is, we want to make a little trip, to another city, you see, and I don't want to upset the local constabulary. So, you see, I thought, if you and Bryan could come along, it might be all right. Especially in light of what you just told us." Jason was grinning his big, goofy grin again, and Bryan and Mackenzie looked completely confused.

"Plus," I put in, " with you and Jason and Bryan here bein' such good friends..."

"I know you probably aren't prepared, but we could take care of that on the way, or have my staff take care of it there...."

"I just know you all will have a good time," I said.

"Wait, wait. You want us to come to dinner somewhere - what, out of town? And if Bryan goes, it'll be all right?"

"What do you think, Bryan, would Matheson go for it?" asked Jason.

Bryan rubbed his face for a moment. "I expect he would, so long as you aren't talking about leaving the state."

Jason and I looked at each other.

"Well, actually - "

"Oh, no, you're not! I can't make any promises about what Matheson will say." Bryan waved his hands at us.

"Where are you talking about?" asked Mackenzie.

"Las Vegas," I said, wiggling my toes in excitement.

"Vegas!? Why Vegas? Why not New York City? It's not like they don't have good restaurants there!" Mackenzie exclaimed.

"And just how long are you planning to be in Las Vegas? I mean, I know you said dinner, but who goes to Vegas from New York for dinner?" asked Bryan.

"Well, it's not only dinner. I figured we'd have that after," Jason said.

"After what? You can't just take off like that, Fields. I mean, I know what we said, but it would look strange to everyone - especially a judge, if Matheson let you go like that. It won't happen. How long did you plan to be gone, anyway?"

"One night," I said.

"Well, I suppose it could take a little longer," admitted Jason. "But I'm sure we'd be back by morning. Or mid-day."

Bryan was pacing, shaking his head. "I don't see Matheson allowing it. What is it you want to do in Vegas that you can't do here?"

"Get married," we chorused.

"Oh," said Mackenzie. "Oh!"

"Get married." Bryan looked stunned, as if it were something unheard of. "You want to get married, tonight, in Vegas. And I'm supposed to clear it with Matheson."

I laughed at his muttering and Mackenzie's sputtering. "Look, Jason and I want to fly out to Las Vegas and get married and have dinner. We know it will look bad if he takes his plane that far out of state, and we would really like to have you at the ceremony. You've been his best friends here, and - and I'd like to think you'll be mine, too."

Mackenzie moved over to Bryan's side. "We can, can't we, Bryan? Will Ted really object?"

"Hell, I don't know. Look. If we just go, and if we're back before he tries to contact you, he probably won't even find out. If the public finds out and there are any questions, and I'm with you, I can say I was sent to accompany you. Why now? Why Vegas?"

I answered that. "Las Vegas - because we're doing it in a rush. They aren't so picky about licenses and so on. And why now?"

Sweet Corn, Fields, Forever

Jason and I looked at each other. "Because we want to," we said.

"Said like that, I don't know if you two need a ceremony," muttered Bryan. Then he grinned. "Come on, let's get out of here."

·C·H·A·P·T·E·R· *14*

·T·O·R·Y·

"Wherever one will go,"

- from "Simple Song" by Tory McCloud and Jason Fields

Two hours later the four of us, Bryan in resigned confusion, sipped drinks as Jason's private jet ferried us to Las Vegas. I'd had my wardrobe people put some dresses aboard, and in a minute we'd see what we could make of them in terms of a weddin'. Mackenzie's close enough to me in size that I could outfit her as well, and I knew exactly which dress she should wear.

Jason arranged for tuxedoes for him and Bryan through the hotel. After we arrived at the Bellagio we'd get dressed, head for the chapel he'd arranged, get married, and then we'd have dinner in a private room. Jason's money made a lot of this possible, but it wouldn't have happened if Bryan and Mackenzie didn't support us.

"Peter certainly won't be able to complain about your reputation," Mackenzie said to me.

"He worries too much about things."

"You've been gone a week without contacting him. Surely that's not normal for a performer - to be so removed from their manager?"

"You worryin' because he called you?"

"No. Yes. I thought you were going to get in touch with him."

"I didn't get to it. With Tyler gone, our tour is done. Peter knew I wanted some time to myself. He's busy tryin' to work out the band's contract anyway. I should have checked in with him, I suppose. Once the press gets hold of this I'll need his help."

Mackenzie raised her eyebrows.

"They'll make a lot of the fact I'm marrying the man the police say killed Tyler."

"With as close as you were, and as closely as Peter seems to monitor things, I'm surprised he isn't here insisting on being in on everything. I'd expect he'd take a personal hand in this."

"We-l-l, like I said, I didn't call him. He doesn't know I'm with Jason."

But, that was what was wrong. I *hadn't* heard from him.

It wasn't like Peter not to call me every couple days. I knew I'd been avoiding him. I had enough emotions to handle without him around. I didn't want to answer his questions or have to argue with his advice. Now I realized he hadn't intruded at all.

"Maybe he's tryin' to respect my privacy for once. He knows how close I was to Tyler," I mused. "And he could do most of his work without contacting me. Fact, he's probably been pretty busy."

"He sounded a bit frantic when he called. Not knowing where you were staying, or if you'd gone back to Nashville or anything."

"Hmm. I don't know, Mackenzie. There's a lot about Peter I don't understand. Daddy was the one who hired him in the first place. Maybe, maybe I need to think about changing managers. Things could get awkward, what with him and Jason bein' at odds with each other. Plus if I go solo, I might need someone with a different approach. Someone who understands female artists better. Peter's a little bit of a chauvinist, know what I mean?"

Mackenzie nodded and added some cola to her glass. "Does that mean you'll keep on singing?"

"Oh, sure. I probably won't tour as much. Not that distance should be a problem." I patted the seat rest. "Once Jason is cleared of this mess and Tyler's murderer is found, we'll be able to do whatever we want." I blinked my eyes and tried to smile.

Mackenzie spoke softly. "How do you do it, Tory? What kind of strength lets you stand by Jason and agree to marry him on such short notice? How do you reconcile pain and happiness in such close quarters?"

I shrugged. "I don't know, Mackie. It's there. I feel them both. Sometimes even at the same time. You know, people talk about one door openin' when another one closes. It's like I've slipped from one room of my life, straight into the next, no pause, no threshold. One endin', one beginnin', just like that."

I caught sight of Bryan smiling at Mackenzie. Even ten feet away the man's eyes were an unearthly blue.

"He sure is cute, Mackenzie."

"What?"

"Your Bryan. Sure is cute. Awfully in love with you, too."

"Um - I guess so."

"You only guess so? He hasn't told you? Come on, let's get his attention proper."

I unbuckled my seat belt and headed toward the back. My assistant popped up. She'd come along to mind the clothes and, in her words, "Try her hand at the red-and-black again." I might have to keep an eye on her. I didn't need to have another gambler on my conscience.

"Ashleigh, bring the dresses out now. Two at a time, okay?"

"Tory, she looks so young!" Mackenzie exclaimed.

"Everyone says that. She's twenty-four, really." She did look young. Her bushy red hair and the freckles that competed so much for space that the girl looked like one long blush made her look young and countrified. But our Miss Ashleigh had worked most of the casino jobs in Vegas a girl can have. She had an eight-year-old son who stayed with his grandmother while Ashleigh traveled with me. Sometimes he got to travel with us, too, but I made sure Ashleigh had the time she needed to give young Roberto a good life.

"Tory!" Jason called back. "Don't choose the silver one, the slit's too high for a wedding dress."

"Jason! You weren't supposed to look!"

"I didn't. I just knew you'd bring it along."

"I'm not the groom. Can I have a look?" Bryan asked.

"No you may not," said Mackenzie. "It might not be bad luck, but it'll be very annoying. I want to surprise you, too."

"You surprise me every day, Mackie, every day."

"Tory, where are those dresses?" she asked me, hiding a blush herself.

"Right here," said Ashleigh, carefully laying them out on the couch in the back.

I already knew which one I was going to pick, and it wasn't the silver one with the slit. I'd had Ashleigh bring along a dress I'd had stashed in the back of my wardrobe. It was white with an iridescent overlay and narrow sliver lace edging along the hem, up the skirt in a swoop, across and up the bodice to circle the strapless top. The waist was tiny, and the skirt rose nearly straight from the ground. I'd fallen in love with it the day I saw it.

"Ooh, Tory. That is gorgeous, and just right for you. How do you have that with you? Surely you don't use it in your show!"

"I've been carryin' this around for a while. Not for the show. More like just in case I needed it. Ashleigh takes wonderful care of my things. You'd never know this thing was nearly twelve years old, would you?"

"Twelve years? Isn't that - "

"Shh!" I jerked my head in the men's direction.

"You weren't kidding when you said you came back to get Jason, were you?"

"Nope. I meant it. Every last word. Look, Mackie, this one - no that's not it. Ashleigh, go get the one in the gray zip bag. Bring that out. Check to see if the veil is in the white bag. I should have that with me, too. Mackenzie, trust me, you will love this gown. It may not look like your style; it's a show gown, but it is going to look perfect on you. It would please me ever so much if you'd wear it."

There were several minutes of fussing, and a couple of warnings given to the guys to 'stay put and keep eyes front', but Mackenzie had the gown on. Ashleigh nodded and slid open a mirrored door for Mackenzie to see.

"You're right. On both counts. It's not my style at all, but it's perfect with your gown."

Instead of silver lace, Mackenzie's gown had trim made of silver cord that discreetly criss-crossed the bodice and became spaghetti straps. The gown started off in a deep midnight purple setting off a gradient that fell through violet and lilac to a snow-white hem. Strands of sliver shot through the purples. The effect was of stars in a darkening winter sky over a bank of snow. Ashleigh held out a pair of silver heels to complete the outfit.

"Honey, you're not much taller'n me, and with your dark curly hair and that dress, you'll look like the dark night precedin' the coming of the dawn!" I giggled, and Mackenzie joined me. "Mackie, I reckon you have to grab your happiness when and where you find it, even if it's in the midst of sorrow. Maybe - " I glanced toward Bryan, deep in conversation with Jason, "Maybe you better do the same thing."

Mackenzie watched Jason and Bryan a minute. They were laughing, Jason's rumble encompassing the whole jet. Bryan's laugh was lighter, more tenor. Her expression changed.

"You may have something there. Right now though, this is about you and Jason. Let's wrap this up."

I watched as Mackenzie picked up the gown and studied it determinedly.

Not much later our flight was in. The four of us deplaned and were whisked to the hotel. Not so fast that we didn't take in the airport décor though.

"Slot machines!" exclaimed Bryan.

"At the airport?" Mackie chimed in.

"Oh sure. Cute, huh? Gives you something to do when you're waitin' on a plane. Want to try one?" I fished around in my bag for some leftover tokens I carried.

"I think the car is waiting," murmured Jason.

"I don't think I could anyway." Bryan seemed dazed. He started walking again, muttering to himself. "Legalized gambling! Trouble. Pure trouble."

The ride to the Bellagio involved driving a stretch of Las Vegas Boulevard, or the Strip. Tall palms, lights enough to make it day, and water: fountains, ponds, cascades. I hadn't noticed it so much before, but it was as if Las Vegas were purposely throwing its water in the face of the desert.

Mackenzie and Bryan peered out the limo windows as we passed Mandalay Bay Casino. Three pirate ships sailed in a private 'bay', their actors and singers playing to a standing crowd a block long and three bodies deep. The Bellagio was home to a classic fountain display dancing to a broadcast of the National Anthem, complete with cannons and fireworks that ran every half hour. Next door was Caesar's Palace, with its bigger-than-life statuary and bigger-than-life celebrities. Further down the street you could see the huge electric billboard with Trace Adkins's picture on it. The city was an opulence of water and light that seemed obscene for a desert locale. Vegas.

Mackenzie and Bryan were being very cool about this whole thing. I expected that, but I also saw a hint of surprise and wonder in Mackenzie's eyes. Bryan looked intrigued, but he scowled more. I reckoned it was professional cynicism. Vegas can hit you that way, too.

Inside the Bellagio we were treated like royalty. It was different being a guest than being part of the entertainment. Jason was known here. For the first time I started to realize how my life was going to change. Our check-in was expedited, and we took a hushed elevator ride to the penthouse suite. Invitations to their restaurants, dining rooms, and their in-house spa reclined discreetly on the credenza, next to an enormous arrangement of bromeliads, date palms, and lilies, with a silver bucket of champagne.

I wanted to stop for a toast, but Jason caught my eye, tapped his watch and inclined his head toward Bryan. He didn't want Bryan to think we were dawdling and worry about us gettin' back on time. So I hustled Ashleigh to get our dresses out, and Mackenzie and I changed. She put on her gown, but I slipped on a long, layered sequined skirt and one of my performance vests. I was takin' no chances on Jason sneakin' a peek at my wedding dress. It would take only minutes to slip it over my head, set the veil, and step into my dress heels.

Jason made a face at me when we met up in the hallway. He knew what I was up to. I held his hand in the elevator, feelin' the rush of emotion as I thought about what we were doing. I could hear Bryan and Mackenzie behind us, and it made me smile.

"You look spectacular." Bryan's voice was barely above a whisper.

"Thank you," she answered, a little prim. "Bryan, are you okay with this? It was pretty sudden, asking you to come out here."

"Mackenzie Wilder, I'd go anywhere with you, don't you know that? Even if you didn't look like you do now."

The conversation was cut short by our arrival at the lobby, and then by the scene on the street. They both gaped, while Jason and I exchanged grins. One more way Vegas will do you.

Cabs with unbelievable ads for nearly naked shows mounted proudly on their trunks. Giant showgirls stared down - sometimes with glittering gyrations - from electronic billboards. Everything around seemed to be doubled by huge ads, so that you couldn't always tell whether it was the name on the venue, or a billboard, or even the real deal. Traffic was heavy. At one point the limo had to go around an SUV stopped by two patrolmen on bicycles. Then, as we came up on the turn onto Tropicana where the chapel was located a few blocks off the Strip, an ad for Reba McIntyre took over the horizon.

"Tyler and I opened for her out here at the Hilton last year. She really liked our set. She's awfully friendly, and she made a point to come back to our dressing room and compliment us. Told us we could send her a couple songs to look over, if we wanted." Jason wrapped an arm around me and took my hand. Bryan and Mackenzie were quiet.

The chapel was huge. Outside it, columns rose up, topped by cornices further topped by giant black-mullioned lanterns. Stonework drapes cascaded across the doorway. Rosebush topiaries lined the glittering concrete walk, a burbling brook playing peek-a-boo serving to water them. Wreaths of white roses hung on the door with silver gauze bows hanging down.

"This is huge," whispered Mackenzie, echoing my thoughts.

"What do they do here? Mass weddings?" asked Bryan.

"It's a complex of chapels," explained Jason. "Each one is tailored to size and taste, even color. I've picked out one I think you'll like, Tory."

First we were faced with a hotel-like lobby with desk clerk who summoned a page to escort us down a long hallway to the back. The chapel was dressed like a simple church. Two rows of seats for those who succeeded in bringing friends along. Brown varnished woodwork stood out against crisp white walls; a small lectern stood central behind a rail, and to one side rested a small clavichord, with a guitar, saxophone, and an accordion, all resting on racks alongside.

I smiled at Jason, and gave him a quick kiss. Then Mackenzie and I stepped into a spacious dressing room off the back of the chapel. As Mackenzie dropped my wedding gown over my head and rustled it into place, I told her, "Thank you. With my family - gone, it means a lot you're here. I love Jason. I've loved him since the day Daddy brought him home. I want him to become my husband in front of God and everybody. Thanks for bein' part of everybody."

"It's nothing, Tory. I'm proud to be your witness. What happened to Tyler is so awful, but in a strange way, he brought you and Jason back together. I think he'd be happy about that."

"I know. It's like he's here, with us, helpin' us have this time before the storm."

"Storm?"

"The storm it's gonna be to get Jason off. I know how many people think he killed Tyler, but you and I know he didn't. I know you said the police don't really think he did, but we still have to prove it. Tyler'll help prove he didn't."

"How?"

"I don't know. I know how silly it sounds, but Tyler never could stand to see a wrong go un-righted. So I know he'll stick around to help us prove Jason innocent. After I marry him!" I started rooting around for my shoes.

"Does Jason know he's marrying an unstoppable force?"

"Oh, I think he knows. It's too late if he don't." I grinned at her and stepped out the door.

Jason's and my wedding was as simple as the chapel itself.

Bryan's eyes glowed as Mackenzie preceded me down the aisle, but once she crossed to the altar, I looked at nothing but Jason. He whistled low as I came closer, and that drew a frown from the chaplain, but his assistant smiled.

The words were traditional, like I wanted, but before the final 'I do's', I held up my hand.

"May I add something here?"

"It's your wedding," said the chaplain.

I'd only thought of this when we came in and saw the instruments. I almost took up the guitar, but instead I handed my flowers to Mackenzie and seated myself at the clavichord. I keyed a few chords to get the feel of it, then I began to sing, and Jason began to smile.

My voice took up the melody, weaving in a child-like sing-song.

> "It seems so simple,
> so true and so simple;
> two shall become as one.
> - So soon they become; in truth they become; two become as one.
>
> So much complication
> in modern situations,
> that no one can believe;
> we all must self-deceive.
>
> But love is so simple,
> So true and so simple
> If only we could see....

So true and simple,
Too easy to believe."

I looked at Jason and sailed into the next section. He pulled out the hand he'd had in his pocket. Just like I'd dreamt so many times, he pulled out and unfolded a tattered rag of paper. In a voice that surprised everyone by being as light as mine he sang along from the words scribbled all over the paper we'd wrote the song on so many years ago. Our voices wove around each other, harmonizing, criss-crossing, gliding in tandem, the way we wanted our marriage to be.

"Look at Jack and little Jill
Hand-in-hand upon the hill,
Wherever one will go,
the second one will follow.

Children and their rhymes
seem to get it right;
Why is it only grown-ups
Who fail at love's first sight?

For love is so simple,
so true and so simple;
two shall become as one.
- So soon they become; in truth they become; two become as one."

Mackenzie said later that she thought the song was sweet, but it was our grins that undid her. We looked like children, she said, rediscovering a favorite game. Even Bryan seemed to be convinced, applauding and whistling as we kissed after the final vow. The chaplain wiped his brow. No telling what he'd thought was going to happen.

As soon as the kiss was done, Bryan was checking his watch. Jason caught him at it and bent to whisper in my ear. I sobered, but it was all right. I'd expected it. I kept my hand resolutely in Jason's.

"Give us time to change, Bryan, and we'll be right out."

"We're going right back?" Mackenzie asked. "What about dinner?"

"We'll eat on the plane. Mackie, we have to," Bryan told her. "Jason is basically in my custody. I can make this escapade acceptable, but only if we're back before anyone knows we've gone."

"For heaven's sake, they just got married!"

"Jason and I decided this right before the ceremony, sweetheart. He knew it was going to be this way. Our bags are already on the plane, and I believe a catered supper as well."

"We didn't check out!"

"Jason arranged it. It is nice to have money. I'm sorry, but you'll have to wear that gown home. Well, not too sorry."

"I - oh, well. It's not uncomfortable. Hope they turn down the air conditioning, though."

We were whisked away yet again, back aboard the plane, and homeward bound.

·C·H·A·P·T·E·R· *15*

·M·A·C·K·E·N·Z·I·E·

"Mid joys, trouble, tears"

- from "Christmas Fires" by Jason Fields and Tory McCloud

O
n the flight home, Jason and Tory were sort of wrapped up in each other.

I was only a little sleepy. Sitting next to Bryan was enough to keep me alert, though he seemed pre-occupied.

We held hands loosely, his palm warm over the back of mine. He'd leaned the seat back. His eyes were closed, a furrow between his brows. I wanted to stroke it, but that little patch of uncertainty kept my hand still.

He opened his eyes and sighed, rolling his head to one side to look at me, tightening his grip on my hand.

"You okay?" I asked.

"It's been a long day."

"Sorry I roped you into this."

"That's okay. Seeing Jason marry Tory crosses one worry off my list." He flashed a smile, but it faded.

"What is it?"

He grimaced. "It's not tonight, Mackie. I'm glad to stand up for Jason. It's what went on earlier."

"Earlier?"

"Remember - the trial?" The furrow deepened as if in displeasure.

"I remember *a* trial. You had to testify today, didn't you? How'd it go?

"Oh, it went fine. They'll probably convict the guy."

"That's good, isn't it? Doesn't he deserve to be convicted?"

"He's guilty," Bryan admitted. "The guy screwed up on a car repair and didn't put the brake lines back together right. Brakes failed and the car slammed into a sidewalk full of teenagers waiting to get into a club. Two of them died. It's just - "

"He didn't mean to? Do the courts give a lot of weight to that? I mean, he's still responsible."

"I know, I know. But, the two girls who died - one of them was his minister's daughter. This guy was careless, but it wasn't malicious. We've had him on a suicide watch."

"If he's that remorseful, why did you even have to testify? Did he not confess?"

"It's one of those weird cases. The insurance company demanded it before they would concede it really was his fault."

"So, you've got a guy who confesses and accepts responsibility, but everybody has to go through the trauma and expense of a trial anyway? Unbelievable!"

"I know. This guy will punish himself for the rest of his life. It's not the same as putting away some guy who's shot someone during a home invasion."

"I'm sorry it's so hard for you." And I was thankful I wasn't in the same sort of position. *What would living with this, with Bryan having to deal with this sort of thing, look like?* The tone my little inner voice used was distasteful.

"Just makes me question things sometimes. Sort of depressing. Sorry."

He wrapped his hand around mine again, his fingers teasing mine, trying to cheer up, but definitely closing the topic.

"So. Did I tell you what I picked up on eBay the other night?"

"No, what did you pick up on eBay the other night?" I responded.

This had become a recurring conversation for us. In-between the patients, the criminals, and the investigations I get myself wrapped in, we had normal conversations. Like hobbies - mine was the boating, and Bryan's, as I had come to learn, was collecting. Specifically, memorabilia. More specifically, space memorabilia. Didn't matter what, so long as a story came with it.

"I picked up some Challenger memorabilia."

"Some what?"

"Some stuff about the space shuttle Challenger."

"Oh. For a minute there I thought you meant you'd bought a piece of it!"

"Well...," he said slyly.

"Uh-oh."

"Hey.... This guy was okay."

"Bryan, what did you do?"

"Actually, I bought three separate items. One was the official investigative report of the Challenger's final mission. Then I got a large photo print of the ship on the launch pad, and that came with a commemorative coin and one of the patches worn by someone on a previous mission."

"Really?"

"Yeah. The patches are sold with NASA approval. I've got a couple from other missions."

"What else did you get?"

"A written tribute to the Challenger crew - written for kids, mainly, but pretty good." He cut his eyes around to me. "You'll never guess what's coming with that."

"What?"

"A piece of the ship."

"Bryan! How? Is that legal?"

He grinned as he waggled his hand at me. "We-l-l - This guy has a good story on it."

"I'll bet he does!"

"Shhh." Bryan glanced back at Jason and Tory. "Don't worry. Seems he was in the Everglades the day the ship blew up. Pieces came raining down. About a dozen of them landed right in the part of the swamp he was sitting in."

"He was sitting in the swamp?"

"Countin' 'gators, he said."

"Oh, boy."

"Somebody's got to count them. No, seriously, he's some kind of game warden or environmentalist researcher. His job is to track the alligator population. So, he's out there, and these pieces fly by him and drop into the swamp. In the write-up he says the water steamed and sizzled wherever they went in. Scared the 'gators."

"But, a dozen pieces? What did he do?"

"Well, according to his listing, most of them were either too big or too hot to retrieve. He only took two. The rest he reported to NASA authorities who went out and picked them up. They never missed the ones he kept."

"Right."

"Well, probably. The pieces he kept were small. They might have come off a door or something. He's keeping one and sending the other one with the booklet." He let out a sigh and stretched his long frame back in the seat.

I chuckled at him. Still, didn't NASA or the Federal government go after people for stuff like this?

"How many pieces does this make?"

"Not that many, unless you count the rocks. Then it's kind of a lot." His eyes dared me to ask.

"How many?"

"A hundred twenty-seven."

One hundred and twenty-seven pieces of NASA memorabilia. Bryan's private obsession.

"Unless, of course," he continued, "my bid on the refracting lens went through this afternoon. I need to check when we get back."

I laughed at him. "Hey, did I tell you that I think Andrea is truly smitten?"

"Again?" he teased.

"This time it may be for real, because if Ted Matheson's confusion is any sign, it just might be reciprocated."

"Andrea - and Ted?"

"That's what it looks like. I think she thought she'd be afraid of him. She never met him, you know, not really. She stood up to him the other day when he was giving me a hard time. Then she fed him cake. I swear, by the time I left, he was following her around my waiting room like a puppy and asking for her number."

"Ted Matheson and Andrea. Wait 'til I see him!"

"Bryan! You can't say anything until we know it's for real. And even then you better be careful!" I swung at him playfully, glad he'd told me what was troubling him earlier, glad that somehow telling me had lightened his burden.

A shadow passed over us as Jason approached from the back of the plane. Tory still lay curled up on the couch, her long lashes making fuzzy lines against her cheeks.

"Bryan, thanks for making this possible." Jason extended his hand. "Don't get up. We'll be landing soon. Tomorrow we'll have to contact Peter, much as I wish we didn't have to. He's been working on setting up a new tour for the band. I know he expects her to go with them. I hope he doesn't cause problems. He hates to have his plans disarranged, but - " He grinned. "- That's how life is: disarranging. Especially an elopement!"

"This means getting back to reality," Bryan warned.

"I know. But you know? With Tory behind me, I can face the people who think I killed Tyler. So long as you keep trying to find out who did." He looked back at the sleeping Tory. "Partly of course, for her. She loved him so much. But then," his voice wavered, "so did I."

·C·H·A·P·T·E·R· *16*

·M·A·C·K·E·N·Z·I·E·

"Cause the end's in the beginning,"
- from "The End's in the Beginning" by Tyler McCloud

We got back into town in the wee hours, all of us as frazzled-haired as Jason normally appeared. In our rush to get to our respective cars, we skipped right by the airport shops with their magazines and newsstands. Bryan headed for home, and I went straight to bed. So I didn't know what Jean was talking about when I came down the next morning. She stood at the stove scrambling eggs, muttering away about how now she'd have to carry a kitchen knife in her car to go with the small twenty-two caliber pistol Arthur'd given her for protection.

"Can't tell what's going to happen anymore," she said, sliding a platter of eggs onto the table, which was already laid out with toast and juice and tea for us both. "Look at it." She pointed to the morning paper folded over and laying on my chair.

"MESSENGER SHOT!" read the fifty-point headline. I read on, wondering why this earned a super-sized font.

A messenger employed by the Pepsi Arena was shot just after 1 a.m. as he was on his way to deliver word to manager Peter Himes of country music singer Tory McCloud's marriage to multimillionaire entrepreneur Jason Fields last night in a Las Vegas chapel. Fields is currently under investigation for the murder of Tory McCloud's country music star brother Tyler McCloud, to whom Fields lost a copyright dispute.

Bobby Fleming, 19, of Colonie, was employed by the Pepsi Arena as a general laborer and had been sent by Dobro player Joe Lauper to tell Himes of McCloud's marriage. McCloud called the band at their rehearsal to check in and share her news. Lauper was to get word to Himes. Fleming, who ran errands as well as crewing events, was picked to make the call. He never reached his destination.

The body was found on Lark Street, three blocks from the hotel where Himes was staying. When reached for comment, Himes said only that he was cooperating with police, and that Fleming had never come to his rooms.

Albany Police Department will investigate. Department spokesperson Gail Woodruff said the Homicide Division will work closely with State Police investigating the murder of Tyler McCloud to see if there is a connection between the two deaths.

"Oh, God," I groaned.

"You've got that right," said Jean. "I could have told you this was only going to get worse."

"Jean, I doubt if even you expected this!"

"I knew something was going to happen. Bound to the way you attract trouble."

"Hey! I - "

The phone rang.

"Did you see it?" Bryan, in official voice.

"Yes, just now."

"They're putting me on it, but not alone. They don't want any questions. When they found out I was actually Fields's alibi last night, Chief said I might as well stay on it. "

"You mean they were looking at Jason for this? Why?"

"Take it easy. You know they can't stand it when one person is so near to two murders."

"Except this time he was nearly three thousand miles away," I argued.

"I know, I know. They'll need a statement from you sometime today. We need to let the newlyweds know. Any idea how Tory will take this?"

"No. It's not like she knew this Bobby Fleming or anything. You'll just have to see."

"Uh - well, here's the thing. Since you know her so well, I was going to ask you to go with me to talk with her."

"What? I don't know her that well. And I have patients to see."

"On a Saturday?"

"I've started keeping Saturday morning hours every other week. I meant to tell you. This is the first weekend." I knew how defensive I sounded, but darn it, my job is important, and he doesn't tell me every little thing either. "Why do you need to talk to Tory? How can it help?"

"It's the connection. It's weird this should all be happening around her. You and I know she didn't have anything to do with it, but the department hates coincidences, so I have to talk to her. Besides, I'd like to see if she knows anything about him. She strikes me as the kind of person who pays attention to the people around her."

"Maybe she'll have something to say. But if this keeps up, I'm putting in a bill for my services. I thought I was a doctor!"

"And a darn good one too. I'll call when I'm ready to leave."

"Fine. I'll be at the office all morning." That sounded more curt than I intended, but I couldn't help myself. Somehow Bryan had managed to get on my bad side in one short phone call.

Jean's expression was as baleful as ever when I left. Maybe I should have paid better attention to her. Despite the pretty day and the enervating gusts of wind that buffeted me as I descended the stairs from my front yard to the crossing that led to my office, despite the sunshine and the smiling faces in my waiting room, despite the confidence I felt that Tory and Jason had absolutely no connection to this latest murder, despite all of that, I should have known there was more to come.

Andrea's eyes were shining and her face was flushed. She'd worn her hair up in becoming swirls, and I was just about to compliment her when I spotted the cause of her blushing cheeks emerging from the darkest corner of the waiting room.

"Hello, Dr. Wilder."

"Hello, Trooper Matheson. I'd say this looks like an official call."

"It is." He scanned the room and raised his voice. "Don't worry, folks. I have to talk with Dr. Wilder for a few moments. Then she'll get to you. I won't be arresting her." He smiled at the laughter this generated.

"Gee, thanks," I said, turning to face him as I closed my office door. "Any other gems you want to share with my patients?"

"Sorry. I was just trying to put everyone at ease. You know you aren't under any suspicion this time."

"Thanks again. Sit down, Ted. Is this about Bobby Fleming?"

"You saw the paper?"

"And heard from Bryan. You know they've put him on this?"

"Yeah. Don't understand it, but I heard. You going to talk to him again?"

I nodded.

"Tell him I'll get with him as soon as I hear from Nashville."

"Nashville?"

"We decided to look into Tyler McCloud from that end, see if there's been any trouble that might have followed him up here. I'm supposed to get a report by two o'clock." He played with his hat. "It may be that whatever this is had its start in Nashville. Could be music, could be drugs, who knows? I've known bands that smuggled diamonds in their instrument cases. These people get in all kinds of trouble."

"That doesn't ring true to me. I mean, I never met Tyler, but I know Jason pretty well, and Tory is - Tory is just Tory. She's exactly what she seems."

"Sometimes that makes its own trouble."

"Whatever. I'll bet almost anything, Nashville has nothing to do with this." I frowned at him. "What else did you want, Ted?"

"Two things. One. What do you know about plants?"

"Plants? You mean growing plants? Green plants?"

"Well, yeah." Ted looked puzzled.

"Good. For a minute I thought you wanted me to know about things planted on someone."

"Doc!"

"Sorry. Anyway, I know a little. Why?"

"The Medical Examiner found traces of plant matter on Tyler McCloud's trouser cuffs. Not surprising. She found some of it in his mouth, too."

"His mouth?"

"Yeah. It looks like he might have been chewing on it. She identified it as some sort of wild mint."

"That makes sense to me. What's your question? I mean, if she identified it, I'm sure she can tell you if it had any effect on him, or anything else pertinent to his ingesting it. "

"You know the property RFD is on, and you know the situation. I could have my men go out there and search for wild mint, but asking you may give us a jump on it. Where would he have picked up something like that? He'd have had to be walking through it to pull some up to chew on. Maybe that wasn't an unusual habit for him. Maybe Ms. McCloud would be willing to share that with you. The big question is, where could he have found it that night?"

"Do you know exactly what it was?"

"McBride said it was - " he tilted his head toward the ceiling and squinted his eyes in thought. "She called it Mentha xpiperita L. You can ask her for more details. I'll authorize her to release information to you."

I smiled. Last time around, he hadn't been so eager to give me a go-ahead. Medical Examiner Betty McBride and I went pretty far back. Besides friendship, there was a mutual respect.

"I'll talk to her, but, if I'm not mistaken, that's just peppermint. What good will it do you to know where he got it?"

"We're trying to figure out how he - and the murderer - got into the complex to begin with. If we can trace his steps, it might tell us not only how they got in, but where else they were. That might locate some witnesses."

"All right. Sure. I'll see if I can help. What else?"

"Huh?"

"You said you had two questions for me. What else?"

"Oh. Yeah." He reddened, and he turned his hat round and round, but he didn't let his embarrassment stop him. "Uh, question number two. How do I go about getting a date with Andrea?"

"Andrea?"

He nodded eagerly.

"Andrea. My nurse."

"She is a nurse, then? Not just a receptionist?"

"She's a fully licensed nurse. She likes keeping busy, so she claims. She won't let me hire anyone else for the office. Which is all right by me," I added. "Why don't you just ask her out? It's no big deal."

"Oh I don't know, Doc. I think it is a pretty big deal. She's an attractive young woman, and a professional, too. You have to be careful around women like that. You must know how that is."

"Um, sure. I think. Ted, Andrea is very easy-going. I'm sure if you simply ask her to go out with you, it will be fine."

"No. No. It's got to be more than that. I've got an idea." With that he swung his hat onto his head. "Tell Bryan I'll be in touch." He marched purposefully out my door, passing right by Andrea's desk with nary a word.

A moment later she brought me the files of the three patients waiting for me.

"Dr. Wilder, do you know if that trooper is seeing anyone?"

I wanted to giggle. "No, Andrea, I don't think he is. You be nice to him, okay? I don't know how much experience he's had with professional women."

"Professional women? Doctor Wilder, I am not!" She flushed to the roots of her curly hair. "You didn't mean it that way, did you?"

"No, but remember what I said about being nice to him. Now, what have we got this morning?"

She was still blushing. "Okay. You've just got two in for shots, and Mrs. Wickowskey's fall allergies are acting up. I swear, she comes in on the exact same day every year. I should just pencil her in on this date for the next ten years. I'll send the Wiestmullers in for Tommy's hepatitis shot first."

She hustled out, and I picked up Tommy's chart.

We finished quickly, and there were no more patients. I took the opportunity to get my records in order and make notes for the following week. I'd just put my pen down from signing the last note when Andrea put through the call from Bryan. It was ten fifty-seven.

·C·H·A·P·T·E·R· *17*

·M·A·C·K·E·N·Z·I·E·

"We'll say the things you say to soothe the one you love."

- from "It's Never Over" by Joe Lauper and Tyler McCloud

I didn't get it," he grumbled at me.

"Didn't get what?"

"The refracting lens. Guy outbid me by a hundred and fifty-five dollars. Damn! I'd feel worse if it had been close, though."

"I'm sorry." I waited for something more, but the line was silent. "Is that all you called about? "

"No, actually. I need to ask you a couple things."

"You too?"

"What, why? Who else has been asking you questions?"

I laughed. "Matheson. He stopped in earlier. Among other things he wanted to know how to ask Andrea for a date. Plus he had a mission for me, and a message for you."

"Message?"

"He's contacted Nashville, they're checking out the music business angle on Tyler. He said he'll get in touch with you after they get back to him."

Bryan grunted. "What's this about a mission for you?"

"Something to do with Tyler chewing on mint. I'm supposed to see if there's any mint around the RFD complex."

Another grunt. Did I sense disapproval in this one?

But it appeared his train of thought was moving on. "Have you heard from Jason or Tory? Or, did you call them?"

"No. Why would I call them?"

Bryan cleared his throat. "I thought you might have already called to see if they'd heard the news about Fleming."

"No, I was waiting for you. I was supposed to wait, wasn't I?"

"Sure, sure. I just thought you might've gone ahead anyway, the way you do sometimes."

"I suppose you agree with Jean that I attract trouble, too!" I could feel my skin grow hot. *What was with everybody today?*

"No, I don't think that."

"Good."

"You're just a little independent, is all."

"Bryan, I told you I didn't call them."

"Okay, okay. So, can you meet me at their condo? I'm ready to ask Tory those questions."

"Why exactly do you want me there?"

"For one thing you're observant. You'll notice if she's hiding anything, or if she says something significant."

"First thing, you'll be asking the questions, so *you'll* notice anything significant. Second thing, why on earth would she be hiding something? Surely you're not suspicious of her?"

"I - well, no - well - oh, hell - "

"Bryan, what is going on? Be straight with me."

"Mackenzie, I'm being as straight with you as I can be under the circumstances. The Chief is not happy that you're so involved in a case again. You know I'm not completely comfortable with it either."

"The Chief isn't happy about my involvement, neither are you, and yet you are asking me to go with you on an interview? Really?"

Sigh. "Inconsistent, huh?"

"Only very. Bryan, either I am helpful or I am not. I'm going to stay involved in this case. No more explanations or excuses. I am what I am.

Take it or leave it." *Did I just say that? Well, I guess I had to be blunt about it sometime or he'd never get it.*

"I'll take it." His answer was prompt enough. "I don't know what the Chief will say."

"When the case is solved, he'll say 'good job'," I told him firmly. "I'll meet you at Jason's. I'll help you question Tory, but I'm going there as much for her as to help you. Because I don't think she has anything to hide."

Bryan groaned. "I don't think so either. But she could hold back something pertinent without knowing it. I just want you along."

"I'll meet you there. Fifteen minutes."

Actually it took longer than that. Travel on the River Road and then I90 to the upper end of Albany where Jason's condo was located took me about twenty minutes. Bryan's trip from the South End took less time, but we were both stymied by a lack of parking space when we got there. Two news vans and a pack of older cars and a Jeep clogged the small tree-dotted lot in front of the condo. I parked next door while Bryan turned on his blue light to convince the Channel 10 van to move.

A driver in the Channel 6 truck was eating a sandwich. He raised a Coke in salute as I scurried past him. Before either Bryan or I could reach the steps, Peter Himes pushed through the crowd. Somebody must have recognized him, because suddenly they were accosting him instead of the front door.

"When did they get married? Did you know what your client was up to?"

"What about the police? Is Jason Fields in trouble for jumping bail?"

"How's Tory taking news of last night's shooting?"

"Did she know this Fleming kid?"

"Hold on, hold on." Peter had reached the steps and turned to face the cluster of reporters. He waved hands laden with wine and white roses over his head. He looked at them in surprise as he lowered them, as if he'd forgotten the stuff was there.

"Look, Jason and Tory took a quick flight to a little chapel in Vegas and got married. I understand they had a police escort - " his eyes flicked to Bryan and me "- and a good friend to stand up for them. They got in early this morning. I don't know if they know about last night's incident yet. If you'll let me talk to them, I'll be sure to inform you of what they do know." He spoke to us directly, "I imagine you're here to see them, too?"

"Yes. We came out to see how they're doing." Bryan reached a hand towards me.

The reporters shifted glances between us, unsure of who we were, or what we were to their stories. One narrowed his eyes at Bryan,

"Aren't you Bryan Jamison? Homicide?"

Bryan slipped his bland expression over his face. "Yes. I'm also a Protestant, a softball player, and her friend." He pointed to me. "I wear a lot of hats, friend, but right now it does not include interviewee." He raised his voice. "All of you need to leave. You heard Mr. Himes say he'd talk to you later. If you have any other questions, the Public Relations Officer at South End Station will be happy to answer them, or you can read the latest release from their office. Otherwise, you can go."

"Sounded more like you were dismissing them from interrogation," I whispered to him as the journalists filed past.

One cameraman walked backwards for a last shot. The print men were still scribbling or adding notes to their smart phones. One looked over his shoulder at us, a thoughtful expression on his face.

"Come on, let's get inside," said Peter, herding us through the door.

I wondered how it was suddenly open. I watched Peter pocket a key and then call up the stairs.

"You all can come out now, Tory." he called. "Jason?"

Tentative steps came from the hall behind the stairs.

"Are they gone?" whispered Tory.

"They're gone, sweet thing," said Peter, hugging Tory. "Now, where's that new hubby of yours?"

"I'm right here, Himes. Looks like I need to thank you for getting rid of those reporters. Who'd have known they'd make such a fuss over a little wedding?"

"Tory's bigger than you realize, Jason. We've worked hard to get her where she is." Peter kept his arm around his client and moved her toward the sofa. "How are you doing, Tory?"

"Actually, I'm fine, Peter. I should be getting you all something to drink. Bryan? Mackie, you want anything?" She jumped up, ready to play hostess, but I could see a darkness in her eyes that wasn't due to our late night adventure or even other post-nuptial celebrating.

"Tory, you don't need to wait on every - " began Peter.

Jason broke in, "I'll get us all drinks, Tory. I think Mrs. Foote left some lemonade in the kitchen."

"Lemonade!" snorted Peter.

"I'm sure we can add something you'll like, Himes. Bryan, maybe you can come fill me in on why you're here." The two men went to the kitchen.

I wasn't sure what to do, but Tory smiled at me. I smiled back, and said, "Thanks for letting me be a part of things, Tory. It was fun."

"Thank you all for standing up for me, Mackenzie. Peter, I'm sorry we didn't include you. It was just so sudden, and I knew you weren't happy about my being with.... Well, I was afraid you'd be mad."

"Does this look like I'm mad?" Peter stretched his arms wide. "Look, flowers for the bride and wine to toast with. Come on, Tory, sweetie, you and I go way back. I'm happy for you. Have to admit, I'm not all that fond of Fields, but hell, I can adjust. Least he knows what the music business is like."

"About that, Peter. I don't know if you should include me on this tour you're settin' up."

Peter nodded. "Now, hon, you can't let the band down. Everyone, and I mean everyone, expects you're gonna carry on.

"Just this one. After that, I'll do some tours, but I'll be cutting back. I'll still record, Peter," Tory said hastily. "It's not like I'm leaving the music business."

He frowned. "We'll hash all that out later."

Jason and Bryan came back with a tray of drinks. Jason gestured to the bar as he handed Peter his. Then he went and stood behind Tory. He leaned down and whispered something in her ear. Her hand went to his where he rested it on her shoulder.

"Bryan?" Tory asked. "What's happened?"

"Tory, I just told Jason about this. Something happened last night. I'm sorry to bring you bad news today, but it can't be helped."

"Bryan, you're scarin' me." Tory giggled.

I raised my eyebrows slightly. Nerves. Was it just the unknown nature of Bryan's news that had her rattled? Or was Bryan's approach itself unsettling her? I turned my eyes on him, so I could warn him off if necessary.

Meantime Jason was squeezing her hand. Peter took her other one. Tory turned a frightened face toward him. "Peter? Do you know what this is about?"

"Yes, I do. It's all right, Tory. It's not like before. It's not like Tyler."

I saw Bryan's eyebrows go up. "He's right, Tory. This isn't like when your brother died. Someone did die, though, and he was murdered. I need to ask you some questions."

"About who? Who died? When did this happen?"

I watched her now. As upset as she appeared, her questions were coherent.

"Last night you called one of your band members, the Dobro player Joe Lauper, to tell him about your marriage to Jason, correct?"

"Yes, I did. We're like family. I wanted them to know. Did somethin' happen to Joe?"

"No, Lauper is fine. I needed to confirm what he told us."

"Bryan, tell me what happened."

"After your call, Lauper decided to send a messenger over to tell Peter here about the wedding."

"He did! Peter, I'm sorry, I wanted to tell you myself. Joe shouldn't have done that."

"I have a question, Himes," said Bryan. "For you. Why didn't Tory - or even Joe - just phone you? Why send a messenger?"

Himes smiled a modest smile that somehow conveyed superiority instead.

"It's like this, Jamison. As manager, I run twenty-one-hour days. Most of the time I have to be knowledgeable, diplomatic, friendly. So when I quit for a day, I really quit. I disconnect any direct phone lines, I tell the desk to hold calls, and I turn off my cell phone. If the venue has a messenger service, I make use of it. If they don't, I have the desk screen the calls according to a prioritized list I give them. That way I'm left undisturbed, even by reporters who have a bad knack of finding all my phone numbers. Pepsi Arena doesn't have a messenger service per se, but they agreed they'd send a gofer any time I needed to get a message. That's why Joe sent this Fleming kid last night. Only he didn't make it to my hotel room."

"Fleming kid? You mean Bobby?" Tory looked horrified.

Bryan shot me a look. "Tory, did you know Bobby Fleming?"

"Yes! Tell me what happened, Bryan!" Her face paled and she ran her hands through her short red hair, pulling it into spikes of distress.

He gestured towards Peter. "You heard Himes here say Fleming didn't make it to his hotel room. His body was found about three blocks from the hotel in an alley that ran behind it. He'd been shot."

"Oh, no! Poor Bobby!" Tory clung to Jason's hand.

"Mrs. Fields, you seem to have known Bobby Fleming. Would you explain to me how?"

Bryan's face looked pained as he switched to the formal terms of address and pulled out his notebook. Tory swallowed once, then folded her hands like a little girl about to recite.

"Lieutenant, I met Bobby Fleming when he helped the boys set up the night we came into town. Tyler sent him for food, and he came back with all these Northern sandwiches, sayin' how he wanted to prove that - that Southern food wasn't the only good food there was. We all laughed, and shared everything with him. I pulled out some of the goodies we carry with us and gave him some. You know, Goo Goo Clusters and pralines and such. We had such a good time that night. He made us feel welcome. We told him he must have Southern roots, he was so hospitable. He blushed and asked if he could have some treats for his baby sister." Tory stifled a sob. "He was a good kid!" she sputtered, then broke down fully.

"Tory, this isn't your fault! You barely knew the kid! Just because he died trying to give me your message doesn't make this your fault." Peter put his arm around her. "You can't act like it does, or the papers'll pick up on it. They're already printing stuff about you being connected to so many deaths."

Jason glared at him, for his words or his actions, I wasn't sure, but the look he gave him was ferocious.

Tory gasped, her eyes widening. "Bryan! I heard Bobby giving Tyler some kind of driving directions right before he went out the night he was killed! Maybe he was telling Tyler how to get to Jason's! I mean, I heard him say something about crossing the river and going south on some road. Maybe, maybe Bobby knew who killed Tyler! Maybe he killed Bobby!"

Bryan stopped taking notes. "That could be what happened. There'd have to be a connection between Bobby and the killer, though. We still don't have any real suspects other than Jason."

Jason registered surprise and caught my eye. I shook my head very slightly. I didn't know why Bryan said that.

"Too bad, old man," said Peter, but I swore he was concealing a smile as he reached for his drink.

Still no love lost there, despite the good cheer and wedding gifts.

"I don't know, Bryan," said Tory. "It seems too much of a coincidence that that poor boy is dead now, and Tyler died going to the place he gave directions to. I hope someone's looking out for his baby sister. Peter - "

"I know, I know. I'll send flowers and a check."

"Don't make it sound so tacky!"

"Tory, is there anything else you can tell us about Fleming? Anything else you remember from the night Tyler was killed?" Bryan asked.

"You do think it's connected," I said.

"I think it may be, so I need Tory to tell me whatever she can about him."

"There was the thing with the directions, like I said. And - and when I got the news about Ty, he seemed to understand. He saw me crying, and he said something about hoping his baby sister cried over him when he was gone like I was crying over Ty - Oh!" Tory sobbed hard this time, and Jason sat down with her.

Peter stood up and poured himself a real drink from the bar. Bryan studied his notes to give Tory time. They'd started to talk again when my cell phone went off.

"Doctor Wilder? It's Andrea. That State Trooper, Matheson? He wants you to have Lieutenant Jamison call him when you see him."

"Andrea, Bryan is right here. Can Matheson call him on his cell?"

At the sound of his name, Bryan turned his head, that stray curl falling into his eyes.

"Doc, Matheson here. Let me talk to Jamison. Uh, please."

I held the phone out to Bryan. Maybe there was new information. While he took the call out to the foyer, I leaned over to Tory and hugged her. She leaned into me for a minute, and sniffled, never letting go of Jason. Holding on to him seemed to comfort her. And even Peter's presence apparently helped.

I gathered up the glasses - Peter kept his, half-filled for the second time with Jason's bourbon. I carried them out to the kitchen on the tray and looked in the fridge for more lemonade. I found ice and added it to the glasses. A pitcher half full of lemonade was on the top shelf. I poured some into each of the glasses. Three quarters was better than nothing.

I wonder if this is from a mix or what. Maybe I should make more. It wouldn't hurt to look for more in the cupboard. I pulled out a box of tea and a jar of instant coffee, but I couldn't see anything else in there. It probably wouldn't matter.

"No! No! It can't be! No!" Tory was screaming.

"Tory! Wait!" I heard Jason call out.

Two sets of feet clattered up the stairs.

I rushed into the front room. Bryan stared helplessly up the stairs. Peter examined the smoke swirling up from the tip of his cigarette.

"Bryan? What happened? Is Tory all right?"

"She will be. I think. Honestly, I don't know. This was apparently an added blow for her."

"What was?"

"Matheson got word from Nashville." Bryan handed me my phone.

"Did they have answers for him?"

"I don't know if answers is the right word. It seems this past week they made a rather gruesome discovery in some place called 'Printers Alley' down there. A body was found in an empty storefront off the alley. It had been there about a week." Bryan's voice was grim.

I noticed that Himes was focusing even more intently on his cigarette. Gore affects some people that way. It makes other people run.

"Is that what upset Tory?" I asked.

"It's worse than that. Matheson's query raised a flag to some of the Metro detectives down there. They called as soon as they identified the body. His name is Auggie Haynes. He was a roadie, and his last employer was Tyler McCloud. Tory was a friend of his."

"Oh, no! Bryan!"

"She took it pretty badly. Screamed and ran upstairs."

"I'll check on her. Two shocks like this...." I turned to go up the stairs, realizing my hands were empty. "Um, there's lemonade in the kitchen if you want. Mr. Himes, do you know if Tory has any allergies to medications?"

"No, Doctor Wilder, I don't think she does. Jamison, I think I'd better step in here to protect my client."

"Are you a lawyer, Mr. Himes?"

"Yes, I'm a lawyer, damn it! Although I'm more of Tory's manager, I handle all her legal work as well. She's my friend; she's family. So, I don't think there will be any more questions today." He stood firm in his small square body, clearly considering himself a more than adequate obstruction.

"Mr. Himes, you must have known Auggie Haynes, too. Doesn't his death bother you?" I asked pointedly.

"Hell yes his death bothers me. Right now I need to look out for Tory's interests. That's my job." He puffed his cigarette so hard I expected to see smoke curling from his ears.

"Himes, if you knew him, you can answer my questions," Bryan said. When Himes looked like he was about to protest, Bryan added, "so Tory won't have to," and started in.

My attention was divided, listening to them with one ear while trying to decide whether or not to intrude on Tory and Jason. I didn't follow the whole conversation. I was about to turn back to the stairs when a white-faced Tory appeared at the top with Jason behind her.

"I'm sorry, y'all. Bryan, I'm sorry. I shouldn't have run away like that. It's just, it's so awful about Bobby and Auggie. Please. I know I have to answer your questions. Let's just everyone sit down again."

Jason followed her to the couch and sat close beside her. Peter stood where he could watch them.

Bryan sat across from them, leaning in to reassure Tory. "Mr. Himes was good enough to give me some information. I understand this Auggie had worked for you and Tyler for a while."

"Yes. Actually, Auggie was with us for about four years." Tory clutched her tissue in one hand and twined her other through Jason's.

"And he did... what?"

"He was a roadie."

Bryan glanced up encouragingly.

"He helped set up and tear down, load the truck. If something needed to be fixed, or picked up, or bought, he took care of it. He drove the truck sometimes."

"So, when did he quit? Or did you fire him?"

Tory's face crumpled again. "That's just it, Bryan. We didn't fire him. And he didn't quit. Well, that is, I don't think he did. He was supposed to be on this tour with us."

"He was?"

She nodded her head frantically. "He was supposed to be with us. But he didn't show up. He didn't show up the night we left." She glanced at Peter once, then she buried her head in Jason's shoulder.

"Himes? What about this? Why didn't you say something?"

Her manager gave an elaborate shrug. "Look, as far as I knew, the guy quit. That's what a no-show means. It happens all the time."

"So, you didn't file a report or anything?"

He shrugged again. "What's the point?"

Jason rolled his eyes. "Can you see the point now?"

"Look. I can't keep track of every Bubba who decides he doesn't want to work. These guys either show up and do their job, or they don't. They don't, they're off the payroll. It's not like they're family."

Tory pushed away from Jason. "Peter! Auggie *was* family!"

"What?"

"Okay, you don't know, but you should by now - Auggie and Tyler and I - we grew up together! All through school - and church. Church camp! Auggie beat up the first boy who tried to kiss me. Auggie toured with us because he loved us! He was *family*!"

"Tory, sweetie, I had no idea this Auggie was so important to you. You and Ty never said much about him. Why'd I never meet him?" Peter demanded.

Tory sniffled. "Auggie was in the Army when you came around the first time. Jason didn't know him either. He was one of the best friends

Ty and I ever had. The most reliable roadie in the business! I told you that night it wasn't like him not to show! I thought I asked you to make sure his wife called Metro for missing persons."

"Hon, you're upset. You probably don't remember right. If you'd told me to do that I would have. Maybe he would have been found before now." He swung toward Bryan. "How'd they find him, Jamison?"

"Apparently the guy in the bar next door was tracking down an odor," Bryan said.

"Oh!" Tory covered her mouth.

Jason held her close. "Tory, what can I do? Do you want to send something special to the family? Do you want to go down there?"

"Oh, Jason, could I? Teresa's gonna need some help. They've got twin boys - they're three - and it's gonna be so hard on them."

"Sweetie, you've got a tour to think about. Records, songs. You're fans'll understand about you getting married and all, but haltin' everything to go to a roadie's funeral?" Himes protested.

"Peter! You should be ashamed of yourself! What would your mama say?" Tory scolded. "You don't know the fans as well as you think you do if you think they'd hold it against me for goin' to Auggie's funeral!"

I wondered if Peter would listen to Tory any better than he would his mother. Bryan had an objection, too.

"Jason, don't you think of going. I was able to cover you leaving the state for Vegas, but you can't leave again now. Not even though you're not - " he glanced at Peter, who was listening intently, "- being kept in jail. You're still under suspicion, and you can't leave the state again."

I looked pointedly at Jason, who raised his eyebrows in return. He'd caught it, too. Whatever reason Bryan had for doing it, I hoped we could cover. Tory concerned me the most. She was overloaded right now. I didn't know if she was aware enough to play along.

Jason waded right into battle with Bryan, his expression fierce. Whatever Bryan was doing he would help it along, to protect Tory. The protectiveness from him was sweet - unlike the kind from Peter.

"That's ridiculous!" he shouted. "No one takes those charges seriously. Tory can't go alone!"

Tory tried to wave off Jason's concern, but Bryan was already arguing back.

"The Chief and the D. A. both take those charges seriously. You can't go."

"You all, I'm a grown woman. I can travel by myself if I want to."

"Fields, I'm her manager. Tory, if you want to go down to Nashville to see this guy's family, I'll take you. You need lookin' after, and I guess I need to go anyway. Is that all right with the local sheriff?"

"It'll work," said Bryan evenly. "So long as Jason stays here in town."

"Great," said Peter, pouring himself another drink. "I'll make arrangements this afternoon. Jason, Tory, I'll call you later with the details."

"Great," muttered Jason, with a black look.

"Great, then," I said, surveying them all. "So now there's just one question: who killed Auggie?"

·C·H·A·P·T·E·R· 18

·M·A·C·K·E·N·Z·I·E·

"Close ties, new starts - "

- from "Christmas Fires" by Jason Fields and Tory McCloud

My question didn't win me any prizes. No one had any answers, and no one knew if the body in Nashville was related to our New York murders or not. All we knew was that Tory was devastated. Our gathering dissolved inside of minutes.

I didn't hear from Bryan for a week, except for a quick call to tell me Tory was indeed going to Nashville with Peter Himes; Jason did not get to go. I didn't hear from Ted Matheson either, although there were plenty of signs of him about the office.

There was the copy of *The Bone Lady* by Mary Manhein, for instance. And a copy of Shakespeare's sonnets. And one of Jean Kerr's *Please Don't Eat the Daisies*. Apparently Ted was a reader with eclectic tastes, which had Andrea totally confused. UPS dropped off the first book at the office on Monday. On Wednesday the second one was waiting in the office mailbox, while the third book apparently was delivered to Andrea's house by hand on Sunday while everyone was in church.

Well, most people. I had taken the morning off from fellowship, only to find myself on the receiving end of Jean's scolding righteous tongue.

"I see from your clothes and the position of your car that you didn't go to church this morning," she commented, dropping her purse on one of the dining room chairs. "You sick?"

"No," I said, snugging my robe closer. "I decided not to go for one Sunday. I usually go. You know that. Rachel and I are going out to the farm later today. I had some stuff to get ready."

"Hmph. You're still here. You had time to go to church."

"What are you? My mother?"

"Don't be silly."

"Then quit trying to run my life. What are you doing here anyway?"

"Somebody needs to keep track of you. I'm here to make up chicken and some casseroles to keep you fed while I'm in Maine the first part of the week," she said, tying her apron over her Sunday dress.

"Thank you. I'd almost forgotten you were going. What do you do in Maine this time of year?" I crossed to the counter and poured myself a cup of tea.

"The trees in Vermont and New Hampshire are starting to turn. And the beaches aren't crowded this time of year. It's peaceful." She pulled some plastic containers out of the cupboard. "Here. I'll pack some of my chocolate cake and some fruit for you and Rachel this afternoon."

"Okay. Isn't there food out at the farm?" Our goal was to keep both larders well-stocked, so that it never mattered which house I went to. I added a bagel to a plate and sat down at the kitchen table.

Jean shook her head at me as she packaged the goodies. "That refrigerator is almost bare. I swear those workmen are stealing food from me - you - us, oh, you know!"

"I do know, Jean. It's okay. I doubt they really are, but I guess we'll have to keep track. So, who's going with you to Maine?" I bit into the bagel slathered with Jean's quince jelly. Perfect.

"Mildred Davenport is riding up with me. We'll stay at the Oceanside in York. Just a few days." She pulled a roasting pan out and headed for the 'fridge to get the chicken.

"I didn't realize Mildred Davenport liked long trips like that. I'm surprised you're not taking Arthur."

"Dr. Wilder! Really! Mildred Davenport was friends with my own mother. This is a trip we all used to take together. She likes a long walk on the beach as much as I do." By now the chicken was rinsed, seasoned, brushed with olive oil that had sun-dried tomatoes crushed into it. In a few minutes she'd have it in the oven.

"That looks great. Don't overwork yourself, though. I can manage a few days without you. Rachel will appreciate the cake, I'm sure," I added as she set the container at my elbow. "I'd better run."

And run I did. I dressed in jeans and tee and sweatshirt, for there was no telling how the day would turn out weather-wise. I pulled up Bryan's long drive, and Rachel ran out and hopped in the car.

"Daddy just left. He got called in, but he knew you'd be here soon. I got all my homework done, so I don't have a curfew. That means I can stay all day! If that's all right with you?"

"No problem, kiddo. We've got a lot of planning to do if we want this camp to open next summer. Did you talk to Lucas about it yet?"

She brushed strawberry blond wisps of hair away from her eyes. "It's Luke now, Mackie. I told him. He asked me to ask you if he could get his dad to buy him one could he keep a horse at the camp. I told him I thought you were going to let me, so I didn't see why you'd tell him no. I hope that's okay."

I chuckled at her rush of words. "I think we can find a way to accommodate him."

She frowned at me.

"I mean he can probably keep a horse out there."

"Oh. Good. And Mackie?"

"Yes?"

"Can I have a club house at the farm?"

I laughed out loud. "I don't see why not. Don't tell Jean right away. She thinks I'm crazy enough as it is."

"Okay. It can be our secret. And Luke's."

"Can we tell your dad?"

A big decision. The two of them were so close. I bet myself she wouldn't be able to shut him out. Not quite.

"Let's not tell him yet. I want to surprise him when it's all done. Do you think the workmen would help us?"

"I think we can get them to help. Maybe we can make a contract with them."

"Ooh. Great. I want it to have two levels. One down low, and one up in a treetop. Maybe two rooms in the lower level. And windows, and a porch...."

"Whoa, girl! You're worse than I am! Let's see what's going on out there today, and maybe we can pick out a site for this castle you're describing!"

A flush crept along her creamy freckled skin. She pulled her hair back in a ponytail and fastened it with a holder. "Mackie! Look! They've cleared a road down to the creek! And there's an open space there! Oh, boy!"

She leapt out of the car and raced across the road. I waved to Brett, the chief carpenter. Across the road and down the bank roared a bulldozer and front-loader while dump trucks idled nearby. This had been my surprise for Rachel. When she'd been here last, this road and clearing were only so many words the grown-ups were throwing about. Since then we'd acquired permits, insurance, an architect. The horse camp was building into a reality, mostly due to her.

"C'mon, Mackie! I want to see this!"

"Wait a minute. Brett, I know I'm paying overtime, but I hadn't expected to see them working on a Sunday. Or you either. What's up?"

"I just stopped by to look in on them. That's Horowitz and Diamond over there. Horowitz is Jewish and Diamond decided he's Seventh Day Adventist. Boss lets them work on Sundays so they can have Saturday off for church - whatever. So, they're not really getting overtime. They're about to quit for the day anyway. You'll have the place to yourselves in twenty minutes."

"Fine by me. Rachel, you and I are going down to that temporary barn we've put up out back. By the time we're done there, we should be able to go down and check the site."

"Why can't we just go over now? Do we have to wait?" She spun around, denim jacket flaring in impatience.

"I think we have to wait long enough to saddle up, or don't you want to ride down there?" I waited for her reaction.

"Ride? Ride? Did you say ride?" Her eyes flew open as wide as they could possibly go.

"I said ride." I grinned and explained. "Our first two horses, yours and mine, arrived the other day. That's what the temporary barn is for. They'll stay there until we've either got the stable built across the road, or until the new barn is done, whichever gets done first."

The new barn was to replace the one that had burned down last spring. Already the foundation was restored and the first floor laid in. There were some modifications from the original building, but it was true in its design. Difference was, this one would house goats and rabbits and chickens. Only a couple horses. Most of them would be in the camp stable, down where we were soon to ride. One more ambitious project I was only too happy to spend my time and money on.

Rachel flew ahead of me, down the hill and up to the barn door. Two large box stalls flanked a central opening, a mere breezeway between doors. This shelter wasn't much bigger than a trailer, but it was adequate to protect our new friends.

"That's Ginger Peach." I pointed to a rosy Palomino nibbling at the straw in the corner of her box. "She's seven years old, sired by Gingeroot out of Peaches 'n' Cream. She's mine. Hey, Peachy," I added softly. Then I turned Rachel toward the other stall.

"Ohh!" She drew breath and held it in. Gently she tiptoed to the stall door, resting her hands lightly along the top.

Inside stood a slender red gelding, his black tail trailing almost to the floor. His features were delicate, but he had a wide-set forehead and a full chest on sleek legs. He stood a only fifteen hands tall, and he was six years old. I passed this information to her as we gazed over the rail.

"What are they, Mackie? I mean, what kind of horses are they?"

"Ginger Peach is mostly American Quarter Horse. Your horse is a Morgan; his name is Red Allen's Justice."

Rachel wrinkled her nose at me. "Yuck."

"Well, the papers said his sire was descended from a famous Morgan trotter called Ethan Allen 50. And his dam was Sweet Justine."

"But, Red Allen's Justice? What can I call him?"

"Well, you could call him Red, or Justy...."

She wrinkled her nose again. "I don't think so. I'll work on it." She pulled open the stall door. "Here, boy. How are you, fella?"

The horse stretched his neck in her direction, blowing softly and stepping toward her. He draped his head over her shoulder and stood calmly while she patted his neck. I saw her eyelids close as her lips parted to move in soft whispers. Red - or Justy - flicked his ears forward, following every word she murmured.

"Ready to saddle up?"

"You bet!"

"Stuff's over there at the end of the stall. Bring him outside and tie him first. Watch the halter."

We brought both horses outside and tied them to some low-hanging branches. I helped Rachel wrestle out the saddle blankets and saddles, and she stroked the horses while I lifted them into place. I showed her how to buckle the girth, cinching it just tight enough to slide her hand between it and the horse's belly so it wouldn't slide but wouldn't hurt either.

"Now, let's get these stirrups the right length. Hold up your hand," I told her.

She shot her hand straight up in the air, grinning at me.

"No, silly. Careful not to spook them," I added, as Red Allen's Justice took a step sideways. "Put your fingertips here, at the top of the stirrup strap. Now, hold the stirrup up to your armpit."

"Yeah, armpit," she intoned.

"Um, yeah. Okay, see how this strap is hanging low? It needs to be right up next to your arm. Let's tighten this thing."

"Yeah, tighten," she repeated, bobbing her head.

Hoo boy.

We adjusted the stirrups on both saddles and moved on to the bridles. Like the saddles, I had to do these. Even though these weren't big horses, Rachel's reach didn't quite make it. We'd have to come up with some sort of arrangement for her and others of her stature. I made a mental note of it. I wanted all of our campers to attend to their own horses whenever possible.

At last we could mount up. Here Rachel didn't need so much help. She'd ridden before, and was probably a better trail rider than I was. My riding up 'til now had been mostly in the ring.

The horses' hooves clopped softly over the weeds and gravel and dirt as we moved from the lower field along the tractor path and past the barn. We guided them carefully through the construction with its pickup trucks and boards and circular saws, up the rocky incline that circled the barn and out onto the road.

I watched with dismay as Rachel suddenly tightened her reins, clapped her little legs against Red's sides and jogged off down the road. I wanted to shout a reminder about cars, but they really didn't come along that often out here. I wanted to call out, "hey, wait for me!" but pride wouldn't let me. An equal sense of pride and responsibility wouldn't allow me to let her get too far ahead. Let's face it, I was afraid Bryan would be mad.

Still, I hadn't ridden in years. Never like this!

Always a first time.

That voice in my head was getting mean.

I kicked Ginger into a jog with a mental eye-closing of resignation. *This is it!* Ginger obligingly jogged, taking slightly longer strides than Red. We caught up in no time, causing me to wonder if my horse felt as maternal towards Red as I did towards Rachel.

We came to the turn-off. Here our pathway was soft earth, rutted by the construction vehicles and dump trucks. On our left was Wexford Road, running between Routes 9 and 20, bisecting the farm. Our path, which would eventually be the access road for the camp and the surrounding acreage, descended parallel to the paved road. The hill that rose to our left was covered in weeds, surmounted by saplings and a few older trees that had been there most of my lifetime. To our right was the overgrown forest of my parents' creation. This had been one of our fields of Christmas trees. Planted so long ago under plans to be sold at the holidays, they'd accomplished their ultimate purpose of reforesting the field. They stood tall in a solid mass, branches reaching toward us as if curious to see who was disturbing them.

I'd told the guys to leave as much of the forest as they reasonably could, allowing for buildings and riding ring, trails and hiking paths. They hadn't disturbed anything along here yet, and the Scotch pines and blue spruces loomed over our heads, shutting out sun and sound alike. Red's and Ginger's hooves thudded on the packed earth. The road right-angled ahead, in front of the creek, making it look as if we were riding into the mountain of black sand that rose beyond the water. Chopped up by diggers and sand trucks as first my family and then subsequent owners sold sand to the cement companies, it was an environmental wreck, an eyesore waiting for Nature to heal it.

With a little help from her friends. I had plans to incorporate what was left of the sand bank into our camp, and then leave the rest to recover. I knew what was around the bend. Rachel didn't. She hadn't been where she could see what the workmen had accomplished. I was eager to catch her reaction. Cautiously I kicked Ginger into a lope.

I grinned at Rachel as I passed her. Ginger's lope was nearly as easy as a Tennessee Walking horse's rolling trot. Rachel hurried Red up a bit, but kept it to a jog. Ginger and I reached the turn in easy time to circle up and face them as they came up.

"Better put your tongue back in your mouth. You'll bite it like that."

That only made her stick it out farther. She always stuck the tip of her tongue out of her mouth when she was concentrating hard. I could see her position her hands just so, gripping her thigh with one hand while she kept her other hand precisely over the pommel of the saddle. I could almost hear her telling herself to grip with her legs, pull back on the reins, ease up in the saddle to let Red know she was at rest. All that concentration kept her busy, and when she looked up, it was with complete surprise.

"It's beautiful! Mackie, the cabins, there's six of them?" her voice squeaked on the 'six'. We only discussed having four. "And the ring, it's so big! Where does that path go? Is it one of the trails? Is there a cook house - oh, what did Jean say?"

"Easy, now, you're getting Red upset here." I reached out to fend off Red's shoulder where he was sidestepping closer to Ginger. She moved her feet, but seemed unconcerned about her livelier companion. "Slow down a little. Let's ride on up and I'll show you around. Head over there, alongside the fence."

We went along the rail of the ring whose outer edge was the very first thing you came to after you turned the corner at the creek. One side of fence ran right along the creek bed, lined as it was with sumac, maple, oak, and elm. The side we rode along ran about a hundred feet before turning another corner towards the cluster of cabins. Three were complete. Two more were underway, and the foundation for the sixth raised its white blocks above the gray-brown piles of dirt.

Beyond the fencing lay the mess hall where campers would eat, gather, and learn the work aspect of camping by taking turns preparing the meals and cleaning up after them. We rounded the corner, passing Horowitz and Diamond as they climbed into a midnight blue pickup and backed around to leave. Diamond raised a hand to us as they went by, a freshly-lit cigarette between his fingers.

We kept jogging, the new fence smelling of pine and tar and fresh dug postholes. It went on for a long ways. This area was going to be pasture as well as riding ring. As we approached the framework of the new stable, we passed where the dividing fence would be. Multiple stable doors would allow horses to be turned out in either area; a gate would allow them to pass between.

I took a quick glance sideways at Rachel. She couldn't turn her head quickly enough to see it all. It must have impressed her; she hadn't said another word. Beyond the stable's exterior wall lay another small fenced pasture. That had a gate at the end of it that opened into the trailheads. Three trails were being cut into the woods. Our campers would be limited to using them until we could safely create more. I wanted to disturb the woods as little as possible, so we were going to take our time about it.

We reined in at the gate and turned the horses so we could look back. The sun brought the scene into sharp contrast with the wooded surroundings. They made a coniferous green frame to the bone-colored earth, brilliant white stone, and bleached two-by-fours.

Rachel pushed herself up in the saddle; her head panned the scene, the ends of her hair quivering with the intensity of her inspection. Her saddle creaked as she swiveled to see me better.

"Mackenzie, it's grand!"

" 'Grand'? Not 'awesome' or 'cool'?" I teased.

"Nope. Grand. It's the only word for it. Only - "

"What, hon?"

"Only it looks kind of - chopped up, the way the trees are cut back and everything. Is it gonna stay like that?"

I chuckled. "Not if I know this place. Those trees and the grass and brush will fill right back in. We'll probably bring some stuff in to help fill it in, too. Kind of give it a helping hand. I take it the camp has your approval?"

"Oh, yeah!"

"Well, come on, we should get the horses back. We have to curry them down before we put them up."

"Can't we try one of the trails first?"

"Not this time. They're not really ready yet. Besides, like I said, we have to take proper care of the horses. Come on. We have to get them done before Brooklynne gets here. She's picking you up, remember?"

"Oh, yeah. So you and Daddy can go out to dinner again."

I hunted for any sound of criticism in her voice, but there was none. Not that I expected any, but you never know.

Even though it wasn't far and the horses were thoroughly at ease, we took it easy going back. I wasn't familiar enough with the state of the terrain to rush it, and there really wasn't any need. Sure enough, though, Rachel urged Red into a lope as soon as we hit the road. I watched her seat - her riding seat, that is. She'd taken to riding a new horse with the same ease her father played baseball.

I showed her where to tie the horses up to groom them. Without any further instruction she put the saddle and bridle where they belonged and hunted down the currycombs. A thorough currying with the metal and rubber combs and we were done. I showed her where to get water and where we stored the grain. After we'd settled them in the stalls, Rachel lingered, switching from one stall to the other.

"Do we have to leave them? Who'll take care of them at night?"

"They'll be fine. No one is going to bother them out here, and one of the workmen will check on them every day until I hire whoever is going to run the stable for us. One of Bret's men has horses himself; he said he'd do it."

"Okay," she murmured, but I don't think she was entirely satisfied with the arrangement. She sighed what seemed to be a sigh of contentment over her ride and kept looking back over her shoulder as we climbed the hill back to the house.

Bret was gone. The yard was deep in grass and newly fallen leaves from the maple and ash trees that lined the road. The sun was busy working its way down into our own personal colorama behind the trees where the road led off into the distance. There it would rest briefly atop the distant mountains before it sank beneath purpling clouds. It wasn't dusk yet; the afternoon was developing that golden amber color of a closing autumn day.

"Let's sit on the porch to wait for Brooklynne," I said. Rachel followed me in silence. She kept to one side of me, the side away from the barn. The memories of last spring, I suspected, when she'd had to help rescue me from where I'd been suspended over an old haymow. Everything had worked out fine, but it would have surprised me if there hadn't been some residual effects on her.

"Well, what did you think? Do you have any ideas for our camp?" I asked her as we sat down on the cement steps that crossed the face of the ancient porch.

"Not yet. But I know I will. I - Wait. Do you hear a car?" She held up a finger. "Yeah, there it is! I bet it's Aunt Brooklynne. Hey, no, wait a minute! It's Mrs. Cooper! Luke is with her!" Jumping up, she ran to meet the champagne-colored Corolla as it pulled down the driveway from its entrance by the barn.

·C·H·A·P·T·E·R· *19*

·M·A·C·K·E·N·Z·I·E·

"My heart kept sayin' "It's not fair."

- from "It's Never Over" by Joe Lauper and Tyler McCloud

I hadn't seen Naomi since that day in my office, and I wasn't sure how she'd act. One thing: I was glad Tory wasn't with us today. I became apprehensive though, when Naomi didn't look directly at Rachel as she ran up to greet them.

"Luke! Wait 'til you see the horses! The first ones came!"

"Really? Hello, Dr. Wilder."

"Hi, Luke. Naomi, how are you doing this week?"

"Hi, Rachel. Yes, go see the horses, you two. I'm going to sit here with Mackie." She plopped down beside me on the front porch. "Doing better now that I know what's going on. Bob, of course, was thrilled, though not so much when I reminded him I'd have to stop work for a while."

"The kids excited?"

"Mhm. Luke here is worried about me. I can't seem to convince him that this is a natural procedure and that I've been here before. Everybody else seems to be taking it in stride." She laughed, a little bit of hesitation coming through.

I joined in to reassure her, but my own laughter didn't ring entirely true either.

Awkward silence.

"Naomi, I hope the other day didn't upset you too much. There's a couple things you should hear."

"Mackie, it's okay. This isn't your fault. In fact, it's not Tory McCloud's fault, either. She's not responsible for what her brother did, and she obviously loves him as much as I love Braeden. I wish there were a way I could apologize to her."

"Actually, I can help with that. It seems I'll be getting to know her a bit more than I'd expected." I went on to outline the boat ride and wedding trip.

Naomi listened thoroughly to my story. "That's very interesting."

"Why interesting?"

"Well, where did you stay?"

I smiled. "Jason put us up at the Bellagio. We weren't there long. We actually came right back after the ceremony."

She took a deep breath and leaned back, stretching her back and brushing her hair from her eyes. "You know, after the other day, I went home and sat down and had a good cry. Then I went through a bunch of Braeden's things. Found a couple that I'd forgotten about. Did Tory say anything about Tyler owning a house in Las Vegas?"

"No, she didn't. What makes you think he did?"

"I have the deed, with his name on it."

"What? How - Braeden left that to you? How did he get it?"

"He had the deed - a copy of it, because he was co-owner. He and Tyler McCloud owned a house together in an upscale neighborhood of Las Vegas."

"Did Braeden live there?"

Naomi shook her head. "I don't know. It's not his usual address. I don't know what Braeden did with the property. Or Tyler either. Even though I have the deed, I don't receive any correspondence on it, no taxes, or anything. I've been assuming that it went to Tyler when Braeden died. So, I don't know who has it now. All I know is that it's only one of the weird things about this situation."

I looked at her, raising my eyebrows. At first she seemed reluctant to elaborate, then she sighed, as if she knew going ahead was the only way.

"Okay. This is painful, and I know it sounds like I'm blaming Tory or something, but can you really tell me she didn't know about Tyler and Braeden? Braeden worked for them, and he wasn't just some roadie, he worked directly with their manager. According to Braeden, Himes never let the McClouds do anything without his okay. If he was so close with them, how could Tory not know who Braeden was?" Her expression was uncomfortably accusing. I was squirming mentally even before she added, "Then there's the money."

"I know you said that Braeden lost everything."

"It wasn't just that he lost everything, Mackie. Braeden was borrowing money to gamble with. He'd never done that before. He had contempt for people who couldn't keep their gambling under control. Came from growing up with our father, I guess. Braeden had never, *ever* borrowed money that way. If he went bust, he left the table." She shook her head, eyes tearing up again. "I don't get it, Mackenzie. It was against Braeden's nature."

"I don't know, Naomi. Sometimes people change in ways we don't expect. Especially when there is an addiction like this involved."

"Is that what you think gambling is? An addiction?"

She looked so hopeful. Would it help to tell her that yes, gambling was addictive behavior as much as drugs, drinking, or even certain styles of overeating? I was opening my mouth to speak when something she'd said finally registered.

"Naomi, I thought you said Braeden had lost everything."

"I did. He did."

"Well, if he still had part ownership in this house with Tyler, he hadn't lost everything. Why didn't he sell it to Tyler? Or to his creditors?"

She shrugged. "I don't know. I assumed Tyler wouldn't buy it, or else he wouldn't let Braeden sell it to anyone else. I guess I was so mad at him, I didn't stop to wonder about it. It is weird."

"Mom! Mom!"

Lucas and Rachel were running back to us from down the hill, Luke in front, Rachel trailing, a doubtful expression on her face.

"Mom! Are you all right? You're not upset or anything, are you? Your voice was loud." He directed a look at me that was suspicious if not downright accusing.

"No, honey, I'm fine. Mackie and I are just talking things over. Did you see Rachel's horses? What do you think?" She pulled him down on her lap, yet he didn't wriggle loose. Instead he turned sideways and draped an arm over her shoulder as he talked.

"They're really cool, just like she said. Please can we get a horse and bring it out here when they're done? You know I'll take care of it. And then, when we ride, I'll have my own horse and won't have to ask to borrow one of Dr. Wilder's. It would teach me responsibility," he wheedled. Just like a boy who knew his mother well.

Naomi laughed. "You know I said I'd talk it over with Dad. Most likely - I said, most likely - the answer will be yes, but don't count on it 'til it's done. Okay?"

"Okay!" Luke wrapped his arms around her in a huge hug. Then he pulled back sharply. "Is it okay if I do that?"

"Hug me? Sure! I don't ever want you to stop giving me hugs!"

"No, I mean, can I hug you that hard? I don't want to hurt the baby. You have to be careful. Watch what you eat. Don't overdo. Don't get upset."

I felt a sharp poke to my rib cage. "Rachel?"

She was standing at my side and slightly behind me. She'd been silent this whole time. She leaned down and wrapped herself around me, putting her face by my ear. "I need to talk to you afterwards. Luke said some stuff about you. I'm kinda mad at him."

I rubbed Rachel's arms in a half hug and nodded slowly. I caught Naomi's eye, she shrugged and continued reassuring Luke. At last she released him.

"Why don't you two go raid the refrigerator?" I suggested. "I'm pretty sure we've got some fruit and maybe some cookies hiding out in there. There's cake in the cooler in the car!" I called after them.

They were halfway down the driveway. Suddenly Luke stopped and retraced his steps to in front of the porch. "Don't upset my mom, Dr. Wilder," he told me, quite directly, quite seriously. Then he hurried after Rachel to the car.

"Lucas!" Naomi looked at me with big eyes. "Mackenzie, I am sorry. I don't know what's come over him!"

"It's okay. Probably a good reminder." I was a little embarrassed that a ten-year-old thought he needed to remind me to be nice to his pregnant mother who was both friend and patient. Not that Naomi was delicate physically, but there was no need to abuse our relationship. The circumstances themselves were odd and stressful enough without aggravating things by thoughtless behavior.

"Where were we?" she asked.

"You told me Braeden had borrowed money to gamble with Tyler, something he'd never done before."

"Absolutely. He despised our Dad for losing us two homes that way. He'd never have borrowed unless he was pressured into it or had gotten in too deep to think of any other way out."

"You found this deed that said he was co-owner of a house in Vegas with Tyler."

"Yes, but you know what? Maybe he wasn't any longer. Maybe he did sell it, or turn it over to Tyler, and this was just an old copy."

"That could be. We'd have to look up the ownership with the county records to know."

"You don't think Tory would know?" Naomi asked.

"Not based on anything she's told me so far. I kind of hate to disturb her now. She's very upset over all these murders. They seem to be happening all around her. She and her manager have gone down to Nashville to visit the family of another young man whose body was found there. You know, maybe Peter knows something about this. You said he contacted you about Braeden, right?"

Naomi wrinkled her nose. "He did. He brought us a check. He said it was a life insurance policy the McClouds had worked out for all their employees. Didn't matter that it was suicide. The policy took care of all the arrangements, paid his debts, and actually, it gave us almost the value we'd have expected if Braeden hadn't lost all that money. It was ironic. Mr. Himes was very sweet about it. He knew I was angry over Tyler. He tried to make it seem like Tyler had insisted Braeden take the policy, but I kind of got the feeling that Mr. Himes was the one behind it."

"Really. I have to confess, I don't get the warm fuzzies from Peter Himes. Probably because he so clearly doesn't like Jason. He seems to relish Jason being in trouble."

"We all know how loyal you are to your friends," Naomi teased. "Luke! Time to go."

We stood up, and Luke came careening out the front door, two cookies in each hand. "Mom! You all right? She's not arguing with you again, is she?" He slid to a stop and looked his mother up and down as if I might have been beating on her with a bat.

"Lucas Cooper! You apologize to Dr. Wilder. Whatever are you thinking! She is my friend and my doctor and she would never mistreat me." When he wouldn't look at me, she bent down and firmly turned him around by the shoulders. "Luke, she is my friend, and friends can disagree. Now apologize."

He grimaced. "Sorry."

Taking a cue from Naomi, I bent down a bit, too, although for me it wasn't far.

"Luke, your mother is a strong woman, physically and mentally. There's a bit of a puzzle going on right now, and we're trying to solve it."

"Does it involve those country music people?" he asked. "And Uncle Braeden?"

"Yes, it does. Those music people are my friends. Tory lost her brother too. There's a lot of sadness and worry going on, but it doesn't have to touch your mother too much. We'll be careful of that. Okay?"

"Yeah, it's okay. If it's just about Braeden and that friend of his." Luke stuffed a cookie in his mouth.

"Uncle Braeden, young man," his mother reminded.

"Whatever."

"What friend did you mean?" I asked. "Did your uncle ever introduce you to Tyler McCloud?" *How funny that would be.*

"No, not Tyler McCloud. That would have been cool. He introduced me to the guy who's always in a suit. His boss, Mr. Himes."

Naomi fixed a frown on him. "Luke, are you sure you're remembering correctly? I introduced you to him that time he came to the house."

"No, Mom, that was the second time I saw him. Uncle Braeden introduced us that time we went to visit him in Las Vegas."

"You were such a little thing!"

"Mom, I was six! I didn't like him much, though."

"Why?" I asked.

"He didn't know kids. After Uncle Braeden introduced us, he slipped me ten bucks and told me to go get him a coffee from downstairs in the casino. Mom, even when I was that little I knew I wouldn't be allowed to do that. He just wanted to get rid of me, and he didn't know that was a bad way to do it."

Naomi grinned at her son. "I always knew you were a smart kid. What about the ten?"

"I put it in with the money I brought from my piggy bank so I could get more action figures."

"I wondered where all that had come from. Luke, you go ahead and get in the car. I'll be right there."

Rachel came outside and stood beside me.

"Who knew?" Naomi asked. "Look, don't take Luke's attitude too seriously. He'll settle down as the pregnancy moves along. He's just really protective of me right now.

"He takes after Bob. It'll pay off in the long run. I'll see you in four weeks at the office. And, if you don't mind, I'll tell Tory and Bryan what we talked about. Maybe we can find out something that'll lead to Tyler's killer, and find you some peace as well."

"We can hope. Bye, Rachel." She headed to her car. Luke barely looked up. Rachel stayed at my side, waiting for me to turn to her. When at last I did, she threw her arms around me and hugged me as only Rachel Jamison can hug.

"Okay, thank you, but what was that all about?"

"Mackie, Luke was being so mean! I know he's worried about his mom, but honestly he shouldn't be, she's had kids before, loads of times, and he shouldn't be mean about you!"

Her words were getting garbled in her hair, so I pushed it back. "Come on, sit here and tell me before your aunt gets here and it's time to leave. What happened in there?"

"Oh, I don't know. He was complaining to me about his mom having another baby. You know, one more person to take care of, more diapers, then he started going on about it affecting her health. He's awfully worried about her. He started saying how you weren't a very good doctor if you let her get all upset the other day, because everyone knows you shouldn't upset pregnant ladies." Rachel hiccupped. We both giggled.

"I think we got it covered, Rachel. Don't let it upset you. I've got pretty thick skin."

"I told him you know your job, and that it wasn't your fault if you found a body and then made friends with its sister. You're just you and that stuff happens to you. Kinda like it happens to my dad.

"I told Luke something else, too," she said, looking up at me with blue eyes beneath strawberry blonde hair that refused to behave. "I told him it was kind of neat having parents who have such cool adventures. Race you to the barn!"

She took off before I could react. It was a wonderful thing for her to say, even if it wasn't strictly accurate.

·C·H·A·P·T·E·R· 20

·T·O·R·Y·

"I made you cry."
- from "It's Never Over" by Joe Lauper and Tyler McCloud

By the Thursday before Mackenzie's horseback ride with Rachel I had decided to tackle the trip to Nashville to see Auggie's family. Not with Jason, like I wanted, but with Peter. I wasn't crazy about havin' him along - he was so indifferent to Auggie's family! But then I decided it was a good way to have a long talk with him. It was time. I wanted to let him down easy, but there wasn't a good way to do it. Like I figured, he blew up.

On Sunday we flew down to Nashville in Jason's jet. He had arranged a car for us. He'd even gotten Ms. Greenwood to hunt down a roadie who'd known Auggie to be our driver, so it wasn't any trouble finding Auggie's little ranch house out in Mt. Juliet. The house looked like it might on any of Auggie's workdays: tricycles in the yard; a couple basketballs, one regulation, one child-size; grass that had been newly-mowed (people need to mow their grass on into November 'round here). Only thing was, there was a giant, fussy potted hydrangea on the front stoop, and Auggie's truck was parked by the garage. Auggie. of course, wasn't home.

Peter shifted from foot to foot with irritation as we waited for Teresa to answer the door. I could hear pots banging in the background, and a pouty whimper by the door. When Teresa opened up, Ty and Terry were right beside her, Terry with his finger stuck in his mouth.

Teresa's eyes lit up, and then she seemed to melt. I knew how that was. We hugged, hard, and Ty started to slip out the door.

"Hey, kid - little boy!" called Peter, stepping back, which allowed both boys to slide past him and start to the stairs.

"Ty and Terry, you two get back here! You know you aren't supposed to do that. You could get - hurt," Teresa self-edited as she took each boy by the arm and directed them back inside. "Please come in, Tory. And Mr. Himes."

Peter looked at me. "Ty and Terry?" he mouthed the names.

"Told you we were close," I whispered back. "Teresa, what can I do? Can I help with the boys somehow? How about I sing to them?"

"No! Read! Read this book!" Tyler ran over to a bookshelf flanking the fireplace and picked up a copy of "Night before Christmas" that was almost as big as he was.

"No, don't sing. Read this book!" Terry ran over to the opposite shelf and brought me another copy that was a little smaller.

Teresa laughed. "They always agree on what to do, but not always how to do it."

"Are you guys sure you don't want me to sing?" I asked, joining them on the couch. By some tacit agreement between the boys, the big book leaned against the front of the couch, while the more manageable one occupied my lap. I had a twin snuggled under my arm on each side.

"No, read!" was the chorused command I got.

"Hey, we're talkin' a million dollar voice here. You kids don't know what you're turnin' down! Ms. Haynes, I thought your family knew the music business."

"We know more about bein' polite, and about what little boys need."

Grief had stripped away Teresa's hospitable nature. I could understand her. I didn't know what had gotten into Peter.

"Peter, it's fine. I can read just as well as I can sing."

"I'll get you some water, Tory." Teresa headed towards the kitchen. "Mr. Himes, is there anything you want?"

"I'll take some water, too. Got anything to go with it?" I heard Peter ask. *Lord, where were his manners?*

"T'was the night before Christmas," I began, pulling the boys closer, trying not to recall how excited Auggie had been the year they were born and he read this to them the first time. It was going to be a family tradition, and I knew that even last year the boys had started bringing him the books to read to them as early as August. He'd joked that if they kept this up, soon he'd be reading it to them three hundred sixty-five days a year. And he didn't care. He loved it. He loved his boys, and Teresa, and music, and us.

I sniffled and Ty reached up to touch the teardrop on my nose. "S'okay, Aunt Tory. Mommy cried today, too."

"I cried this morning," put in Terry. "So did Tyler."

"Did not cry this morning," insisted the little man on my right. "I cried last night, when Daddy couldn't read to us."

"Mommy says he won't be able to read to us again. But if we listen real close, with our eyes shut tight, we might be able to hear him in our heads. 'Cuz he loves us so much, he's still with us, she says."

Both boys nodded their little round heads at me solemnly. I sniffed again and grabbed them tight.

Peter wandered in with his glass of water. "They still awake? How long does it take to read a book?"

Terry stared at Peter. "I don't like you."

Tyler stared, too. "No, we don't like you. You can go 'way now."

"What the hell?" Peter said, then tried to pass it off with a laugh.

"No swearing in my house, if you please." Teresa spoke almost automatically. "Come on, boys. Aunt Tory will come in to tuck you in for a nap in a little bit. You can take the books in and look at them 'til you fall asleep."

"Hang on, Teresa." I was really gettin' annoyed with Peter. Did he not know how to act around bereaved families or little kids? "I have an idea. Boys, did you know that there is a song that tells this same story?"

"Night before Christmas?" Ty asked, his eyes wide.

"Really?" asked Terry, his eyes widening, too.

"You bet. You settle back for a minute. I can't read the way your Daddy did, but I can sing you the same story." I swung into the classic Fred Waring version of "T'was the Night Before Christmas". Course, it don't sound the same without a full choir, but the gist was there. And it was familiar, because ever since we first went caroling in our Nashville neighborhood, Tyler and I had sung this song together a dozen times a year. It was even on the Christmas album we had coming out this year.

I finished the final "and to all, good night," hugged the boys and turned to Peter. "I want to dedicate that Christmas album to these boys, Peter. I want you to make sure that happens."

Teresa took the boys off for their nap with a glimmer of a smile on her face. She returned carrying glasses of sweet tea, slowing her steps infinitesimally as she neared the table. She set the glasses down and gestured to the chairs, mostly ignoring Peter as he sat with us.

"Tory, thanks for that. The boys loved it."

"No problem. You know I'm always here for you."

"I know. It means a lot." She glanced at Peter out of the corner of her eye, hunching over her glass of tea. Her hands encircled the glass, one finger playing with the condensation drops as they slid down the side.

Peter spoke, "I hope you know, Ms. Haynes, that Auggie will be sorely missed by the crew.

"Really?" Teresa raised her head. "Is that why it took one of *them* to call me and tell me he hadn't made the tour? That was the first clue I had that he was missing, you know. The second was that measly termination check you sent."

I stiffened, turning towards Peter. "Termination? What?"

"Hey, Tory, you know I have no patience with these guys. Someone's a no-show, they're fired."

"But, you told me he quit."

"Same difference. Like I said, if they don't show, it tells me they quit."

Teresa bristled. "You know that Auggie was always responsible and business-like. Not showing is unprofessional and he wouldn't do it. Besides, he'd never leave Tory and Tyler in the lurch like that."

"You should have come to us, Peter. We'd have known something was wrong. Maybe he would have been found sooner. Although, I don't know if that matters, really." He would have already been dead, I thought, but it might have saved Teresa some grief. *I don't reckon I like Peter's attitude very much. Partin' ways with him is lookin' better 'n' better.*

"It might have mattered, Tory." Teresa spoke in low, anguished tones. "Auggie - Auggie was hit over the head with something, the police aren't sure exactly what. Then he was dragged into that old bar down at the end of Printers Alley, know where I mean?"

"I know."

"Then - then that murdering bastard, whoever he was - shot him and left him there. They say he wasn't dead yet. That he might not have died if he hadn't been left. I have to talk to the police again tomorrow. They know I don't know anything. I know they don't know anything.

We just keep talking. Talking. I'm getting so tired of it. I want Auggie back!"

Her shoulders started to shake. I got up and went 'round to her and held her as she cried. Peter looked bored and got up to start pacing.

"I'm going by to see the police this afternoon," I told Teresa as the sobbing slowed. "After Tyler's death and all the others, they want to see me. Here's hopin' they don't suspect me!"

It was supposed to be a joke. Peter stopped his pacing mid-stride and faced me, his expression neutral, but his eyes giving away that he was thinking fast. Teresa froze in my arms, swiveled in her chair, staring at me. I backed away. She sipped her tea in silence, gazing at me over the rim of the glass with dull eyes. I tiptoed around the end of the table to my seat. *What just happened here?*

Teresa didn't take her eyes off me as I sat back down.

"You do have the money to pay for something like this," she said, speaking in a reasonable tone. "Did you have a reason for wanting Auggie and Tyler out of the way? Out of your way?"

I felt like my insides were collapsing. "Teresa, honey, think about what you said. What earthly reason could I ever have for wanting your husband, one of my best friends for years, or my brother, whom I adored, out of the way? I know your world is cavin' in, honey, but, not only would I never hurt either of those boys, I could never kill a living soul. You know me better than to think that."

I sat still, watchin' emotions play across her face. It crumpled, and she stood up and reached across the table to me.

"I'm sorry. Oh, God, I'm so sorry, Tory. I don't know what I 'm saying. It's not real to me yet that Auggie's dead. I don't want it to be real. I don't know what to think! I - " she started sobbing again.

I held her hands, releasing one sometimes to brush her hair to one side. She cried for nearly ten minutes, the two of us standing there, reaching across her dining room table. Midway through I caught Peter watching. His face was still neutral, still thoughtful, but I didn't know what those thoughts were.

"Aunt Tory, are you gonna tuck us in?" Tyler stood in the doorway, rubbing at his eyes. "Why's Momma cryin'?"

Before I could answer, he said, "Oh, it's because of Daddy. Don't cry, Momma, Daddy loves you. I know."

"I'll take care of him, Teresa." I left the room, taking Tyler by the hand. When we reached the boys' room, Terry was curled up on one bed against a big pile of pillows. Tyler climbed up beside him, laying his head against his brother's, his tucked body a mirror image of Terry's. Terry's eyes were nearly closed, and he held out his arm and draped it over Tyler's shoulder in a hug. Tyler did the same, and the picture they created was very nearly a perfect heart. I slipped off their shoes and drew a light quilt over them.

"Tyler, that was very nice, what you said to your mommy."

He slid his eyes at me over his shoulder, never moving his arm from his brother. "I wanted to make her feel better. 'Course, Daddy does love her. Aunt Tory, why did you bring the mean man here?"

"Huh? What mean man, Tyler?"

"That man who came here with you. We don't like him. He ran over our truck last week."

"Are you sure it was him?" I asked. *How could it have been Peter? He was on tour with us. Tyler must have seen someone else.*

He nodded his head once, then nestled into the pillows. "He doesn't like kids."

I smiled. Well, he had that right. Trust a child to know when an adult is uncomfortable around him. Right now, I didn't much like Peter myself. I didn't think Teresa did either. I closed the blinds and left the room. I had three uncomfortable chores ahead of me.

"Teresa, we'll be leaving soon. I want to stop back and see you. After I'm done with the police and everything. Peter, if you're - " My cell phone chirped its email signal. "Just a minute, let me check this." I pulled up the screen as I crossed to the couch in the front room. I never liked opening emails around other people, not even when I was reading the small screen of my phone.

It was a long one, from Mackenzie. I stifled an exclamation as I read the second paragraph. Naomi claimed Tyler owned some house in Las Vegas with her brother! What on earth? The only real estate we ever owned was Daddy's house in Brentwood. We'd never been able to agree on a place for any other home, and we were never in one place long enough anyway, exceptin' Nashville. I didn't know what kind of stunt her brother had been playin', but Tyler never co-owned anything with anybody except me, and that was the bus we toured in.

I'd have to ask Peter about it. If he wasn't too mad after our talk.

"Teresa, we're goin' now."

"Was that more bad news?" The question was too apt.

"Not exactly, but I have to run those errands. I'll stop over later. You see if you can't get some rest."

She nodded, but I doubted she would. Teresa would stay up, take care of the boys, keepin' busy ten minutes at a time until she wore herself out. Then she'd get up and do it again, busyin' herself until she healed. Heck, it was what I was doin', but I had Jason.

The driver straightened up in a hurry as we came down the steps, but I'd already seen the tell-tale paper and pencil and the guitar on the seat beside him. Everyone in Nashville's a songwriter.

"Do you know where the main police station is in Nashville?" I asked our driver.

"Probably downtown. There's one on Broadway. I think it's the Central Precinct. That what you mean?"

"Sounds right. Can you take us there, and then we'll be ready to go out to Brentwood. Peter, do you want to be dropped at your place after we talk with the police?"

"What we? I don't have time for these bozoes. You can tell them anything I could. You knew Auggie a whole lot better'n me. Besides, you're the one who's going to have to defend herself from his wife's accusations." I swear he snuck a look at me to see how I took that. "Are they going to ask you about J.D., too?"

"J.D.?" I repeated.

"Sure. They've been sayin' how these are probably all connected. Sweetie, it's lookin' like you might be the connection. I know you're not responsible, but you've got to admit, it doesn't look good. You may be in for as much trouble as that new husband of yours."

"Peter!"

"Hey, it's the truth, isn't it? You pay me to advise you, and I'm advising you that you need to be prepared to face some tough questioning."

I was startin' to boil, but Peter seemed not to notice. "I would think, then, that as my advisor, you would be insistin' on comin' with me to the station, rather than letting me go in there on my own."

"You'll do fine. These boys probably know who you are. Just charm them and you'll be fine. It won't matter whether you're guilty or not."

"That's enough, Peter. In fact, it's all enough."

"What is?"

"I've had enough of the bossiness, the lack of confidence, the remarks. I think we need to talk separation here."

He turned sharply. "Hold on there, Tory - "

"Look, I was going to bring this up anyway, because of circumstances, but you've really pushed the limit, you know? How dare you make it sound like I could have anythin' to do with all these deaths!"

"No, now look, wait a minute, Tory. I'm sorry. I don't know why I said those things. It's just - well, yes I do know why I said them." He paused, his face a study in misery. The harsh lines of sarcasm and hardcore PR savvy had melted. In their place were shades of disappointment. *And fear?*

"Okay, then," I said, crossing my arms. "Suppose you tell me why you think you have to say such hurtful things to me."

"Tory, can't you figure it out?" His voice softened. His hands lay upturned in his lap, as if he were helpless. "Tory, it should have been obvious, the last six years. I'm in love with you. I've wanted nothing more than to look out for you, protect you, be with you. Believe it or not, that's all my work is about; it's all about you."

His eyes, maybe for the first time since I'd ever known Peter, focused on me as if I were the only person on the planet. In all the years we'd known each other, even when we were so-called dating, I didn't recall him ever looking at me the way he did now. It felt dirty.

"Peter, you do remember that I'm married now, right?" My discomfort with the situation showed in my awkwardness. "I mean, telling me you're in love with me, here, now isn't exactly appropriate."

"I know," he said smoothly, "but I'm telling you anyway. I don't care if you are married to the big, famous Jason Fields, I am telling you that I have been in love with you for years. It hurts that you up and married Jason like this, on some ridiculous whim. I don't know, maybe you figured it was the way to save him from the cops, but it's not going to work out. I wish for you that it would, but it's not going to happen. He still might be the one that killed Tyler. He might hurt you, too."

"Peter! Peter, look. You're wrong about Jason, and you're wrong about me. You don't really love me. If you think you do, I'm sorry, but I don't love you. I'm sorry." I hesitated. I didn't know how much he could take right now. As if I'd forgotten just how sharp he was, he reminded me.

"I know, I know. I'm fired. Just as well, I guess. I don't think I could stand being around you as half of a newly-wed couple. Not if I wasn't the other half."

I swallowed. "I'm sorry, Peter, but I do think it's better. It will be easier for you."

"What would be easier for me would be for you to return my affection. But, hey, I know when I can't win. I am going to insist on a couple things, though, business-wise."

I raised my eyebrows, and he smiled. "I want you to buy out my contract. It's only fair, and you only have to pay out this year. Second, I want to stay on with the band. They'll need me, especially if you're taking time off like you said. Third, well, third thing is, if things don't work out with Jason, don't look me up."

"Don't?" I asked.

"No," he answered, and took my hand. He tried to twinkle his eyes at me and failed. "Because if things don't work out for you and Jason, I'll be right there for you. The farthest you'll have to look to find me is right behind you." He released my hand. "Until then you can reach me with the band. As for now, why don't we drop you at the police station, and James here, or whatever, can drive me home and come back for you."

"All right," I agreed, uncertain as to whether or not it was the best idea. The driver was scowling at me, or Peter's way of referring to him, I'm not sure. What I was sure of was that he wanted to get rid of Peter right now, and he wanted me to tell him to. "We can do that," I said.

The driver nodded agreement. Peter sat back and busied himself with his cell phone.

Me? I sat back and tried to figure out what had happened here, and how I felt about it.

Relieved, that's how I felt about it. R-E-L-I-E-V-E-D.

·C·H·A·P·T·E·R· 21

·T·O·R·Y·

"Guess I'll be in the neighborhood."

- from "Don't Lock the Door 'til it Stops Swingin' " by Jason Fields

I hate to admit it, but Peter was right. Everybody at that police station knew who I was. It didn't take much Southern charm - and I'd've thought these men would be resistant to it, but no - to get me out of there with both the information and the spotless record I wanted. I don't know if they got what they wanted, and after going through all that with Peter, I didn't care.

Auggie'd been shot, like Teresa said. He'd been shot with the same sort of gun that Bobby Fleming had been shot. That wasn't necessarily significant, the skinny young detective told me. Then another detective, older and built like he'd been huggin' his desk for a while, tried to explain to me about statistics and probabilities and how there was a certain likelihood that the two crimes were related, but that you couldn't base an investigation that way. He talked long enough to dissect three crimes instead of two. By the time he was done I knew he was just tryin' to impress me. Sometimes bein' pretty and talented and famous is not really at all it's cracked up to be. Except for the fact that no one wanted to think I was even remotely the cause of any of this. They asked me a few questions about Tyler and about Bobby, apologizing all the while for their questions, then they let me go, sayin' they'd get whatever else they needed from the police workin' the cases in New York.

It was a relief to be picked up by the driver again.

"I'm sorry to keep runnin' you around like this," I told him.

"No problem, ma'am. I knew Auggie, too. By the way, I've always admired your music." He smiled in the mirror at me.

"Did you drop Mr. Himes at his home?"

"No, ma'am," he said, negotiating a U-turn on Broadway that was sure to get him stopped if anyone from Metro PD saw it.

"No? What happened?"

"He said to take him to the airport. Said he reckoned he might as well get back with the band as stay here."

"That's weird. I figured he'd want to spend some time catchin' up here. Okay, if you would, take me back out to Mt. Juliet. I'll be there about an hour, I think, and then I'll need you to take me out to my house in Brentwood. I'll head back to New York tomorrow. I'll let you know what time to pick me up."

"Not a problem, ma'am. I'm paid for the week."

Jason! I'd been so focused on what I was doing here in Nashville, I hadn't thought about him in hours. I was too new at this wife stuff. Knowing how he'd arranged for this made me smile. He was a part of everything in my life now. We were a team.

We'd gotten on to I-40. Cars rushed by in the ever-expanding Nashville rush hour. I spotted a tour bus up ahead, made by the same outfit that had done ours, but I didn't know who was on it. A black and silver guitar with mother-of-pearl trim saluted me from a billboard as we left town. Trees still lush but taking on autumn color pushed closer and closer to the interstate, Nature's endless attempt to overturn the concrete Nashville kept laying down. The city tried to strike a balance, but Mother Nature would never be happy until she ran things again. *I love Nashville.*

We hadn't talked about it, but Jason and I had enough money to have several places to live. I knew he liked Nashville well enough, and I certainly didn't want to give up our house there. I didn't know exactly how many homes Jason had. There was the suite at the Bellagio and the condo in Charlotte where his NASCAR team was headquartered. He'd lived in London and Baltimore, and I knew he spent time in Europe, and now New York State. This could get excitin'. Once we got out of this mess.

We pulled off the interstate to take Mt. Juliet Road to Teresa's and the boys'. I felt a buzz from my cell phone. Text messages.

'Did you learn anything about house owned by Tyler with Braeden Snyder in Las Vegas?' that was from Mackie.

No, I didn't find out anything about that. The conversation with Peter hadn't exactly gone as planned.

'Word back from racing chief. J.D's car may have been tampered with. Call me.' From Jason.

No, oh, no!

'Btw, half the Nashville house is deeded to me. Am putting it on the market so we can split proceeds.' From Peter.

What the hell does he think he's talkin' about?

I was so stunned, my mind didn't know which question to tackle first.

Suddenly, all I could think of was the swing set. The swing set in the back yard that Daddy had built for us. It had a fort attached to it that Tyler always thought was his. He tried to prove it, too. Like most little sisters, I proved otherwise.

The set had started out as one of those redwood kits so many suburban homes put up. Daddy, however, was never a person to do anything small. Mama, near as I can remember, just encouraged him. So our set looked more like something out of a theme park. The slide - the bigger one - was several sheets of polished metal lapped and bolted together. Five kids could slide down the long gentle expanse seated side-by-side. Tyler preferred rolling down it sideways. He had more than one scar on his arms from that. The swings were those strap style swings you used to see on playgrounds. Fact, Daddy might have purchased them as surplus from the city schools. We had six of them, allowing each of us to have two friends over at the same time and still not have to take turns.

The fort was ten by ten, with a look-out perch above and a platform below the main floor. A fireman's rope, a ladder, and a cargo net completed the build. Two eighteen foot see-saws stretched on the ground, so big you couldn't get hurt because they moved so slow.

Daddy had never taken down that swing set. When he died, Tyler and I, past our teens, slept out in that fort for four days straight. It had been Daddy's and Mama's gift to us, as sure as our music heritage. It smelled of Daddy's tobacco with a touch of beer, and sweat and stain, and a big dose of the reassurance of our parents' love.

While Peter Himes might say he was in love with me, that text message told me he wasn't so much in love with me he wouldn't destroy some of my happiness by sellin' my home and my precious memories. Nevertheless, the swing set meant nothing to him. If I couldn't stop him sellin' the house, I'd have to find a way to get that set out of there.

I hadn't let go of that thought yet when we arrived at Teresa's. I got out of the car, and this time the driver - named George Box, I found out - came with me. He had to stand aside as Teresa flew out the door and grabbed ahold of me, wrapping her arms around me. She didn't seem to be crying, but she hung onto me fierce.

"Teresa. Teresa, hon'. What is it? What's happened?"

"Tory, the police got him! They found the guy who shot Auggie!"

"They did! When? They sure didn't say anything about it while I was at the station!"

"They just called me. They're bringing him in now. They had prints or something from where they found Auggie's - Auggie, and they got the guy who matched them!" she hiccupped, pulling away from me. "It's not enough, but at least they got him." Her eyes were almost black.

"C'mon, let's go inside. Are the boys back up from their nap yet?"

"No, not yet. George, I'm glad you're here. Would you like somethin' to drink?"

George gave her a big hug. "I know my way around out there. Let me get it. Ms. McCloud?"

"Time you called me Tory. It's goin' to be Tory Fields from now on."

George ambled back to the door. "Terry, when the boys wake up, I'll take 'em while you two finish talkin'."

"Thanks, George. You and Shelby have been a big help. Shelby's his wife," she told me.

"You know if you need anything, you just have to tell me." I reached over to put my hand on hers.

"I know. And I will. Which brings me to earlier. Sorry I acted like that. When your whole world is upside-down, you can't always tell what's real. I know you wouldn't have anything to do with Auggie's death. But, that Himes made me so mad, I didn't know what I was sayin'. Why did you bring him with you?"

"Honestly, I was annoyed with him, too. I wanted to make him see you as a person, as Auggie's wife, and the boys as his kids. I hoped he'd apologize. That was before I knew about the - "

"The severance check?"

"Yeah. That. Teresa, I had no idea why Auggie hadn't shown up, or that Peter really thought he'd quit. I figured Peter was handling it. I should have called you myself!"

"I wish you had. I knew Auggie wouldn't up and quit. So that meant he was missing. When I went to the police, they started lookin' in his usual places. It just took a couple days after that to find him. It wasn't soon enough." She paused, clenching her fists, jabbing at the air as if the murderer were in front of her. "I hope that guy rots in hell!"

"You and us both, Terry." George had returned with tea and some cake he'd found.

"What do the police have on him, anyway?" I asked.

"Just the fingerprints, I think. He's a troublemaker around Printers' Alley anyways, they said. They've been waitin' for this guy's temper to get the best of him and get him in trouble. But why, why did it have to be my Auggie!" She hunkered down in her chair and laid her head on her arms.

I was burnin' inside. I wanted to talk about Peter, who I was rapidly growin' to hate. I wanted to ask if Auggie had ever mentioned anything about Tyler gambling or owning anything with Braeden Snyder. I wanted to call Jason to find out more about J.D.

"Teresa? Teresa, did Auggie know J.D.? J.D. Lazenbee?" Roadies hung together. J.D. and Auggie both went way back with us, just in different ways.

"Lazenbee? You mean the guy who used to hit on you when you were younger?"

"That's him," I said with a grimace. "If you know that much, Auggie must have, too."

Teresa smiled. "Auggie was the one who saved your butt. Along with George here."

"You worked for us?"

"Nah. I wasn't doin' this stuff then. I hung out with Auggie a lot though. Back then, he and I and whoever was handy from your crew used to meet up down on Second Avenue or over at Tootsie's for some beers and the music. Funny how you can't get away from it. Anyways, there was this night J.D. came along with us. He was goin' on and on about what a cute little thing you were and how he'd like to - well, you know."

"Yeah, I know." I rolled my eyes and stuck out my tongue.

George snickered and stretched his long legs under the table.

"Well, you should have heard Auggie. First off, he knew J.D. had got help writin' songs from your Daddy. And you'd gone and given him a decent job. Yet here he was, bein' disrespectful about you, in public even."

Teresa shook her head, a dreamy, remembering kind of smile on her face. "Auggie always hated it when men were disrespectful to women. He was a knight in shinin' armor."

I snuck a quick glance at her. That *was* tea she was drinkin', wasn't it?

"So Auggie, you know how big Auggie was," George went on. "he pulls J.D.. up by the scruff of his shirt and he starts whalin' on him right there in the bar. Punched him a couple times, slapped him in the face, holdin' on to his shirt and lecturin' him about how to treat women the whole time. J.D.'s holdin' his hands up, tryin' to fend Auggie off, but he never tried to hit 'im back. J.D. finally slumped down in the chair, and Auggie sat down across from him. He made J.D. promise to leave you alone; told him he'd have his hide if he ever heard anythin' about him abusin' women again. J.D. promised. You know what? He lived up to it. Heard he even started goin' to church and goin' to Wednesday night suppers and helpin' out in the kitchen. Started datin' a Sunday School teacher, too."

"Sara Hunt. That's her name. I talked to her last week when I heard about J.D. She's taking his death hard, too. Like me." Teresa's words slurred, and she punctuated her sentence with a soft hiccup.

I glanced at her again. When I turned back to George, he nodded gravely at me, looking me straight in the eye. Oh. I turned back to Teresa; she was sliding down to rest her head again.

"Hon, let's get you into bed. You need a little nap."

Between us George and I settled her into a bed. We headed for the master bedroom, but Teresa roused long enough to protest, mumbling, "not in there". George knew where the guest room was, so we tucked her in and returned to the dining room, peeking in on the boys, still sleeping cuddled together.

I was wondering what to do next, when George pulled out his cell phone.

"I'll call Shelby to come over and stay with her. Then I can get you back to your house. You need me tomorrow?" He started punching in numbers.

"Yes. I'm not sure yet what I'm doin', but I'll at least need a ride to the airport."

"I'll be there at eight o'clock. That okay?"

"It'll be fine."

While we waited for Shelby, I asked George about somethin' that had been on my mind most of the trip.

"George, did you *ever* work for us?"

He smiled. "No, Tory, I haven't had the pleasure."

"Well, I'm relieved to know I wasn't overlookin' you, too."

"Auggie always said you were concerned about the people who worked for you. 'Course, he was your friend, too, wasn't he?"

I nodded, my lips pursed. "I always prided myself on knowin' everybody and a little somethin' about them. I'm findin' out I didn't know as much as I thought I did."

"It's hard to keep up with that, 'specially if you're big enough to have a manager like Peter Himes. Those guys get in there and take over your business and you end up knowin' nothing about what's going on."

"I'm afraid that's what's happened. I'm not comfortable with it, either. It shouldn't be that way. I'm seein' now that between Tyler and Peter, there's a lot that went on that I didn't know about."

"That's what Auggie said a couple weeks ago."

"Huh?"

"Couple weeks ago, before Tyler died, Auggie was tellin' me that he thought you didn't know enough about how things were with your outfit. He thought you should know what was goin' on."

"He didn't say anything to me about that." I was indignant and sorry all at once. Auggie was gone. I'd miss all the advice he could offer.

George shrugged. "He would've gotten to it eventually. If he hadn't been killed."

"If he hadn't been killed."

There were too many people in my life that phrase applied to right now. The more it echoed in my brain, the heavier it felt, pressin' in on me like a giant tombstone.

My morbid thoughts were interrupted by the doorbell heralding Shelby's arrival. Brief introductions, and then George and I left for my house. I insisted on sitting in front so we could talk.

I was havin' trouble gettin' my thoughts in order. Those text messages kept runnin' around and scramblin' up my brain. Felt like I was under attack by a pack of mosquitoes. Big ones. By the time we were back on I-40 and headed to Brentwood, I remembered what I wanted to ask George about.

"Now you said that Auggie thought I - or was it Tyler and me? - didn't know enough 'bout what was goin' on with what - the band? The tour?"

George shook his head at the traffic and scratched his ear with a large hand attached to a muscular forearm. The forearm had a tattoo of a guitar entwined by a vine with roses on it. The roses stood out in shades of red, from a salmony-pink to a deep wine red.

"Auggie wasn't real clear on it. It was just talk over a couple of beers. Let me see." He squinted his eyes in thought. *Hope he doesn't have to think too hard about this, or we'll be drivin' blind.*

His words came slowly. "Auggie was worried, bugged about somethin'. I remember askin' him if everything was all right at home. He brushed that idea off in a hurry. No, he said, it was things at work. He didn't like seein' his friends get manipulated, he said. He thought everybody ought to know what went on in their business, so no one could ever take advantage of them."

"Okay. I can see Auggie thinkin' that way."

"Then he said somethin' I didn't quite get. He said he had to head out Charlotte way for a couple days. Said he wanted advice, and he wanted to see somebody he hadn't seen for a while. He got all satisfied with himself, said that was the answer."

"Dang. That still doesn't tell me a whole lot. Who could be takin' advantage of us? Peter had that covered. I don't think anyone could get past him. I know how sharp he is," I added blackly, thinking of the house. "Guess that just shows how little I do know about our business. Reckon I'll be learnin' more."

George glanced at me, but I wasn't goin' to continue. After a turn off the interstate, we got onto the road that wound around to our house, as close to outside Nashville as you could get and still be part of Davidson County. He asked me what I'd meant about Peter being sharp. "Sounds like he did something you didn't like."

I snorted. "You might say that. See, he and I used to date a little. He always looked after Tyler's and my business real good. He was sweet to me, too. We sort of had a thing going. I was never much serious about it. I've been in love with Jason Fields most of my life. Peter, well, he was nearby, and he was protective, and I didn't know if I'd ever see Jason again. I went along with him. Until I found Jason again. We got married last week.

"So, this afternoon, I had to tell Peter I was letting him go as manager. Partly because I'm not going to need a manager for a while - I'm takin' a break while Jason and I get used to marriage, and while this whole investigation is going on. I was a kinda miffed with some of Peter's behavior towards everybody, too. I never realized he didn't understand that you're supposed to treat your crew like family." I paused, thinking to myself. No, I never realized he didn't know that, but he didn't, and that bothered me.

"I take it Mr. Himes didn't react so well to the news?"

"You could say that. He seemed all smooth about it. I mean, there was a lot of stuff about how he loved me and he'd be right there if things don't work out between Jason and me, but he made a reasonable deal to end the contract. Or so I thought."

"What happened?"

"I got a text message. Somehow, I don't know how, he owns half mine and Tyler's house, and he says we have to sell it and split the money. I don't know if he can make that happen, but if he can, it'll break my heart. It's not like he'll let me buy him out. I know that without even askin'. I don't understand how he can be like this! I don't understand how he owns half the house for that matter!"

George laughed a curt laugh and shook his head. "Just goes to show."

"Goes to show what?" I asked

"The man really loves you, Tory."

"What?"

"He said he loves you and will be right there if you and Jason break up, right?"

"Yeah."

"That's like a last-ditch pitch. He acts all understanding when you're firing him, right?"

I nodded. "Pretty much. Yeah."

"Then, after he's left, he stews in his own juices for a while, gets mad, and does somethin' to hurt you. Do I have that right?"

"You sure do."

"Classic. The man loves you like crazy. And I mean crazy."

"Huh?"

"Look a lot of guys will go ballistic when someone breaks up with them - "

"But I didn't - "

"Basically you did. Other guys will go all noble. But the ones who turn around and hurt you, they're hurtin' bad. If they're unpredictable, if they do something really mean or cruel, they're a little bit crazy."

That made me think. What he said felt true, was true. "Unpredictable?"

"Well, would you have expected him to sell your house out from under you?"

"No. I didn't even expect to hear that he was in love with me."

George threw a skeptical look at me.

"Well, I didn't! I thought we were beyond all that."

"Apparently he didn't think so. You need to watch yourself. Man like that can be trouble. 'Specially as powerful as he is in this business."

"I've got Jason to protect me. Peter's still with the band, but he can't really touch me. It's just the house."

Which we were pulling up in front of. Which had a sign on the lawn. That said, 'For Sale'.

"Son-of-a-bitch!" I said, shoving the door open. "That son-of-a-bitch!"

I ran to the sign. Bayford Realty. With a lockbox on it. I looked up at the porch, then ran to the door, fumbling my way into my purse as I ran.

I stopped at the bottom stair and zipped my purse shut again. It was pointless. There was an MLS lock on the house. I had no way to get in.

·C·H·A·P·T·E·R· 22

·T·O·R·Y·

"Through fights and flights and sleepless nights,"
- from "It's Never Over" by Joe Lauper and Tyler McCloud

I stared at the door, at the lock. I thought about breakin' in from the back - who knew better than me where I could manage that? I thought about the swings. Then it all came crashing in again. All I could tell was that I had to get to Jason. I choked back a sob and clenched my purse into my stomach. I *had* to get to Jason.

George came over to me, his big hands wrapping around my shoulders. "Tory! Are you okay? What can I do?"

One more look at that MLS box.

"Take me - " my voice cracked. I cleared it. "I hate to impose. But, can you take me back out to the airport? I've got to get to Jason. I'm sorry. I know you were headed home."

We were already walking toward the car. "Airport's on my way. No problem."

He stowed me in the back, and we got back on the road at full speed and then some. Once we hit I-40, it only took fifteen minutes. He dropped me at the terminal with my luggage.

I hailed a porter to ask how I went about getting the Fields jet in order and authorized to leave. In minutes I had the pilot on the phone. Several apologies and a promise of a healthy bonus got him out there in record time. My apparent urgency seemed to grease a few wheels, too, or else the Metro Airport Authority was simply used to the bizarre travel schedules of country music stars and other celebrities. I wasn't yet used to flyin' that high.

In a few hours we were in the air. I'd spent my wait time eatin', texting Jason, and tryin' to figure out what Mackenzie's message meant. For some reason I couldn't reach her to ask.

And I set there doin' a lot of thinkin'.

About Tyler.

About Peter.

About Auggie, J.D., and this Braeden guy I'd never met - I'd almost swear to that, regardless of what his sister Naomi said.

I didn't think about Jason. I didn't think about Jason because I wanted to throw myself in his arms, and because I had enough evidence in my texts that he was waitin' to catch me.

There's a way of knowin' you married the right partner. When you know instinctively that you are facing everything together, when you know that person has your back and will drop everything to take care of you, you know you've married the right one. I didn't have to think about Jason; I knew he was there for me.

I didn't turn up much in my thoughts. Except that somehow, all this was interconnected. Even Bobby Fleming. All these deaths were related. What scared me was that they all seemed to be related to me! Peter had said as much. Even Teresa had wondered about it.

Would suspicion turn from Jason to me? Would the police find the situation compelling or circumstantial? What could I do about it?

I doodled on a piece of paper. Circles and words all intermixed. Not much different than writin' a song, I thought. What else did these men have in common besides knowin' me? The easy answer was music. Country music. At least three of them had song-writin' in common. And actually, Jason had that in common with them, too. So did I. Did this have anything to do with writin' songs?

I teased at the notion, pickin' at it, trying to pull together threads of an idea. There had to have been some kind of problem behind this.

People don't get murdered over nothing. I shivered. I'd been avoidin' using the word murder. It was too heavy, too weighted to use, even if it were true.

The only problem I knew regardin' songwriting was that writers didn't get paid enough, especially not at the beginnin'. That never stopped anyone with the bug for country music. Not even Jason. He hadn't stopped writin' because of the money - or lack of it. He'd stopped because of the lawsuit between him and Tyler over that one song.

I understood the situation a whole lot better since Jason and I had talked it over. I'd always thought Peter had actually defeated him in court. Probably because Peter wanted me to think so. But even Tyler had seemed to think that was how it was. Right down to the publicity releases that were put out for the tour. Like the one they found him carryin' in his pocket.

I frowned. That one had never made it out, had it? Although I'd seen a couple articles along similar lines. Had Peter sent them out? Or the fan club? They were the only ones authorized to do that sort of thing. Now that I knew how that court battle had been decided, those press releases didn't feel right. And why had Tyler been carrying it around with him? I was beginnin' to understand how the police were thinkin' now.

The waitress came by and cleared my table. She made a show of leavin' me my ink-covered napkins. "I love your music, Ms. McCloud. I'm terribly sorry about Tyler. Nashville will miss him. I hope you're gonna keep on singin'. Writin' a song tonight?"

"I'm sort of workin' on an idea, yeah."

"Well, you sit here as long as you like. We aren't that busy. I'll bring you out some sweet tea."

I glanced around. I'd thought the place was busy, but maybe it wasn't as full as it could be. Funny how different airports were. The one in Albany felt smaller, more industrial and business-like than Nashville's. Nashville piped in country music whenever possible, and sometimes they still ran the tape of Miss Minnie Pearl callin' out "Howdy!" to welcome people to Music City. Las Vegas, of course, had glitz and glamour and the slot machines.

I looked down at my notes. Braeden Snyder. Slot machines.

That was it! I *had* seen Braeden Snyder once, at the slots. Now how did I know that when I didn't remember knowing him or even recall what he looked like? There must have been something about - wait, it wasn't just the slots. I remember someone telling me I was seeing Braeden Snyder. Something about how he was Tyler's new best buddy - why didn't that memory come all the way up? What wasn't I remembering? Naomi said Braeden died last year. When would I have seen him at the slot machines?

I tried to pull up the memory. It had an unpleasant feel, a sort of nasty taste. Something that I hadn't liked. Dang! What was it?

My cell phone chirped. The pilot was ready. I put my phone away slowly and gathered my notes, my brain still searching. I'd have to figure this out on the plane. There was something about Braeden, and it did seem to involve Tyler, and someone else, if I could only recall who.

Before we took off, I received one more text from Mackenzie. It had a photo attached, of the copy of the deed Naomi Cooper said showed her brother and mine owned a house together in Las Vegas. Mackenzie wanted to know one thing. Was that Tyler's signature?

I studied it, then thought really hard as our flight got under way.

It didn't take much to reach a conclusion. In fact, my thoughts started to wander, playing with my situation, playing with words. I began working on a song in earnest. The airport waitress would be pleased.

The songwriting process is hard to explain. Anything can set you off, and usually does.

Someone else's song.

A word.

A look.

A broken date.

A drunk.

A child.

Something stirs a response in you that you have to frame in terms a listener can understand.

Words are usually my trigger, but this time it was an image. Two images. The swings in our backyard as I'd seen them last night, standing in shadows cast by the night's full moon.

And the image from my cell phone screen of Tyler's name on a deed to a house in a high-maintenance suburb of Las Vegas.

Two ends, two extremes of my brother's life. A musician's life. Tears stung my eyes, but my brain was over-run with words, phrases, gibberish that would eventually sort itself out into a song for Tyler.

A Song for Ty

From the blessed dark of
 Lying on a blanket
Under Daddy's watchful eye,
Seeking constellations
Filling up a country sky

To electric star-glitzed
Buildings held by
Music City's sway.
With booty garnered up
And stashed for rainier days -

All hell broke loose
We all went bust
Life's deadlier urges
Became a must
Gone back to lust,
back to lust -
We all come back to dust.

We all come back to dust.

I paused. This was dark, way too dark. Not how I wanted Tyler to be remembered. Where did this come from anyway? Probably from the mess this had all become. I sighed. Mackenzie was so much better at this. I had no idea who wanted so many people around me dead.

I shivered. People all around me dead. Tyler. J.D. Auggie. Bobby. It felt like they circled around me, closing in. If I were at the center, it would seem like I was either the murderer, or the ultimate victim. Well, I wasn't the murderer. I shivered again.

Why would I be someone's victim? We're not talking random. This was a plan.

Someone didn't like me. Enough to kill me, or, as another thought occurred, set me up to look like the killer.

Oddly enough, the idea that someone disliked me enough to do these things is what bothered me the most. Performers exist to be liked. It's our livelihood, and for a lot of us, it's the reason we begin performing. I'll admit I like being the center of attention. I love music and creating it. I was used to being criticized. I don't like the feeling of being disliked. Not at all. Who had I ticked off so much that they wanted to do this to me?'

I didn't reach a single conclusion by the time Jason picked me up at the airport. I was nearly neurotic by the time we landed, frustrated at not being able to do anything about this, scared that I was a target. Just touching Jason calmed me, and we were both ready for more than that. Not 'til morning did he tell me the details about J.D. I told him about Teresa and Auggie, and Peter.

"So they got the guy? At least that's one we don't have to worry about."

"I'm not so sure. I mean, I know they think they have the guy who actually did it. Maybe he did, but maybe someone paid him to."

Jason's eyebrows went up. I told him about my feeling I was at the center of it all.

"I don't mean to sound all ego and everythin', but this makes me awful nervous."

"I don't think it's overstating it to think carefully about how this looks to the police. You are at the center of it. They *could* suspect you -

even though we know better. Some of Peter's remarks don't help, you know?"

"I know, all right. He's developed a real knack for saying stuff that makes us both look bad. What are we gonna do about him and the house?"

"I'll take care of that. I know he wouldn't let it sell to either of us, but it's no problem to have someone buy it for us. That's something my lawyers are particularly good at. I'll make a call later. Today, however, we have something more important to do." The mischievous sparkle was back in his eyes.

"What's that?"

"We have a date with Bryan and Mackenzie this afternoon to go out in Mackenzie's boat. It's one of her last runs for the season, she said, and she's determined to get Bryan out on the water."

"Uh-oh."

"I know." Jason grinned.

·C·H·A·P·T·E·R· 23

·M·A·C·K·E·N·Z·I·E·

"It's not where the circle takes us,"

- from "The End's in the Beginning" by Tyler McCloud

J ason and Tory were grinning when they came into my office. I didn't know why they were grinning, but I took it as a good sign.

"Have you told Bryan what he's in for today?" asked Jason.

"What? Oh, not exactly. I sort of thought I'd tell him when he gets here. Why?"

Those matching grins seemed to be laughing at me as Jason asked, "You think he'll be okay with that?"

"Sure." My words - word - sounded a lot more confident than I felt. I didn't understand what Bryan's problem with water was. Brooklynne had said he'd have to tell me himself; did that mean it was serious? Or was this just some pet peeve of his that he was embarrassed to admit? I'd imagined everything from a failed rescue attempt to him nearly drowning as a child. I hoped to find out the real story today, if he didn't get mad at me.

"Let's go on out back. Andrea, tell Bryan where we are, won't you? Andrea?"

"Hmm?" She looked up from her book. "Sorry. I'm trying to finish this before I meet Ted. I want to be able to discuss it with him." She wrinkled up her nose. "It's kind of a peculiar book for a trooper to read, don't you think?"

I glanced at the title, *The Guernsey Literary and Potato Peel Pie Society*, by Shaffer and Barrows. "Uhhh...."

"I've read that," said Jason. "I'm a little surprised that our Trooper Matheson has, but it is about World War II. Plus, you have to have an understanding of people to be in law enforcement."

I stared at him. "That's pretty generous, coming from someone in your position."

Jason shrugged. "He's just doing his job. We all know that. Besides, I think Bryan has a pretty good understanding of human nature, and he's a cop. You agree with that, don't you?"

He was confusing me. I think we all get confused by stereotypes versus the people we know - and love. "I think it's fine Ted has such diverse taste in literature. Keeping up with him will be interesting for you, Andrea."

"I don't know...." She wrinkled her nose again.

"I didn't think there was anything you didn't know, Andrea," teased a friendly voice.

"Bryan!" I slid between Jason and Tory to kiss him hello.

"You told me to be here, remember?" he teased. "I changed before I came, like you said. Now, what's up?"

"Come on outside, won't you?" I tugged at his arm with one hand and motioned Jason and Tory with the other.

They kept exchanging grins. Fat lot of help they'd be.

"Mackenzie," Bryan said in a warning tone. "I'm not going to like this, am I? I thought I explained...."

We were around back and heading up to the boathouse.

"No, you didn't explain," I began, "You just said you didn't - Bryan, it's happened again! Look!"

"I'll be damned." We broke into a run, a confused Tory and Jason right behind us.

The *Emma D*, my newest boat, bought after the *PsyKe* was destroyed in last year's barn fire, bobbed placidly dockside once again, its ropes coiled in precise concentric circles and secured properly to the cleats, its cover pulled neatly over the cockpit, its nose headed away from shore, ready to go out. Only, I hadn't left it this way.

"Bryan, this has got to stop! I don't know if someone is joyriding or what, but it's got to stop! Check the *Amiga*, will you?"

"Mackenzie, what's goin' on? Is this what happened before?"

I nodded. "Pretty much, Tory. Outside the boathouse but properly moored and all tidied up, as if I'd brought it back from a run. Only I didn't; someone else did. Someone who keeps messin' with my boats!" I yelled to the world at large. Maybe whoever was doing it would hear me.

Bryan came back out shaking his head. "The *Amiga* is still in there. They only seem interested in the *Emma D*. Any idea why?"

I scowled. "I have no idea why 'they' are doing this at all. One of these days I'm going to come here and find my boat wrecked. You wait and see." I started unfastening the cover. "Come on, let's go."

Bryan sighed. "I don't suppose we have a choice, do we?"

I glared at him.

"I didn't think so. Better check the gas, though."

"Why? All they ever do is pole the thing out here and tie her up."

"What about the time she was run aground behind your office? Surely that time they ran the engine," he said, helping me fold the tarp.

I shook my head at him. "No, even then. The pole was aboard, and it was wet. I found the painter in the reeds and sand. Somebody pulled it ashore."

"How many times has this happened?" asked Jason, kneeling down to steady the boat for Tory to step aboard.

"At least four now."

"It's never damaged?"

"No. But it's only a matter of time. Besides, I'm a bit possessive when it comes to the *Emma D* and *Amiga*. Honestly? There's never been any sign that someone's run it. They just move it around. I figure, though, that it's got to be tempting them. I don't want anything to happen to these. I already lost one boat."

Bryan was quiet, holding the folded tarp, staring down at the boards that made up the inner decking. His lips were moving silently, and he closed his eyes.

Prayer? Oh, my.

"Let's get aboard," I said, hoping my enthusiasm would override whatever emotions he was struggling with.

His climbed in with minimal effort and the perfect timing of an old hand.

So, how'd he do that? Unless it was a fluke of his natural athleticism.

The engine caught. I busied myself idling us out into the river. I'd get my answer later.

I steered the boat out into the main channel and turned it upstream. The day was sunny but brisk in that full-blown autumn kind of way upstate New York has. Whitecaps popped up here and there along the expanse of water in front of us. There wouldn't be too many more runs before I had to pull the boats from the water.

Although, maybe.... I'd have to speak to Gary at the Boat Club, or maybe Art Swandeck, Jean's beau, to see if they thought I could keep the boats in the boathouse over winter. I couldn't recall if the river froze all the way or not. If the boathouse stayed ice-free, maybe they could winter over in the water. I'd heard of some people doing that.

I snuck a look at Bryan. His profile never failed to thrill me. Tall forehead, high cheekbones, a slight tilt to the tip of his nose - which he claimed to hate - a shallow cleft to his chin. He was so handsome, and solid-looking.

Right now that solidity did not appear to be the least bit shaken by being out on the water. His shoulders were relaxed, his hands open, resting along his thighs. He wasn't even squinting into the sun or breeze.

Really? He hates being on boats?

"Hey, Mackenzie? Where are we all headed?" Tory shouted from the back.

"Up to Kings Island. I figure we can picnic up there, and talk without any interruption or eavesdroppers."

Bryan turned to me in surprise. "Eavesdroppers?"

I nodded. "I'm probably over-cautious, but do you realize how many things have gone haywire in my life because someone overheard something?"

He flushed, probably because one of those 'things' had involved Vince Lamberson hearing him make a date with me and resulted in Bryan's ex-wife being killed by mistake.

This time Tory overheard Bobby Fleming giving directions to Tyler to go someplace the night he was killed, possibly RFD. That was bothering me. Somehow I felt Tyler's murderer had to have overheard as well. After all, the murder weapon was a guitar string. The murderer must be a musician, and this whole series of murders must be related to country music and the world that Tory and Tyler and, to an extent, Jason inhabited.

All I said, however, was, "Besides, it'll make a great picnic. I've got Jean's cake with me."

"Is that the cake you've been tellin' me about?" asked Tory.

I nodded, my hair whipping around in the wind. My hand slipped a little on the wheel as I shook strands out of my eyes. Bryan reached over and steadied it with his hand. He released it as soon as I cleared my face.

"What else have you got in your picnic basket?" asked Jason.

"The usual," I said. "Sandwiches - subs, actually. Some chips. Fruit. Cider." It was a fall day, after all.

"This is starting to remind me of a certain strategy session we had the last time there was trouble," Jason commented.

"What are you all talkin' about?"

Jason reminded her of the skeletons found on my parents' farm when I moved back here. "A group of us met at Mackenzie's over food to try and piece everything together."

He was right. There were similarities.

Bryan looked at me with concern.

"You all right?" I asked.

"Yeah." He shifted his long legs around the confining cockpit. "I was wondering if you were."

I pulled the throttle back to accommodate the changing current. We were getting close to King's Island. "I'm fine, actually. Jason's right. This is a little too reminiscent of last year."

Bryan grunted. "I don't like it now any more than I did then. I don't like you putting yourself in danger."

"Me? I'm not in any danger. I think it's Tory we need to worry about. I think she's the one in danger." The words came out of my mouth without any conscious thought, but it rang true...and urgent. "Bryan, we've got to solve this before something happens to Tory."

I swung the boat around and eased it towards the rock-strewn beach of King's Island, the island for which Kings Hill was named. Situated as it was across from Jason's facility, he'd taken it upon himself to have his grounds people clean it up. It still bore remnants of people's campfires, but the monumental amount of litter that had built up over years was gone, and people seemed to be making an effort to keep it that way.

He'd also had a makeshift pier put in. Bryan leapt out as the boat came alongside, cursing briefly as his well-shod foot dipped into the water on his transfer. He steadied the boat for us and helped pull it close enough to tie the long bowline to the pier. His face grew red with frustration as he fussed with the rope. He appeared to be struggling with the knot.

He must dislike this an awful lot, I thought, climbing out to get the other line secured. He stood frowning at the boat and the water.

"Good job, thank you." I offered as I moved past him. He grunted.

We collected the picnic basket and a couple blankets from under a seat and headed for the flat rocks that stood out over the beach near forest's edge. Bryan and Jason spread out the blankets, and Tory helped me with the food. No one spoke.

We arranged everything and passed around individual bottles of cider. I was biting into my sandwich when Tory spoke up.

"We heard what you said, Mackenzie. I've been feelin' like these murders were circlin' all around me. Since I know I didn't do any of them, it must be that somehow they're all aimed at me."

Her voice broke. She was such a tiny person, even if she was some sort of fireball. I watched for tears or a break in the hold she was trying to have on herself. Hysteria was not unexpected, but her next words were.

"So what do we all do to stop the buzzards that are tryin' to make hash out of Jason's and my life?"

·C·H·A·P·T·E·R· *24*

·M·A·C·K·E·N·Z·I·E·

"but how we make the ride."

- from "The End's in the Beginning" by Tyler McCloud

B ryan nearly choked on his sandwich, but Jason grinned. The fireball was in control.

"I guess that's what we're doing here, Tory. Maybe we better start by making sure we all know the same things. Bryan, do you have a note - ?"

He sighed. "Notebook? Sure. I'll take notes. However, I'm going on record as saying that whatever we come up with has to run through my department and Ted Matheson. No one here is going after this guy, whoever he is. As many murders as there have been, none of you are equipped to deal with this person. Agreed?"

"Got it," I said, trying to mask my annoyance. *Did he really think we'd go after someone like this on our own?* "So, where do we start?"

"I think we should list exactly who has been killed, when and where," said Jason, his hand on Tory's shoulder. She leaned into it, as if she were drawing strength from his touch.

Somehow that made me feel a little forlorn. I gave myself a mental shake and began. "There was Tyler, first."

Bryan interrupted immediately. "We *think* he's first. We'll have to check coroner reports."

"As far as we know, Tyler was first," I said firmly. "At Jason's company. Then J.D. Lazenbee, at the track. Next was Auggie Haynes, back in Nashville. Finally, Bobby Fleming, here in Albany, on the street near Peter's hotel."

"What about Braeden?"

I looked at Tory over the edge of my bottle of cider. "What about Braeden?"

"He died before Tyler."

"True, but he committed suicide."

Bryan's eyes narrowed. "Braeden? I haven't heard about this. Mackenzie?"

"Braeden Snyder, Naomi Cooper's brother. I told you about him the other night. You said something about contacting Vegas about his suicide, remember?" *Had he not taken me seriously?*

"I remember, but I turned that over to Matheson. He hasn't got back to me on it."

Tory started to explain. "Mackenzie, I know he killed himself way before all this, but I think he's part of it somehow. His papers claimed he owned that house with my brother, and - "

"Wait. 'Claimed'?"

Tory nodded. "That's one of the things I need to tell you all about. That is *not* Tyler's signature on that deed. Actually, it's not even very close. He - we both - worked at developing a distinctive signature. See, when you autograph something, it goes so fast, nobody can really read it. So we both decided we needed to make our signatures special enough that even when you couldn't read it, you'd recognize it as ours. Some folks have different signatures for autographing - different from their regular ones? Tyler's and mine always looked the same no matter what we signed. Tyler always wrote left-handed. I don't think that person - whoever signed his name - knew that. I think he must have been right-handed or something, because the angle isn't right." She popped a couple potato chips in her mouth and crunched them down.

Bryan frowned. "Tyler - left-handed? His guitar didn't look any different."

Tory shook her head, her mouth too full of chips for her to speak. Jason answered for her. "Tyler was unusual. He was right-handed in everything except his handwriting. He showed me once. Dared me to imitate his signature. You can't do it well unless you are left-handed, too. I agree with Tory. Judging from Naomi's photo, Tyler did not sign that deed. If we can see it, you can bet a handwriting expert will know."

"Okay, okay, let me think." I squeezed my eyes closed. "Just because Braeden's dead and someone forged Tyler's signature doesn't necessarily mean we should count him."

"I don't know about that," said Bryan slowly. "These things sometimes have long roots. It seems to center around the music industry and Tyler and Tory. Braeden is part of that, so maybe it is tied up in this. Maybe his suicide needs to be laid at the door of whoever killed Tyler."

I wasn't sure. "Do all of you think this?"

Tory and Jason nodded.

Bryan pursed his lips. "It can't hurt to put him on the list. Braeden Snyder. Las Vegas. If nothing else, this guy gets around."

I continued. "How about means, how each one was killed? Sorry, Tory."

Her face had gone white, but she rallied. "It has to be said. Okay, Tyler was strangled, with an E string."

"J.D.'s car had a broken tie rod that was only broken because someone cut it half through right before he drove it for qualifying. That's in the forensics report that was supplied to the crew chief." Jason's voice was low but firm.

"Auggie was shot," Bryan noted.

I turned to Tory. "I thought you said the Nashville police had his killer in custody."

"They arrested someone because they found his fingerprints on the gun, and he couldn't remember what he was doing when Auggie was killed. I'm not sure they have the right guy."

"Neither are they," said Bryan. "According to Matheson."

"Oh." I stared at the apple I was eating. Every piece of information we had held an unknown element, something that didn't fit or that we didn't know or weren't sure. How would there ever be enough evidence to pull this together?

"Bobby Fleming was shot, too, with a gun of the same caliber as the one that killed Auggie." Bryan spoke as he wrote.

"Don't forget to mark Braeden down as a suicide." I added.

"Do we know how?"

"Naomi told me. He jumped."

"Jumped? Jumped where?"

"Bryce Canyon. If he hadn't left a note and if his car hadn't been there, they might never have found him."

Bryan frowned as he noted: Get report on Snyder suicide. "You know that unless we can prove it was actually murder, this one won't count."

I nodded. *Obviously.*

Jason swallowed the last of his sandwich. "Does it seem at all odd to anyone else that someone from Vegas would drive all the way to Bryce Canyon just to kill himself?"

"Does it matter where he killed himself?" Tory sniffed, her face twitching.

"It could. Suicides tend to fall into certain patterns of behavior. Sometimes they're unpredictable, but mostly not. If something doesn't fit some kind of a usual pattern, well, then, maybe it's not suicide."

"What are you saying, Bryan?"

He shifted around on the blanket. "It's like this. Even if there was undue influence, or someone put him in bad circumstances, a suicide is just that, a suicide. Not a homicide. People have sued in court that someone else is at fault, but those cases are not easily proven. Chances are that's why Naomi never said or did anything. However much she may blame Tyler, there is no legal recourse to lay blame at his door."

Tory muttered something undistinguishable. Jason put his arm around her again. She seemed cross more than distressed. "Damn gambling anyway!" she said more loudly.

Bryan continued. "However, if his death is too far out of the patterns of suicides of this type - jumping - then maybe we need to investigate further. Maybe it wasn't suicide. Maybe it is one more murder, the first murder."

"Naomi's brother murdered? But who - oh!" I didn't dare look at Tory.

"Look," she said, standing up. "Tyler did not murder anybody, no matter what Naomi thinks. Braeden must have committed suicide. Besides, if the idea was that Tyler killed him, then who killed Tyler?" She stomped around kicking at pebbles.

"I'm not saying Tyler killed anybody," Bryan said. "No. I'm wondering if the same person could have killed both of them. And the others."

"Where does that come from?" asked Jason.

Bryan shook his head. "I wish I could give you a real answer. Call it instinct. But I think it makes the most sense, based on what we know. The question is who, and why."

"So, it's back to connecting things again. Who is connected to all of them?"

Again, we all wanted to look at Tory, but none of us did.

"You know, silence is as loud as shoutin' sometimes. I know what you're all thinkin'. You're all thinkin' you don't want to say how this all points at me. I didn't kill anyone, and you all know it!"

Bryan got up then, and went and put his hands on Tory's shoulders.

"We all - " he smiled self-consciously "- know that you did not kill anyone, Tory. We know Tyler didn't either. Somehow, you *are* at the center of it all. Do you have enemies? Stalkers? Maybe someone who thinks you did them a wrong in the music industry? Because that's the commonality."

She closed her eyes and shook her head at him. "No, none of those. If I did have a stalker, you'd think he'd have gone after Jason here. And no one has. Nobody's touched him."

"You don't think so?" I asked.

"What?"

"You don't think trying to frame Jason for Tyler's murder is going after him?"

Tory stared at me, but Jason turned his eyes on me with a more speculative glance.

"Elucidate, Mackie," he said.

"Look, from the beginning - well, the beginning here anyway - this has not only been about killing Tyler, but about making it look like you must have done it." I started ticking things off on my fingers. "The location, the timing. Then, the innuendoes in the paper. Press releases, speculation, references to the lawsuit between you and Tyler...." I paused to think.

"That wasn't really Tyler," said Tory. "Peter was the one who pushed the lawsuit. Peter always led me to think he'd beaten Jason in court. I didn't know until Mackenzie told me that he let the judge decide in Tyler's favor. I reckon Peter wanted to impress me."

"He never liked me," mused Jason. "I used to think it was because I was simply better at most things than he was. I could have won that case in court, you know. After what you told me he said in Nashville, maybe it was all about you. He was in love with you even then."

"What?" I choked on my sandwich, catching crumbs of bread that tumbled from my mouth.

Tory nodded at me. "When we were talking about the elopement and everything, when I was firin' him, he told me he was in love with me. Said he'd be there if Jason and I ever broke up."

I shivered. "There's something creepy about that. Not that it would ever happen."

Bryan was frowning again.

"What is it?" I asked. *What's the criticism this time,* my little voice wondered. I was surprised at the words myself.

"Has Himes ever been in trouble with the law?" he asked.

"Peter?" Tory said, astonished.

Jason snorted. "Bryan, he's a lawyer. Lawyers like him are experts at skirting the law without getting caught. You're familiar with that, I'm sure."

"Yes, I am."

Something about his tone gave me pause. "Why, you don't think Peter could - ?"

"Think about it. Would it bother Peter if Jason were framed for Tyler's murder? I don't think so."

"Hell, no," said Jason in one of his rare swearing moments.

"Peter knew Braeden. Knew Auggie. Knew J.D.?" he asked, his eyebrows raised.

Tory answered, "I don't know how well he knew J.D. There wasn't much overlap in their times with us."

Jason put in. "They knew each other. When J.D. called to ask about the testing job, he had a long litany of complaints against our Peter Himes."

"He definitely knew Bobby. He knew Tyler. He knows you, Tory, and wants to, let's say, know you more." Bryan being delicate. "Peter Himes is, in fact, the only person we know that knew each and every victim.

A pall descended on us. The wind lapped at the blanket edges, and the air felt ten degrees colder.

"I just found out that Peter thinks he loves me," Tory began. "Now you're wantin' me to think he's killing people I love? How does that even make sense?"

Bryan raised his hand, starting to say something in reply, but then his hand dropped, and he shook his head. "I don't know, Tory. I'm not sure. Maybe I don't know the guy well enough to judge. I'm not comfortable with the picture, you know? I'm just not."

His pronouncement put the final damper on the picnic. I started gathering up trash, determined to leave no footprint on the island. I circled out from where we were sitting, pulling bits of litter out of the weeds, pausing to look at some of the ones too stubborn to call it quits. Probably the reason weeds prevail.

"Hey, Bryan? Come look at this. Isn't this the mint Matheson told us to look out for?"

He scrambled over next to me. "Could be."

Jason joined us. 'Mint? Oh, that. Yes, that's what's known as Mentha xpiperita L. There's a bunch of it over on the RFD campus."

"Well, that's exactly where I'm supposed to be looking for it. Matheson said Tyler had some in his mouth the night he died."

"He did that, you know?" Tory had come over too. "Tyler was always puttin' somethin' in his mouth. Probably 'cause he used to smoke a lot. He was always pullin' up blades of grass and stuff to chew on. Mint was always good, because you really could eat it."

"It looks like he did that night. It could give us an idea of how he got onto the property. There never were any alarms or anything, were there?"

Jason answered. "No, that's one of the things I didn't understand. No records of him signing in through one of the gates. No intrusion alarms or barking dogs." He shook his head. "I can show you where the mint is. There's a lot of it, but it only grows in one place. In the ditch."

"What ditch?"

"The one alongside the River Road, just before the turn-off to the access road. He must have come along through there."

"Bryan, do you suppose there could be anything there that would help? I mean, tire tracks or anything?"

My wonderful cop smiled a little too indulgently. "Mackie, you're thinking like a TV show again. I doubt that there are any tire tracks that would be useful. There's no telling how many cars have come that way and driven on the shoulder."

My irritation - or at least my disappointment - must have shown, because he backed down slightly.

"That's not to say there might not be something there. We need to check. I'll call out - "

"Look, why don't we just go over there now? I can pull into the public access dock. It'll be faster. If we find anything, then you can call for somebody."

It was his irritation that showed now. "The boat again."

"Yes. The boat. We kind of have to go by boat. It's how we got here." I smiled at him in a lopsided, goofy sort of way. "Bryan, what's the deal? Why is it you're scared of the boats?"

He snorted. "Scared? Who said I was scared? I don't like them is all. Let's go. I don't know how much daylight we have left."

We finished packing up and climbed aboard. Once again I noted how easily he moved. *Really? Not at ease on the water?*

Oh well, I thought, and turned the engine over. It came on with its usual unmuffled roar. Bryan cast off and pushed us away from the dock. I eased out into the channel, heading on the diagonal for the public access dock Jason had built near the RFD. In five minutes we were halfway across, skipping jauntily across the waves.

The engine sputtered once, then caught.

"Hunh. Shouldn't do that," I muttered, glancing at the gauge. Everything seemed fine. Then it coughed again. Once more. Then it quit.

I drew in an irritated breath. "Hold on a minute," I told the others. I switched off the ignition and went back to check the engine and tank.

"Damn! I knew it! I knew it, I knew it, I knew it!"

"What? What happened?" asked Jason.

Bryan turned around in concern, his hand back on the wheel to hold the boat steady.

"I knew someone had been out joyriding in this. There should've been over a half tank of gas in there! It's nearly bone dry! Now what do we do?" I bit back the other curse words I wanted to use.

"I knew you should have checked the gas," Bryan muttered.

I glared at him. "Not exactly helpful."

"Now we row? Right?" Jason managed to keep a bright tone.

I wondered how many motorboats of this size he'd ever rowed. Or how many any of us had rowed. It was what we had to do, but it wasn't going to be fun. I started pulling up the paddles from their holders along the sides of the boat. I passed one to Jason and the other to Bryan.

"It'll take both of you."

"You seem prepared. This happen often?" Jason asked with a grin.

"Let's just say similar things have happened often enough that I never go out without at least two paddles. Sometimes three. If you two get too tired, Tory and I can spell you."

"We'll be fine. It shouldn't be too bad in this direction." Bryan glanced at us. "Sorry, ladies, but we're in better shape than you are. At least I am."

Tory and I exchanged glances, her eyebrows raised to my scowl.

"I can handle it if you get tired," assured Jason. A good-natured competition began.

"I'll stay with the wheel," I told them. "That will help some."

I edged past where Bryan was setting up mid-cockpit, marveling at how nonchalant he was acting.

He grunted and settled in, leaning into the extended handle, feeling his grip, adjusting to the rhythm of the task. His biceps bulged with the effort of the stroke. The muscles in his back stretched and rippled as he turned and the paddle responded with long, smooth strokes.

"My guess is this isn't going to endear boats to you either, is it?"

He snorted and shook his head. "One more bad memory."

"Huh?"

"Boats. Like I said, I'm not afraid of them. They bring up bad memories, is all."

"Memories? You mean, Deb? His ex-wife," I told Tory when she gave me a puzzled glance.

He looked ahead as he began his next stroke. "Nothing to do with her. Look, I don't really want...." He trailed off. "Oh, what the hell. If I tell you, then you won't worry about it. Because, you know, you don't need to worry. It's not your problem, it's mine."

Jason stretched out his arms to maneuver his own paddle, his eyes narrowed in the effort to catch Bryan's words. Though it was quieter without the engine, a stiff breeze still blew Tory's and my hair around. I gripped the wheel maybe more tightly than necessary. If I was in for any surprises from Bryan's revelation, I wanted to hold onto something.

Bryan spoke in rhythm with his paddling, pausing only when he needed to shift his the paddle around.

"Look," he began, "it was something that happened during training. We were doing rescue training, covering a lot of ground. This was one of those sessions run for groups made up of law enforcement, fire, and rescue teams. We were running multiple scenarios. I don't know exactly know how it happened, but I screwed up. Big time, and in front of a lot of people." He paused for a few strokes.

"What happened?" I prompted.

"It was a practice swift water rescue. I was steering the boat; only the second time I'd ever done that. It should have been easy, but I was trying to move as fast as I could. Something happened to the boat, the steering or something. I came up on the rescue location too fast. I swung the boat around - it was a little outboard, small enough to navigate a thirty-foot wide, eight-foot deep creek - or small river, whatever you want to call it - I swung it around, thinking it would slow us down. I wasn't experienced enough to realize how strong the centrifugal force would be. It threw my two partners out of the boat. When I reached out for Ryan, the wheel spun back, out of my hands, and I went out, too."

"Oh my lord!" exclaimed Tory.

"How bad was it?" asked Jason.

I stared at the windscreen, unable to imagine what that must have felt like. Not the going overboard part; I knew what that could feel like. No, what it had felt like for this to happen. Bryan was always the knight in shining armor, the sheriff riding in on his swift horse. What did it feel like for things to go wrong, even if it was a practice?

"We were all okay, eventually. I had a few bad minutes stuck under the boat - it overturned on me. The real rescuers - " his voice turned bitter "- got me out okay. I twisted my shoulder, though, and I wasn't able to finish the training."

"So, when did you go back out?" asked Jason.

Bryan raised his head. "As a rescuer? Never. I never had the opportunity. I started moving up in the division, and left that sort of thing behind."

"Did you never go out on a boat since?" I asked, suspicious because of what I'd seen earlier.

"Only when I absolutely had to. Every time I do, it reminds me of that failure."

"But, you only failed at the rescue attempt, and it was a training exercise. Not everyone gets things right the first time."

"I know," he said, but he sounded like my reasoning didn't matter.

"Bryan, I'm sorry I made such a big deal about going out on the boat. I shouldn't have insisted."

"Don't apologize, Mackie. It's not anybody's problem but my own. I'll deal with it." He fell silent and paddled. We were nearly across.

"Seems like a lot of pride to me," said Jason. His words came tightly. "You can't let pride get in the way like that."

"I know. I know! It's my problem, like I said. All right?" The defiance in his voice and face silenced us.

It did seem like mostly a matter of pride. I knew how Bryan always felt about being the person who helped other people. It was his nature to be strong, to expect himself to be able to handle danger and play the rescuer. He might be overreacting to things, but that was because this was so important to him.

I knew now I couldn't ask him to make a regular thing of going out in the boat. He'd never share my joy. However unnecessary, he was too disappointed in his own actions to get past this. It wasn't just pride, it was disappointment.

"Mackenzie, you're awfully quiet. What's going on up there?" He kept his voice light, trying to clear the mood.

"I'm looking for a good docking place. We're almost there, but I think we need to go around to the other side. Can you guys keep going a few more minutes?"

"I'm okay," called out Jason.

"Tell us where you want her and steer her in. We'll do the rest," Bryan said.

We worked it out and tied up to the dock. Again there was that efficient ease with which he handled himself, putting up the oars, helping Tory out, extending a congratulating hand to Jason. Surely this thing was something he could get over. *If he wanted to.*

"We'll gas up first," I said, and went over to the pump master, explaining our problem. He produced a fuel can and helped me fill it with the right mix and bring it over to the *Emma D.* He whistled when he saw her and started asking me questions as we transferred the fuel.

He waved good-bye and we headed up the dock.

"Sure am glad you included that fuel station, Jason. This could have been so much worse."

Bryan reached over and took my hand. Was it my imagination or did he seem more relaxed now? Must have been the rowing.

We walked past some curious eyes. Some people pointed to the boat, others reacted to us personally. It was true you didn't usually see four well-known locals casually docking a polished piece of boating history at the public pier.

"Does your boat always cause such a stir?" asked Jason.

"I think it's more the company I'm keeping...Hi, Ms. Thierry. How're the sinuses?" I asked a middle-aged homemaker who had a cottage business bottling and selling clover honey made by bees she kept in the back yard.

"Doing better. You'd think the Lord would take pity on me and make it easier to earn a living without the extra bother of sinus pressure when I'm working. Lovely boat you've got. Reminds me of one Charlie Osterhout used to have. 'Bye, Doc." Her terrier pulled her away, rushing to yap at the water at the end of the pier.

Bryan was shaking his head. "How is it you know more people than I do, and you've only been back a little over a year?"

"You work in Albany, I work here," I said. "Let's cross."

We dodged River Road traffic, such as it was, and approached the stretch of road that lay to the southern side of the driveway to Jason's company.

"This is where the mint grows," said Jason. "See? Whole patches of it."

"It smells wonderful," said Tory, inhaling deeply. "Mmm, can I pick this to make some mint juleps?"

"When we're done looking, you can pick all you want, but not before," said Bryan. "Let's get started."

We spread out along about fifty feet of road.

"Work from the shoulder of the road in. Don't miss anything. Move the grass and mint around carefully. Something could be caught in the stems, or hidden underneath."

"Bryan, do you think we'll really find anything?"

"Probably not, but we don't want to overlook anything. I have to take some samples of the plant in for Matheson. Make sure we're looking at the right stuff." His voice was muffled as he bent down, combing the plants with his long fingers.

I took a cue from him and started gently brushing among the patches of mint where I was. It was thinner here, and thinned out more behind me, where Tory was searching. She squatted down among them, careful not to kneel on anything.

"There's some trash back here," she said.

"It might not be trash," Jason warned. "Let me get you a bag from Bryan." He stepped over plants, lifting his long legs gingerly, and fetched us a couple of the evidence bags Bryan always carried.

"Pack anything you find, Tory," Bryan called.

She nodded, head bent to the ground once more. I resumed my own hunt.

Beneath the mint leaves and browning grass, the shoulder was covered in gray gravel, scattered on a regular basis by cars speeding along the road. Dark ruts and tracks lay closer to the pavement, while taller, healthier weeds filled the ditch where gravel gave way to actual soil.

I dove in.

Beneath the tiny leaves of mint and multiple stalks of grass crept sickly stems of salvia with their dried purple flowers. Plucky, stumpy balls of white clover dotted the undergrowth as well. I pushed further. Flecks of foil, strips of plastic wrap, twigs, pebbles, detritus. Nothing. I brushed aside some more. At last, a Bic lighter, totally dry with its mechanics all rusted. Nothing, I was sure, but Bryan would say bag it anyway. I found some more: paper scraps, an envelope, two paperclips entwined with thread. Nothing that could yield any clues, I was sure. I tried to imagine what impressions would look like - tire impressions, footprints, walking sticks - what brought that idea into my head? I saw nothing. I felt frustrated, but I had to remember that at least I was eliminating possibilities.

"Hey! Bryan! What about this?" Jason pointed to bushes of mint whose tops were crushed and broken. Bryan went over and squatted to examine them more closely. He frowned, then pulled out his phone for pictures. He looked about when he finished, and sort of duck-walked to another section. More crushed mint. He squinted, then stood and stared at the ground, then looked up and down the road.

"I'd have to get someone else out here, but I think we can be pretty sure someone was here with a car. Recently, but not too recently. Of course, it could be anyone, any car, who knows?" He sighed. "Anyone find anything else? Mackie?"

I shook my head. "Just junk. I bagged it, but even if it's from that night, I don't think it will give you anything. Tory, what about you?"

She shook her head. "I'm tryin' to sort this real careful, but I'm not findin' a thing. Everything here is just green or brown. Hey, Mackie?" she made a gesture for me to look behind me.

A man was walking up. He wore spotless jeans and a sweatshirt over a plaid shirt. The sweatshirt looked like it was either new or freshly ironed. He might have been fifty or he might have been sixty, but his face exhibited concern for us.

"You young people may want to consider moving that boat of yours. Dock's getting crowded. You don't want that pretty thing banged up. Especially when those afternoon people get in. They don't pay any attention to what they're doing."

He watched Jason as he pawed through his patch of mint once more.

"Be careful there. You don't want to bruise that."

Jason nodded.

"You know what that is, don't you?"

"Why, yes." Jason flashed a smile. "Mentha xpiperita."

The man grunted and fished around in his pockets. "I've got a pocketknife here if you want to cut a bunch of it. You can rub some on your forehead if you're gettin' a headache." He peered at Jason.

"My colleague over there might need it."

Bryan was talking on the phone again. He frowned when he saw a civilian invading his investigative scene

"You familiar with the mint family?"

"You might say. Mentha x piperita. Peppermint. One member of a diverse species with varieties exhibiting nuanced flavors, known familiarly as orange mint, chocolate mint, spearmint. Edible, peppermint is often used medicinally. While this is the only patch on this property, it is also on Kings Island, and I am sure in many other yards locally,"

Looking Jason up and down, the man seemed to arrive at some conclusion or other. "You must be the fellow that cowboy wanted to see."

"I'm Jason Fields."

"Oh, that's your name, huh? Funny how he chose to see you at that fancy shindig. He sure was eager to see you." He looked from one to another of us. "You're not looking at this mint for fun, are you?"

"No, no, we're not." Bryan spoke as he approached where the man and Jason stood. "I'm afraid you'll have to excuse us. We - "

"Bryan, wait a minute. This gentleman - um ?"

"Keith Zavier."

"Mr. Zavier has just said something I think you might find interesting." He nodded to the older man.

"Oh, I was just saying how eager the cowboy was to see Mr. Fields."

"You met a cowboy who wanted to see Mr. Fields? Where? When?" Bryan rattled off the questions while throwing sharp glances at both Jason and Mr. Zavier.

"The other evening, the night of the big opening. He kept asking me if I was sure this was Jason Fields's new headquarters. Like I said, he was eager to see you."

"I guess you could say that, since he got himself killed trying," said Bryan.

"Killed? That young cowboy? That's a shame."

Jason raised an eyebrow at Bryan, who moved in closer to speak with Mr. Zavier.

"You didn't know someone was killed here that night?"

"No. I assume it was in the news? I left town on a family emergency later that night. Got back a few days ago, but I've been dealing with the aftermath of that emergency. Coming down here to fish is the first I've been out since I got back."

"It's continued to be in the news, Mr. Zavier." A cop-like skepticism crept into Brian's voice. "You didn't hear anything on the TV news? See something about it on the Internet?"

"I'm not a fan of either of those two pursuits, young man. Now, what can you tell me about what happened?"

"Maybe you'd better tell me a few things first. You didn't know about the murder, but you knew Tyler McCloud was coming here to try and see Jason Fields that night?"

"Like I said, he told me."

"*He* told you?"

"First thing he said when I told him to move his motorcycle out of the mint so it wouldn't get bruised. Most people would've blown me off, but he seemed to get it. Moved his bike over there polite as you please."

"Could you show me exactly where he moved his bike to?"

"Sure, he parked it - right - yeah, right here by this tree. I remember because we laughed about how no one would care if that one was crushed. It's a sumac."

"Did he say anything about why he had come here? Or why he was parking down here instead of going on up to the reception?"

"Well, he said he wanted to see Mr. Fields, pretty bad, it seemed. Didn't really say anything about parking - no, wait a minute. He said something about not wanting to be noticed. Of course that cowboy hat and the red shirt would've done it. Fine-looking young man, too."

By now it was obvious to all of us that this man was telling the truth. He had too many details. Except Tory had never said anything about Tyler riding a motorcycle. Maybe she didn't know?

Mr. Zavier went on. "We talked a couple minutes, just chit-chattin', you know. Then he said something about it never being too late to apologize, but how once you know you should, you need to get it done."

I wanted to know more. Tory would want to hear this, too. I waved for her to join me as I moved closer to where the men were standing.

·C·H·A·P·T·E·R· *25*

·T·O·R·Y·

"And then we stared at one another once again."

- from "It's Never Over" by Joe Lauper and Tyler McCloud

I caught the motion of Mackenzie's hand right away. I hadn't exactly heard what the men were sayin' but the way Bryan moved around and frowned and hopped on his cell phone told me something was up.

I grabbed the stuff I'd collected and stood up to go to her. Something slipped and made a soft thud among the mint leaves. Damn. I felt around with my feet. Found it. I picked it up carefully.

"Whew." It was my old iRiver drive. Part mp3 player, part recorder, part flash drive. A lot of musicians get into the habit of carrying some kind of gizmo around so that they can record ideas or rehearsals and play them back or put them on computer at will. It had dropped out of my pocket. I snagged it and joined the others, slipping it back into my jacket.

The boys were deep in discussion, Bryan lookin' fierce, Jason thoughtful. He reached out for me when I got there. I snuggled up under his arm and looked at this person they'd been talking with so urgently. He seemed like a kind man, I thought, looking at his white hair and the character lines down his face. He put me in mind of the man in the music video for Craig Morgan's "This Ain't Nothin".

Bryan and Jason introduced us and brought me up to speed. This was the last person to see Tyler, the last person my brother saw. A kindly face. A friendly person who seemed to care about what happened to a stranger, even someone met just one night and never seen again. I had to fight the tears.

Bryan was wrapping things up. "Thank you, Mr. Zavier. I'll give the State Police your contact information, and someone will call. We'll need to come up with a timeline of everything, folks. Mr. Zavier will help us with what happened out here that night. Then we need to backtrack - I'm sorry, Mr. Zavier, of course you can go. Thank you very much for your time. You've been more help than you can know."

"Well, I'm glad to be of help. There's nothing worse than murder." He turned to go.

"Wait!" I scrambled out of Jason's arms and ran up to Mr. Zavier, stopping short of hugging him, but grabbing both his hands.

"Mr. Zavier. Thank you. Thank you for caring about my brother."

"That's all right, Miss. I couldn't do any less. I don't think anybody could."

"Thank you anyway. It means a lot."

"You're welcome. Now, don't worry. These officers know what they're doing. They'll get whoever did this to your brother." He waved good-bye and crossed the road.

I returned to the others where Bryan was back in organizational mode.

"This case is getting more complicated and hard to follow by the minute. We need to take the time to sit down and really sort things out. I think building a timeline from everyone's information is the best way to do it."

"Bryan, can I help?" I asked.

"I was counting on it. You know more of the history than anyone, Tory. I'll need to ask you about Tyler's motorcycle, too."

"Motorcycle?"

"Yeah, apparently he rode it here that night. But it's not here; no one said anything about a motorcycle on the property. Any reason you didn't report it missing?"

"Bryan, I don't know anything about it. Last motorcycle Tyler had was back in Nash - Wait a minute. He might have picked one up on the tour. He'd do that with stuff sometimes. I wouldn't find out about it until we got back home."

"Where would he keep a motorcycle on tour?"

"Dean would know. He's in charge of transporting heavy gear. Anything like that, if Tyler bought it, Dean would handle it."

"Dean's one of your men? Can I have his last name?"

"Sure. Dean Dechard. Peter could - no, never mind. Um, Joe would know. Joe Lauper, in the band." It felt weird, discussing things this way, but it was working toward a solution. Anything to catch the man who killed my brother.

Bryan finished writing down what I'd told him. He continued to organize, "Mackenzie, I'll need your help with some of the other dates - hell, you know? We all need to work on it. Can we go back to your place? I'd like each of us to work up our own sequence of events, then combine them and see what they tell us. Did anyone find anything on the ground?"

"Here are my bags. I don't think there's anything important there." I handed him the stuff I'd found. Something dropped to the ground when I did. Bryan snagged it and turned it over.

"Why didn't you bag this? It could be important, and now any prints will be - "

I shook my head at him. "That's mine. It keeps fallin' out of my pocket."

"Oh. Here, then." He handed it back. I started to put it in my pocket and thought better of it. "Mackenzie, will you put this in your purse 'til we get back? I don't want to lose it. It has some songs on it that Tyler and I recorded." I sniffed. "The last writing session we ever did, too. I don't reckon that song'll get done now."

We picked up fresh-made pizza from D'Amore's on the way and got to work on it and our lists as soon as we reached Mackenzie's. By the time the pizza was gone and Mackenzie was done searching the refrigerator for Jean's chocolate cake and stash of ice cream, we were comparing and combining our lists.

"Tory. What about this here, did you tell me about that?" Jason asked.

I looked at my list where it lay on the table next to the others. "That? Yes. Remember? It came up in conversation at Teresa's. I didn't think anythin' of it at first, but when we started listin' stuff, I thought I better include it. It seemed odd, since none of us knew he'd gone anywhere. Those boys don't like him at all."

Mackenzie read off the list, "'Ty and Terry Haynes, Auggie's twins, said that the man named Peter Himes ran over their truck when he was there the week Auggie was killed.' Are you sure that was the week?"

"Mhmm. They're only three, but they're sharp. They recognized Peter, and they referred to 'last week'. That was the week Auggie died."

"What did Peter say?" asked Bryan.

"I didn't tell him. Or ask him either. It was right after I fired him."

"Is it significant, Bryan?" asked Mackenzie.

"I don't know," he murmured. "We need to know if it's accurate, first." He looked at Jason.

"I don't think we need to mention this to anyone else," Jason said, moving closer to me. "In fact, we probably shouldn't mention any of the things we have on this list. Just as a precaution," he said, looking down at me with troubled eyes.

I knew that look. I was getting just a teensy bit fed up with all this special treatment. *Okay, I got it. Don't talk about this, because it could be dangerous. Just say so already.*

I sat down with my chocolate cake and some butter pecan ice cream, pulling the lists over to me. I studied them as I spooned ice cream into my mouth, leaving the spoon dangling there as I paused at some of the entries. Some of them didn't make sense.

"Auggie made a mysterious trip to Charlotte. When did he go to Charlotte? Do we know for sure he really did? I mean, I know Teresa said he wanted to get in touch with somebody there. Or was it George who said that? Anyway, do we know if he did?"

"We can infer he did. That's why we're doing this list. We'll check it out."

"Bryan, I can do that for you. Let me talk with the people at the raceway and my garage. They should know," Jason offered.

"Right. Thanks. Tory, I want you to talk with Teresa and George again. Take notes on what they say. Confirm some of this stuff you've got here from your trip. Get Teresa to question those boys of hers."

"Bryan, you make it sound like an interrogation. They're just little boys!" said Mackenzie.

"I know. That's why it's their mother who'll do the questioning. I want some leads."

"You know you've got two references here to press releases," Mackenzie pointed out.

"That's right. The one in his pocket that was tampered with, and the one that was released to the paper."

"Why that one?" I asked. "Wasn't that one just speculation or something?"

"It was used to inflame people about Jason's history with your brother. It referred to him as the 'losing litigant' in the court case."

"So? I mean, I know Jason and Mackenzie told me different, but everyone thought he lost the case. That's what Tyler - "

"- And Peter," put in Jason.

I nodded. "And Peter - let everybody think."

"But the official record says differently," said Bryan. "Anyone could look it up. Or ask Jason. Whoever wrote that release knew people thought he'd lost, and they wanted to encourage people to *keep* thinking it."

"Like Peter did," I said softly. "We never found out who sent out the release. Anybody who didn't look it up would probably still think Jason lost the case."

"Only the killer would have a reason to perpetuate that idea, since it would incriminate Jason. The release had to have been sent by the killer. No one else owns up to it."

"It still could have been anyone with a grudge against both Tyler and Jason. Not necessarily Peter."

"True. It could be someone else. Frankly, I don't see Peter Himes as a multiple murderer anyway. I don't think he has it in him. He does have plenty of reason to hate Jason. He *might* have a reason to hate Tyler as well. Or fear him." Bryan continued, "We don't have enough to go on yet. We need more answers."

"I think it would help if we broke down this list a little," said Mackenzie. "We need to see some order. I wrote everything down in the order I uncovered it. Maybe we need to put things in the order they happened, too."

"That changes the order of the - the killings, too." I stumbled over the word. "I mean, the way we saw it, Tyler was the first one killed. Then Auggie was the last one we discovered. But we know that Auggie was killed before Bobby Fleming. And Braeden was the first one of all."

"Okay, so we need to put things in the order they happened - or at least the order in which we think they happened. I'd like to separate them out, too. We have five people dead, so we need to think of them as five different cases, related to each other. We need separate lists of clues, thoughts, and evidence for each person killed. Then we can figure out what we still need to know."

We looked at each other and groaned. This was going to be a lot of work.

Two pots of coffee and a pitcher of tea later, a second round of pizza gone, ice cream and cake consumed, we finally had the lists we wanted.

The first was of the events in the order we thought they had happened. This superseded when we discovered things - bodies, mostly - because the order of discovery wasn't relevant in the world of the killer. The second list, once we made it into a table, broke everything down into factors on individual murders, and it looked like this:

Order of Discovery →	Tyler	J. D	Braeden	Bobby	Auggie
↓ Clues/Info					
#1	Murder weapon E-string from guitar	died in car crash same weekend as Tyler murdered	*Peter took insurance check to Naomi after Braeden's suicide last year	shot on way to give message to Peter re Tory & Jason's wedding	Peter didn't report Auggie missing or tell Tyler & Tory
#2	boat prank (?)	car was tampered with	*not Tyler's signature on Braeden's house deed	didn't reach Peter	*Peter sent severance ck to Teresa
#3	Mint in mouth - pinpoints entry to R&D	had written songs based on stories told by Tyler's dad, same as Tyler & Jason	*Tory vaguely recalls seeing Braeden with Ty at the slots	Bobby overheard giving directions to Tyler	*shot w/ same type gun as Bobby
#4	tampered PR release			*shot w/ same type gun as Auggie	planned to talk to Tyler &Tory re: Peter; made mysterious trip to Charlotte
#5	conclusion: 2nd PR leaked by killer. No ID				Auggie's twins saw Peter at their house near Nashville the week their daddy diappeared
#6	*not Tyler's signature on Braden's house deed				
#7	*Tory vaguely recalls seeing Braeden with Ty at the slots				
Note:	Peter nearby	Peter nearby?	Peter nearby?	Peter nearby	Peter nearby
Actual Order of Killings	Braeden	Tyler	J. D	Auggie	Bobby

"I see you've got a question mark by the boat pranks." noted Mackenzie.

"Yeah. I'm not sure they're actually related," said Bryan, scratching his earlobe.

"They started that night."

"I know. But they've been pretty random. No harm's been done."

"Could Ty's killer have used it somehow? Maybe to escape?" I spoke hesitantly. It was one thing for Mackenzie to question Bryan, but I had to ask.

Mackenzie threw me a look of gratitude. Bryan, however, shook his head.

"I don't think so," he said. "The boat was docked too neatly, and with no sign - that time - of having actually gone anywhere. We haven't evaluated things from today yet, but I think we'll find the killer traveled by land." He paused. "And none of the other boat pranks tie in with any of the other activity. So, I don't really think so. I'm not ruling them out. Just saying I'm not sure."

"Okay, okay. Tory, what's this about something you remembered? Number seven?" Mackenzie pointed to the sheet.

"That. I can't remember who it was. I just remember seeing them across the room, by the slots. They'd been gamblin', but that didn't mean anythin'. Or at least, I didn't think it did then. Tyler and Braeden were standin' there talkin' when somebody walked up."

I scrunched up my eyes, picturing Tyler in his show gear, Braeden in jeans and one of those preppy blue polo shirts. And someone, somebody also in country clothes came up. Another performer?. He was shouting - no, he was drunk. Of course, who was always drunk at that casino?

"Frank Haltemann. Damn, that's who that was! It was Frank Haltemann! Frank Haltemann! You know who I'm talkin' 'bout?"

"You mean the guy who sings comic songs about hillbillies, policewomen, and NASCAR drivers?" asked Bryan.

Jason's shoulders shook with contained laughter. "I love country music."

"That was him," I said, excited I'd remembered at last. "Whenever he goes to Vegas he ends up gamblin' away any money he's brought with him, then he maxes out his credit card getting' drunk. But he always sobers up for his show. He's never missed one yet."

"I love country musicians," said Jason.

Bryan was scribbling down notes. "Any idea how we could find this guy?"

"He records for Sony. They could put you in touch with his agent. If I knew who his agent was, I'd call him for you. He was more Tyler's friend than mine. He never paid me much mind."

"I'll track him down. Thanks. We need to check on all this stuff. Jason, you said you'd check on J.D. We need to know if he was who Auggie went to see and why. If we can even find that out. We also need to stay on top of the investigation of the crash. How was it possible for someone to get to his car to sabotage it?"

Jason nodded and started making notes in his smart phone.

"Tory, can you come up with some samples of Tyler's handwriting so that we can definitively prove that it's not his signature on the deed?"

"Peter would have that. He's got our contracts," I began.

Bryan shook his head. "No, not Peter. I don't want Himes to know we've even talked. I realize you've fired him, but he's still around, and he can hear things. No one is to know about this information or that we're back-checking things any more closely than before."

He rubbed his head. "I hate having civilians involved in investigations. I'll talk to Matheson, and he'll put his people on a lot of this. Still, some of these are things you can get hold of quicker. Do not involve Peter, but find a letter or something with Tyler's signature on it and get it to Matheson.

"Mackie, document the boat stuff. Write it up; you'll remember more than I will. Turn that in to Matheson, too, in case it turns out to be related. Tory, call Auggie's wife and get her to talk to the kids. She should try to pinpoint when they saw Peter, and judge whether or not it was really Peter that they saw. I trust a mother's judgment on that sort of thing."

Mackenzie spoke up then. "Is there anyone else who might have heard Bobby giving directions to Tyler? Somebody who might have seen whoever was in earshot?"

I shook my head at her. "I've been going over and over that in my head. I want so bad to remember something, someone. A bunch of us were standin' backstage. The crew was goin' over the equipment. Putting it up for the night."

"Wait," said Bryan. "You mean there was a stage full of people there while he was giving Tyler directions?"

"Well, not a whole stage, Bryan. There was Tyler, and me and Joe, Bobby, of course. I think Tommy and Alan were covering up the drums and stashing drumsticks and stuff. Sammie was there. The lighting guys. Tyler had them wait until he was done with Bobby, 'cause he wanted to change the lighting sequence. Probably Dean was there, too. But you don't have to worry about any of them."

"I don't? Why not?"

"Well, because none of them had any reason to kill Tyler is why not. Besides, they all were as mystified as I was when he didn't show up later for the interview."

"*What* interview?"

"Bryan, no need to shout. The WSM interview. Tyler and I were supposed to do it together and play a number with the band, but he didn't show up. The band and I handled it." My fingers were cold. In the chaos of all that had happened, had I actually forgotten the interview? How could I not mention to the police that Tyler had been noticeably AWOL that evening? "Bryan, I'm sorry. I don't know why I didn't say anything."

He was shaking his head. "Tory. If I weren't so sure of your innocence, I'd seriously be wondering about that omission. Don't you see how that looks?"

"No! Bryan, how can you - No, I don't see - " Except I did. From Tyler's death on, I'd been surrounded by the murders of people I knew and loved. The bodies were stackin' up higher and higher, just as Peter had said. I shuddered. "Peter was right. This does look suspicious. No wonder he was worried about my image."

Jason made a thoughtful clucking sound. "Bryan. Bryan, notice who else didn't say anything about this?"

"What do you mean, who else? *Nobody* said anything about Tyler being absent from an interview session." He stopped and swung back to me. "Tory, who knew Tyler was supposed to be there?"

"Well, everybody. The radio station recordin' the interview to send back to Nashville, the band, me, Peter, even Bobby. Everyone who was there when he didn't show."

"What, did you all come to some sort of agreement to keep silent? Would it have looked bad for the band to admit Tyler wasn't there?" Bryan looked skeptical.

"Actually, sort of. I mean, Peter told the radio station that Tyler had someplace else he had to be. To cover, you know? He was mad as hell that Tyler wasn't there. So, he told them that story and told us not to say anything. I guess we took that part too literally. Then he left, and we just did the interview as if it was normal. It does happen a lot. People not keepin' their appointments, I mean."

"You said Peter left?"

"Yeah. He had some other business, he said. And he was going to check the hotel and a few bars for Tyler." I caught the look that passed between Bryan and Jason. "Now, Bryan, no. I know you don't trust Peter, and Jason doesn't like him, but Peter wouldn't kill anybody. He couldn't kill anybody. Especially not Tyler!"

"Why not?"

"We go back too far, you know? He and I were almost engaged. He thought we would be eventually. I think I did, too, until I saw Jason again. Plus Peter was so close to Tyler. It's not something he could do. There has to be someone else. Maybe someone connected to all the stuff in Vegas. With Braeden." I added vaguely. I rubbed my head. I felt a little strange, light-headed even.

Jason took my hand. "About Las Vegas. You said the man who joined Braeden and Tyler that evening was Frank Haltemann. Why would it be important that he was talking with Ty and Braeden? He was just another musician, wasn't he?"

I wiggled in my seat. "He was another musician, but he was, well, I guess you could call him a musician with bad habits."

Jason raised an inquiring eyebrow at me.

"Well, he drank. And he gambled. And he could be really coarse sometimes."

"Drugs?"

"Not that I know about." I hesitated. "But there is something else. It's always sort of been floatin' around that Frank was 'connected'."

"'Connected'?"

"You know. That he had friends in the Mafia. Family. I mean, real family. As in his family was part of 'The Family'. You know?"

Bryan was nodding again. "I thought the name sounded familiar. That leads us to some interesting possibilities."

"I know," I said, sighing. "I don't want to think about them. Except, at least it would be a logical explanation for so many bad things happening, wouldn't it? It would mean the killer wasn't anybody we knew." *It would mean it wasn't Peter.*

·C·H·A·P·T·E·R· 26

·M·A·C·K·E·N·Z·I·E·

"So much complication"

-from "Simple Song" by Tory McCloud and Jason Fields

We all had our jobs to do. Most of it seemed to fall on Tory, until Bryan sat me down after they left to give me my own assignment.

"Mackenzie, I need you to get Tory and Naomi talking. We need to figure out the relationship between Braeden and Tyler, and we need to see if it included Peter. What were those boys up to out in Vegas?"

"Bryan, you know you're demanding the impossible. Tory already thinks Naomi blames Tyler for Braeden's death. And when Naomi hears some of what we discussed, she *will* blame Tyler. She's not predisposed to believe Tory like we are. You're demanding the impossible." I started clearing away our litter, setting aside the stack of lists and notes we'd made, putting boxes and napkins in the trash, dishes in the sink. Bryan followed me from point to point.

"Ah, but I'm demanding it of the right person," he said, and pulled me aside to kiss.

"Hey, no fair!"

"Really? No fair?" He kissed me again, and for a while I forgot the impossible task he was setting me. The task almost as impossible as setting up the Hallowe'en party I was planning with Naomi and the others.

I don't know what I was thinking when I agreed to help them out. I had no idea how to run a party for kids. What do pre-teen kids like anyway? And now I was going to have to find a way to get these two very different women to talk to each other! I never said I was brilliant at human relations.

And the next day it showed.

"Doctor Wilder," Jean said, greeting me with a cup of fresh tea when I came downstairs. "I hope you plan on having a talk with Bret about the men he has workin' for him out at that house of yours."

Uh-oh? "Why? Have they done something wrong?"

Jean sniffed. "Not if you don't mind two-by-fours scattered across the lawn or sacks of mortar hardening in the open air or the risk of roofing nails in your car's tires when you pull in the drive. Heck, no. They've done nothing wrong."

"O-kay," I said. "Jean, is it as bad as all that?" I'd heard her complaints before, but usually they were based on her high standards of workmanship. There were times I had to stop her from taking over a project because she had such definite ideas on how to do things.

"Yes, Doc, it is." She wiped a last dish with her towel and put it in the cabinet. "I don't suppose you've noticed anything."

"Well, I haven't been out to the farmhouse yet this week. Last time I was there was with Rachel, and - "

"- and I'll bet you didn't notice the paint job in the kitchen or the new tile I put up in the bathroom. Got the black latches put on, too. And the window shelf you wanted for that little kitchen window. Seems backwards to me, though. What you need there is a greenhouse window on the *outside* of the window. That was all my work." She started wiping down the refrigerator, even though its stainless steel was both stain-free and spotless.

"Thank you! I hadn't realized you were working so hard out there yourself. Thank you, very much!" I set my teacup down and chased her down for a hug.

"Quit, stop that!" she tried to push my arms away, but I managed to get a good hug in nonetheless. Her face flushed, she straightened her shirt and clucked at me, but I knew she was pleased. Her next words, however, were not. "You aren't the only one not noticing my efforts. Arthur was supposed to be out there helping me, but he never showed up! Told me he forgot about it."

"Maybe he did. He might have gotten busy."

"That doesn't excuse poor behavior. Forgetting an appointment - and that's what this was, make no mistake about that - is plain rude!"

"When did this happen, Jean?"

"I don't know. I've been working on that bathroom for two weeks now. Can't get it done any faster, what with working around Bret's men and trying to do my duty here, too." Her voice wasn't so grumbly now, and I recognized the ingredients she was pulling out were those that went into her latest coffee cake creation. "What I do know is that Arthur is up to something."

I hesitated. "Jean, do you mean, is Arthur seeing someone else? You think he's seeing another woman?"

"A new girlfriend? Doc, how could you ask that? Of course he's not seeing anyone else. Wouldn't care if he did. All I know is, lately he's never around when I want him!"

Then she - gruff, rough, tough Jean of the steel-gray helmet hair, the build and forearms of a farmwoman and the cynicism born of observing too many fools - burst into tears. She grabbed a large bandanna out of her pocket, held it to her face, and began a coughing fit to hide the fact that she was crying big wet tears as if her heart were breaking.

I didn't know what to do. Jean Hesford, a drill sergeant of a housekeeper, stood falling apart in my kitchen, and I had no clue what to do for her.

Abruptly the sobs ceased. She wiped her face, blowing her nose at the end and re-pocketing the bandanna.

"Jean," I began.

"Hold it, Doc. Don't say anything. I'd be happy if you didn't refer to this little outburst. It never happened, okay? Doc?"

"Okay, okay. As long as you're sure."

"I am. Let me get to work, and I won't stay mad at you over what you said about my Arthur. You'd better get to work, too, not stand around cluttering up my kitchen." She shooed me out of the room, so I headed upstairs to change for work.

Where my dealings with people did not improve.

I walked into the office to find Brooklynne waiting for me. She seemed sort of antsy. She stood near Andrea's desk, reading over her shoulder. She'd straighten up as she finished a page and glance from floor to wall to ceiling while she waited for Andrea to catch up.

Andrea, on the other hand, was so subdued, she never objected to Brooke reading over her shoulder that way.

Maude Davenport and Bennie Osterhout were there, too. Maude waved me over.

"Good morning, Mackenzie. I'm here on a social call. Had Bennie here bring me over, because I wanted him here to verify what I said."

"You've got me intrigued, Maude," I said, dropping onto the waiting room couch beside her. "What's this all about?"

"I told you last year that Charlie Osterhout had always had some boat or other on the river. Remember?"

"I remember you comparing my old boats to one he had a long time ago."

Brooklynne smiled at my comment as she wandered across the room to pick up a magazine.

"Because he always had at least one old boat, usually more. Charlie loved the water, and he passed his love of the water on to his many children. He had six, you know. Bennie here is the youngest."

Bennie nodded to me. "Tell her about the *Moira Finn*, Mrs. Davenport."

"I told you, call me Maude. So long as you're polite about it. I'll get to the *Moira Finn* in a minute." She turned a prim smile back to me.

"Mackenzie, I had never realized what a pack rat Charlie was. His children have insisted now that he clean up his house. They expect he'll need to either move in with one of them or into some kind of senior housing within ten years, and they told him he'd better start now, before they lose patience."

Bennie spoke up, "Dad's really attached to his things, but they've gone beyond clutter. We're afraid for his health with all the dust and potential mold. We figured if we gave him a hand - and a deadline - that maybe he'd have time to say his good-byes to his mementos. That would be a lot less traumatic than us coming in and throwing everything out."

"You're pretty generous giving him ten years," I said, without a trace of sarcasm. "Most family members put up with stuff like that until they can't stand it, and then they just rush in. It makes it a lot harder all around when they do that."

"That's what we thought. Anyway, Maude here had told Dad about your interest in boats - "

"Antique boats, Bennie," put in Maude.

"Right, antique boats. Thing is, it's hard for me to think of them that way. We grew up with Dad's boats. They're the only ones we've ever known."

It wasn't hard to see where this was going, but I didn't want to rush things. I wasn't even sure I was in the market for another boat yet. "So, which of you is going to take on his old boats?" I saw Brooklynne raise her head and laugh as I asked. She could tell what was going on, too.

Maude grinned. "*They* aren't. They may have grown up with the boats, but not one of them is a river rat. In fact, I don't think a one of them remembers how to put a boat in the water."

"Hey, now, Maude. That's not fair. I've put my share of boats in the water. I'm just not that interested. I like baseball, and I like archeology. I've got a real appreciation for these boats, but they'd be wasted on me."

I looked from one to the other. "Okay, but clarify this for me. What exactly brings you to me, other than the fact that I love old boats?"

"Dad wants to give you his boats."

"Did you say 'give'? I won't take them that way. I might buy them, but he can't just give them to me. It wouldn't be right."

"That's what I said," said Maude.

"That's what we thought, too, if you'll pardon me for saying so. We think Dad should be selling them. He's insisted we give you first look, and that we make you a good deal. He's more concerned about them going to someone who cares than anything else. He knows there's a limited audience for them here in Kings Hill. I mean, besides you and Art Swandeck, I don't think there's anyone here who would care. Arthur doesn't have a place for them, or the means for upkeep either."

"Are they in the water someplace? Or in storage?"

Bennie snorted. "Dad puts them up every winter, and he has them put in the water every spring. All done by Hawkins Marina up at Lake George, regular as clockwork. He pays them enough to do it."

It was tempting. Even though I had no idea what kind of boats we were talking about. The idea of adding to my boat collection was very, very tempting. "So, what kind of boat - boats - are we talking about?"

Bennie took the floor. "There are three boats, actually, but I don't expect you'd want to buy three more boats all at once."

Brooklynne seemed to be overtaken by a coughing fit. Maude and Bennie looked her way.

"You all right, Brooklynne?" asked Maude.

"I'm fine, thanks. Don't mind me." She spoke to Maude politely, but I saw the laughter she was holding back.

Bennie resumed his pitch. "Dad's really hoping you'll take two of them. One is a little white Lyman outboard runabout. Small, open cockpit, four-seater. It's in wonderful shape, we actually had it out once or twice this past season. Engine runs well."

His proper English caught my ear. I'd spent so much time listening to Tory talk, I'd subconsciously expected Bennie to say 'runs good'. Which made me wonder, would Jason and Tory be interested?

Bennie had segued into describing the second boat. "I think you already had a Chris Craft, Dr. Wilder, but you probably haven't seen one like this. It's a two-seater, a 1955 Chris Craft Cobra. Dad named it '*The Moira Finn*' because of the gold fiberglass fin on top. She's got a 131-horsepower, six-cylinder engine in her."

"How big is she?"

"Eighteen feet. She's powerful enough to tow half a dozen water skiers. I know, because that's what my friends did for recreation."

"Mmm, I don't know. I like my boats all wood."

"Dad'll let her go cheap. He wants her to have a good home. But maybe you'll want the other one. I am sort of saving the best for last."

"What is it?"

Maude interrupted. "Wait until you hear. Actually, wait until you see."

"Maude's right. Dad's other boat is a 1936 twenty-eight-foot cabin cruiser. Another Chris Craft. This one is in prime condition. Practically all original. It's been taken such good care of that there isn't even a replacement part on it newer than 1950. All mahogany and teak. He picked it up in Florida in 1975. The story is that it was reputed to have belonged to Al Capone's wife. It's even called 'Sonny' - that's what they called their son."

That intrigued me. There was something about Al Capone in my father's history. I couldn't remember exactly what. I felt myself wavering.

"Tell Charlie I don't think I want the Cobra. I'm still an all-wood girl. Although I can ask a couple people I know if they'd be interested. I'll come talk to him about the others."

Bennie helped Maude stand up. She put a hand on my arm.

"Don't you worry about Charlie wanting to give you these boats. He always was generous to a fault. I'm sure you'll work out a deal that will satisfy everyone, even Bennie here." She tilted her head in his direction.

"I'm just trying to make sure he'll be taken care of." His expression was pained.

Maude snorted. "If you can't trust Mackenzie Wilder, who do you think you can trust in this town?"

"I suppose so, Maude. Hey, why did I end up doing all the talking? I thought I was just going to back you up."

"Oh. Is that what I said?" Maude asked, winking at me.

After they left, I turned to check in with Andrea, only to find her shaking her head and clicking her tongue at me.

"I think you messed up, Doc."

"What do you mean?"

"I mean you should've taken them up on that third boat. And you should never turn down something that's free."

"I couldn't do that, Andrea. I can easily afford to pay for what I want."

Andrea shrugged. "I just make it a policy to never turn down free stuff, that's all. Who knows? They might be worth a bundle, and you'd be living up to what Mr. Osterhout wants."

"I wouldn't feel right about it, that's all," I said, perhaps more sharply than I'd intended. The temperature in the room dropped about ten degrees.

Andrea sat very still. "You know, there are other things in life besides always being concerned about what's 'right'. Some people can't see that. I guess you're one of those, too."

Too?

I dropped into the chair in front of her desk where I could see her eyes. "Andrea? You okay?"

Her response was a twist of the lip and shrug of the shoulder.

"Um, is this something to do with Ted?"

The phone rang. She pursed her lips and picked it up, looking right through me as she answered.

After a minute, she told the caller, "Could you hold, please? Doctor, I'll tell you about it later. This is some guy named George, from Nashville. He asked if you were the Mackenzie Wilder who was helping out Tory Fields."

"I'll take it in the office. We'll talk. Brooke? I'll be back after I take this." She nodded, and I slipped into the office and settled in my chair.

"Doctor Mackenzie Wilder? This is George Box, callin' from Nashville. I'm a friend of Terry Haynes, Auggie's wife? They're friends of Tory McCloud - er, Fields. Terry asked me to call you."

"Yes, George. Tory told us how great you were in Nashville. How can I help you?"

"Ma'am, it's Tory you might need to be helpin'. Teresa wanted me to call you all with some information Tory asked for."

"Oh?" Tory had gotten to her friend already? The girl was quick! "But, why call me? Rather, why is Teresa having you call me? Why doesn't she call Tory?" I didn't have time for niceties in this case anymore.

"Ma'am, I appreciate you wondering. See, Terry told me and my wife about Tory's questions. As we were talkin' I started rememberin' a few things, so I figured I needed to call up there myself. And, Tory, well, Tory is a little bit of a thing, and we thought - frankly, we thought she might need a little protectin'. She seemed kind of impulsive back here in Nashville. Maybe even a little reckless."

"Like she might jump into something without looking out for her own safety?"

"You got it. So I thought maybe I should call someone else, someone close to her who could help her out, look out for her sort of. I didn't know about callin' her husband, but she'd mentioned your name as someone helping with this investigation? Is that right?"

"Yes." *Well, it was right, even if it was unofficial.* "What do you have to tell me, George?"

He seemed to relax.

"Well, Doctor Wilder, first off, Terry wanted me to answer a couple of the questions Tory asked her. They were mostly about the boys. You know, Terry's twins? Yeah, well, the first thing was that, yes, the boys' truck was wrecked a few weeks back. Terry said it looked like it was run over by a heavy car. She couldn't figure out how it happened - none of her neighbors or friends would have done somethin' like that without ownin' up to it, and there hadn't been any strangers by in a long time."

"Tory said that the boys insisted it was Peter Himes who ran over their truck," I stated, checking.

"Yeah. I don't get it, but they're stickin' to that story. Somethin' about seein' him in the driver's seat of a big black car. They're smart boys, and generally truthful, but I don't see how it could be. Terry said she didn't see anything, and Tory insists Himes was on the road that whole time. Then there's the other thing."

"What's that?"

"The boys both said they overheard their daddy talkin' with Tyler 'bout time off to go over to Charlotte - the boys said the racecar city. Auggie's taken them over to Charlotte to the track before. They think Charlotte's just all one big racetrack. They said they heard him on the phone sayin' that he'd meet up with the tour. Funny thing is, those boys were right. Auggie told me himself he was takin' off."

"Do you know exactly where he was going, or who he was going to see?"

"All I know for sure is that he was real pleased about it. I reckoned he was going to see some driver he knew. He talked about going right to the track when he got there. Wanted to get a look at his buddy in action. Said he hadn't seen Jackson race in a couple years, and he wanted to see if he'd gotten any better. "

I frowned. "Was that the drivers' name - Jackson?"

"That's the only name he used."

"Hmm." I scribbled a note to myself to check out with Jason. *Could Jackson be J.D.?* "Teresa didn't say herself where Auggie went or who he was going to see?"

"She didn't mention Auggie's trip at all. I don't think she knew he went. It was right before he got killed. Way Teresa talked, she thought he'd gone on the tour. Didn't help matters any that Himes didn't report him missin'. Tory sure was mad about that."

"She had every right to be. Auggie's death tore her up. At least they've got that guy. We were wondering, though, is there a chance the guy who killed him could have been hired to do it?"

"Maybe, but we'll never know."

"You don't think he'd tell?"

"Don't matter if he would, he can't. Hasn't Metro police got in touch with Tory?"

I sat forward in my chair. "Not that I know of. Why?"

"Damn! I knew she was in danger. Doctor Wilder, the boy they arrested for Auggie's killing is dead. He died in the jail two days ago. Almost right after Tory went back up North."

"He's dead! What happened?"

"That's just it, they aren't sure. Or they ain't sayin'. There was a report that he was dead is all. Maybe they don't know yet, or they're tryin' to keep things quiet. I don't like it that somebody in custody is dead. I think Tory needs to be very, very careful."

"That's a conclusion we'd already come to. Can you tell me anything more about this guy?"

"Not much. Guy I know works for Metro didn't think much of him. Said he didn't think he was smart enough to kill somebody and then stash the body. Said the guy was too wasted most of the time to do anything that took that many brains. I gotta wonder somethin'. What if he didn't do it? Whoever did might be worried he'd eventually be able to remember for real what happened, and then he'd tell. Maybe somebody wanted to erase that possibility."

"Do you think so? Or are we being too melodramatic here?" I asked.

"It's murder, ain't it? How can you be too melodramatic about murder?"

"George, can you give me your number? I want to have Bryan Jamison give you a call. He's working the case on Bobby Fleming, the kid who was shot with a gun similar to the one that killed Auggie. And Ted Matheson is a New York State Trooper working Tyler's case. They both might call. Please, please, call back if you think of anything else we should know - official or otherwise." I paused to take down his information and give him some in return. Setting down my pen, I asked. "Do you think

Teresa knows anything more? Should we ask? Or would it be better to leave her alone for now."

"She's pretty emotional. I can pass along anything she thinks of. The one thing my wife and Teresa and I do agree on, this ain't over. Tory's probably in danger. She needs to be careful."

"We'll watch out for her, don't worry. Thank you, thank you very much for calling me." We hung up, and I finished making some notes. The suspect was dead and Nashville hadn't told us? Or at least Tory? When did they plan on telling her?

I went to the outer office to see about Andrea, but another surprise awaited me. Nadine Cooper had joined Brooklynne. The two sat in chairs next to each other, deep in whispered conversation. What were they up to? Another phone call interrupted before I could find out.

"Gary Henry for you, Doc." At least Andrea smiled at me when she handed me the phone, and she was back to calling me 'Doc'.

"Hi, Gary. What's up at the other end of the street?" Gary was another old school friend. Besides being a local Justice of the Peace, he was also president of the Boat Club. He spent so much more time at the dock than in his office that he finally gave up and simply put in another office dockside so he could do both jobs at once.

"Mackenzie, things are fine except for one little barnacle on my butt." Gary loved to lapse into what he considered sea lingo.

"Why? What's the matter?"

"You remember me telling you you couldn't dock your boats here?"

"Of course I do. Made me mad. Still makes me mad, but you know I only dock there when I'm seeing you or using the shop or gas tanks."

"Then tell me why I'm sitting here looking at the *Emma D* rocking on the swells in the slot usually reserved for the police boat, which just so happens to be in dry dock to fix the hole those joyriders put in her hull? Can you answer that?"

I ran out the back door with the receiver to my ear, startling Naomi and Brooklynne. I hustled up the path to the boathouse. It was closed up tight, locked on this side.

"Gary, are you sure? Because my boathouse is shut." I made my way along the dock and around the side of the boathouse.

"You better look inside, because if this isn't your boat, somebody's stolen your name and registration numbers. Its got *Emma D* all across the stern. Are you telling me you didn't bring her up here?"

I came around the corner of the boathouse. The doors were wide open. The *Amiga* was still inside, just like I'd left her. The *Emma D* was nowhere to be seen.

·C·H·A·P·T·E·R· *27*

·M·A·C·K·E·N·Z·I·E·

"we all must self-deceive."

- from "Simple Song" by Tory McCloud and Jason Fields

S hit!"

"Mackenzie?"

"Shit, shit, shit, shit, shit!"

"Mackenzie, what is it?"

I ran my free hand through my hair, more frustrated and angry than ever over this nonsense. "Gary, that's the *Emma D* all right. You mentioned joyriding? Well, I think that must be what's going on. Dammit!"

"Okay, I believe you, but you still need to get this boat out of here. The members won't like it; you know that. How soon can you get here?"

"Gary! I've got patients today." I started walking back to the office. "I've got to get there to move the boat, but I've got to make arrangements to get my car back here, too. That's going to take time."

Brooklynne met me at the back door. "What's going to take time?" she whispered.

I shook my head at her, then covered the receiver. "One of my boats has turned up at the Boat Club dock. Gary wants it out of there. I need to pick it up, but I won't do that until after your appointments."

Now Brooklynne was shaking her head at me. "We don't have appointments. Except for our hair. We were stopping by to see if you wanted to go with us." She glanced at her watch. "Actually we have to go now. Lloyd's waiting out front. You want a lift?"

I uncovered the phone. "Okay, okay, Gary. I'll be there. But for the record, I did not dock my boat at your stupid Boat Club. If anyone complains, tell them to stuff it!"

Brooklynne broke out laughing. "I don't think I've heard you talk like that since we were fourteen and you were trying to be tough. Gary must be stunned."

"He didn't say anything back. Like I gave him time to. Thanks for the ride. I wish I knew what was going on with these boats! One of them is going to end up crashed to smithereens," I added as we re-entered the waiting area.

Andrea's eyes grew round at my words. I hastened to explain.

"I'm riding up to the Boat Club with Naomi and Brooke. Some idiot took out the *Emma D* again and docked it up there. I'll bring it back down the river after I talk to Gary. If anyone comes in, tell them I'll be right back."

"Well," Andrea drawled, glancing between Naomi and Brooke. "It's not 'til later in the day, but these two here are your only appointments."

"I thought you said - " I began, but Brooke just rolled her eyes and made a whistling motion with her mouth.

"Oh, all right. I can't deal with any more mysteries right now. Let's go."

They dropped me off with much fanfare and continued to their appointments amid promises to explain it all to me when they got back. I turned, and there was the *Emma D*, floating primly as you please dockside. I paused as I marched my way to the door of Gary's office. On inspection I found every rope coiled correctly, all loose equipment properly stowed, and both wood and chrome polished to a shine.

So, whoever is taking this boat out is taking good care of it. What the heck is going on?

I took up my march again, landing myself at Gary's door and barging in without hesitation. Gary left his seat as I entered his office.

"I hope you realize I meant every word I said. I did not bring my boat down here. Not to make trouble, not to show off, not even to fuel up. Someone has been out joyriding in my boat!"

"Take it easy Mackenzie. Now that you're here, we won't have to do anything to apologize to the membership."

"Apologize to the membership? For what? Something I didn't even do? That's ridiculous. Apologizing to them for anything is ridiculous anyway! That boat is duly registered with the State of New York. It is totally seaworthy and it can outrun any of these blasted yachts. I have every legal right in the world to tie up here, and you know it!"

Gary shook his head and sat down, his sky blue polo shirt matching his eyes, his khakis rumpled from a little too much sitting.

"Mackenzie, actually, you don't. The Boat Club owns these docks, and technically they are private. However, it is usually too much trouble to enforce the rules of ownership, so we tend to overlook most visiting boats, provided they adhere to our rules and don't overstay their welcome." He paused.

"So which is it?" I asked, still steaming.

"What?" He seemed startled, as if I'd interrupted his train of thought.

"Which is it? What rule did I break, or did I simply overstay my welcome?" The bitterness of my tone betrayed how stupid I thought this all was. It must have betrayed how hurt I was by it as well.

Gary spoke softly. "Now Mackenzie, I know we've seemed unfair, and inhospitable. We haven't meant to. One of the reasons we don't receive antique boats is for their own protection."

I raised an eyebrow. This was sounding remarkably like old-time segregationist reasoning.

"No, I mean it. The wooden boats are fragile compared to the larger fiberglass boats. The members - who, by the way, don't really care what boat a person sails - they're concerned about liability if a wooden boat gets crushed, or even scratched. You know how obsessive some classic boat owners are." He cleared his throat. "Don't you?"

Ouch. I scrunched up my face as I felt the wind go out of my ego's sails. "Yes, I do. I'm sorry, Gary. I'm sort of wrought up with all these murders going on. This boat business is one more irritation. Seriously, someone has been taking out the *Emma D* without permission. I don't even have any idea who's doing this! It's driving me a little nuts. Although, I'll tell you one thing. They're taking good care of her. I checked the boat on my way to your office. She's tied up perfectly, all the lines coiled the right way, everything totally shipshape. Just the way we've always found her when she's been taken out. I have no idea who is doing this, but they respect the boat, even if they don't respect the fact that she's mine!"

Gary leaned back in his chair, and I caught a reflective attitude in his eyes. "You know, Mackenzie, I think every time I see you, you're upset about something. I don't remember you being like that back in school."

I stepped around and flopped down in the chair in front of his desk.

"I am, aren't I? Just your luck. I'm really not upset all the time, even if it seems that way. How are things?" I grinned at him, and he grinned back.

"Pretty good. The Boat Club's going well. Having a fundraiser for scholarship money for some local kids. Not too much going on at the Justice's office; just enough to keep me busy."

"You keeping up with your health?" I asked. There was something about him that looked a little off to me. "I'm not drumming up business. I want to make sure a friend is taking care of himself."

Gary snorted. "I didn't think anything showed. I've got a couple problems. My doctor's working on a diagnosis. Doesn't want to worry me, he says. Why do doctors do that? Tell you not to worry and then do stuff that makes you worry? Anyway, I think I know what it is, and not worrying isn't an option."

"Gary, if your doctor said he doesn't want to worry you, that means he doesn't know what it is yet. He can't tell you what it is you might have to worry about. So, the idea is, don't worry until you know what it is.

Worry doesn't do anything except rip you up unless you know what the problem is and your worry is aimed at fixing it."

He stared at me a little glassy-eyed. "Sure, yeah," he said. "Of course, I have to convince my wife, too. She worries twice as much as I do. Heck, I'm sure it'll be fine. I guess everybody is sure whatever they've got must be something peculiar or fatal, like cancer. A sign of the times. Anyway, let's check that boat of yours. I'll help you cast off. You did say you were taking it back now, right?" He held the office door for me.

"Yes, Gary, I'm taking it back now." My tone was exasperated, but I was smiling. At least I knew where the darn thing was. I glanced out from the stairs to his office. Art Swandeck was coming across the parking lot.

"Doc!" he called, stopping in his tracks. "What are you doing here in the middle of the day? No patients?" He glanced behind him as he started across the driving lanes.

"Hi yourself, Art. Gary here called me. Seems the *Emma D* brought herself down here to the Boat Club. I came to pick her up."

We met up at the boat. Art stared down at it a moment. He seemed focused on the perfectly coiled rope.

Gary reached out his hand to shake. "Hey, Art. I came down to help her shove off. Listen, you're the local expert on these boats. Are Mackenzie's boats as good as she's always saying?" He threw me a quick smile to show he was teasing.

Art answered seriously. "Dr. Wilder's got a couple of the finest vintage boats around. Not just that she can afford 'em, either. She takes good care of them. Never leaves them out in bad weather, cleans 'em, polishes 'em. She treats her boats as well as she treats her horses. Wish everybody'd do that."

"Hey, Art! Arthur!"

"Mr. Swandeck! Look at what - "

Three young people raced across the parking lot to where we stood, twirling half-eaten ice cream cones around their lips as they secured every drip that tried to escape. All three of them were kids I knew. Luke was one. His older cousin another. Leading the charge was a long-legged strawberry blonde whose fingers gripped a cone overflowing with her favorite strawberry. Rachel.

"Mackie!" she yelled, her eyes as wide as her smile.

"Dr. Wilder!" Luke braked to a stop at our feet.

"Hi, Doc!" Luke's cousin kept things cool, but I saw him glance at Luke. *Not so cool as he'd like to be, now is he?*

"Hi! What are you kids doing here? There's no school today?" I looked at Rachel.

"Nope. Teacher's conferences. We're just hangin' out together." She looked at me from under her bangs. "In fact, we're supposed to meet Luke's mom and Aunt Brooklynne at your office to get picked up. Mr. Swandeck said he'd take us."

Art sort of shrugged. He was still staring at the boat, although now it seemed like it really was the boat he looked at, and not just the rope.

"I could take you."

"You could? Where's your car?" asked Luke.

"Back at the office, actually," I said. "I'm here to take my boat back. Somebody brought it up here and docked it."

"Who did that?" asked Rachel, while Luke began studiously licking his ice cream.

"I don't know, Rachel. Someone's been taking my boat out without my knowing about it. Didn't your Dad tell you?"

She shook her head at me.

"Well, if you see it someplace and I'm not around, let me know. I've got to stop whoever is doing this. Nothing's been damaged yet, but I can't help but feel it's only a matter of time. You haven't seen anybody else with the boat, have you?"

Now I had three heads shaking furiously at me.

"Okay, okay. Thank you. So anyway, if you want to go back with me, it's a boat ride. Hop on in!"

"I'll - uh, I'll get a ride back to my house with Art. Is that okay, Art?" said Luke's cousin, whose name I still couldn't remember.

Art shrugged again, but then he smiled at me and stepped back for me to climb into the *Emma D*. He turned and clapped Luke's cousin on the shoulder, and the two of them set off across the parking lot. Gary untied ropes while Luke and Rachel clambered aboard and I started the engine. Luke and Rachel each pulled a line aboard and started stowing them. They did a pretty good job considering I hadn't had the chance to show them how. Maybe Luke knew boats. Gary waved us off, and we headed down river to my office.

It never fails to surprise me how close I am to the Boat Club by water.

As we sped back to my office, I was also struck by how matter-of-factly the two kids were taking this ride. I'd been talking up the boats with Rachel for nearly as long as I'd been back here. She'd commiserated with me when the *Psyche* burned; I knew she was excited about the prospect of riding in one of 'those old boats'. I thought she'd be asking questions or begging for a chance to steer.

Maybe she didn't want to exhibit too much enthusiasm in front of Luke. Maybe it wasn't cool. Everything was about cool. Or maybe she'd decided she liked horses better.

"Mackie, what's *that*?" Rachel pointed to something cruising out in deeper water.

I slowed the *Emma D,* turning my head to see the prettiest, strangest little vintage boat I'd ever seen. She was small, only eighteen feet or so, with a mahogany hull and a deck that gleamed a fiberglass white. The roof was part orange, and two giant wings sprung open from the center top, a lot like the doors on a modern DeLorean car. She'd pulled far out into the river, about a football field's distance away. She circled into a position headed upriver, and suddenly picked up speed.

"Rachel, I'm not sure what kind of boat that is. She's pretty though."

"Is it an old boat?" Luke asked.

I wondered if he was as perplexed as I was at the fiberglass finish.

"I'm not sure. It could be, although I don't think it's made all out of wood. I've never seen anything like it. I don't think it can be older than 1960, though," I added.

"Wow, that *is* old," breathed Lucas.

"It's beautiful, don't you think, Mackie?" asked Rachel, her eyes tracking the boat and its spray as it pulled away, the hull lifting off the water, the wings looking exactly like the wings of a gull.

"Yes, I do." I switched my attention to Rachel, so young, so concentrated and focused on this relic of days past. Her face glowed, the breeze lifting the light veil of her hair away, her torso pulled forward by her mind's fascination. I didn't know which awed me more, the young girl or the old boat.

Clearly Rachel liked *some* old boats, even if they weren't mine. Before I had much time to think about this or, worse, develop hurt feelings over it, we were back. The kids helped dock, again showing more prowess than I'd expected. Luke caught me watching him. He sort of half-shrugged.

"Uncle Kip takes me out on his boat sometimes. Us out." He pointed to Rachel and back. "He's taught us how to cast off and tie up."

Rachel nodded her head vigorously. So they had some experience. Oh well.

When I opened the door to my office, both Naomi and Brooklynne were already in the waiting room. Sandy Cooper was there, too. They sat on the new waiting room couch, talking animatedly, looking embarrassed when we interrupted them by coming in. In fact, they jumped apart as quickly as three musketeers caught plotting the dethroning of a king. Luke and Rachel prevented any comment from me on this by launching themselves to Naomi's and Brooklynne's sides.

"Mom! Mom!" Luke wrapped himself around his mother, ever careful of her burgeoning midsection.

Rachel, not inhibited by the presence of any impending cousins grabbed Brooke and held on tight. "You should see Mackie's boat, Aunt Brooklynne! It's awesome!"

Aah! She was paying attention.

Brooklynne steadied herself against Rachel's onslaught and sat down, laughing and pulling Rachel with her. "I have seen it. It's quite the boat, isn't it? Did you get to steer?"

"No, but I bet Mackie will let me next time, won't you Mackie?"

"We'll have to see. I want to make sure you know what you're doing, first."

"Oh, I do. I mean, we've been out with Luke's uncle a bunch. We've learned a lot. Although, I suppose there are things that are different with an old boat." She seemed to be giving the matter some thought, her head to one side and a tiny frown line between her golden brows.

Sandy's brows were slightly elevated. "I didn't realize Kip - "

"Mom! Mom! Did you have your exam yet? Dr. Wilder, have you checked out my mom? Is she all right?" Luke's face wore that anxious expression again.

"No, I haven't seen her yet today. I will. Although, this isn't your regular appointment, is it, Naomi?" I glanced past her to Andrea for confirmation, but that young lady was engrossed in one of Ted's books again.

When I returned my gaze to Naomi, I caught her in a sly exchange of smiles with Brooke and Sandy. What was going on here?

"Actually, Mackenzie - " Naomi began.

"Actually, Naomi and Brooke are here because I asked them to meet me here. You know I talked to you about helping us plan the Hallowe'en party? With all the Cooper cousins, Rachel, and their friends, it's turning into a big bash. We need more space for it. We thought if you didn't mind, maybe we could use the horse camp facilities. A campfire would be great for telling ghost stories."

"Oh! Well, I don't know. The cabins won't be ready for a few more weeks. I don't know if they'd make the deadline. Plus I'm not sure about campfires yet. The pits aren't finished, and with the wind and the dry grasses, it might be too dangerous." The idea was appealing, but I wasn't sure it was the right location.

Rachel hopped up and sat on the arm of the couch. "What if we had it down here? Your house here is big, and the cave would make a great haunted house. Or even, we could use the boathouse. Maybe you could give rides in one of your boats. I know! You could dress up like an old fisherman, or maybe a Victorian lady, and be the ghost of the river giving tours. Or maybe - "

"I get it, I get it!" We all laughed. "What do you think, Sandy? Switch it down here? We could have the party inside if it was too cold - remember the year we were in high school and it snowed two days before Hallowe'en? There's the fireplace. And - oh, I haven't told you! I've had the attic refurnished. It's set up dormitory style with six twin beds, just for something like this. We could use the whole house, if you like. Of course, we'd have to do some planning." As I said the words, another idea popped into my head and started to grow.

Brooke was nodding and laughing, a bit of a gleam in her eye, maybe mischief over what I was letting myself in for, but I didn't care.

"You know, I bet we could get Tory Fields in on this. I'm sure she'd like to help plan something like this." *You don't know that.* "Maybe she'd even sing a little at the party itself." Okay, so I thought she would if I asked her, but the real reason I was bringing this all up was to get Naomi and Tory together.

Naomi looked only mildly uncomfortable at the suggestion. Then she tossed her head. "Well, I said I should get to know her better. I guess this is as good a way as any."

Brooke turned to me. "You know, I think I remember Dr. Kesselman having parties and using his garage for some of it. He had a big sound system he could hook up to it, and the band or DJ would play from there."

"Dr. Kesselman had parties with DJs? You're kidding!"

"No lie. My parents went to some. He only stopped having his annual summer bash about three years ago. You should write and ask about them."

"Maybe I'll have to." I glanced at Brooklynne. She looked tired all of a sudden. "You okay?"

"Oh, I'm fine. Just a little tired. You forget, we came in for check-ups, not just to plan a party."

"Well, we'll have to have an official planning session anyway. Maybe get together over here to set it all up. I can have Jean come, as well as Tory." *Aha, sealed the deal. Bryan will be proud of you.*

"I'll help," said Andrea. "I love planning these kinds of things. Ms. Kerns is right, Doc. You're supposed to be having appointments with them."

"Wait a minute. Naomi, what am I seeing you for? You seem to be in fine shape, new hairdo and all. I like it, by the way. Yours too, Brooke. I see you didn't get your usual color done. Making a change?"

Brooke dropped her head, smiling to herself. "You could say that. I didn't want to risk the chemicals. I know it may be silly, but I don't want to take any chances." Her smile grew broader. Sandy and Naomi were smiling, too.

When I didn't say anything, Brooke leaned over and touched my arm. "The appointment isn't for Naomi, Mackie. Or Sandy. I'm the one you need to see. Dr. Green told me yesterday. He confirmed I'm pregnant."

Ten seconds of shocked silence erupted into whoops and hollers and hugs and a cry from Rachel that she was calling her dad. I hugged my best friend and cried into her shoulder. Not exactly professional, but Brooke and I went too far back. From half-pint milk cartons shared over a kindergarten table to tight blue jeans under caps and gowns marching down the auditorium aisle to her bringing me back to Kings Hill. I knew how much she and Lloyd wanted children. Now her dream was coming true. Rachel was going to have a little cousin after all.

"Oh, wow. And I thought planning a Hallowe'en party was going to be exciting." I wiped the tears from my eyes. "Tell me, do you want me to see you through this - well, I will anyway, but I mean, do you want me or

Dr. Green to be your doctor? It's okay with me, either way. I'll be there for you regardless."

"It's funny. Now that Dr. Green's gotten me pregnant - I mean, overseen me getting pregnant - stop laughing at me! Anyway, he seems to have lost interest. He has no problem with you taking over, if you will, Mackenzie. I'd love to have my best friend and practically sister-in-law deliver my baby into the world."

·C·H·A·P·T·E·R· 28

·T·O·R·Y·

" Don't lock the door 'til it stops swingin',"

- from "Don't Lock the Door 'til it Stops Swingin'" by Jason Fields

I hate wakin' up from bad dreams. Even with Jason beside me, this one left me feelin' disoriented and scared. In my dream, Tyler was still alive, but he was hurt. Jason was in jail, but I didn't care. I was with Peter. I was with him, and I knew he was manipulatin' my life, but I didn't care. Everything was all right, except for Tyler bein' hurt, and I was kind of impatient with that. Sort of like I was tellin' him to just get over it, because it was spoilin' things. Except underneath it all, I felt like somethin' was wrong.

I sat up shiverin' and still with a bad taste in my mouth. There was somethin' about the dream - maybe it was my subconscious's way of sayin' it wanted to go back to when things were all right, when none of this had happened, before I knew how questionable and manipulative Peter's actions were, and how bent his motives. Maybe the dream was just a longin' for the bliss of ignorance, but because I did know all this stuff, I felt the sense of wrong-ness comin' through. I nodded to myself. Yeah. I had to face up to how things were and deal with it. Keep Peter out of my life, hope that we find Tyler's killer, and that no one else gets hurt.

I always like action better than thought. I swung my legs over the side of the bed, tryin' not to disturb Jason.

I was almost out of bed when he swung his near arm out and around my waist and pulled me back into the covers. I squealed, but he shushed me and drew me closer, kissing me.

"What had you so upset that you were crying in your sleep?"

"I was?"

He nodded, his curly hair bouncing, then drew his fingertip along the corner of my eye. I felt it glide as it hit a fugitive tear and came away wet. "See?"

"I had a nightmare, I guess. Bad dream, anyway. Tyler was alive, you were in jail, and I was with Peter." I scrunched up my face and stuck out my tongue.

"Ouch. That is a nightmare! You okay?"

"I reckon. I don't want to let it spoil my day. Things are crazy enough without that."

"Maybe I can help," he said, his voice dropped, and his green eyes penetrated into mine.

It took us a little longer to go downstairs.

When we did, it was to find faxes coming in, emails on the computer, and two messages on the phone. The first fax was work for Jason, and I didn't pay attention to that. The next one, though, was from an insurance investigator's office in Las Vegas.

Charlie Hanrahan, investigator for LV Midstate Motor and Property Insurance, wanted to inquire as to whether or not this was where the next of kin of Tyler McCloud could be reached, and was she/he the executor of his estate. The executor was sought because presumably any claims on the property would be distributed to the heir, and the company needed to contact them. Dispersal of benefits was being withheld pending investigation into the property's ownership as well as the verdict of arson by person/persons unknown as rendered by the local board. No further action could be taken until the executor and heir of Tyler McCloud's estate could be located for identification and potential questioning.

"Arson? Did his house burn down?" Jason wanted to know. He wore a violet bathrobe over the custom scrubs he used as pajamas, and he was pouring coffee into a mug.

"They don't say. It surely sounds like it." Worry poured back into me. "I told you, that wasn't Tyler's signature on that deed! Should we answer this?"

"Did you ever get that signature sample to Matheson?"

"I did, but I haven't heard anything back."

"You need to check on it, and you need to tell him about this. He'll want to talk to these people. Arson at a house Tyler owned? Meanwhile, I'll put my lawyer on it. You're Tyler's heir. Are you the executor, too?"

"I don't know. I thought he would have made Peter executor." I caught the displeased expression on Jason's face. "This is going to make things complicated, isn't it?"

"Especially if Peter has anything to do with the house." Jason raised his eyebrows at me.

"He couldn't."

"You said that wasn't Tyler's signature. How many people would be in a position to get away with putting Tyler McCloud's signature on a contract?"

"Bryan and Matheson are not going to like it." I sighed and helped myself to some coffee, followed by a jumbo giant pecan sticky bun. Jean had made them for us. Another benefit of being Mackenzie's friend. "What were all the emails about?"

"Mostly work. The new project at RFD. A reporter wanted a follow-up on how RFD was doing since the opening night. Somebody from Country Music Magazine - is that right? - wants to do an interview on what it's like to be Mr. Tory McCloud."

"Some people just have an extremely high quotient of dumb! What else is there?"

"We seem to have one here from Matheson. He says he has received independent confirmation that the signature on the house deed is in fact not Tyler's. That will probably hold up - "

"The payout check mentioned in the fax."

"He's coming out this afternoon to discuss the cases."

I rubbed my head. This was really takin' over our lives. I didn't know how much more of it I could handle. "Jason, I need to rehearse."

He stopped. "Rehearse? I thought you weren't - "

"I know. What I mean is I need to do some singing. Keep my voice in shape. It'll make me feel better. I haven't been able to stand back and wail since - well, since that night at the arena. Reckon Joe could come over with a guitar and amps so we could practice a little? Maybe everybody?"

"Of course. Bring the whole band. They're all still here, right? Why is that?"

I blushed. "You know, Joe talked to me 'bout that the other day. Since they don't have a tour yet, they could all go home. No one wants to. Seems they all want to make sure I'm okay. So, I sort of told them I'd keep payin' 'em. If the tour hadn't ended, we'd all be on the road together anyway."

Jason's eyebrows went up again. They were like radar signals, really. I held back a giggle. Every time he wondered about something, up went those eyebrows.

"Don't they miss their families?" he asked. "And vice versa?"

"Nobody's married, except Joe, and his wife is visiting her mother. Nope, they want to stay here by me."

Jason came over and hugged me. "Anybody would want to stand by you, Tory."

"You don't mind I'm still payin' their salaries?"

"Of course not. We can afford it, and it's only right. Are you paying Himes as well? He did say he wanted to stay with the band."

He had that wary look now, like he might have to disagree with me. Luckily that wasn't going to be a problem. "I bought out his contract. Now he's the band's manager, and *only* the band's manager. I don't know if they've signed contracts or not, but he won't pull a salary until he gets them a booking."

"That's that, then. Do you want to turn the rec room into a rehearsal room? Probably can't in time for today, but we could do it. On the other hand, I do have a designer on speed dial. He's very good at emergency work."

"Jason, it's just the boys comin' over. I'm sure they won't think twice about how it looks. They only care about acoustics."

He nodded, as if expecting something like that. "They'll want a good sound system. I know a top-notch guy who could probably do the room over in a few hours. I could call him," he offered.

"We don't have to rush it. Why not get a speaker system over here for today and figure out what else we need to do later. Is there anything else?"

"No, I don't think so...wait." Jason frowned at his smart phone. "I've got something from the people checking into buying the house from Peter. It doesn't make any sense though. Let me make a phone call."

He turned to go back to his den, and I went to the closet where I'd stashed some music. I started flipping through our book, picking out things to warm up on, a couple old numbers that would stretch my cords, wake them up a little. There was one I was seriously thinkin' about re-writing the voicing on. I'd have to. No one could take Tyler's place on that number. There were too many key changes, and it was written to Ty's range, which was pretty broad.

I swallowed, hard. Things weren't going to be the same; things weren't going to be easy, ever again. No one could take Tyler's place anywhere. I made myself go on, the same urge to make music that pushed me to start writin' a song about Tyler made me sing, made me run my voice through exercises. There is something about music, something universal. There is a reason people turn to it in celebration, and in sorrow. It reaches us at a depth we cannot plumb any other way. There is an African saying I've always loved. "All that sing have the right to be called children of God". Not all my songs are godly, but I definitely feel closer to Him when I sing. I needed some of that today.

I was sortin' through more pieces when Jason came back from his phone calls. He was scratchin' his head, and there was a big frown on his face.

"I can't believe this. I don't like it."

"What?"

"The man they arrested for killing your friend Auggie? He was found dead in his jail cell a few days ago. The realtor in Nashville thought we might want to know. What I really want to know is why didn't the police tell us? Why are we hearing about this through a realtor I happened to contact?"

I stared at him. "Oh, Jason. Does Teresa know?"

"I don't know. Wouldn't she have called you if she did?"

"I think so. I'm not sure." *This feels all wrong.* "Did they say what happened?"

"That's the other strange part. They aren't releasing any details about it. They didn't say if it was suicide, or a fight, or - " He broke off, a startled expression on his face. His eyes widened as he continued more slowly. "They also didn't say if it could have been an attempt to keep him quiet. I don't expect they'll talk to us. We'd better ask Matheson."

"One more thing to talk about this afternoon," I muttered.

"I'm not waiting until afternoon for this, Tory. I'm calling him now."

"Okay, but I'm callin' the band. I can't stand the way things are startin' out today."

A couple phone calls to band members set it up, and then I set about puttin' stuff away. I found my jacket from our outing the other day. One pocket felt heavier than the other as I hung it up. Fishing around deep inside I found my flashdrive. That was funny. I thought I'd seen this in my purse. I picked it up and checked the two compartments. Sure enough, there it was in the second one, where I'd put it after Mackenzie returned it to me. Then, what was this one in my hand?

Oh! It hit me. I'd gotten a new drive with larger memory. Tyler had borrowed my old one.

"Can't have too many memories," he'd joked. Oh, Ty.

I must have picked this up lying around the dressing room and dropped it in my pocket before he was killed. Only way it could have wound up in my jacket. I fingered it. I didn't think I could stand to hear Tyler's voice yet. I dropped it in my purse with the other one. When I'm ready, I thought. When I'm ready.

I heard the bus pull up about forty-five minutes later. I wondered what our neighbors must be thinking. They'd left us pretty much alone, probably figuring all that tragedy would leave us wanting our privacy. Or that tragedy might be contagious. Havin' a busload of musicians show up in a quiet neighborhood in any city other than Nashville can change your thinking. I hoped they didn't mind and that we wouldn't be called upon to play at a spontaneous block party.

The guys - and they were all guys, we didn't have any female band members on tap right then - piled into the condo, each one carrying equipment. I was glad to see them all. Joe set his armload down and gave me a quick hug.

"Hope you don't mind. We had a sorta tagalong." He gave a slight backwards jerk with his head. I followed the gesture and stifled a sigh.

"Where do you want this, Tory?" asked Peter, a mic stand in one hand.

"The room we're going to use is downstairs, Peter, thanks."

He and Joe followed the trail of band members to the stairway. Jason entered from his den, eyes widening as he recognized Peter's retreating back.

"What the hell is he doing in our hou- "

"Shhhh." I touched his lips. "Don't let him know how we feel. I know you think he's got something to do with these killings, but I don't. Either way, though, Peter Himes is not an enemy you want to make. You should know that. We can't go actin' hostile. It'll make matters worse."

He put his arm around me as if claiming protection for me and bit his lip in frustration. "All right. Of course we can't be hostile. It would go against every Southern bone in your body, wouldn't it? And while it's true I fully comprehend how important civility and patience are, I really want to give him a good swift kick in the - Hello, Peter. Have to admit, it's a surprise to see you." Peter had made his way back upstairs to where we stood talking.

"Is it, Fields? I guess it might be. I suppose Tory told you all about the little talk she and I had down in Nashville. Right, Tory?"

"I - well, of course, I did. I don't keep secrets from Jason. Did you think I would?" I heard the irritation in my voice already. I tried to soften it. "Look, Peter, why are you here? I don't know that it's really a good idea. The boys and I are just goin' to rehearse a little. I mean play, not rehearse. I need some practice."

"Well, gee, I don't know if the band has that kind of time. It's not like it's a paying gig or anything," Peter drawled.

Jason glared. "On the other hand, Tory is still paying them a salary. We don't need you here, Himes. I have people who can make sure you leave." Jason pulled out his cell.

Peter froze, and his face went blank. "I don't doubt you do." Then he rubbed his hands together and put his smile back in place. "But, relax, Fields. I don't mean anything by it. You have no sense of humor. Of course she wants to sing with the boys. It'll be good for her. Don't mind me. I'll just hang around. I won't be a bother."

He grinned up at Jason like some pesky younger brother wanting to be a nuisance. Which, of course, he was. A major nuisance. He followed me back downstairs to where the boys had set everything up. Jason came, too. I was glad. I knew he'd keep an eye on things. All I wanted to do was sing.

Tommy counted us down, and we set off with one of my favorite numbers. All I was doin' today was vocal. I'd leave the instrumental work until later.

I closed my eyes and sang. The music welled within me. My voice was rusty with so little use. I was used to singing nearly five hours a day, but that didn't affect how the music made me feel. Like I was a conduit for melody, a pipeline for harmony. With every note I became more a living vessel carrying the lifeblood of song to the hearts of the listeners. *This is why I sing.* It felt good.

We ran through a couple of songs Joe had written, then we started on a set that Tyler and I had used as a fallback whenever we had an unexpected concert date crop up. It didn't happen too often, but we liked to be prepared. I kept an eye on Jason and Peter now. I didn't want them tearin' into each other. Every once in a while I'd hear a phrase or two of what they said to each other. Jason told me most of it later.

Neither said much during the first song. Mostly Jason glared at Peter, and Peter ignored him or made asinine (Jason's word) remarks. Then Peter started needling him some about the police keeping him under suspicion. It took all Jason could do not to inform him differently. Then Jason took another tack - one I wasn't so sure Bryan would be happy about.

"Himes, you do realize that Jamison and Matheson want to talk to you as well. Seems like you've had a lot more opportunity than I've had, and probably more motive as well. After all, I didn't even know of Braeden's existence. I didn't know anyone, really, except Tyler and J.D. You knew all of the victims."

As soon as Jason said it, he regretted it. He waited for the explosion, or explanation, or whatever.

Instead, Peter was thoughtful, even sorrowful. "You didn't mention Bobby."

"Who?"

"Bobby. Bobby Fleming. The messenger. That's the one I regret the most....Oh, don't go reading into that. I regret that he was killed, but I did not kill him. It's just - he was a young kid, and he got killed coming to tell me about you and Tory getting married. So I guess I feel kind of responsible. But - you've got to consider this. Tyler and Tory both knew everyone involved, too."

"And Tyler's dead," said Jason. "So...." He pointed a finger at Peter.

"So, Tory is not. In my estimation, either she's another victim, maybe the intended one all along or, she's the one doing the killing."

"You can't be serious!"

"I wish I wasn't. It's just that I've started looking at this from a different perspective is all. If we're talking possibilities here, we've got to be honest." Peter settled back on the couch, turning his gaze on me.

Jason kept turning his head, first to stare at Peter, then me, then down at his lap. He knew I wasn't the killer; it was the other possibility Peter mentioned that had him worried.

We took a break around eleven. We trooped upstairs and I ordered pizza from Jason's favorite Italian caterers. Some of the guys went out to the bus to grab some zzz's or email. Joe stayed inside, talking with us after asking Tommy to track down some more music. He said he had a new song he wanted me to try.

"It was written for Tyler, but I think you can handle it. Might even sound better sung by a woman."

I shivered inside, shrugging my shoulders in answer. "Maybe" was all I said.

"Sorry, Tory. Don't know what I was thinkin'. Have the police made any progress?"

I caught the sudden movement of Peter straightening in his chair from the corner of my eye. "No. There's a ton of loose ends. The police have practically handed out lists of questions to people. Who went where when? Who knew they went? Who had access to buildings and garages? Was somebody in a certain place - or could they have been - on a certain date? It's like a giant jigsaw puzzle where we don't even know which pieces are missing!"

"Can I do anything to help?"

"Only if you can tell me anything about Auggie. You knew him pretty well, right?"

"Hell, yeah, but so did you and Tyler."

"I'm findin' out that there's a lot of things about this business that I don't know half so well as I thought I did. Auggie goes way back with Tyler and me, but there's a lot about him I don't know. Like what he would have been into that he would have wound up in Printer's Alley instead of bein' on the tour bus with the rest of us! Nobody seems to know where he was!" As awful as it was to talk about Auggie, it was easier than talking about Tyler. No matter how brave I acted, a part of me always fell apart whenever we discussed Ty's murder.

"You didn't know? Auggie went over to Charlotte the week afore we left; reckoned he'd be gone 'til we hit up here. Tyler gave him the time off. Told him he could join up with us either here or in New York City."

"He what? Jason, did you hear this?"

"Yes, I did. Joe, are you sure? Auggie went to Charlotte?"

"Well, yeah. I was with him when he asked Tyler for the time off. So was - so was - " he looked around. "So were some of the other guys. They heard him ask. Fact," he paused, taking a couple steps toward the chair where Peter sat. "I coulda swore you were there, too."

"Peter! You told us he was a no-show!"

"That's what I thought he was! I never heard him ask Tyler for any time off. That must be why Tyler wasn't mad Auggie wasn't there the night we left."

There was no flying off the handle this time. Peter seemed downright thoughtful. I turned back to Joe, who still stared at him, a frown line between his blonde eyebrows.

"I coulda sworn you were there when Auggie asked for the time off," he repeated.

"Nah, wasn't. Listen, you guys done here?"

"Unh-unh. This is just a break. We're fixin' to go back down. It's really good havin' you sing with us again, Tory."

The boys started driftin' back in right then. Jason leaned down and whispered in my ear. "This is something else we'll have to tell Bryan and Ted. I think they'll be very interested."

I nodded. Tommy came up to Joe with a CD in his hands. "Got this for you. Right one?"

Joe looked at it and nodded. "I recorded this for Tyler. Don't know if'n he ever had a chance to sing it but the one time. We were late in the studio, and he pulled out that little mp3 player and taped a couple versions."

I smiled at him. "I've probably got it then. I found his player, but I haven't listened to it yet. I'm not ready to hear him sing."

"I'd like to give that a listen, Tory. Maybe copy the file for myself." Peter laid a hand on my shoulder. "Think you could let me borrow it?"

"I'll make you a copy later. I want to listen to it myself first. You understand. I just - it's private, you know?"

"Yeah, yeah, well, sure. So long as you make me one. Say, can you excuse me? I have to make a phone call, and my phone's gettin' lousy reception in here."

"Sure. I'm not quite ready yet. I need something more to drink. Jason, help me find something for everyone to drink?"

Everyone else headed downstairs. Jason and I were in the kitchen, Joe still in the living room, goin' over the sheet music. I heard Peter's voice as he came back in. He must have said something to Joe, because I heard Joe raise his voice in reply.

"Got everything, hon?" I asked Jason.

"I think so. A variety six-pack, a six-pack of Coors, twelve-pack of Coca Cola, and you've got the ice and sweet tea, right?"

"Right. That should cover it. The water cooler will take care of the water drinkers," I added as I held the door with my foot for him to follow through. Peter was at the head of the stairs, a new briefcase in his hand. He started down when he realized we were coming. Everyone was in place. Tommy and Alan stood up front. Joe was seated at his Dobro. Peter hovered near the couch across from Sammie the drummer. Jason and I set down the drinks, and I headed for the mic.

"Hold on a second," said Peter, catching at my arm. "I want to ask you something."

"What is - ?"

An explosion burst and echoed about the room. I screamed. I know I did, because I heard it, but it got cut short as a ringing took over in my ears. Stands tumbled, ceiling tiles blew up into the drop ceiling or descended to the floor at our feet. Peter was knocked backwards onto the couch.

Jason. I saw Jason lurch to his feet and stumble towards me. Tommy was on the floor, blood on his head, but he was moving, his bass in three pieces across his chest. The others leaned against the wall, checking their instruments, their faces, their hands. Only Joe was out of sight. I turned around, whirled I thought, but probably not, since I could barely balance. Joe was against the wall, too, only he was slumped down against it. Not a mark on him, but he didn't move.

"Joe! Joe!" I yelled, I think. "Jason, help me!"

Jason passed me and knelt down. "Call 911. He's breathing, but I can't tell how well. Everybody, get upstairs. Go outside! Get out of the building. Tory, take the cell. *And stay outside*!"

"Jason!" I shouted.

"It's all right. I can't leave him here alone. Go on. I'll come up with the emergency crew."

Peter reached for my hand. I looked at his eyes. Whatever I saw there, I couldn't identify, but I didn't want any part of it. I avoided him and went to the foot of the stairs and leaned on the railing until everyone else had gone up.

Someone said it took only minutes for the emergency crew to arrive. I couldn't tell. The ringing was still in my ears, and something was affecting my balance. Despite Peter's offers of help, I climbed the stairs alone, one step at a time, grabbin' the rail for support. I figure I pulled myself up those steps hand over hand like some kind of tightrope walker in training.

Once I was outside, Sammie took the cell phone from me and called 911. Then the guys set me down and stood around me, not lettin' onlookers or anyone else get close until the ambulance was there. Paramedics brought Joe up on a stretcher, Jason at his side. Jason was rubbing the back of his neck. I watched as they loaded Joe in, then one of the paramedics pushed past the band members to check me out. He started with questions, spoken firmly, evenly, in quiet tones. I calmed a little, but something weird was happening.

I could see a paramedic by the second ambulance examining Jason's neck. He lifted a neck collar from some equipment box.

In front of me - maybe that was why they were slightly out of focus - two other paramedics checked out the band members. Only Tommy needed bandaging; he walked to the ambulance under his own power. Sammie and Alan got the name of the hospital and told the tour bus driver. He took them and the rest of the band to the ER.

I could see it all happening in slow motion, like an old film, an old, silent film run at half-speed. I was answering the paramedic's questions, the ringing getting alternately louder, softer, interfering with his words. Then, blessedly, the ringing stopped. Just stopped. It felt as if a band around my head had snapped and floated away.

I smiled up at my paramedic, "Hey, the ringing stopped. I - " I cleared my throat. Somehow nothing was coming out. "I said, the ringing stopped." Nothing again. I shook my head.

The paramedic was leaning down, touching my face, turning my head to check my ears, then speaking into my face. I say he was speaking, I could only see his lips moving. I couldn't hear a damn thing.

I started to shake, and to cry. In my head I called for Jason. I must have really called his name, because he was behind the paramedic in an instant. He knelt down in front of me, the silly neck collar looking like it was trying to launch his head off his shoulders. The paramedic spoke in his ear. Jason's eyes glistened as he cradled my face in one hand and smoothed back my hair with the other.

I was tired. I ached. I was frightened. My hearing was gone. Maybe it was just for a moment, but what if it wasn't?

Jason gathered me into his arms. He lifted me, carrying me to the second ambulance like the child I felt I'd become. The ride to the hospital was a blur.

We overwhelmed the ER. Joe was taken somewhere immediately. Tommy was in the bed next to mine. His bandage had slipped, and now he held his right arm as if it were aching with pain. A nurse hustled in and slung the curtain between us. I could barely see through the corner curtain where Alan and Sammie and Guy were in another cubicle, sitting on chairs and the bed. I knew Peter had to be there, too, taking up space somewhere. I didn't know if he was hurt or not.

I stopped thinking about anything else. My body and my mind had gone completely into defense mode. Something was terribly wrong with my hearing, and hearing is everything to what I do for a living. Hearing is important to everyone, of course, but you can't sing without it. You can make music without your eyes. Not without your ears.

I couldn't think. I curled up on my side, weeping into the pillow. Even Jason's hand on my back didn't comfort me. In my little cocoon, I couldn't know what was happening in the rest of the ER.

Soon, though, I could sense that tensions had risen and the pace stepped up. Maybe it was the thudding sensation I felt through the bed. Maybe it was the breeze resulting from people streaming past my curtains. I felt Jason's hand leave my back as he stood. I rolled over to sit up.

I saw a familiar medical bag gripped by a feminine hand, legs in slacks dancing back and forth at the desk. In no time Mackenzie burst through my curtain.

·C·H·A·P·T·E·R· 29

·M·A·C·K·E·N·Z·I·E·

" 'Cause I can't take this anymore - "

- from "Don't Lock the Door 'til it Stops Swingin'" by Jason Fields

T ory looked terrible. Her face was white, her freckles standing out like droplets of blood on a sheet. Her eyes were big and reddened with tears. Her hair was flattened where she'd laid her head down. Her hands wrung each other of their own accord. Mostly it was her expression. Her face wore the haunted look of someone who has lost so much they don't dare breathe for fear it will be their last.

It wasn't just the trauma of the explosion. No doubt her fears about her hearing were eating her up, but coming on top of the shaky ground created by the uncertainties and calamity she'd been encountering, they'd devastated her. I set my bag beside her on the gurney and wrapped her up in a hug. Then I slowly took her face in my hands and spoke directly in front of her.

"It will be okay. I'm going to examine you now."

She nodded, lips trembling with the effort of trying not to cry. I began with looking into each ear, while behind me Bryan and Ted and company completed turning the place into a circus.

Bryan was here officially because this connected to the case regarding Bobby Fleming, and unofficially because Jason and Tory were our friends and he'd already been assisting Ted. Ted was here because of his jurisdiction over Tyler's death.

The situation had already made me wonder. Surely this meant that Metro Nashville had jurisdiction over Auggie's death, and the Charlotte police over J.D. With Braeden's death being ruled a suicide, his case was closed, but if we were right about it actually being murder, we'd have to contact someone in Vegas. This thing stretched across the countryside. Isn't there, shouldn't there be some agency to coordinate everything, share information? Sounded like the kind of job you'd expect the FBI to do, but I didn't know if it applied here.

Thank goodness Ted was willing to work with Bryan.

We also had some bomb experts - who were from the FBI, I reminded myself - as well as a couple guys from the Arson division and Homeland Security. In fact, we had a little bit of somebody from nearly every department related to explosions here, all prepared to run around asking questions. They had been starting with the band members, but now Bryan and Ted were conferring with two men about who would talk to whom when.

Bryan caught me when I turned to check what was happening and hustled over. I knew he'd expect my cooperation. I shook my head at him before he got there.

"No," I emphasized, stopping him at the curtain. "Not now."

"You know we have to talk with her. We need her version of what happened."

"Talk to Jason. Question the others first. She can't answer anything now."

"Mackenzie! You're kidding! Right?"

"Wrong. Tory is not going to answer any questions tonight."

"Well, can't you ask her? At least for starters? We can get a formal statement in the morning."

"You can get a formal statement then, I'm pretty sure, one way or another. But nothing tonight. Bryan - "

"What the hell is going on?" Frustration was becoming anger very quickly.

"Bryan, she can't hear anything. Acoustic trauma. I'm not sure if it's temporary or permanent, but she can't hear anything right now."

"She can't - ?" He swung around to look at her then swung back to me. "My god!"

"I know. Like I said, I'm hoping it's temporary, but we won't know for a day or so. I'm sure after she's rested, though, she'll be willing to write it all down. You know how Tory is."

Jason had moved back to the bed to sit with her and hold her. "Bryan, I'll give you my statement. I know she'll be ready to help after she's had a night's sleep. She's scared right now. This is all too much." He bent his head over hers.

"Bryan, talk to the others. Do what you have to do, but Tory can't handle anything more tonight."

"I - sure. Of course." He brushed the curtain aside to exit, but about-faced and crossed over to Tory. I almost stopped him, but then he leaned in past Jason, who stepped away. Bryan took Tory by the shoulders with a gentleness he usually reserved for Rachel. He touched his lips as if to shush them, then smiled sweetly. He gave her a squeeze, mimed sleep with his hands together and his head tilted to one side, smiled again, and stepped back with a small wave. Then he left to join Ted. Together they went to talk to the band members in the other cubicle.

The sight of him treating her so tenderly, that he thought of her in such a way - my voice caught in my throat as I told Jason, "I'll help her get situated. She needs to be here overnight. She'll be looked after, and she'll be safe. This may disappear by morning. I've got a notepad in my bag. I'll explain to her. When all this is done, I'll make sure you have the room number and that the nurses expect you."

"We can do that?"

"Yes, we can. I'll get it arranged. You go answer questions." I shooed him away and put my words into action. I wrote a note for Tory:

I'm going to admit you for the night. We'll run some tests in the morning, maybe call in a specialist. But for now, I can't see any actual damage. The eardrum is intact. There's just a bit of redness. I don't know how big the explosion was. Were you right next to it?

She shook her head and took my pen, making a quick sketch and labeling where people were. Joe had been the closest, then Tory and Tommy. The others were all further away. She tapped my wrist and held up the pen, then signed and dated and timed the picture, and put a caption it to identify what it was. Then she pushed the paper at me and pointed out the curtain.

"Give this to Bryan? I will," I said, nodding. Then I scribbled again. "I'll be right back. You know, you are tough." I grinned at her and went through the curtain.

I stopped at the desk and told the nurse to see about admitting her to a room, with an extra cot for Jason. I also forestalled the insurance questions.

"Look, I know these folks personally. Even if they don't have coverage, Jason and Tory Fields could put a new wing on this hospital and never blink an eye. They can answer the insurance questions in the morning. Or Admitting can follow them to the room - Jason can answer questions when he comes up - but get her admitted. I'll be back there." I had to bark my best professional bark, but she started pulling up the appropriate screens on her computer, shaking her head, but doing it.

I popped back into Tory's cubicle. On the pad I wrote:

They're admitting you. I don't want you to worry. I think this may just be temporary. Don't worry until you know what it is you're worrying about. Just rest tonight. Sleep. They'll bring you a light medication to make that easier, to help you relax. It may take a couple days, but if this is temporary, your hearing will come back by then. No permanent damage. Until we see if that happens, there's not too many things to do. But - like I said, there's a couple tests we can run. Jason will stay with you as soon as all the questioning is done.

Tory scanned it, and I saw a little of the tension leave her shoulders. She still looked so overwhelmed, though. She frowned a bit and pointed to the word questioning and then back to herself.

I wrote:

You can answer their questions tomorrow. They'll get enough to go on tonight. You keep these and you'll have something to communicate with. I'll take your sketch to Bryan and Ted.

I laid the notebook and pen down and started to turn. Tory grabbed my hand and held it, looking up me with her big blue eyes. She laid her other hand over the top of mine and lightly brushed it and held it to her cheek. "Thank you," she mouthed, and squeezed my hand twice.

My eyes sparked with tears as I went to look for Bryan.

I found him with Jason and Ted and the other two investigators. All were crowded into the cubicle Peter Himes had been assigned. Peter lay on the gurney. He sported no bandages except for one by his ear, but he lay against the pillow as if overcome with fatigue. Perhaps he was. Surviving an explosion can take a toll. We didn't yet know how powerful a blast this was; after all, no one had been killed outright, and only Tommy, Tory, and Joe seemed to have anything resembling serious injuries. Joe was the worst off. Still, both Peter and Jason were beginning to look haggard. Ted and Bryan, however, didn't seem to be giving Peter any sympathy.

I slipped Tory's drawing to Bryan and stood back to watch our men in action.

Peter seemed to have a lot to say, and he wasn't exactly worrying over whether or not his attorney was present. *Maybe he considers he's representing himself?*

"It took you long enough to get around to me. What's the matter, Jamison? Wanted all your ducks in a row before you questioned me? Wasn't going to happen, you know. Because I haven't done anything."

Matheson stepped in. "Settle down, Himes. I'm sure if you haven't done anything you won't mind talking with us. Who knows, maybe you can even help clear things up. Suppose you start by telling us what you know about today's events."

Peter lay back against the pillow, taking a thorough look around the room. He paused and narrowed his eyes when he came to me, but he didn't say anything. He raised his arms and placed his hands on his head. Then he shrugged and flung out his arms.

"Boom!" he shouted, lowering his hands to the covers and his voice as well. "That's all I know. Boom."

"You have no idea what caused the explosion, what direction it came from, or anything?" Matheson's face and tone gave nothing away, unless you'd been through this sort of thing with him before. Peter had better tread gingerly; Matheson would find some reason to put him in jail despite his lawyer's bag of tricks.

"No, Officer Matheson. I had no foreknowledge of the event, nor did I see anything that would have led me to think anything was amiss. We had all gone back downstairs so they could resume playing when - Boom - there was the explosion. I was thrown backwards, and I think I shut my eyes. When I opened them we were all trying to recover. Tory was sort of teetering around, Jason was behind me, I think. Tommy's bass was broke - glad we got that insured - and the other boys were standin' up against the wall."

What about the guy who's having the CT scan right now? I wondered. *Didn't you know where he was?*

Jason put words to my thought. "You're forgetting someone, Himes."

"And you're forgetting you're not the interrogator here, Fields," Peter snarled. "Does he have to be here? He doesn't have any right to, you know. Her, either," he added, finally acknowledging my presence.

"What made you decide to come along to this rehearsal?" asked Matheson, ignoring the interchange. He looked over his shoulder at Jason and added, "surely you weren't expecting to be welcome."

Peter shrugged again, then adjusted the covers. Not for the first time I wondered why he rated a hospital gown and blankets when all anyone else - except Joe - had gotten was a blanket to warm them while they were waiting to be examined. Even Tommy hadn't had to change to a gown, although he did lose the sleeve off his shirt. Was the hospital warding off lawsuits, giving the lawyer extra care? Or had Peter pressed them for it? ER staffs are frugal about their handouts. Either he was hurt in some way he wasn't sharing, or he'd been pushy.

"Look, Mr. Himes, it would be a whole lot easier for me if you would shed some light on your participation in the events that have occurred since you came to the Capital District That can mean I will make it a whole lot easier for you as well."

"Oh, hell. Look, I'll be honest with you here. Provided you keep him" - jerking his head towards Jason - "off my back and give me protection when I need it."

" 'When' you need it?"

"Yes, when. You'll understand after I tell you. If I'm right about all of this, I could be one of the next people on this hit list or whatever it is."

Bryan stole a glance at Matheson. "Ted?" he asked, holding up his notebook and pen. Ted nodded, and Bryan took a seat closer to Peter and pulled over a table stand.

Jason settled deeper into his chair, arms crossed, his face a mask for eyes that never strayed from Peter's face. The other two men in the room, the investigators from other departments, moved in closer, one near the foot of the bed, the other leaning against the only blank spot of wall near the head of the bed. No doubt they would have questions of their own.

"Before I start, I want to know something. I know you've been talking about me. I know you had me under consideration for all this. Why didn't anybody ask me any questions? You should have come right out and asked me. Because I could have told you. I could have told you I didn't have anything to do with anybody getting killed!"

Bryan spoke to that as he scribbled. "If you recall, I did ask you, several questions. About Tyler. About Bobby. About Auggie and J.D. It's not like you weren't given an opportunity to speak."

"What about that, Himes?" asked Matheson. "I talked with you myself. What makes you say we didn't?"

"Okay, so you asked questions. But you didn't ask the right questions, did you?"

Ted lowered his gaze an infinitesimal notch. "So tell us, Mr. Himes. If we'd asked the right questions, what would your answers be?"

Peter stared for a minute, then began fidgeting with the covers again. "All right, all right. Just remember about that protection."

"I haven't promised anything yet, but I'll consider it." Ted shrugged off the disbelieving looks he got from Bryan and Jason.

"Okay. Okay. First, I'll admit, I went over to Fields' place today with the express intention of annoying the hell out of him. He's got Tory. He's got money and fame, hell, he's got the good opinion of nearly everybody around. Most of all, he's got Tory. So if I can get a little of it back by being a thorn in his side, I'll do it. I knew my just bein' there would annoy him. Mrs. Fields wasn't going to be too thrilled with my presence either. So, I figured, what the hell? I like to listen when the band rehearses anyway, and their little jam session was takin' the place of rehearsal. So I tagged along."

"And that was with Tommy who plays bass, Sammie the drummer, your fiddler Guy, and Joe, right? Joe the one who plays the Dobro?"

"Yeah, Joe. And Alan."

"You didn't mention where Joe was when you talked about opening your eyes after the explosion. Did you see him?"

"Of course I did, I mean. I think I did. I must have, right? Where is he? I haven't heard him or anybody talking about him. He's not - he's not dead, is he?"

"No, Mr. Himes, he is not. We haven't spoken with the physician yet, but Joe Lauper is still with us so far as we know. Funny how you forgot to mention him. Think the explosion affected your memory?"

Now the Homeland Security officer cast Ted a dirty look. Apparently he didn't want Peter awarded any excuses for not remembering things.

But Peter wasn't going to hide behind that.

"No, no I think I was just too disoriented in the moment to notice. I was more concerned with making sure Tory was okay."

"I believe that's my job," said Jason in a dry tone that underplayed his fury.

"Look, she married you, but you don't have a monopoly on being concerned about Tory McCloud. Quicker you realize that, the better off your marriage will be. Consider that piece of advice a wedding present."

"I don't quite get who the hell you think you are, Himes, but - "

"Mr. Fields! You are here on my authority, but I will not hesitate to remove you if you keep interfering!"

Both the other investigators exhibited discomfort at Jason's presence. Homeland Security outright scowled. I had to wonder myself. Was Ted risking this for a reason? Even I knew that improper questioning was grounds for not allowing evidence to be admitted into court. Why would Ted risk a mistrial by having Jason here?

Perhaps Jason was having the same thoughts. He rose, holding both hands out. "I'll go find where they've put Tory. You can find me wherever she is. Anytime," he added, his eyes on Peter.

Ted nodded and returned to Peter.

I had to wonder. Ted must have had a reason for allowing Jason to stay, but I didn't know what, unless it was simply to rattle Peter, make him careless. Peter had to have his owns reasons for not objecting sooner. He knew the law. He knew it wasn't protocol to have another interested party present during questioning. Maybe he was counting on being able to cite intimidation to get anything he said thrown out. His bad luck that Jason thought of these things too and removed himself from the scene before Peter had time to put any such ideas into action.

My question was, would a completely innocent man think that way? Maybe a lawyer hedging his bets would. However, Peter was indicating he wasn't completely innocent.

"I don't know anything about today's explosion per se," he said. He seemed to hasten along now, as if once opened up, he wanted to get everything out. Bryan had to lean forward to keep up his notes. "But I'm not really surprised by it. The boys Braeden and Tyler played with were rough, and they were also thorough. Business-like, as it were, if you catch my drift."

"Are you saying organized crime enters into this?"

"More like they permeate it. And organized is an understatement."

"You told us Tyler had no such connections," Bryan pointed out. His voice was quiet.

"I also told you he was a clean and upright citizen, a real Boy Scout. Of course I told you that! Think I want those people down on me, too? Plus I was upholding Tyler's image. He never wanted Tory to know."

"Why would this - group - want Braeden and Tyler dead?"
Interesting way to introduce Braeden's death, Ted.

"Gambling. Too much debt. Braeden was getting indiscreet, and Tyler probably seemed cocky to them. They wouldn't have known it was because he was naive about most of their operation. All he knew about was the gambling."

"Whereas Braeden...?" Ted left the question hanging.

"Yeah, Braeden. Braeden got greedy. Our accounting job wasn't enough for him. Especially with his gambling habit. So he started a small exclusive escort business out of that house he owned."

"You mean the one you co-owned with him that burned down two days after Tyler McCloud was killed." This from the Arson expert, reading from a report in his hand.

Bryan glanced at me, but I was as surprised as he was. Ted, however, was not.

"I didn't co-own the - hell, who am I fooling? Yes, I co-owned the damned house. Scared me witless when Braeden turned up dead. I didn't know if it was really suicide or not, but I wasn't taking any chances. I made sure all his business was turned over to his creditors, along with his insurance check."

"Insurance check? What about the check you gave his sister Naomi?" I leaned forward.

Peter glared at me. "I forgot about you," he said. "Weird how Braeden turns out to be brother to a friend of yours. Yes, Naomi's check. I needed to keep the family satisfied, so I took some funds out of Accounts and presented it like it was a life insurance policy."

"You took the band's money to cover for an employee's criminal activity?" Bryan shook his head.

"Hey, it worked. Everyone was happy, and quiet. Problem solved. I replaced the money. The band never missed it."

We all shook our heads now.

"So that's the real truth about the trouble those boys were in?"

"That's the real truth."

"But you don't know whether Braeden committed suicide or was helped over that cliff."

Peter stared at the covers, then spoke slowly. "I don't know anything for sure except that these people hire experts. They don't like competition or fools who let their idiocy affect business. Braeden had introduced unauthorized activity. That was either foolish, or out'n'out competition. Either way." He shook his head.

Ted looked at some of his own notes. "Mr. Himes. What about the debts that these two boys owed you?"

"Come again?"

"My information says that Snyder and McCloud racked up a good portion of their debt at the Bougainvillea. That would be your casino, sir," he added softly.

Peter smiled a mirthless smile and lifted a glass of water from the bedside table. "Yeah, well, that would be true. However, they were safer owing me money than those other guys. At least I wasn't going to kill them. It just gave me control over them - if not the situation."

Good God.

"Why did they come after Tyler?"

"I don't know exactly. He wasn't the same kind of trouble Braeden was. He did sometimes place bets I knew nothing about. Maybe he reneged on a big one. Or, he may have been going to Jason for money."

"Why? I thought they were estranged."

"Well, Tyler had been talking lately about mending old fences. Maybe Tory'd been talkin' to him. He may have decided to turn a new page and lay ground for renewing their friendship. He wouldn't have told me about it if he had. He knew I'd blow up."

"Why?"

"Officer, I make no bones about my dislike for Jason Fields. We've always been in competition, and I hate losing. Hate it. So, yeah, I'd kick up a stink if I knew Tyler was going back to him."

There was quiet while the four men digested that. I watched Himes.

His hands, though fidgety, moved solidly and steadily. His eye contact had been direct. When he had hesitated, there had been something calculating about it, although it was fleeting and I wasn't completely certain of it. Despite that, he appeared to be telling the truth.

"Besides, I should tell you."

"What?"

"I know I'm saying it was the mob. I'm not entirely sure it was. You've got at least two other possibilities that I don't believe you're looking at close enough anymore."

"What are you talking about?"

"It still could have been Fields. Or, and I hate to say it, it could have been Tory."

I came up off the wall.

He spoke directly to me. "Look, I know Fields is your pet or whatever, and Tory can insinuate herself very neatly into new friendships. I've been thinking about this. Can you be absolutely sure Fields didn't murder Tyler before you ever started your tour and set you up to be there when he 'found' him? Do you people have any more concrete proof that he's innocent besides your blind loyalty to some guy you only met this year?"

·C·H·A·P·T·E·R· *30*

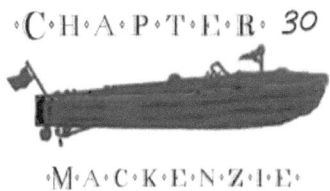

·M·A·C·K·E·N·Z·I·E·

"Don't you worry none, I'll leave."

- from "Don't Lock the Door 'til it Stops Swingin'" by Jason Fields

I glanced at Bryan, hoping he wouldn't glance back. It had been the elephant in the room all along, if one that blended into the background. I had refused to look at the situation from that angle, that possibility, focusing instead on how I was Jason's alibi for the duration of the tour. It was a good thing that the coroner placed the time of death, because if it had been me, I could so easily have been accused of slanting the evidence. Was Bryan was feeling the same sort of guilt?

Ted's face bore a reddish tinge as he responded to Peter. "All right. We'll look into it. Do you have any more details on the organized crime connection?"

He shook his head. "Nope. Not really. Frankly, I don't want to have any more details. Vegas police will know who's who out there, I'm sure. So long as that's not the only direction you're looking."

Just then a nurse came in.

"Mr. Himes? You're being discharged. You don't need any medications. Rest. Keep an eye on that swelling. Call us if it gets any larger or tender, if you have any headaches or vision problems. You can apply these packs to it for some relief. Take an over-the-counter pain reliever for pain. That's it. You can get ready and leave." She glanced at his interrogators. "As soon as you're done here." She turned to leave but Peter reached out a hand to stop her.

"Here, thanks for all the trouble you went to." He handed her a fifty-dollar bill, held out in a flashy sort of way that allowed us to see exactly what it was.

"Oh, no. We're not allowed to take tips. After all, I'm only doing my job."

"No, I insist."

"I - well, all right." With a quick glance over her shoulder she pocketed the cash, then scooted out of the cubicle. I supposed she didn't recognize me as an attending physician. She also wouldn't know that I wouldn't bother reporting it.

"Gentleman, doctor, I think that's your cue to leave," said Peter, sitting forward and slipping the hospital gown off. He was still wearing trousers and socks.

"Not so fast. Do either of you have questions for your departments?" Ted asked of the Arson and Home Security investigators.

"Just tell us where you'll be. We may have more to ask after we've completed our site investigation," said the one from Homeland Security.

"Yeah, and I'm letting the Las Vegas department have that information. It doesn't look too good for someone to be involved in two such incidents in a short time period. We'll both want to talk with you."

"Are you telling me I have to stay in town? Because that wasn't my plan." Peter frowned at the men as he balled up the gown and threw it on the covers.

"We want to know where you are at all times, so that we can contact you. Do we have to insist you stay put for that to happen?"

"No. Of course not. I'll provide you with my cell phone, as well as my office in Nashville. They can always locate me."

"What about Tory?" I asked.

"What do you mean, what about Tory? She's got Fields looking out for her, doesn't she?"

"Apparently you don't know," I said slowly.

"Know what?"

"I've admitted her to the hospital. She still doesn't have her hearing back from the explosion. I'd have thought you'd want to stick around to see what happened to her."

He stopped, one leg suspended over the side of the gurney. "Is she all right?"

"I just said, she's lost her hearing - "

"And I just asked, is she all right? Will she get it back? Is there anything else wrong?" He glared at me in a way that made my spine quiver. "Why the hell did you wait until now to tell me? Kept me busy with all this shit. You didn't tell me what really mattered!" His hands clenched and unclenched. Then he pounded the gurney. "Damn it! Damn Fields for getting her hurt!"

"You can't blame this on Jason!" I protested.

"Can't I? It's all his fault. None of this would ever have happened if Fields had stayed out of the picture. None of it." With that he blew by me and out the cubicle door.

Bryan and Ted both raised eyebrows while Homeland Security and Arson exchanged weary looks.

"I'm sorry. I didn't mean to run him off like that,"

Ted waved my apology away.

"He'd have done something like that anyway. We've gotten all we can for today. Problem is, what we've got."

"Near as I can figure it, Matheson, you haven't got a helluva lot. Himes is right. It looks like something organized crime would do, and they've got a lot of it out there. I can talk to the folks in Vegas, see if they've got any leads, tell them what Himes said, but if it's the mob - we're not likely to pin it down."

"Thanks, Avery. I appreciate the effort. Houston, what're your thoughts?"

Houston? Wonder how many 'we have a problem' jokes he gets in a day?

"I don't see anything here that really falls under my purview. That bomb was a small c-plastic device, not as powerful as your average IED. If anything this guy says is true, this was what you'd call a private issue, not a public safety one. My job is probably done. Although, from the looks of this guy, I'd just as soon it wasn't. He's trouble."

"You've got that right," said Matheson. "You see my problem, don't you?"

Avery and Houston nodded.

"Ted, what are you talking about?"

"I'm talking about having to let Himes go, Mackie. And maybe having to pick up Jason after all."

"What!?"

"You heard what Himes had to say. He's right. The only reason we haven't put Jason in jail is because we're all sure he didn't do it. We don't have any evidence to show he didn't."

"I thought you had to have evidence he *did* do it in order to arrest him."

"True enough. There's also public safety and public opinion. So long as we had other suspects, we could put off bringing Jason in, even if the public didn't know the details. With everything Himes said, there's an equal chance that it was this criminal organization he's so fond of being vague about. Actually, there's a bigger chance of it being them rather than anyone else, a factor I may call into play when I'm asked why I haven't brought Jason in. We have to look into them as well."

"But, but - look at how Peter's behaved. There's something wrong there!" I sputtered. "He has to be guilty!"

Bryan came over to me and put his hands on my shoulders. "Look, Mackie, I agree with you, he's guilty of something, but it may be nothing more than being a class A jerk. We're bound by rules of evidence here. We don't have any real evidence to tie Peter to these deaths any more than Jason. In some cases, there's more evidence pointing to Jason. He knew J.D. as well as Tyler. And he never actually said whether or not he knew Auggie, but he could have."

"He didn't know Bobby. And besides, Bobby was shot while we were on the way back from Vegas anyway! It couldn't have been Jason!"

"Probably. But the window on Bobby's death runs a fine line with our arrival time back in Albany. You can ask our coroner, he'd tell you. A prosecutor would push that line. Besides, someone with Jason's resources would stand a chance equal to that of the mob's of hiring the work out. The fact is, evidence-wise, the one that's our best bet is the one we're least likely to convict, the crime mob."

"You can't tell me you don't think Peter has something to do with all this - or that you think Jason does!"

"Honestly, Mackenzie?" Ted put in. "Right now I'm inclined to follow the evidence and look real close at the organized crime in Las Vegas. It's not just the evidence. We've all seen instances where the evidence was misleading. What Peter Himes said today has plausibility. It makes the most sense in tying all these together. That's one thing we all agree on. Even Braeden Snyder's case. If it's organized crime, especially the Braeden Snyder case, because that's where it all stems from. Tyler and these others are all clean-up work."

"What about today? Jason and Tory? The band? Is that clean-up too? How?"

Bryan had returned to the table to pick up his notes. Matheson straightened his jacket. "I can't answer that. Maybe it was just Tory they were trying to get to. Could be she has some knowledge they don't want let out. Hell, it might even have been Himes they were after, since he knew about their operations. We won't know that until we investigate further. There is one thing. Peter Himes wouldn't have risked his own skin in an explosion, but neither would Jason. So one sort of nullifies the other. I won't pick up Jason, but I will advise him to stay put. I'll mean it this time. I'll go tell them the news."

He headed out. Bryan and I were left together to figure out our own next move.

"It's not going to get solved, is it?" I asked him.

"Honest answer?"

I nodded.

"Probably not. I know you think Himes did it. He hates Jason enough, and whatever love he had for Tory has probably turned to hate, too. I don't know why he'd kill Tyler."

"To keep him from going back to Jason."

"You think? Is that really enough of a reason to kill someone?"

"I don't know. Somehow, I know in my bones, though, that there is something wrong with that man. He is evil."

"Well, he could be evil, but not guilty. Right now, we have nothing to prove he is guilty. We have a pretty good alternative in the mob."

"I know. I know. It's just, just - oh the man gives me the creeps! What more can I say?"

"Last I knew, being a creeps inducer was not yet illegal." He smiled sort of sadly at me.

I rolled my eyes. "I know. If there were only something that tied him to things more definitively."

"Let me know when you find something, okay?" With that he put his arm around me to walk me out.

Daylight outside was surprising. It was only four o'clock, but it seemed like it should have been later.

"Want to go to dinner?" Bryan asked.

"I don't know. Maybe. Where were you thinking?"

"Maybe the Carriage House? Or we could go someplace more casual."

We'd reached the parking lot. "I think casual is better. Maybe we should just pick up some takeout. What do you - "

My cell phone rang. It was Bret, calling from the farmhouse. He was calling to give me a status report, the main part of it being that the bulk of the work on the house was finished. It was habitable. There was one other piece of news for me, too.

Bryan watched me as I listened to Bret.

I pressed the 'end' button and eyed him back. "Bryan Jamison, what did you do?"

"What do you mean, what did I do? I didn't do anything, I promise. I don't think." His grin was not quite so wide as usual.

"That was Bret on the phone."

"Uh-huh."

"He informed me that, one, the farmhouse is pretty much done, as is most of the camp."

"Well, that's great, isn't it?"

"Yes, it is. But that was not his only news."

"No?"

I couldn't decide if his eyes were twinkling with innocence or guilt.

"Bret also informed me that he took a delivery today."

"A delivery? Of what?"

"Of two horses, one pinto American Quarter horse and one chestnut Tennessee Walking horse. He said that they were sent there on your orders, that the pinto is for you and the Walking horse for me." I eyed him severely, shoving out of my head that I'd always wanted a Tennessee Walker.

"Good! I'm glad they're here. Did he say if they were in good shape? I told the seller and the transporter to take extra care."

Was it my imagination or was his smile just a tad too broad? As in trying too hard.

"Bryan, I'm glad you bought yourself a horse, and of course you're welcome to keep it at the farm. Rachel will be ecstatic to have you ride with her. But a horse for me? I don't know." There was no way he should be spending his money on me that way.

"It's a gift, Mackenzie. A special gift from me to you."

"I get that," I said, watching the ground where we walked. I didn't want to look into his eyes. I didn't think, either, that I wanted to have dinner with him tonight. More than anything else, I realized, I wanted to be alone, to think. I didn't want to hurt his feelings. I turned to face him, stepping closer.

"Bryan, thank you. A horse is a beautiful gift. I just hope it wasn't too extravagant a gift. Can you meet me out at the farm tomorrow morning to check them out? Maybe around nine? Tonight I think - if you don't mind - I think I want to go home and think. I want to think about a lot of things, and then I want to come back and talk to you about them." I smoothed his shirt and patted his shoulder.

He took my hands and clasped them between his at his chest. "Mackenzie, couldn't you think things out with me there? I mean, I want to be with you, not alone." He pulled me closer until my head rested on his chest and his chin atop my head.

"No," I said softly.

"What?" He pulled back, frowning.

"No," I repeated. "Bryan, I can't explain it, but I need to think some things through. I think - I don't know. I understand why the police have to officially back off Himes as a suspect. Maybe he's not even guilty. Still there's something, something my radar is telling me, and I can't figure out what it is with you - or Ted or anybody else - around me to influence my thinking. I'm worried about Tory, and I think there isn't much time to solve this thing. It's - it's as if we solve it very soon or it doesn't get solved at all. I want to think it all over."

Bryan couldn't have looked more crestfallen if he'd tried. I wanted to take back my words, but at the same time, I meant them. I watched him, anxiety tearing at me.

He took my face in his hands and pulled me toward him to kiss me gently, very gently on the forehead. The crestfallen look had been replaced by a twitchy smile that tried not to be sad.

"I get it. I really do. It's one of the things I love about you. Your dedication - whether it's to a principle, a patient, or a friend, even a boat - you give everything in your life everything you've got. I'll meet you out at the farm at nine a.m. At which time we will discuss the gift of horses, and horses' mouths, and hoof-and-mouth disease and how to take one's foot out of one's own mouth and anything else you want. Will that work?"

I was laughing and crying all at once. "Yes. Yes that will work nicely. See you tomorrow."

Before we exited the ER, I'd checked on Joe. He was still unconscious, no clear diagnosis. The ER attending told me, "Honestly? Other than his getting a conk on the head from the blast, it's like he decided to take a long nap."

As Bryan and I went our separate ways, I started listing all the people I needed to check up on the next day. It was getting to be a long, long list.

Sweet Corn, Fields, Forever

·C·H·A·P·T·E·R· *31*

·T·O·R·Y·

"You don't know when I might sneak in "

- from "Don't Lock the Door 'til it tops Swingin' by Jason Fields

L osing your hearing suddenly is a weird thing. At first, it's as if everyone has gone quiet, like in church when you're gathering your thoughts before the service. Then, it starts to become oppressive, like when the teacher says you have to be silent during an exam. You want to shake your head, clear it of the silence and let some sound in again, but you can't. You can't shake the silence out of your head the way you clear your ears of water. That's when the panic starts. You keep trying to hear, and there is nothing there to hear.

After the nurses got me set me up in the room, they left me pretty much alone. Far as I was concerned, that was about the worst thing they could have done. I tried layin' on my back starin' at the ceiling tiles. The sun made a terrific pattern on them. It was a distraction until I realized how much grime was ground into them from the airborne city pollutants. The thought was depressing.

As were my next thoughts. Worry about the guys in the band crept in, especially about Joe. Then grief. Tyler. Auggie. Everybody. Jason bein' a suspect. Now my hearing. I was feelin' real sorry for myself.

It helped when Jason came upstairs. Even then I realized somethin', somethin' I'm afraid isn't going to change. See, I thought when you got married, everything you went through, you went through together. Jason and I are a team. I know that. Jason is right here for me. But, he's not here *with* me.

He can hear.

He feels this need to protect me. He's not inside this - this bubble with me, feeling the silence, the worry, the pain. He's not inside here with the frustration of trying to cope and worrying about how I can defend myself if I have to. I'm not helpless. I don't want to be helpless. But I am, at least until I learn how to handle this.

He's on the outside. He still has all his faculties and abilities, and he doesn't have to rethink everything he wants to do. Even if this is temporary, it's not like I can get right up and handle myself as usual. I can't even talk to people! Or know if someone is coming up behind me. Which right now especially is not a good thing.

Even though we are a team, Jason is not part of me. There's stuff I have to go through alone, even as happily married as I am, and I reckon that's how it will always be. Jason is here, he will be here, but there are parts of my life he will not experience, because it is my life. Not his. Not even ours. Just mine.

Dang.

I spent most of the night holding Jason's hand as he slept in the cot next to my bed, watching him snore, marveling at how weird that was when I couldn't hear it. I watched the dawn come up. Jason rose, stretched, made funny faces, and wrote me a note that he was going out to bring us some breakfast.

I still couldn't hear. When he left, I picked up the pad and re-read the notes he'd written me on the statements Peter had made. I couldn't tell if I was more angry or sad over what Peter said about himself and Braeden and Tyler. Lord, things had been so different from what I thought!

I considered Jason's inbred dislike for Peter, and Mackenzie's wariness of him. I considered the legal view that there was not enough evidence, that it was plausible organized crime had taken the life of my brother.

I rolled over on my left side, away from the door, clutching the notepad to my chest. Tears oozed out of my eyes and onto the sheets. Organized crime. Or Peter. No. It couldn't have been Peter. He loved Tyler too much. He loved me too much. Truthfully, he had too high a regard for his own skin. I almost snorted at that. Peter had always had a high regard for himself. That much wasn't news to me.

What I couldn't get over was that while Tyler and Peter seemed to have loved me enough to try and hide their bad sides from me, they didn't love me more. They didn't love me enough to *let* me see them. At that thought I just shut my eyes and lay there.

I didn't know, then, when Peter came up to see me. I didn't know how long he stood in the doorway watching me sleep, stepping aside when the nurses passed, watching as they deposited my food tray for me to wake to. I didn't know he'd come to say certain things to me, about how much he loved me, how he was sorry for what had happened and what he'd done, how he'd give anything for things to be different. I don't know if I would have understood it better if I had heard more.

All I know is that gradually, very gradually I heard the sound of someone's voice. Just the voice, then the cadence and rhythm of speech. At last I began to hear words, words spoken softly, in sort of a croon, words that were, at best, confusing.

"Coulda, woulda, shoulda.... How can I say what should have been? How can I make what could have been be what would have been? How can I make it up to you?...Tory, this wasn't how I wanted life to turn out. I wanted you with me....You took it all away. I want to give it back, but you took it all away."

I pushed myself up with one arm, shaking my head. Too fast, maybe, because my head swam. I faltered. Almost instantly, Peter was at my side.

"Nurse! Hey! I need help in here!"

Footsteps coming through the door. I waved at Peter as I steadied myself against the bed.

"She's sitting up, but she was pretty woozy there."

"Ma'am? Mrs. Fields?"

"Here, come this way. She can't hear you - "

"Yes! Yes, I can. Peter, I can hear you!" I grabbed on and hugged him. "I can hear!"

"Tory! Tory! Darlin', I'm so glad!"

"Mrs. Fields, steady. I'll have the resident come and check you out. Will your doctor be in today?"

I nodded. "Yes, she'll be here around eleven."

"Well, that's all right then. I'll still have the resident stop by. Mr. Fields, can I get you anything?"

Peter froze. I froze.

"This isn't - " I began.

Peter put on a stiff smile and turned to her. "I'm not Mr. Fields. I'm just a family friend. Mr. Fields will be in later, I'm sure."

"Oh! I'm sorry."

"Yes. Mr. Fields will be back shortly. He went out to pick up some breakfast. The tall man who was here last night?" Okay, I was being a little pointed and testy.

"I'm sorry. I just came on duty. I didn't see your husband before. My apologies." Then she scurried from the room.

This was beyond awkward.

"Peter, I'm sorry. That was terrible."

"Nah, don't worry about it. Darlin', I am just so glad you got your hearing back. How'd it happen?"

"I - I don't know. I was layin' there, thinkin' about Tyler and - and all, and then I sort of started to hear you talkin'."

"Oh? You did, huh? So I get to take some credit for this miracle?" he teased.

"I don't know about that. At first I couldn't make out what you were sayin'. I just heard some of the last of it. You writin' songs again?"

"I - what - oh. The coulda-shoulda-woulda thing. That's what you heard?"

"Yeah, that's where I started really pickin' up words. Everything before that was a blur."

"Well, yeah. Um, this is sort of embarrassing. I'm glad you didn't hear it all. I mean, I didn't think you could hear me. I - well, I know it doesn't make any sense, but I wanted to apologize to you. But I didn't want to actually say those things to you out loud. I figured by saying them in your presence, sort of, that it would count, sort of. Damn, Tory, it was a private moment between me and - and your spirit, something like that. I never actually wanted to face you over it. I just wanted to say the words."

"Oh, Peter. Thank you. It helps. Knowing you wanted to apologize helps. Don't be embarrassed. I think it was sweet. And you should take up songwriting again. You weren't bad at it."

"Spoken diplomatically as usual."

I smiled at him, the first comfortable smile I'd been able to manage with him since Tyler died. It felt good. "Would you hand me my purse, hon? My brush is in there, and I know my hair is a sight."

He handed it to me, peering into it with typical male superiority as he did so.

"You still carry all this stuff? Wallet, lipsticks - three that I can see, mp3 player - hey, is this what has Tyler's song on it?"

"Yeah. Peter, why don't you go ahead and take that? Make copies or whatever you want, just make sure I get it back, okay? It's the least I can do." I was feeling generous. I'd wanted to listen to it first, but that didn't matter so much. I wanted to make a goodwill gesture to match Peter's. Oh, I knew his 'apology' wasn't that much, but then, that sort of thing comes real hard to Peter Himes.

"Really?" he asked, almost as if he couldn't believe I was being so generous.

"Yes, really. Take it. I know you'll get it back to me."

"Himes, what the hell are you doing here?"

Jason strode in carrying bags from Stewart's and Dunkin' Donuts. He placed them on the stand and glared at Peter.

"Darlin', it's all right. Peter was just stoppin' by."

"Well, he wasn't - Tory! Your hearing is back!"

"Yes, yes it is!" I laughed and let him pull me into his arms.

"That's wonderful! Does Mackenzie know? Has she been in yet?"

"No, not yet. Peter here is the only - " I stopped. Peter wasn't here, now. I turned back to Jason. "I reckon he couldn't stand seein' us together after all."

"A man can only take so much," Jason said. "I can't believe I'm being that generous, but you being okay makes me feel generous with the world. Know someone we can donate a million dollars to?" he joked. Then he hugged me again, swinging me up off my feet.

He put me down gently and resettled me on the bed. "I've got some other news for you, too. Joe's okay."

"He is! What did they say? Where is he?"

"Hang on. I tracked down the ER doctor - that's why I was late getting back. He told me Joe's room number and said they were keeping him a couple days for observation, but the tests all came back negative. Doctor said he thought it was just an exceptional concussion. Joe woke up today as naturally as could be. I understand he was demanding pancakes and bacon and wanted to know what happened to the Dobro. So I think he's all right."

A thought proven when Mackenzie showed up later.

"Well, hey, the nurses tell me you got your hearing back!" She bustled over to me and gave me a hug.

"Shoot! I wanted to tell you myself! It came back this morning while Peter was here."

"Peter! He was here?"

"I know what you're thinkin', but he was really rather sweet. He kind of apologized. And I accepted his apology," I added sternly, with a look at Jason. "I don't think he's stickin' around here much longer. I didn't want to end things on a bad note."

"Okay, okay." He held his hands up in surrender. "Frankly, I'm still not convinced he's completely innocent."

"Hey, Tory! Can anybody join this here party?"

"Joe! Come in, sit down!" Jason moved aside for the musician to find a spot in the room. He leaned on a cane, grimacing as he did so.

"They're makin' me use this stupid thing. Told 'em I was all right, but they said it was this or the wheelchair. Don't want me fallin' down, I guess."

"That's absolutely right," said Mackenzie, pulling a chair over for him. "They're not sure why it took you so long to wake up, and they don't want to take any chances. Are they having you stay overnight?"

Joe nodded. "I can't seem to convince 'em to let me out of this place. 'Course, the Dobro's out of commission, too, so it wouldn't do me any good to try to go home and play it, I reckon." He glanced around as if checking for spies. "As for not wakin' up, I kin tell you why I didn't wake up. It was my daddy."

"Uh-oh," I said. *Here it comes.*

"Your daddy?" asked Mackenzie.

Joe replied with a solemn nod. "Yes'm. My daddy, he always told me if I was scared or nervous, I should just shut my eyes so's I couldn't see what was scarin' me. When that blast went off, I was out for a bit, but then I sorta came to in the ambulance. I didn't know what was gonna happen next. It seemed like Armageddon or maybe it mighta been terrorists, but I knew I wanted no part of it, so's I kept my eyes closed. That's when I saw Daddy. It was like he come to keep me company. He set there, and he kept tellin' me to keep my eyes closed, and he'd take care of me, and I'd be safe from everything around me. Finally, this mornin', I had a real hankerin' for some eggs and bacon, and I decided I'd better wake up and see what had happened to me and get me somethin' to eat. That's why I didn't wake up until this mornin'."

"Uh - really," said Mackenzie. She was reaching for my hand and trying to steal a look my way. I could see her brain at work, tryin' to diagnose which kind of trauma Joe might be in for as a result of his conk on the head.

"Mackenzie, you need to know that Joe here loves his daddy, but he is a bit of a storyteller."

"Oh, you mean, he doesn't really mean - ?"

"He means it all right, in the best storytellin' tradition of the Appalachians. Joe, you 'fess up, now!"

"Oh, Tory, all right. Dr. Wilder, I don't know why I didn't either die or wake up, 'ceptin' all the men in my family have exceptionally hard heads. Why I had an uncle out in Texas who - "

"Joe, cut it out!"

His eyes twinkled. "Yes'm, Tory."

Mackenzie gave a sigh of either exasperation or relief, I didn't know which. "I'm glad you came down here, Joe. You're both lucky you'll be all right. We want to keep an eye on you for a day or so. Tory, you'll be spending the night, too."

"Wait! I thought I could go home! My hearing's back. I feel - well, maybe not fine, but okay. Do I have to stay?" I felt myself starting to whine. Which was probably a sign I wasn't totally okay. I never whine.

"It's just for one night. I'm sure Jason isn't going to leave your side."

"Especially after finding Himes here with you this morning." Jason fairly growled. I was so glad to be able to hear him that I just shook my head at him. I wasn't going to complain.

"Why was he here?" Mackenzie asked.

"I - I think he was just checking on me. Like I said, he sort of apologized."

"I daresay Peter Himes has never truly apologized for anything in his life," said Jason, rolling his eyes so hard he nearly sprained his neck.

"Did he say where he was going when he left, Tory?"

"He didn't really. He actually sort of just - left."

Mackenzie made a sort of face, flattening her mouth as if tasting something bitter.

"Joe, I wanted to ask you, the night Bobby Fleming was sent out to tell Peter about Tory and Jason getting married. How did that work?"

"Ma'am?"

"I mean, they said you asked him to go. Why not just phone Peter, or wait until morning? And why Bobby?"

"Ma'am, you got to understand the set-up 'round here. Bobby was a good kid. We were always tryin' to think up ways he could make some more money, givin' him extra errands and such. He liked hangin' around late, and he was as helpful as a Southern boy to his momma. Liked goin' that extra mile, like givin' directions to people. Himes almost always turned off his cell phone when he left for the night anyway, so we just went ahead and sent Bobby to tell Peter about the weddin'. He was glad to do it. Peter always tipped real big."

"That's if he was happy with what you did," I put in. "I'm not so sure he'da been happy with what Bobby said."

"Wait a minute. Peter showed up at your place the next day with flowers and everything. He knew that you were married. How'd he find out?" Mackenzie's nose fairly twitched.

Jason and I exchanged looks. "I don't know. I just figured he'd heard it from the band or saw it in the papers."

"Could be. I'll have to ask Bryan what he said about that. But, look there's something else, too. Didn't Peter say Bobby never got there?" Her nose was twitching again, and there was a frown line between her eyebrows. It was like a dog on a scent. I'd never seen Mackenzie this way before. Did she know her nose twitched like that?

Jason answered her. "You're right. He kept insisting he'd not seen Bobby at all. Said he must have been shot before he ever got there. Why?"

"I was over at the coroner's this morning, reading the report and going through the bag of Bobby's things. He had a fifty-dollar bill in his wallet. Nothing else."

"A fifty-dollar bill?" Everyone knew about Peter's habit of flashy tips. Still, I wondered, "Surely Peter's not the only person who tips big."

"No, Tory, but his is the only tip Bobby would've had on him, 'lessin' he picked up another errand along the way. He'd already passed along his tips to his sister that day." Joe's face darkened.

"So maybe he did make it to Peter's. Peter doesn't want anyone to know." Jason's speech was thoughtful, but I recognized the thundercloud on his face.

I said the first distracting thing I could think of. "Mackie, was his baseball cap in with his stuff? Do you think they might release it to his sister? Bobby was never without it, and it would mean a lot to her, I'm sure."

"Baseball cap? No, no I don't remember seeing one. There was no listing of it in the report either."

"Really? He wore that cap wherever he went. A bright red Boston Red Sox hat. I teased him about it bein' so clean an' all."

"Nope. No cap. Now, his having fifty dollars might not be all that important, but maybe Bryan could - "

Joe cut her off. "Ma'am? Pardon me, but that's got to be wrong. 'Lessin' it got lost in the street, but don't the police check for stuff like that? Can't figure why a cap would stray far from somebody goin' down bein' shot, but don't they check?"

"Huh?"

"What are you saying, Joe?" asked Jason. I felt myself go cold.

"Bobby was wearin' that cap when he left to deliver that message to Mr. Himes. You sure it wasn't with his stuff?"

"Joe, are you absolutely sure?"

"Yes, ma'am, I am."

Mackenzie stood up. "All right. Jason, I'm calling Bryan. Tory, Joe, you two are staying the night here, and if I can arrange it, you'll be in adjoining rooms. Jason? Take this - " she scribbled on a prescription pad. "Wave your money around and make sure the hospital moves them quietly today. I'll tell Bryan, and maybe they can spare someone to keep an eye - "

"I'll get my people. No sense tying up one of Bryan's bunch. Besides," he said grimly, "call it paranoia, but right now I'd rather deal with people I know and trust."

I spun my head from one to another, following what they said even if I was a little short on what they meant. One thing was clear. They thought Joe and I were in danger of some sort. Apparently from Peter.

The next few days were a confusing disappointment, an exercise in waitin', which I am not good at.

Mackenzie got Joe and me moved into the same room. He and Jason and I spent a lot of the night playin' cards and tossin' around song ideas. It was good to see Jason wantin' to write again, even if Joe did laugh at him. The next day Jason and I moved into Mackenzie's farmhouse. It was private, sort of remote, and best of all, no one knew where we were. We sent Joe up to visit his Yankee cousin in Maine.

Mackenzie said she'd taken her ideas to Bryan and Ted, but they didn't have anything more to add. Bryan sent people to check out Peter's hotel again, especially since he'd checked out of there after Bobby was killed. Any time we asked, all Bryan would say was 1) anybody could have put a fifty-dollar tip in Bobby's pocket and 2) they hadn't found anything else at the hotel. I reminded him about the baseball cap, and that he should talk to Bobby's sister. He wrote it down in his little book, but his expression was tired. I could tell he didn't think we'd ever really know for sure who killed my brother. All I knew was it wasn't Jason, and despite everything, I didn't want it to be Peter.

Saturday was coming, a day I'd dreaded ever since Mackenzie brought up the notion.

She wanted me to come to her house to plan a Hallowe'en party for her friends' kids. Her friends were fine, but this included Naomi, and I didn't feel up to dealin' with her any more than she'd be wantin' to see me.

"Come on!" Mackenzie had begged. "It will be fun, eventually. I need the help. I love Sandy and Naomi and Brooklynne, but I don't know kids that well, and I know these ladies will steamroll me into something I can't handle! Did I tell you that Luke and Rachel want to use the Underground Railway cave as a haunted house? They're going to plan it out, and then see if we'll okay their ideas. How do I know what's a good idea or not?"

She was talkin' so fast, I stared at her. "What are you tryin' to get me into, Mackenzie? You're up to somethin', and I can tell. 'Fess up."

She groaned and flopped down at the hard maple table she'd had Bret build for her in the new kitchen at the farm.

"I knew I couldn't do this. Okay. I need you and Naomi to talk. First of all, you two need to get past the grief and the anger you both feel over your brothers. I think you could be friends, and you'll need that if you and Jason spend much time here. Besides, I can't have the two of you sulking on opposite sides of my living room at parties."

I didn't think that was all. I kept lookin' at her.

"Okay, so maybe if the two of you talk, you'll come up with something we can work with about Braeden and Tyler. Like what was Braeden into? How much did Tyler know? And maybe, maybe even a name or something that will be a lead for the cops in Vegas."

"I knew you were up to something! This get-together is all about gettin' me and Naomi to talk!"

"No, the kids' party is for real. They asked me to do it. Although why I agreed, I'll never know. I don't know how Sandy and Naomi do it. Now that Brooklynne's pregnant, it's like she's gone over to the other side."

"You tryin' to tell me you don't want kids, Mackenzie Wilder?"

She scrunched up her face like she'd made some mistake, or like she didn't want to own up to somethin'. "No, it's not that. I do want kids. I don't know how to handle them. I mean, Rachel is older, and she's delightful. I have no problem taking care of her, but if I ever have my own, or if somehow I end up with a lot of kids, I just don't know. There's so much involved in raising children. It scares me."

"Probably a healthy way of lookin' at it, so long as you don't let it run you off completely. So, when's this all likely to happen?"

"What? Saturday, at the River Road house."

"I don't mean that. I mean, when are you and Bryan fixin' to get married?"

"We aren't fixing - great, now you've got me doing it - we aren't getting married. I mean, maybe someday, but neither one of us has said anything. I didn't mean anything specific by it. I was owning up to my fears is all."

"Mhmm." I studied her a minute. "I'll come to your plannin' party or whatever. *You've* got to promise me that you'll stop thinkin' about this in the negative and start thinkin' 'bout all the good things that come with gettin' married. Especially to someone as handsome and talented as your Bryan."

We ended things there, and Saturday morning, come nine o'clock, I was due at her house to plan a Hallowe'en party, chit-chat with her lady friends, and try to untangle the angry web Naomi and I were caught up in to see if we could uncover what happened to our brothers.

·C·H·A·P·T·E·R· *32*

·M·A·C·K·E·N·Z·I·E·

"Darlin', you're gonna grieve."
- from "Don't Lock the Door 'til it Stops Swingin'" by Jason Fields

S aturday morning.
      I had to be out of my mind. I had to be out of my flippin' mind. Whose idea was it for me to host a Hallowe'en party for kids? How did I let them rope me into this?

Never mind that this is supposed to be a way to get Naomi and Tory together and who knows how that will go. This isn't even the actual party and I'm already a mess!

Jean watched me pace between kitchen and living room where mounds of decorating supplies and party bags filled every chair and most of the couch.

"You'd better pull yourself together, Doc. It won't do for these kids to see you thrown so easily," she told me. "Besides, you pull out any more hair and you won't have any left to pull back in that ponytail you been sporting all week."

Rachel wandered in. She'd come over early with Brooklynne and the supplies. They'd had breakfast and were planning to spend the day, regardless of how our planning session went. Considering Tory and Naomi, that could be a long time.

"Can Luke and I go down to the cave when he gets here, Mackie? I've got a tape measure and my notebook and the nails and string."

"Nails and string? What are they for?" I asked, my mind turning circles already.

"Remember you said we could use it for the haunted house? The tape measure is so we can tell if the sarcophagus will fit, the notebook for writing stuff down" (*she said that with a straight face!*) "and the nails and the string are to make the feelers and the antennae."

"The what?"

"The feelers and the antennae. You know, for the giant cockroach. Oh, and thread for the spider's web."

I shivered. "Okay. Enough. I can only take so much. You two handle that part. Take a broom and flashlight with you. You'll need to sweep out the dirt and the real cobwebs before you put up your own."

"Ew, gross."

"Good idea about the notebook."

Rachel went off to the gallery to watch for Naomi and Luke. I had mixed feelings about their arrival, but we had to get things underway.

Andrea bustled in the back door. "Doc, I brought over the papers Bennie Osterhout dropped off on those boats. You're actually going to buy *two* boats?"

"What?" asked Brooklynne, setting down her decaffeinated tea and soda crackers. Her system wasn't taking too well to the early stages of pregnancy. She regarded it as a badge of honor.

"I'm buying two of Charlie Osterhout's boats. I thought about buying all three of them, but Jason decided to buy the *Moira Finn* for Tory. She loves speed, and he thought she needed 'a new toy'. I'm getting the little Lyman runabout and - ready for this? a Chris Craft Cabin Cruiser. Built in 1936, twenty-eight feet long, and absolutely gorgeous."

"Twenty-eight feet? What do you do if this one runs out of gas? Get the oarsmen from a college rowing team?"

"Don't bring that up. I am so mad that someone keeps using the *Emma D*. I don't know who it is and it worries me sick. That boat is going to end up smashed to pieces someplace. Somebody'll probably get hurt in the bargain! Why do people do that sort of thing?"

"It's probably just some kids messing around," said Brooklynne.

"I know that, but it doesn't make it any better. Don't parents teach their kids not to mess with other people's stuff? I bet you will."

"Aunt Brooklynne will what?" asked Rachel, wandering back through. "Luke's not here yet."

"Teach her kids not to take what isn't theirs. Like your dad taught you."

"Oh." She swung around and headed back the way she came.

"Doc, if you're really going to buy two new boats, you've got to sign these papers."

"Give them here, Andrea. Thank you for managing this for me."

"It's not like I have anything else to do," she said, sinking into a chair at the kitchen table with Brooklynne and me. "Aren't we supposed to be planning? Should I be taking notes or something?"

"Sandy and Naomi aren't here yet. Neither is Tory." I glanced at my watch. "I thought she was coming early. You taking notes is a great idea. Thanks."

"I'm glad you think I have good ideas."

"What does that mean?" Brooklynne set down her teacup and opened another sleeve of crackers.

"It's just that - tell me, *do* I have good ideas? Or am I stupid?"

"Stupid! Andrea! Not in a million years!" I turned to face her. "Who's calling you stupid?"

"Ted."

"What?"

"Not Ted! Really?" Brooklynne snapped a cracker in half and slipped one in her mouth.

"Well, not exactly. He doesn't call me stupid. It's just that I feel so stupid next to him. I mean, I like that he gives me books to read, but I like to pick out my own subjects, you know? It's like he thinks I need improving or something. It kind of makes me feel bad." Her mouth, usually round and bubbly had closed into a flat, straight line.

"Andrea, Ted doesn't give you books because he thinks you need improving. He gives you books to share an experience, so that you can enjoy what he's enjoyed. I am absolutely certain he does not think you need improving. At. All."

"You think so, Doc?" A little glow of eagerness lit up her face.

"Yes, I do. Ted may be trying to impress you, but not by making you think you're ignorant. He asked me what kind of books you liked. I didn't know what to tell him. He said he thought maybe sharing what he liked to read would be a good way for you to get to know him. He was really taken with the idea. He was so worried about how to approach you! Did you know it took him three tries to work up to asking me if I thought you'd go out with him?" I watched as she processed the notion, a shy smile flirting with its acceptance. "So don't you fret thinking he wants to improve you. He thinks you're just about perfect."

"I suppose I'd better finish that book he left at my place last - Oops!" she blushed.

I grinned at her discomfort. "Don't worry. It's not like I'm surprised."

Brooklynne smiled over her tea. "Love."

Rachel wandered back in. "Mackie, where're Luke and his mom? I thought they'd be here by now. Even his Aunt Sandy's not here. Are they *all* mad at you?"

"Rachel!"

"Sorry, Aunt Brooklynne. Was that rude?"

"Rachel, I - " *Oh, great.* "No. They're not all mad at me. At least, Sandy isn't. I hope Naomi's not."

Rachel hugged me. "Mackie, nobody could stay mad at you. I'm sorry I said that."

"It's okay, Rachel. I don't know why no one's here yet."

Andrea looked up from her notebook. "I've broken the party down into zones. The living room is Zone 2 - for games and dancing - No?"

Rachel was shaking her head and scrunching her face.

"Okay, no dancing. So, maybe storytelling. The kitchen is Zone 1 - for eating refreshments. And your haunted house makes Zone 3."

"You *are* organized! Let me see that." Brooklynne pulled the notebook over.

"Can we have food in the living room, too?" asked Rachel.

I considered. "Some. Mostly you'll eat in the kitchen. The big refreshments like pizza and soda. And the messy stuff you're making that's just for Hallowe'en."

"Oooh, you mean like the eyeballs and guts?"

"Yes, like the eyeballs and guts," I laughed.

"Are we going trick-or-treating, too? I told everyone we would. Daddy said he'd take us."

News to me, I thought.

Brooklynne stepped in. "If Bryan said he'd take you, he will. That's one thing Mackie won't have to worry about."

I brightened. "True. Sure, Rachel, you can trick-or-treat with your Dad. No problem."

"I can see some problems, Doc." Jean stood in the kitchen doorway in her usual hands-on-hips stance, feet square under shoulders. "Chocolate stomped all through the rug and smeared on the floor. Water from the apple bobbing." She shook her head. Then she added, "Where the heck are those friends of yours, Doc? I've got food waitin' here that won't wait much longer Do any of your people ever arrive on time?"

·C·H·A·P·T·E·R· *33*

·T·O·R·Y·

"But it's not over."

- from "It's Never Over" by Joe Lauper and Tyler McCloud

T he condo was quiet; peaceful and comforting as a warm cozy blanket. Given all that was going on, I needed that.

Jason was out someplace with Bryan, checking on files in his office about J.D. Then they were supposed to meet with Ted Matheson to see if there was any news from Las Vegas. I was getting ready to go to Mackenzie's little get-together. I was a bit worried about Naomi, but if Tyler had really been into all that gambling and stuff, I wanted to know about it. Maybe if we worked together and really looked at everything, we could figure out why our brothers died.

I'd got up early, because I couldn't sleep. I drove out to the condo to peek at the damage the explosion had done. We were allowed back in to get stuff, but we couldn't move in until it was all repaired. Luckily there'd been no structural damage. Holes in the ceiling downstairs sure looked like they were structural, but the experts said no. Tommy's base still lay in pieces, and bits of insulation hung down like pink hay.

I plunked down on the couch on the main floor and hunted through my purse, looking for the mp3 player. I'd use it to make notes about the murders. I'd make some here where it was quiet, so I wouldn't forget anything when talking with Naomi.

I pulled it out and clicked it on. Right away I saw the filenames. This wasn't my mp3 player. This was Tyler's. Somehow I must have given Peter the wrong one the other day.

I sighed. Now I'd have to make a point of seeing him to swap them out. Or, I could just make a cd of Tyler's song and mail it to him. I'd still have to get my player back of course. Once we knew exactly where Peter was. I sighed again. As much as I wanted all the murders solved, sometimes I just wanted to walk away.

I could use a dose of Tyler. Maybe listening to his song would make me feel closer to him. Maybe it would help, so that when Naomi and I talked, I'd remember more. Maybe - I just needed my brother.

I found the recordings. The last three were all named the same, but with different suffixes. The song title matched the one Joe had shown me. "It's Never Over". On paper the words were haunting enough. Hearing them in Tyler's voice undid the sinews that held my bones together.

We said good-bye;
I made you cry.

But it's not over.

You thought I didn't care,
My heart kept sayin' "It's not fair"
We never should have gone there.

I heard you say
"It's over."

But it's not over.

We said the things you say to hurt the one you love;
I told you there were women;
You said there were some men.
And then we stared at one another once again.

Each of us believing,
it must be over.

But it's still not over.

We move as one joined throughout time.
I will be yours and you'll be mine,
Through fights and flights and sleepless nights.
Tight-rope walking the highest heights.
We'll say the things you say to soothe the one you love.

Because with us,
It won't be over.

It isn't over.

It's never over.

It was a song intended for lovers, but it could have been about me and Tyler, too. We'd always be brother and sister. Family is never over, either.

Which meant, I thought, that it wasn't over for Naomi.

I clicked through the mp3 player files. Sometimes Tyler left notes in the voice recordings about changes he wanted to make in a song. Maybe he'd left notes; if he did, I wanted to keep 'em. For potential changes to his and Joe's song, and just to hear his songwritin' voice one more time. Our collaborations had been some of the best times we ever spent together.

I bet this was it. A voice file also labeled 'neverover'.

Sure enough, Ty's voice came up.

"Joe, I'm makin' notes here. Get back to me after you listen to this. What do you think about makin' this a duet? You know, break up some lines or verses? Kind of like "Whiskey Lullaby". Tory's voice'd be perfect."

I smiled. We always did look out for stuff for each other.

"And I want to work on some of these rhymes, make 'em more complex. You know what I mean."

I certainly did. The simple rhymes were good for the old stuff, but country fans wanted a little more sophistication in the construction of modern country songs. A tribute to education, I reckon.

"I want to run this by Tory when we're done. See if she has any suggestions to make."

"I have one."

That was Peter's voice. I frowned.

"Himes, what in hell are you doin' here?"

"That song could be about us, Ty." Eew. He continued. "About you and me and Tory. Our relationships."

"I told you you were fired, Himes."

"Did you tell Tory?"

"I haven't spoken to her yet. I'm tellin' her tonight. Since you won't be at the show."

"How do you plan to explain why you fired me? You can take it back, you know. I won't hold it against you. We'll just call it a little overreaction to the circumstances."

I clicked it off. I was breathing hard, as if I'd been running. Or punched in the gut. Tyler fired Peter? And they were arguing. Arguing on the day - I checked the date on the file - on the day Tyler died.

·M·A·C·K·E·N·Z·E·

"Luke!"

"Hey, Rachel."

"Luke, come here - Mackenzie! Can Luke and I go down to the Underground now to check it out?" Rachel raced into the room ahead of Luke. Behind them came Naomi.

"Hey, Rachel, did you know 'underground' is what they call the subway in England?"

"Yeah, and who cares? Our Underground is way better than that."

"For a haunted house, well, yeah."

Naomi and Sandy and I smiled at their constant one upsmanship. "You can head down there, yes. Take the flashlight, and don't forget to make notes. Oh, and remember the broom from the garage, too. You might as well sweep it now."

"But we want the cobwebs. They'll be cool!" protested Rachel.

"I think we just want ones that we put there, not the genuine article," said Naomi.

"Oh, Mom," groaned Luke.

Looking at the two kids, I realized that Luke was now half a head taller than Rachel. And I knew she'd grown three inches in the past year. Time was speeding by.

"Rachel, take some of Jean's post-it notes with you. Mark any stuff you want left in there, and write down anything special about how you want it used. Like if you want to put a skeleton on the iron bedstead, for instance."

"Oooh, we could put bowls of guts and eyeballs on the table in there!" said Luke.

"And hang flying bats from the root that grows across the ceiling of the cave," Rachel said as they left the room.

"Like we don't have enough of the real thing around here," I muttered, laughing as I stood up to hug Sandy. Naomi had joined Brooklynne and Andrea in the gallery. Jean was still fussing around the kitchen.

"Everybody here now but that Tory, is that right?" Jean asked.

"Mmm, Maude Davenport said she might drop by, too. She claims she used to give the best kids' Hallowe'en party around, back in the day, as she put it. Says she has a couple of unique ideas we could use. But she wasn't really sure she was coming. Other than that, Tory's the only one left. She might run a little late. I told her to get rested up this week. Go ahead and put out some munchies, Jean. I'll call if Tory's not here pretty soon."

"Phthpt," went Jean, and I went back to the other room to see if I could prep Naomi, brainstorm party ideas, and dodge any other actual responsibility for the party myself.

·T·O·R·Y·

When my heart stopped pounding, I clicked the mp3 back on.

It was Tyler speaking again.

"I'm telling Tory the truth, Peter. It's time she found out what a saint I'm not, and what a sinner you are."

"My, aren't we all self-righteous and religious here."

"No, I'm just speakin' truth. I've messed up. I've got a lot of cleanin' up to do to straighten things out, but I aim to do it, and I'm startin' back on day one."

"With Jason Fields." I could hear the bitterness in Peter's voice, even through the recording. Bitterness, and something else. Some edginess.

"Yes, with Jason, and with Tory. They both need to know what you did, what you made me do. They need to know who you really are."

"Ha! That's rich." Peter laughed. "What I am? What about what you are? An addict. A gambling and drug addict who can't control his habits and who keeps questionable company at best. How much money do you owe? How much do you think little sister would adore you if she knew what you wasted on drugs and cards? Me? I keep you out of trouble. I make sure no one knows. It doesn't get in the papers, and you never get caught. Ever since I made you file that suit against Jason Fields for stealin' your song, I've been watchin' your back and takin' care of you and then takin' care of Tory."

"Don't say her name like that!"

"Like what?"

"Like you own her!"

"You don't get it, do you? You - I own. Tory, Tory - I love. If it weren't for her - ahh, well, and the money - I'd throw you to the mob's wolves in a heartbeat. You're gettin' to be more trouble than you're worth."

I stopped the player, my blood running cold. God, Peter really did love me. Where before that sincerity had sort of mitigated the discomfort I felt with him, now it just gave me the creeps. This wasn't a good sort of love. I pressed the button back on.

"Himes, I'm going to see Jason Fields and tell him what happened. I'm going to pay my debts, even to you, you bastard, and I'm startin' over. I'm goin' to be exactly what everybody thinks I am. And even though Tory doesn't know about you yet, she doesn't love you, you know. She doesn't."

"Ha! You don't know what you're talkin' about. We're like that." I could picture Peter crossing his fingers.

"Nope. She told me. She's been pushin' for this stop on this tour for a long time, right? Why do you think that is? She found out Jason lives here. She's invitin' him to the concert this week. She and Jason are goin' to have themselves a reunion! Once I've talked to Jason, that'll be that. It'll be over. You're over."

"You haven't been listenin', have you, boy? What's your song say? It's never over."

"We'll see."

"Hey, where do you think you're goin'? I'm not done talkin' with you yet. Tyler. Tyler!" Peter's voice was fading off the recording.

Tyler's next words were a little breathless, like he was walkin' fast. "We'll just see. Damn. I should have done this a long time ago."

There was a fumbling noise, then the recording stopped.

·M·A·C·K·E·N·Z·I·E·

I came back into the room from the gallery where I'd sought some privacy to try and call Tory. Words and names and colors swirled around me like ghosts of the season.

"We'll need some kind of dinner food so that the kids don't fill up on all that sugar."

"Are they bobbing for apples? I know it's old-fashioned, but it's so much fun!"

"Black crepe paper, orange crepe paper. Do we want black tablecloth with orange plates or vice versa?"

"Do we need tablecloths? Won't they just get messed up?" Andrea spoke innocently enough. I was wondering the same thing.

Sandy and Naomi looked at Andrea like she was trying on a third head.

"Of course we need tablecloths!" They chorused.

"They may be kids, but they appreciate decor, especially in the right colors," explained Sandy sweetly. "I actually have a tablecloth done in gourds and pumpkins and apples, all the fall colors."

"And I have black paper plates from the Party Town sale last New Year's," put in Naomi. "Andrea, you were telling us about - what did you call it? Eyeball Cocktail? Do you suppose you could make those for the party?"

"I, well, sure." She blushed.

"Let's get the refreshments down," said Brooklynne, suddenly taking charge.

Jean snorted. "If you can call Gummie things and electric KoolAid refreshments."

"Well, we've got the spaghetti and rigatoni entrails pie, and the Jello brainiac. Those are wholesome," argued Brooklynne.

"You're really into this, aren't you?" I asked, putting down my phone and crossing my fingers. The max it should take Tory to get here was twenty minutes. If she wasn't here by then I was calling Bryan. And Ted. And Jason. And the National Guard, I thought wildly.

Brooklynne shrugged and smiled shyly. "I've always loved putting on kids' parties. Now that I'm pregnant, it feels legit." She glanced at me. "It'll happen for you, too. If you just go ahead and marry Bryan."

I guess my smile was a little tight. I wasn't thinking about marriage, but until I knew more about Tory's whereabouts, it was as good a topic as any.

"I can't exactly marry him until he asks."

"You could ask him."

"Un-unh. Not my style. Besides, I don't know if he's ready. I don't even know if I'm ready."

Brooklynne glanced at me, hesitating. "What would you say if he did ask?"

"I don't know. Honestly, I don't. I love him. I love Rachel. I think being married to him would be - " I searched for the word. "Easy. Even given the professions we're in."

"And your propensity for finding dead bodies?" she teased.

"Don't say that," I said, and walked away.

"Mackenzie. Mackie! What is it?"

She followed me, casting a backwards glance at the other four women. Andrea was in earnest explanation about making zombie dirt - a sort of bread pudding made with broken chunks of red cake and mushy mocha frosting.

"Come over here," I said, pulling her into the gallery. "I'm worried about Tory."

"Why? Oh, she's late isn't she? Did you call her?"

"I did. And there was no answer."

"You two coming back? We still have a lot to talk about." Sandy waved us back to the group.

I tried shrugging at Brooklynne. "I'm giving her twenty minutes." I glanced at my watch. "Make that fifteen." *Where is she?*

We sat back down with Andrea and the others.

"What about games?" Sandy was asking. "I mean, besides the apple bobbing."

"We could set up a sort of scavenger hunt through the house - that is, if you don't mind, Mackenzie." Brooklynne, at least, thought to ask.

"She may not mind, but I don't want people traipsing all through my fresh-cleaned house. Especially not kids. They've got to learn some boundaries, you know."

"Um, Mackie? How do you feel about it?"

I studied my watch, recalculating. Tory was over forty-five minutes late. What I felt was worried. The hell with fifteen minutes, I needed to call her now.

·T·O·R·Y·

It was Peter.

Peter.

It didn't matter that we'd sort of suspected him all along. It didn't matter that he'd made me angry by not telling me the truth and uncomfortable by declaring his love for me when I married Jason. Maybe I shouldn't have been, but I was surprised that it really was Peter.

Peter. Peter killed Tyler. And - and Auggie? J.D.? Bobby, and probably Braeden? And tried to frame Jason into the bargain!

He also tried to kill you and Joe.

I began to shake.

He had. He had! That's what the explosion was all about. He tried to kill us!

I had to get out of the house. Yes, I was supposed to go to Mackenzie's, and I'd made myself late listening to Tyler's recording. I had to get to Mackenzie's. I'd be safe there.

I dropped the mp3 player into my purse. We'd need that. It was the proof to convict him. It was Tyler speaking from the grave, and it would convict the son-of-a-bitch.

Tears were dropping off my face, but my mind was clearing, clearing in a cold, white-hot way. How dare he!

I pulled open the door, keys in hand.

Peter stood in front of me.

"I hadn't expected to find you here," he said.

"Then why are you here?" I snapped. Angry. I had to be angry, or the fear would show all over me.

"Uh, well, I was going to leave you a note and - are you all right? You're upset, aren't you?"

"Yes, I'm upset, but it's none of your business." I brushed a hand over my eyes. Hide the fear. "I thought you were leaving town."

"Yeah, I am. I wanted to give you this." He held out his hand. The other mp3 player lay in it.

I stared at it. He kept talking. "You gave me the wrong one the other day. Must have got them confused, but this one just has some of your files on it. I - uh, I kind of like that song you're working on. I suppose it's about Jason?"

His eyes were dark, hopeful. Tender. He didn't want to hear that song really was about Jason. I swallowed.

"Actually, actually, no. It's - it's one I started back in Nashville. Before we came up here. I, uh - I, it's kind of funny. I started writing it after that trip we made to Italy, you know? So, you sort of, inspired me." I swallowed again and took the player from his hand. "I have to go now. I have an appointment, and I'm late."

I took a few steps over towards my car. I needed to get in it and drive, I thought.

Peter kept pace with me.

"Yeah, well." He smiled. "Kind of funny about those two mp3 players. They must look exactly alike."

I nodded, concentrating on opening the car door. I climbed in, put the key in the ignition.

Peter took hold of the door and closed it for me. He tapped on the window, and instinctively I put it down, trying to play it out.

"Did you listen to Tyler's song yet?" he asked softly, and grabbed my wrist and pulled my arm up and out the window.

"Ow! Peter, that hurts! Let go!" I looked him in the face as he grabbed my chin with his other hand. I gasped at the force, and at the fury in his face.

He squeezed my face tighter and tighter and leaned in as close as his grip on my arm would allow. "I'll never let go, don't you know that by now?"

I heard my cell phone ring from my purse. Instinctively I started to turn my head towards it. He yanked it back, then slid his hand to my throat and gripped it while he lowered my arm to where he could pull at the door handle. The force of his hand on my throat was paralyzing. He reached in and grabbed my collar, let go of my throat, and dragged me from the car. Before I could recover, he'd grabbed my arm again, twisted it behind me, and produced a small efficient-looking gun, which he thrust in my side.

"Come with me, Tory. We're going for a ride."

I thought then that he was taking me to his car. Instead he maneuvered me to the other side of mine. He pulled handcuffs out and fastened my hands behind me. Then he lowered me into the passenger seat and proceeded to fasten the seat belt.

"Tsk, tsk. You forgot to put one on before. I couldn't let you drive away like that. It's better if I drive." He yanked the seat belt in a way that forced me tight against the seat. He had some kind of lock or adjuster that he fastened onto it that kept it from slipping loose.

Then he closed me in and got in on the driver's side. He reached to start the car, then paused. He felt in his pocket, and out came a roll of duct tape.

"Peter, you can't be serious! No, that's too - " I struggled against it, but he slapped a piece of the tape over my mouth, pressing it tight against my lips.

"Your lungs are way too powerful. I can't let you keep screaming for help, now can I?"

My eyes must have told him what I was thinking.

"Yes, I did plan this. You'd have been all right if it hadn't been so obvious you were scared of me. The only reason for that was if you'd heard the recording." He was backing the car down the drive. "You've forced my hand. I don't have choices anymore. Sounds like one more country song, doesn't it?"

My cell phone rang again.

He slammed on the brakes at the curb and grabbed my purse, yanking my phone out.

"Mackenzie Wilder," he read off the screen. "That's where you were headed, wasn't it? Well, I don't like Mackenzie Wilder any more than I like Jason Fields. Let's just go see her, and then maybe we'll invite Jason to the party as well. Damn, I hate havin' so much cleanin' up to do. My own fault I guess. I couldn't seem to give up on you. If only you'd loved me. You realize that? If only you'd loved me, none of this would have had to happen."

·C·H·A·P·T·E·R· *34*

·M·A·C·K·E·N·Z·I·E·

"All hell broke loose"

- from "Song for Ty" by Tory McCloud

T he line rang. And rang some more. She didn't pick up. Was she driving? Maybe that was a good sign.

I shook my head at Brooklynne and shrugged. "I don't know. Maybe she's on her way."

"Mackie? Brooklynne? Come on, you guys. We have to talk about the sound system."

"Sound system?" I whispered to Brooke.

"For the scary sounds in the haunted house," she whispered back. "Do you suppose we could borrow something from Tory?"

"I'm sure she'd be delighted to let us borrow anything." *So long as she's all right.*

·T·O·R·Y·

I can't breathe. I can't talk, because of the damned tape. I can't breathe because this is so horrible. I'm scared. Peter is - Peter is sick. He's evil. He's - oh dear God Almighty, he's actually doing this!

In my car, driving down the street, as if nothing was happening. We stopped at a red light. I looked to my right, hoping the driver would look at me and see the tape and my frightened eyes and realize something weird was going on.

The driver was a little old lady who probably could barely see, and she clutched the wheel like the side of a pool that's over her head, staring straight at the lane in front of her.

I know Peter's talking, but it's really hard to focus on what he's sayin'. I don't want to listen. I don't want to hear this. I don't care what he has to say about why!

"I don't understand it. I don't understand it, darlin'. Why couldn't you have loved me? Even a little? What does Fields have that I don't? I'm not bad looking. I'm talented, intelligent. Bet you didn't know my IQ is one-fifty-seven."

He paused as we came to another light. This time no cars at all pulled up next to us.

Where is everybody? This is Saturday! Where are they all?

"I hate Jason Fields!" Peter yelled, pounding the steering wheel. "I hate him! Damn it, Tory, why did you have to love him!"

His eyes were wild. My heart jumped every time he hit the wheel.

"Why? Damn it, why!"

Just as suddenly he calmed down and looked over at me. Fondly. Tenderly, almost.

I feel like I'm going to be sick.

"Tory, I'm sorry you have to go through this. It wasn't what I wanted. I love you. You know, I truly do, darlin'. I will always love you. Like the song. I will always love you."

Then he stepped on the gas, and we turned down the River Road.

We couldn't be more than ten minutes away now. My heart was beating so hard it hurt my chest. I couldn't move anything. My hands were numb from the handcuffs and the pressure of being fastened behind me.

Who is at Mackenzie's this morning? Besides Naomi. Sandy, she said. And Brooklynne. Brooklynne and Naomi are pregnant. Oh, God, Peter, you wouldn't do that, would you?

I turned to stare at him. What made him like this? What did I do to drive this - this obsession? How could I have inspired - is that the right word? Inspired him to do all this?

"You know, you were so cute, no, so beautiful that first time I saw you, when I talked to your daddy about managin' you and Tyler. So talented. I knew right then I wanted you for myself. I knew I had to get Fields out of the picture. Even then, before he realized it, I knew he'd decide he'd want you. You were so taken with him.

"When he wrote that stupid song and submitted it before Tyler did, I knew I had a way to split things up. Tyler was still a kid. He liked the idea that his song was really better. Didn't take much to convince him that maybe Jason had stolen some of his ideas when he wrote it. He never thought about it just bein' that they were inspired by that old story your daddy told. Gettin' to court was a piece of cake, and it didn't matter that Jason conceded. It was obvious he didn't want to face up to me in court. I was always a better lawyer than him. Probably could write better songs, too."

That's how far back this goes? To the very beginnin'? It's like Tyler's song.

> *You have to ask the question: where have we come, and how?*
> *'Cause the end's in the beginning,*
> *And the beginning's in us now.*

Tyler was right. The end of this love story was seeded from the very beginning. *Only here we are, at the end.*

Tears rose in my eyes, spilling over a couple drops. The end. The end of something I never wanted.

I don't care about Peter, or his feelings. If he really loved me, even hurt, he'd never do anything like this. If he's anyone worth loving, he won't do it. As much as I fear him right now, I hate him more.

Hate makes fire in your belly.

There are other lines in Tyler's song.

Like: "Sometimes a new beginning is someone else's end,".

Jason's and my beginning is going to be Peter's end, dammit! I am not going to let him end it all like this. He's done enough! I've had enough!

With that, I started to plan. I listened to Peter's words with full attention now. I wanted to be ready for any opening I could find in what he said, what he did, anything. If there was any chance I could warn someone or catch him off guard. If I watched now, while I couldn't do anything else, I could be ready when the opportunity arose.

Peter slowed the car.

"I want you to understand something. I loved Tyler like a brother. If he hadn't planned on going to you and Fields about how I was running things and the problems he had, if he hadn't decided he had to tell you all what was goin' on, I never would have killed him. I swear I never would have killed him, But I couldn't let him do that. I'm sure you understand.

"Auggie and J.D., same sort of thing. 'Course, I wasn't fast friends with either of them, but if they hadn't figured on telling Jason about the way I ran the business, why, they'd still be alive today, too. Same thing with Bobby. Well, not quite. The kid wasn't too bright. Wanted to know how come I got so upset when he told me about you and Fields.

"Well, I couldn't have anybody knowin' what I said, now could I? It just made me so mad! Here I'd gone to all the trouble of stoppin' Tyler and runnin' down to Nashville to shoot Auggie and hirin' someone to fix J.D's car so's it would wreck, and you go off and marry Fields anyway! Damn it, Tory, it wasn't fair!"

He was pounding the steering wheel again.

"I'll tell you one thing. I did not kill Braeden Snyder. Fool took his own life. Cost me money, too. But I didn't kill him. I only killed the people I had to."

'Had to'? I narrowed my eyes.

"Don't look at me like that. It's true." He shook his head. "True now, too. I'm sorry, Tory. I know better than to ask you to come away with me. If you won't do that, well..." he shrugged. "But I promise you, I will always love you. There won't be anyone else. My love for you will never be over, sweetheart. Never."

I closed my eyes to shut out the pain. *There has to be a way out of this. There has to!*

·M·A·C·K·E·N·Z·I·E·

I was getting jumpier by the minute. I'd tried Tory again, but got no answer. I tried Bryan. Same. I thought he was with Jason today, but there was no answer there either. Great time for them to be in some unreachable hollow in the geography of cell phone service. Ted seemed to be out of reach as well.

I stomped back and forth, scowling every time I answered one of the crazy questions Sandy and Naomi had for me. Brooklynne was the only one who understood why I was acting so antsy. And maybe Jean. Jean always knew when there was trouble going on. She just didn't know exactly what.

"Jean, do me a favor?" I called out.

"I will if you'll tell me what's going on with you."

"I can't exactly, because I don't even know myself. I'm nervous that Tory hasn't shown up and that I can't reach her either. When the kids come back from the cave, make sure they get some food and then make sure they come in here with us. I want to be able to keep an eye on them."

"Why? Surely you don't think those two kids are up to anything, now do you? I've never known any two kids less likely to be in trouble in all my life. Those two never do anything wrong!"

"No, no, it's not that at all. I agree, they're terrific kids." *I want to keep them that way.*

"Sure, sure. I'll feed them and then see they get in here."

"Mackenzie! Mackie? I think we've covered about all we can today. Sandy and I will look into the rentals, and we'll go over Luke and Rachel's lists so we can get what they need. We'll need a day to set everything up. We usually get together the afternoon before a party like this and do all the cooking and decorating. Sort of have a little party ourselves. The thirtieth's on a Thursday. All right with you? I'll call you with more details." Naomi was gathering her tote bags together.

Another get-together like this one? Gulp.

"Let me know if Tory can't let us use their equipment," said Sandy. "I'm sorry she didn't make it here to join us. It would have been nice to settle this together before we left."

"As soon as the kids come back, we'll have to go. I think we've done really well." Naomi looked around. "I don't think I've left anything - oh, here's Luke's cell phone. You know, I hate when he makes a big deal over having one already, and I hate when he leaves it around. If he had it on him I could call him - hey, Mackenzie, can you call Rachel and have them come upstairs?"

I shook my head. "Bryan is a little old-fashioned. Rachel doesn't have her own cell yet."

"Well, for heaven's sake!" said Naomi.

"I think Bryan told her she could get one when she turns thirteen. He said something about everything else going crazy then, so he might as well throw a cell phone into the mix."

We all laughed. They were leaving, and Tory hadn't made it here yet. If everything was all right, I was going to be awfully mad at her. I shook my head at myself. There was no reason to think anything was wrong. It had to be my nerves.

Which jumped when my phone rang.

"Excuse me," I said, moving to the kitchen.

"Mackenzie?"

"Ted! Just the person I wanted to - "

"Is Bryan there with you?"

"Uh, no. In fact I haven't been able to reach him. Jason either. Or you, for that matter. I wanted to - "

"Listen, we've got some odd information out of Las Vegas. I need to tell Bryan and Fields about it as soon as we can get hold of them. The bottom line is that, not only did Snyder and McCloud not owe any money to the mob, the reason they didn't is that Himes bought up all their debt. The only person they owed money to was Peter Himes. He didn't have *some* leverage over them. He had complete control."

I didn't know exactly how this affected things, but right now my blood was chilling faster than a patient packed in ice.

"I've got some other bad news for Tory." Ted's voice was heavy. "Her brother was into drugs as well as gambling."

"She won't take that well," I said.

"Yeah, most folks don't. There's more. I finally heard from the fan club president. She did not send out that press release. In fact, she said Himes told her not to send out any more until further notice. He would be in charge of press releases. One more thing, and I only tell you this because I want you to be careful. Dean Dechard told us the motorcycle was in a trailer they were keeping parked behind the hotel where they all stayed. We checked it out. It was there, and the tire prints match the ones on the River Road. Dean told us he'd seen the bike being put in the trailer after midnight the night Tyler was killed. He said he couldn't be positive, but he'd thought at the time that it was an odd job for Peter to being doing, seeing as how he doesn't like his clothes being messed up. I'd say we've got him. We're going to pick him up. Listen, tell Bryan what I said. Have him call me."

"I will," I replied. "But Ted? I'm worried. I haven't been able to reach Tory all day, and she was supposed to come to my house."

"Hmm. You said you've been having other cell phone trouble. Maybe that's all it is."

"Ted, we both know it might be something else."

"I know. She's still at the farm, right? I'll send someone out to check."

"Thank you! I'll give Bryan your message." He switched off, and I put the phone back in its cradle. Finally I'd reached *somebody*! Ted would handle it. I turned to go back into the gallery.

Someone was at the door. There hadn't been any noise of a car driving up, but that happened sometimes. The handle rattled as someone fumbled with it, then it swung open and Tory stumbled in.

I grabbed for her arm to steady her. I froze at the sight of the tape over her mouth. Then I saw Peter behind her. Peter, with a gun, and he looked serious. I know it sounds stupid, but the look on his face frightened me more than the gun in his hand.

·T·O·R·Y·

I kept tripping. My feet were numb from the fear and the car ride and the awkward position I'd had to sit in. My mouth was dry and still taped, and I couldn't make a sound as Peter turned the handle of Mackenzie's door.

I'd seen the cars outside. I knew everyone was still there. I knew this was going to be awful. My little bits of fight and hope were slipping. *We're never goin' to get out of this, not alive.*

Mackenzie caught me as I came through the door. Then she saw Peter.

"Dr. Wilder, just the person we wanted to see, isn't she, Tory? Now we'll make some phone calls and - hey, what's going on? Who are these women?" He frowned.

Mackenzie's housekeeper Jean and her receptionist Andrea were there, standing this side of the brick fireplace in the living room. Naomi and Sandy were there, too, Naomi on the couch with her huge purse open in front of her on the coffee table. Sandy looked like she'd just stood up. I thought I saw Brooklynne back in the shadows of the gallery. Maybe if she stayed there, she could - Peter pulled me back, away from Mackenzie.

"Doc, you picked a helluva a time to have a party. Okay, listen to me everyone. This isn't how I wanted to do things, but my hand keeps gettin' forced. You all sit down nice and easy, all on the furniture right there. You, in the back, come join your lady friends."

So much for what Brooklynne can do.

"Now, so I won't have to do so much explaining, and so that you can understand how serious this is, I'll have Dr. Wilder remove Tory's gag. I'm going to keep ahold of Tory, here, and I'll have the gun on her all the time. No cooperation, no Tory. Plain enough?"

His hand on my arm tightened.

I caught the eye of each of the women individually and nodded. They had to do this. Maybe I could keep the damages down to a minimum, but they had to do what he said.

After they sat down, he motioned to Mackenzie to remove the tape. She positioned herself squarely in front of me, and she kept glancing from my face to Peter to the kitchen.

Why not stand off to one side? The way she was now, it was nothin' for Peter to see all of us at once. No chance for him to miss any of us movin'. W*ait, what's she watchin' for behind me?*

"Sorry, Tory. I'll try not to hurt you. Turn your lips in as far as you can manage."

Peter snorted.

She picked at the corners of the tape until she could slide a finger under each one and grip it to tug.

"Okay, I'll try to do this steady, but not so fast it will tear the skin."

I closed my eyes, shutting out everything except the tickle of her fingernails and the pain I anticipated. I even shut out the gun in Peter's hand. It felt good.

The tape peeled off me like a reluctant second skin, leaving each cell burning with the friction. The pain made me gasp, and that made me cough.

Peter pulled me up short. "Now, you and Dr. Wilder are going to join the other ladies. Doc, I want you sitting in that chair over there, and I want Tory in the one on the other side. Do not talk to one another, any of you. Tory, you just explain to everyone how you happened to bring me here. I will stand right here. When Tory is done, I will be making a couple phone calls, during which I expect quiet. Tory, be sure to make it clear that I am an excellent multi-tasker. And don't assume I don't know my way around guns. I do. Tory can testify to that as well."

So I told them. The effect seemed split right down the middle. Sandy and Naomi and Andrea turned white. Jean looked dour and mad. Brooklynne and Mackenzie both looked grim, as if they'd had to deal with this before, which, I reckon they had.

I tried not to feel guilty over bringin' Peter here. That was what he wanted me to feel. I felt responsible for puttin' them in danger, but he was the one doin' this, not me, and I wasn't feelin' guilty for the actions of a lunatic.

As I talked, I kept glancin' around. That's what performers do, and even in this situation, old habits don't vanish. Peter was watching all of us. The ladies were mostly lookin' at me, as if struck motionless with the enormity of it all. Only Mackenzie and Brooklynne kept slidin' their eyes toward Peter and the kitchen. I expected they were sizin' up the possibilities. Only I didn't know what those possibilities included.

·M·A·C·K·E·N·Z·I·E·

This feeling was all too reminiscent of last spring. Helpless. Captive. Frightened. And worried about the kids into the bargain. There was no way for us to know when Rachel and Luke were coming back upstairs.

I pictured them running in from the garage. Peter turning at the noise. We'd try to rush him or something, that urge would be strong, but he'd start firing at the noise he heard. In my mind's eye, I could see it.

Down went Luke.

Down went Rachel.

I wanted to die.

Tory was telling us how Peter was behind all the deaths. Except Braeden's, she noted. But he'd killed all the others. Because of her. Her voice went small on that.

I looked back to the kitchen, watching the corner they'd have to turn coming from the garage. My glance slid past Brooklynne, head turned and eyes directed right where mine were going. She knew it, too.

My heart skipped a beat. I'd caught the sound of a door closing. Only faintly, because the house carried sounds in the way old houses do, and I was pretty sure only I knew it for what it was.

I made myself cough.

Then I started to yell. Not for help, but at Peter. I went for shock value, borrowing some of my rebellious father's favorite invectives.

"Peter Himes, you son-of-a-bitch. Who the hell do you think you are? You think you're so tough and so smug and smart! Well, you aren't worth a damn, you know that? Coward, killing people because you can't get the girl you want. You're a damn coward, that's what you are, you sorry son-of-a-bitchin' bastard!"

Tory and the others stared at me, mouths open. Andrea looked shocked as well as scared. I caught a suspicion of a satisfied smile on Jean's face. Only Brooke narrowed her eyes at me. She knew. The cop's sister knew.

Peter came at me in a rage. Backhanded me across the face. My tirade stopped, but his began. Perfect. I could hope.

"Shut up! This is as much your fault as it is hers, you know that? If you'd kept your nose out of things, everybody would have assumed that Jason Fields had killed Tyler McCloud. He'd be in jail, and I'd be the one running Tory's show and callin' her my wife. Auggie and them would still be alive. So don't think you're not at fault here!"

"You killed Auggie before you killed Tyler," I snapped back. "Right? And J.D. as well. It wasn't all fear, was it? It was a plan calculated to save you the most trouble. Wipe out everyone who knows and you won't get caught. It's not about Tory, either! It's about getting what you want. It just so happens that you want her!"

He raised his hand at me again, but then another look came into his eye.

"You think all I do is kill people? Is that it? Well, I can be generous. I'm not stupid. I know the cops will be able to prove it's me. I'm not as good at this as I hoped. But I've got connections who can get me out of the country, so I just need time. And the two of you. So, listen up - "

"Wait!" Brooklynne yelled. "Wait!"

"What?" Peter turned to face her. "What the hell do you want?"

I sneaked a peek towards the kitchen. The rubber toes of two different-sized shoes overhung the edge of the doorway I'd been watching before, and slender fingers grabbed the jamb. Carefully I turned my head as if listening while Brooklynne explained that she and Naomi were pregnant. She had to go to the bathroom, and Naomi probably did, too. There were no windows in the bathroom, it was an interior room. Couldn't they just go?

I rolled my eyes past their talk and caught Jean watching. I tilted my head a fraction toward the kitchen. She caught it, and her eyes widened as she saw what I'd seen.

The kids were here.

"Mr. Hines!" she yelled, with all her drill sergeant authority thrown behind it.

"Himes. Now what? *You're* not pregnant, are you?"

"No I am not, but suppose you just tell me what you plan on doing? You said you can be generous. Well, how about it? What's your generosity consist of?"

"You stay here," he told Brooklynne. Then he swaggered over to Jean, his back towards the kitchen. "Listen, lady, if you all would just shut up already and let me talk, I'll explain this. In detail."

As he started to explain to Jean - and the rest of us - I snuck one more look at the kitchen. The telltale sneakers and fingers were gone. Didn't know how or where they were, but they were out of sight, and Peter hadn't seen them. Maybe Luke would let Rachel use his phone to call Bryan. Or he could call - the thought died as my eyes fixed on Luke's forgotten cell phone.

Damn!

I looked across at Tory.

·C·H·A·P·T·E·R· *35*

·T·O·R·Y·

"and the circle goes on spinning."

~ from "The End's in the Beginning" by Tyler McCloud

I didn't know what Mackenzie and Jean were up to. I felt frozen in place. As I watched, though, I realized something. Peter was capitulating. He was actually not goin' to kill these women! I realized that whatever reservoir of hatred and pain he'd drawn on to enable himself to kill Tyler, whom he'd known and loved like a brother for years, whatever resources he'd pooled to help him carry out the other murders, he was out of his element here.

It's not easy for a man like Peter to think of killin' a woman. More to the point, he had more people on his hands to manage than with any of the other murders, and he was improvisin', somethin' else he wasn't too keen on. Peter might be an excellent multi-tasker, but he was always a planner. He thought far enough ahead that even in these circumstances and as rattled as he was, he knew one thing. If he started killin' us in a group, the others wouldn't let it go on. He was goin' to have to manage this carefully. So maybe we still had a shot.

Although, I was goin' to have to worsen my own odds in order to make sure the others were okay.

It was me and Mackie he was after. So it would be me and Mackie he would get. Maybe between us we could do something.

From what Peter was sayin' to Jean, my idea was right in line with his plans. Good.

"Peter," I called, my voice breaking with disuse. "Look, if you lock them all up, you'll only have me to manage."

"Tory, darlin', I just said that. Only it'll be you and Dr. Wilder here. Got to have something to bargain with when we call Fields and the Lieutenant. Jason's going to want to play hero. Doc'll give me some leverage, enough to slow him down, anyway."

This was such a bizarre discussion!

"Ladies, like I said. I can be generous. If you will just proceed to the bathroom, I will lock you in there. Cell phones out, first, if you please. And just think, you pregnant ladies can pee all you want to."

He waved his gun to herd them along. Sandy and Naomi were scared to death. Andrea was beginning to seem a little defiant now, but a stern look from Mackenzie settled her. Mackenzie must be thinking like I was. Now if there were some way we could let Jason and Bryan know what was goin' on before Peter lured them in.

·M·A·C·K·E·N·Z·I·E·

I watched as Peter closed the door on the five women. At least now they'd be safe. Somehow I thought even he would be intimidated by the thought of killing that many people at once.

He strode back to where Tory and I sat and gathered up the cell phones from the coffee table. He carried them to the gallery. Opening one of the windows, he tossed them one by one into bushes in the yard. Satisfied with that, he closed the window and returned to sit on the sofa, still clutching his gun,

"Now, Dr. Wilder, Tory, I've been very reasonable here. Your friends are safe. So long as they don't do anything stupid. The question is, how are we going to play this out? Should I have you call Lieutenant Jamison, Dr. Wilder? You could tell him you've discovered something about the case. Or, Tory here, could call Jason saying she had car trouble and he should pick her up here. No. I don't like either of those. What do you think?"

Tory spoke softly. "Why bring them here at all, Peter? It'll just complicate things. Take me. Maybe, tie up Mackenzie or something like that, take me and we'll leave town. I'll - I'll go with you. I won't give you any trouble, either. Just let my friends alone."

He cocked an eyebrow at her, and then cocked his gun. "Your friends? Jason is your husband now, as you so often like to remind me, not just your friend. Do you think, even for a minute, that he wouldn't come after us? I want to control the situation, thank you."

"Mr. Himes," I said. "We're not that far from the Canadian border here. You could take any number of roads to get there. There'd be only a little slow-down at the border, and then you're home free."

"You think so? I didn't realize how close we are to Canada." His voice was easy, musing, then it turned hard. "But if you think crossing that border is easy nowadays, you haven't traveled recently. You need identification, passports. They'd have us stopped in seconds, even if Tory did cooperate. And, sorry, hon, but I don't quite believe you would. You're a great singer but a lousy actress. You couldn't fake it. I'm going to have to make you love me again. I can't do it around Fields. I've got to get you away. For that, I've got to put a stop to our Mr. Fields. And anybody else that might hold us up.

"So. I think we'd better find you a working phone, Doc, and have you call your friend Jason, and tell him - tell him he should surprise his lovely wife by picking her up here. Yes, that should do it. Then, after he shows up and I deal with him, the two of you will come with me. Once I know we'll get out of the country, Dr. Wilder, it'll be just Tory and me." He looked at me, calculating. "Depending on the circumstances, you might wind up back here safe and sound in a few days. Maybe. Tory, would you appreciate that?"

"Yes, of course I would." Her face was white and her eyes were big, but Tory's voice was steady. And he said she couldn't fake it.

"I've tried calling Jason today, Mr. Himes. I haven't been able to get through. Same with Bryan."

"Where are they?" He fingered the gun.

"I don't know, but wherever it is, they don't seem to have cell phone service."

"Well, we'll just have to keep on trying, now won't we? Here. Use my throwaway. Start dialing. Keep trying until you reach him. Don't try to be clever and tip him off. That would be incredibly stupid. Get him to come out here."

I picked up the phone and dialed Jason's number. I don't know which I hoped more, that he'd answer, or that he still wasn't in range. For the first try, it was the latter. And for the next twenty tries as well.

Peter didn't take to waiting easily.

He went to the bathroom door and rattled the handle. I could only imagine how that made my friends feel. He walked along the gallery, flipping curtains so he could see the road.

He walked over and sat on the end of the couch nearest Tory. There he took her hand, rubbing the back of it with uncomfortable familiarity.

Tory sat quiet. For those few minutes we might have been friends spending a peaceful Saturday afternoon at home. Out of the silence crawled the thought I'd been unwilling to entertain: Where were the kids?

I knew they'd been here. Now they were - thankfully - nowhere to be seen. Where were they? Would they be smart enough, and patient enough, to stay away?

"One thing I don't understand, Peter." Tory spoke to him in a soft voice. "Why do you dislike Jason so much? Now, don't tell me it's because of me. I could see how much you disliked him way before you were ever interested in me."

Peter smiled one of his smug little smiles and patted her hand. "You don't really know how long I've been interested in you. No, I never liked Jason Fields. Everything always came easy to him. He's got money, people like him. He never had to work for everything like I did."

"What do you mean, hon?"

That 'hon' may have been reflexive, but I bet it still cost her. How did she do it?

"When I was growin' up, my father taught me to go after anything I wanted. He'd tell me, 'Work hard, and above all stay focused. It's the only way to succeed. Don't let anything get in the way of your goal.' I did that. It took me through law school. There I was, working hard, staying focused. I had all the drive I needed. Maybe not all the intellect, but I was pretty smart and I knew how to work at it. Well, along comes Jason Fields. Multi-talented, rich. Everything, every class, seemed to fall into his brain and settle there like a cartoon where every seed that falls to the ground sprouts and grows into a perfect garden. It frustrated me to see him have it so easy while I had to work two jobs and study during the little time I wasn't doing those or going to class."

"I didn't know you had to work so hard. Didn't your parents help?"

"Hah. My first year, my dad paid all my expenses. He was proud of me, proud to see his advice had been taken and was paying off. Then, he died. He didn't have anything to leave us. He'd risked it all on a business deal, one he'd been sure would pay off. It fell through, and he died before he could recover our finances."

"What about your mother?"

Tory's question was genuine. I could read the puzzlement on her face. I have to admit, I was curious myself to see what made Peter Himes tick.

He rose and walked back to the gallery, drawing Tory along with him.

I took the opportunity to stand, too, examining my hands quietly. I needed to move, and to be ready to move, but I couldn't alarm Peter.

Luckily he was more intent on checking the road for vehicles than watching me. He still hadn't answered Tory's question, but now he stared out the window, holding her by the arm. Finally he answered her.

"My mother. My wonderful, loving, social-minded mother. No, no, I need to correct that. She wasn't social-minded. She was social-LYminded, and when we no longer had Dad or his money, she didn't know what to do with herself, or with me. Off she went to live with her sister in Chicago. Took what was left in the house, the savings she could access in the accounts, and barely ever contacted me again. Not even Christmas cards, let alone a phone call or a gift. She gave me no money, no support, no love. Proof she never loved me at all."

"Peter, you - you never told me anything like this before. As long as we've known each other, I never knew!"

"Exactly why would I have wanted to share with you that my mother didn't think I was worthy enough to give more attention than she gave her manicure?" He paced around in a circle, ending up right back at the windows. "No. I had to work two jobs to keep studying at one of the toughest schools in the country. People joke about college kids living on Ramen. I was spreading a single pack of Ramen over three days. Lived on that, Kool-Aid, and pain. But I made it. I made it big. Didn't make too many friends, but I made it. It was great, just how I wanted it to be. 'Til along came Jason Fields."

Tory tilted her head in confusion. "Wait a minute. You knew Jason before you met us?"

"Yes, one more thing I didn't tell you. I don't tell people my whole life story, Tory, not even you. Yes, I knew Jason back then. Every time I turned around, it seemed like there he was, acing classes, making money, getting headlines! Every damn thing the man did, people applauded. They loved him." Peter was shaking his head.

While his head was down, I snuck a look toward the kitchen. Where were those kids? I was rewarded with the sight of another shod toe, only this one was much larger than the last. I recognized it, nonetheless.

Bryan!

I took a step toward the kitchen. Peter brought his head up sharply, and I froze. It wouldn't do to attract his attention over there.

Tory was asking another question. "What else was there? I mean, rivalries in business aren't that uncommon. What made Jason's success stick in your craw so bad?"

"How can you even ask that? Tory, I've seen you pitch fits over talent like Kelly Clarkson, even Reba McEntire. Those singers have nothing to do with you. They have nothing *on* you. You're a mega-talent all by yourself. But did that stop you from fuming when Kelly won a Grammy or Taylor Swift took top honors at CMA? Or when Reba's TV show turned out as successful as her albums? But, yeah, there was something with Jason, even before you."

My eyes never left Peter. I wanted to imprint my presence on him. Absorbed as he was in his own narrative, if he could feel my attention on him, he might not notice my movement. With care, I slid one foot in the direction of the kitchen. Straight back, not changing my profile, not showing movement, altering nothing but the perspective of my body's outline.

"It was a case, my first one in patent law. Jason came up, and just like later, he was acting as his own lawyer." He snorted. "You know, it was another infringement case. My client was suing Jason over a patent for a computer device. I knew my client was dreaming. His documentation was good, but Jason's showed when he began work on the device, the steps he took to get it reviewed along the way, and when he filed. I knew all this going in, but I figured I could out-argue him before the judge."

I slid another step backwards, and shifted my weight, making another invisible move. At this rate it would take me hours. What was Bryan doing in the meantime?

Tory was crossing her arms as she watched Peter. It was the defensive posture of a woman preparing to hear something she didn't want to hear. Luckily, she hadn't looked my way yet either. I didn't know if she could maintain her cool knowing that help was in the house.

I repeated my previous moves, three times in succession. No reaction from Peter. I heard a sound behind me.

"Mackie! Stop. Don't come back any farther," Bryan whispered so low I could barely hear him. Yet it brought me to a halt.

"Good. You can hear me. Right? Move your left hand if you can."

I waved my hand as if brushing away lint from my slacks, and held my breath.

"Okay. Are you okay?"

I waved my hand again.

"Is Tory all right?"

I waved.

"Jason's here with me. Are the others still here?"

My left hand waved of its own accord. I hoped he wasn't going to give me instructions this way. In fact, I hoped he'd be quiet. Peter's story couldn't go on forever.

"...so I lost that one, too. Damn Jason Fields!"

"It sounds like you were drawing on history when you instigated Tyler to place that lawsuit against Jason." Tory's voice was cold, but growing louder.

Uh-oh.

"Could be, maybe."

"And it didn't turn out any different, did it?"

"Yes, it did! I beat him that time. I won that case for Tyler!"

"Only because Jason dropped his countersuit! So, that's it? You're jealous of Jason Fields? So you killed my brother and Braeden, Bobby and J.D. and Auggie, because you were jealous?"

"Not just jealous. There was you, Tory! I love you, and if you'd found out about me, you'd go back to Jason and I'd have nothing!" There was the beginning of a tortured plea in his cracking voice.

"Peter, you need to realize a couple things. You never really loved me. This was all about you bein' jealous of Jason and wantin' anything he wanted, just to show him up. And two... I did go back to Jason. Jason is all I'll ever want."

I drew in my breath. What would Peter do now?

First he scratched his chin with the back of the hand that held the gun.

I rolled my body weight forward. I had to get closer if I could, disguise the fact that I'd moved. He frowned at me, but said nothing.

Instead he gazed at Tory with a blank expression, taking hold of her arm once again. I watched as his grip tightened.

Then he spoke. "You know, I don't know what I was thinking. You - you're right, Tory. Perceptive. I guess you have to be to write songs the way you do. This is still all your fault, though. Because if you'd returned my love, even a little, who knows? It might have grown into something real. Now, well, now I know. You're Jason's. So, it won't hurt so much if I have to kill you."

"Fields!" It was a cry from Bryan, grabbing at air where Jason rushed past.

"Jason!" Tory cried.

Two sets of hands pushed me aside. Jason, speeding by me in a blur, Bryan trying to get me out of the way as he aimed at Peter. Jason grabbed Peter's gun hand before he could pull back the hammer, shoving it skyward, popping the shoulder of the shorter man.

Tory screamed.

Echoing screams came from the bathroom, then Jean ordering "Pipe down and stay still!"

I stood frozen, unsure whether to try to pull Tory from the vicinity of where Jason and Peter fought or stay back out of the way. I watched as the unbalanced struggle continued.

Peter still had tricks up his sleeve. Unable to swing at Jason, he allowed the bigger man to overtake him. Then he cut upwards with his leg in some sort of martial arts move, following it with punches that didn't seem to suffer from arm length. Jason went down.

"Hold it, Himes!" shouted Bryan, his weapon now steady and firmly aimed at Peter.

"Hold it yourself!" Peter snarled, and in one swift move scooped his gun from the floor and grabbed Tory's arm, wrenching it and clamping her to him. "Back off, Jamison. I just finished telling Tory how it wouldn't hurt me if I had to kill her. Do I have to?"

Bryan lowered his gun slightly, his eyes narrowing as he sought another advantage.

Peter was grinning now, his eyes fixed and glazed, his shoulders heaving with heavy breathing from the fight. "I want out of here. Tory will be my ticket. And you," he swung around and glared at Jason, glued in place on the floor by the threat to Tory. You will - Aah!"

He'd pulled Tory close. Pinned like that, she cut loose with the only weapon she had left. Tory screamed. Only it wasn't just a scream. It was a holler, a pig holler, and she aimed it straight into Peter's ear.

·T·O·R·Y·

I don't know where it came from. Well, maybe I do. Hollerin' is an honorable old-time tradition, and it works powerfully to keep a person's lungs in shape. I've used it to exercise my lungs for years, and it always bugged Peter. He thought it was too hillbilly. So, maybe I was doin' it for spite; I knew it would annoy him, but if I made it really loud, it would distract him good, too.

He screwed up his face and reached for his ears like there was nothin' else on earth more important than stoppin' that noise. Thank goodness he didn't do the obvious and just shoot the source.

Jason grabbed Peter as he let go of me. I felt another hand on my arm as Mackenzie started draggin' me out of Peter's reach. I didn't notice anything else, because Jason had started hittin' Peter, beatin' him now. I'd never thought before about how powerful his arms would be if used to fight. I'd always thought of them as sturdy fences keeping danger out and security and warmth in.

"Jason! Jason! Stop. Stop! You don't need to keep doing that. Stop, please!" I slumped against Mackenzie, the strength draining from my legs and arms. I covered my eyes, willing Jason to listen. "Stop!"

When I uncovered my eyes, Jason's emerald eyes bored into mine. I read the raw intentions of a man who would do anything to protect me. Even kill. His one hand held down a motionless Peter, his other was still drawn back in a fist, ready to pound away some more.

"Jason." Bryan moved in closer, his gun still raised. "Jason, I've got this. Let me take over."

Jason flicked his eyes over at Bryan, but nothing else of him moved. His eyes came back to me, making sure I understood.

I pushed away from Mackenzie's support and approached my husband. I put my small hand on his huge fist and pressed it.

"It's okay, Jason. I'm okay. We're okay. He - he didn't hurt me. I don't think he can hurt anyone now." I couldn't see Peter breathing.

I couldn't let it matter. This wasn't a time for splitting hairs about being the better man than the killer. Jason needed to know I understood what he'd done for me, that I knew now exactly how much I meant to him.

If Peter had deluded himself into thinking he was murdering people because he loved me, Jason had proven that he would kill to protect me. Because he loved me, he would go to extremes against his own nature to make sure I lived.

No matter how many weeks it had been since our wedding, no matter how close we were when we wrote music, no matter how passionately we made love, this moment was our true marriage. That moment when two people know things about each other and their relationship that no one else will ever know. Our moment.

Bryan stepped in between where Peter lay and where Jason and I stood. It broke the spell, and I moved into Jason's arms, wrapping my own about his waist, creating a cocoon to shelter us both.

"Mackenzie. Mackenzie! Come here. Can you find a pulse?"

"I don't - wait, wait, yes! Call EMS. I'll get my bag - "

There were sirens already. Bryan grunted, not even having completed his call.

"It's Matheson," he called out. "Don't know why he took so long."

There was some groaning.

"He's coming back around," Mackenzie said. "He's going to be in a lot of pain."

"You be careful. I'm right here. Himes, don't move. Don't try anything."

"I don't think he can, Bryan."

I pulled Jason back from where they worked on Peter. We retreated into the kitchen. He sat wearily, and I caught the expression on his face as awareness of his actions sank into him. His shoulders sank correspondingly.

I stepped around and unlocked the bathroom door. Sandy and Naomi spilled out first, Naomi frantic to find Luke. Brooklynne was serious, less openly fearful, but she called out for Rachel. She'd barely said her name when two figures came flying around the corner, whizzing past me into the women's arms. Jean and Andrea came out together, blinking. Jean wore a self-satisfied expression.

"I always knew we were headed for a shootout around here. Doc, you got to stop finding dead bodies!"

Naomi gave a little shriek. Brooklynne looked grim, but resigned. After all, she was twin to a policeman, and Mackenzie was her best friend.

Ted came in through the portico, EMS right behind. They moved past Ted and took over from Mackenzie. She carried her bag over to the table, her hands shaking as she set it down.

"Jason, Tory, you two should get checked out. You especially, Jason. Your hands don't look too good, and you took some pretty heavy blows."

"We'll be all right, Mackenzie," he said, but his eyes and his voice were dull.

"Mackie, do you want to examine us? Or is there somebody you think we should see?"

She looked at me with surprise. "I can check you out. But Jason probably needs x-rays. I'd like him to go to the ER."

"I'll go, too. Where he goes, I go. I'll make sure we get there."

"Look, I don't think either of you should drive. I'll get my - "

"Hold it, Doc. You shouldn't be driving either." Jean scowled. "Bryan. Lieutenant Jamison! I'm taking these three on up to the Emergency Room. When you get your business done, that's where we'll be. Brooklynne, can you handle things here? Rachel, are you all right?"

·M·A·C·K·E·N·Z·I·E·

Rachel! I turned around and grabbed her in a hug.

"Where *were* you? Where were you hiding?"

She grinned at me, but it was a nervous grin, and she didn't say anything.

Luke, however, did.

"Hiding? We weren't hiding! We went and got Lieutenant Jamison and Mr. Fields. We got them here so they could rescue you!"

I looked from one to the other. "You did? That's amazing! Thank you! But, I don't understand. How? They couldn't have been far away."

Jason peered up from under his mop of bushy hair, a sly glint re-igniting in his eyes.

Bryan ambled over to the table. "We were at the Boat Club, trying to reach Ted. These two came up and - "

"You ran to the Boat Club? How? I mean, I know you're fast, but it must be a mile or more - "

"We didn't run, Mackie. We took the *Emma D*."

"Oh, you took - You took the *Emma D*?" my voice squeaked. "My boat? How? What did - ? Wow! That's pretty tricky to get a strange boat that far on the first time out." Something was knocking at the door of my comprehension. "Wait. The boathouse was locked. You didn't break in, did you? I mean, under the circumstances I don't mind, but - "

I broke off. This time it was to watch the EMTs take Peter out to the ambulance on the stretcher, State Troopers flanking it. IVs were already running. He didn't open his eyes as they went by. I'd examined him thoroughly enough to know; his eyes were closed by choice.

I turned back to Rachel and Luke. Their faces suddenly slipped from shining to sheltered. Rachel was giving nervous looks to her dad, who gave her a quiet nod, then whispered to me, "Don't give them a hard time, okay?"

I hadn't begun to figure out what he meant when Rachel spoke up in her thin voice. "I'm sorry, Mackenzie. Really, really sorry."

"Sorry about what? The boathouse? I'm sure we can repair any damage you two did to it. After all, we've had to fix a number of things down there what with all the joyriding going on."

Rachel dropped her head, and Luke grimaced.

"Well, you see, that's what we need to explain. We didn't break into the boathouse today."

"You didn't? Then how did you get the boat out? It wasn't out already, was it?"

I saw their faces light up for a brief second, as if they liked this answer, but Bryan was shaking his head.

Rachel sighed. "We didn't break into the boathouse today. We broke into it the - the night of the open house. The night you found Mr. McCloud. We're the ones who've been taking out the *Emma D*."

·C·H·A·P·T·E·R· *36*

·M·A·C·K·E·N·Z·I·E·

*"The warmth of a circle
binding close friends
outshines the flames
of a blaze we can tend."*

- from "Christmas Fires" by Jason Fields and Tory McCloud

Y ou what?" I looked from Rachel to Luke, and back. "But, but - you're only ten! You've never been out on boats like these before! I - How did you - *why* did you - " I stopped shouting and made myself take a couple deep breaths. You wouldn't think I could get so upset over this after what we'd all been through. On the other hand, maybe that was why I was so upset. They were only kids. Moreover, they were Luke and Rachel.

"Okay, first, you two do know you shouldn't have taken my boat out without permission. You don't do that. And since you had no experience with these boats, that made it just plain dangerous. You get that, don't you?"

"We get it. But, the boat is so great, and we knew you wanted us to ride in it. It's - it's kinda hard to explain, but we're family, Mackie. And families share, right? It didn't feel like it was wrong. Besides, Luke's cousin went with us, and then Arthur. Arthur showed us how to run the *Emma D* and treat her right. He took care of the gas, too, so you wouldn't run out."

Luke was letting Rachel do all the talking. He hadn't moved from his mother's side, either. I guess he figured she'd protect him.

"What do you mean, Arthur showed you how? Arthur helped you?" It was the closest thing to a screech I'd ever heard come from Jean.

"Well, yeah. He was watching the boathouse the second time we took her out. He said he was watching for the vandals that had broken in. When he saw it was us, he said he didn't know what to do. He didn't want to tell Dad." She slid a sideways glance toward her father. "So, he said he'd have to supervise, make sure we knew what we were doing and teach us how to handle the *Emma D* the right way. He really did, Mackenzie! He knows a lot about old boats. As much as you even."

Bryan stepped in. "Rachel, Luke, I know you didn't mean any harm, but you also know that you should ask before using or touching something that belongs to someone else. Especially something as valuable and unusual as an antique boat."

"But, Daddy, - "

"Wait, I'm not finished. Furthermore, didn't you realize how worried Mackenzie was over this? Especially with the danger her friends - and even she - was in? We were afraid that the same person who was behind the killings was behind the stuff with the boat."

I couldn't help but add, "Kids, what if Bryan had been the one staking out the boathouse, maybe even with his gun, waiting to catch the criminal who was messing with the boat? Did you think of that?"

I watched Rachel's face fall. Luke stared at the ground, more mute than ever.

"Mackenzie!" Naomi cried. "These kids have been through more than enough. And face it, if they hadn't been taking that boat out, they wouldn't have been able to find Bryan and Jason and bring them back in time! They're heroes. And even if they were doing something they shouldn't have, they were responsible about it."

"Responsible?" asked Bryan, lifting an eyebrow.

"Oh, you know what I mean. They didn't attempt to do anything they couldn't, and except for using it without permission, they were respectful of Mackenzie's property."

"Okay, okay. We need to sort it out with her, yes, and with Luke, but let's face it, they are heroes." I looked at their faces, which had started to lift a little. "You're right. They've been through enough today."

"They surely have," put in Tory, who wore the face of someone who'd been through way more than enough. "Kids, that was quick thinkin', and I want you to know I appreciate it. Now, your daddy, Rachel, and your mama, Luke, probably should have a little talk with you, and you should listen; but, I think you are both very brave and very, very smart. When you have your party, I'll come by and sing for you and your friends. And now I s'pose we ought to go get checked out? Isn't that what you said, Mackenzie? Jean?"

It was nearly a repeat performance at the ER, only with a few cast changes. Jason and Tory and myself, with Peter there under the watchful eyes of New York State Troopers. I didn't want to think about him. Judging from how closely she clung to Jason, neither did Tory. We were all in for a lot of healing that had nothing to do with physical injuries.

Peter's outlook, his sick take on responsibility, and love, the enormous jealousy. Ambition denied and twisted 'til all reality distorted out of it. I shuddered thinking about it.

What, I wondered, would the Hallowe'en costume for this look like?

Then I realized, it would look like any number of villains, fictional or real, notable or unknown.

Take a positive human condition and thwart it, pour pain and insult over it, bake it with contempt, and you serve up a dish of villainy seasoned with evil. Dissect any number of evil deeds and at the heart you find something has gone wrong in the person's life that he - or she - didn't know how to handle. Not to say they bear no responsibility. I don't mean excuses, but there are reasons why these things happen, and those reasons are usually to be found in the history of the parties involved. If only hindsight worked in reverse.

Friday, the 31st.

I had to be out of my mind. I had to be out of my flippin' mind. *Whose idea was it for me to host a Hallowe'en party for kids? How did I let them rope me into this?*

I stood in the doorway to the kitchen, a tray of 'blood juice' in my hands. To my left, on the floor, sat three of Sandy's kids dutifully going through all the candy they and the younger kids received when we took them Trick or Treating before the party.

Yes, I wound up tagging along. Jean wouldn't let me work in my own kitchen, and Bryan looked so helpless with all those kids. So we all went.

Besides the eagle eyes going over Kit Kats and Gummie worms for suspicious unwrapped versions or protuberances, I could hear a little sharp trading going on.

"But, Cassidy, you don't like Nerds. I'll just take these two packs. You can have my candy corn."

"Did Mr. Duncan give you the candy apple? That's okay, then. Except that he always uses old apples, and they're mushy. But he doesn't put poison in them or anything."

"Mom!"

"What'd I say?"

Over by the couch Luke and Rachel were recounting their boating adventures, not for the first time. With every telling, their roles expanded a little more. I feared the final version would end with Bryan's department hiring them on as undercover agents.

Rachel was finishing her part of the story. "And then Dad brought us back on the *Emma D*. He wouldn't let us drive, because, he said he'd have to go pretty fast. And, man, he did! And then he got it right down by the cave and tied it up, and then we came up the passage. After that, we didn't do much except stay out of his way."

Wait a minute.

Bryan drove the boat back. Now that was an interesting tidbit. He never told me. I glanced around the room to locate him. I spotted him in a secluded chair in the gallery. Watching me, watching him. I smiled at him. He and I were going to have a little talk.

Tory and Jason were at the piano, absorbed in working on a new song and explaining to a confused trio of pirates and one ghost that songs need to be written so far in advance that Christmas songs were often underway year-round. This was going to be a last minute addition to Tory's Christmas album for next year.

"I've got a final round of 'blood juice' here. Any takers? I'm putting it on the coffee table."

"Great, more sugar." Brooke passed by me carrying out a sack of trash from the mask-making craft we'd set up. She looked a little gray around the gills, as Jean would say.

"You okay?"

She nodded. "Just tired. But then I'm tired all the time right now, remember?"

I laughed. "That's supposed to pass. Remember your vitamins, and sleep in tomorrow."

"No question about that. This is my final run. I'm taking Rachel tonight. I promised her pancakes. I figured you might be at your limit for kid activities."

"Thanks. This has been an adventure." I went in to set the drinks out. Naomi, more trash in hand, came over.

"What adventure? This?"

"Yes. I mean, you guys did most of the work, but it's been a real eye-opener. I don't know how you do it."

She shrugged. "You learn. Right now you just have Rachel to work with. Add a baby into the mix, and everything will change, but you'll grow into it right along with the baby."

"Mmm." *I really am not so sure about that.* The pit in my stomach deepened. While I enjoyed tonight's party, the swirl of pre-teen humanity with its burgeoning hormone issues and consequent acting out in all its bizarre social ritual scared me to death. "I don't know. I felt more at home trying to figure out how to save us from Peter last week."

"Speaking of which, thanks, Mackenzie."

"What for?"

"For being patient with me over Braeden. I can't get used to what he did, but now I understand a little better. It wasn't just him. It was the surroundings and the mischief Peter Himes set him up for."

"Then, it's confirmed it was a suicide?"

"Well, either that, or some other criminal he owed money to. But they're saying they actually think it was suicide. I - I have to let it go." She patted her own swelling belly. "That and make sure no one in this next generation falls into that kind of thing. Strong kids. You have to raise strong kids these days."

"Well, you've got a great start with Luke and the others."

"Thanks. And you'll do fine yourself someday. Kids!" She raised an arm and did a 'round 'em up' circle over her head. "Time to go!"

I heard a couple groans, but they all complied. All of them.

"Everybody?" I asked.

"Sandy and I are taking them to her house to sleep over. We do it all the time. I'm staying there, and Bob's coming over in the morning. Why don't you and Bryan and Jason and Tory come, too? I've got breakfast casseroles set to go. Brooklynne and Rachel can join us."

Breakfast with this crowd, too? I loved them all, but....

"Maybe next time. I understand Brooke promised Rachel pancakes, and I told her to sleep in. You might better, too."

Naomi smiled. "No sleeping in with pregnancies after the first one. Not unless you've got someone to take over. I'll catch a nap later. Besides, that's why we're at Sandy's and why I made the casseroles ahead. See? That's something you learn along the way. How to cope."

Cope? No, thank you, said the little voice in my head. I watched as they all located jackets, said final good-byes and left, all the while that little voice providing a running commentary involving words like *freedom* and *dependence* and *ruckus* and *privacy*.

"Doc, hey, Doc!" Jean stood at my side. "We're headin' out ourselves. I'll get the rest of this tomorrow. The kitchen, that is. I'm not venturin' down to that cave to see what those kids have created. You're on your own, there."

"Fair enough. I take it you and Arthur are back together again?"

"If you can call it that. After I yelled at him for helping those kids take your boat, and after he explained that that's where he was whenever I couldn't find him and how he was making sure they weren't in any real trouble outside of not askin' permission, well.... Sometimes you can't live without 'em, you know?"

I glanced at Bryan, fixing us substantial glasses of wine after tucking Rachel into his twin's car. I knew he'd been telling Rachel one more goodnight, but I suspected he'd also been checking up on his twin. I smiled at Jean and patted her shoulder. "I know."

I collapsed onto the sofa, ready for the wine Bryan was bringing me, and ready to ask a few questions myself.

He settled himself beside me, wrapping his arm around me, clinking his glass to mine. We sipped the first sip, and then I said,

"So, you didn't tell me it was you who ran the *Emma D* back here, and to the cave at that." I felt him freeze beside me, but I continued as if nothing had happened. "If I hadn't overheard Rachel talking to her friends tonight, I'd have never known."

I resumed sipping, waiting for his reply. It came more smoothly than I expected.

"It was simple. I didn't want the kids to run any further risks. Plus, I wanted to get here as quickly as possible. No big thing."

"Then why am I just learning about it tonight, accidentally? You could have said something."

He shrugged.

The piano music stopped and Jason joined in, sotto voce.

"He made me swear not to tell you. Kids, too."

"Shut up, Jason."

"You should tell her about that three-point docking maneuver you made. Never seen that done before."

"Fields! I said be quiet!"

"Bryan, what's the problem? You conquered something here. You should be proud." I sat forward, setting my glass on the table and facing him. "You were not comfortable with that boat, with any boat. And yet you took charge and not only sailed it but apparently handled it very well in emergency circumstance. Seems to me you've overcome your fear or phobia or discomfort, whatever it was, that made you dislike the water."

He set his glass down beside mine, his face serious, his characteristic smile subdued. He leaned forward for a minute, elbows on his knees, not saying a word, staring at the grain in the mahogany table.

"I always hated how I felt about the water. I didn't stay away from it because I was scared. Or even ashamed. I know everyone makes mistakes. It was just a training exercise. What I hated, what kept me away, was the fear that I wouldn't be able to do my job. What good is someone in an emergency who can't handle his equipment?

"When the kids found us the other night, Ted had just gotten hold of us to give us the news he'd given you. He told us you hadn't been able to reach us or Tory. Jason wasn't able to reach her either. When the kids showed up, well, then we knew. We needed to get to you fast, and even if I didn't feel sure about using your boat, I knew I knew more than Rachel or Luke. I was the expert by default. I had to step up. I did, and luckily, it worked out."

His voice went sort of lame at the end, as it normally did when he was uncomfortable discussing his own heroics. I wanted to let him be comfortable, but this was too important to just let go.

"So, basically it's like I said. You faced it down, and you conquered it. You can handle a boat when you need to. Even in adverse conditions. You don't have to worry over it anymore."

He shrugged, but his shoulders relaxed, his eyes regained their twinkle, and a tiny satisfied smile set upon his lips.

Sweet Corn, Fields, Forever

We finished our wine. Combined with the exhaustion of the crazy day, it made me sleepy. I rearranged myself on the couch, wrapped back up in Bryan's arms, the piano music and murmuring of Jason and Tory's voices lulling me. They were running through their song again, this time start to finish.

> Christmas fires of pinecones alight,
> Yule logs and boughs
> don't burn as bright
> as new-forged friendship vows.
>
> The warmth of a circle
> binding close friends
> outshines the flames
> of a blaze we can tend.
>
> Fires of love unending....
> Christmas fires of love are blending....
> long mem'ries, filled hearts,
> close ties, new starts -
> Brightened by Christmas love.
>
> Mid-winter, mid-season
> Mid joys, trouble, tears
> T'is love beyond reason
> We seek to draw near.
>
> A love beyond
> measure
> To last to the end.
> The circle of friendship,
> Where circles can't
> end.
>
> Fires of love unending....
> Christmas fires of love are blending....

long mem'ries, filled hearts,
close ties, new starts -
Brightened by Christmas' love.

As the music faded and Jason and Tory went into musical consultation once more, Bryan bent his head near mine.

"You know the horses? I meant them as a gift."

I snuggled closer. "I know. You told me."

"No, I meant them as a special gift."

"Mmm?" I was feeling snug, and lazy, and at ease for the first time in months.

"Any comments, you two?" Jason raised his voice. "We're calling it 'Christmas Fires'."

"Mackenzie, don't go to sleep on me. I want to tell you something."

"I'm not asleep, just ... sleepy. What did you want to tell me?"

"The horses are a special gift. An engagement gift."

My eyes flew open. Bryan's turquoise ones met mine. He was so close.

"Mackenzie Wilder, will you marry me?"

I drew in a breath and sat up higher.

"Hey, what do you think of the song?" Jason called out. Tory played some chords.

I looked back at them. I looked at Bryan.

"I don't know," I said.

·T·H·E· ·E·N·D·

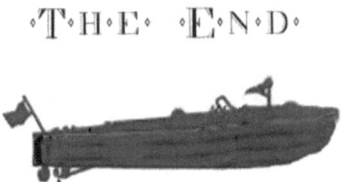

The Songs

" The End's in the Beginning "
by Tyler McCloud

Sometimes a new beginning is someone else's end,
a circular relationship where time begins to blend,
You have to ask the question: where have we come, and how?
'Cause the end's in the beginning,
And the beginning's in us now.

You say you love me as you leave me,
- stories, lies, and misconceptions -
The truth still has its root in lies;
Life is all based on perception.

The truth might have its root in lies;
the end's in the beginning.
Time pursues its ceaseless prize,
and the circle goes on spinning.

Sometimes a new beginning is someone else's end,
a circular relationship where time begins to blend,
You have to ask the question: where have we come, and how?
'Cause the end's in the beginning,
And the beginning's in us now.

It's not where the circle takes us,
but how we make the ride.
If you become a part of me,
and I stay at your side.

If we're lucky to be left standing
within love's golden ring,
We'll have beaten love's unwinding
and taken all that it can bring.

Sometimes a new beginning is someone else's end,
a circular relationship where time begins to blend,
You have to ask the question: where have we come, and how?
'Cause the end's in the beginning,
And the beginning's in us now.

" Don't Lock The Door 'til It Stops Swingin' "
by Jason Fields

You've gone and sent me packin'
Don't you worry none, I'll leave.
But if you want me back in ,
Darlin', you're gonna grieve.

Don't lock the door 'til it stops swingin',
Or it'll stick ajar.
You don't know when I might sneak in
Like some stranger from afar.
If you really want me long gone,
This time I'm gonna stay.
Don't lock the door 'til it stops swingin';
No more games we're gonna play.

You've told me you don't want me,
Not to come around again.
That's the same thing you done told me
When this first happened way back when.

But then you let me back in.
Tho' you swore you never would.
This time I swear I'm leavin',
And it'll be for good.

Don't lock the door 'til it stops swingin',
Or it'll stick ajar.
You don't know when I might sneak in
Like some stranger from afar.
If you really want me long gone,
This time I'm gonna stay
Don't lock the door 'til it stops swingin';
No more games we're gonna play.

'Cause I can't take this any more -
I love you more than my own good.
If you can't close up that dang door,
Guess I'll be in the neighborhood.

" Simple Song "
by Tory McCloud and Jason Fields

It seems so simple,
so true and so simple;
two shall become as one.
- So soon they become; in truth they become; two become as one.

So much complication
in modern situations,
that no one can believe;
we all must self-deceive.

But love is so simple,
So true and so simple
If only we could see....

So true and simple,
Too easy to believe.

Look at Jack and little Jill
Hand-in-hand upon the hill,
Wherever one will go,
the second one will follow.

Children and their rhymes
seem to get it right;
Why is it only grown-ups
Who fail at love's first sight?

For love is so simple,
So true and so simple;
two shall become as one.
- So soon they become; in truth they become; two become as one.

" It's Never Over "
by Joe Lauper and Tyler McCloud

We said good-bye;
I made you cry.

But it's not over.

You thought I didn't care,
My heart kept sayin' "It's not fair"
We never should have gone there.

I heard you say,
"It's over."

But it's not over.

We said the things you say to hurt the one you love;
I told you there were women;
You said there were some men.
And then we stared at one another once again.

Each of us believing,
it must be over.

But it's still not over.

We move as one joined throughout time.
I will be yours and you'll be mine,
Through fights and flights and sleepless nights.
Tight-rope walking the highest heights
We'll say the things you say to soothe the one you love.

Because with us,
It won't be over.

It isn't over.

It's never over.

" Christmas Fires "
by Jason Fields and Tory McCloud

Christmas fires of pinecones
alight,
Yule logs and boughs
don't burn as bright
as new-forged friendship
vows.

The warmth of a circle
binding close friends
outshines the flames
of a blaze we can tend.

Fires of love unending....
Christmas fires of love are blending....
long mem'ries, filled hearts,
close ties, new starts -
Brightened by Christmas love.

Mid-winter, mid-season
Mid joys, trouble, tears
T"is love beyond reason
We seek to draw near.

A love beyond
measure
To last to the end.
The circle of friendship,
Where circles can't
end.

Fires of love unending....
Christmas fires of love are blending....
long mem'ries, filled hearts,
close ties, new starts -
Brightened by Christmas love.

" Song for Ty "
by Tory McCloud (*unfinished*)

From the blessed dark of
Lying on a blanket
Under Daddy's watchful eye,
Seeking constellations
Filling up a country sky

To electric star-glitzed
Buildings held by
Music City's sway.
With booty garnered up
And stashed for rainier days -

All hell broke loose
We all went bust
Life's deadlier urges
Became a must
Gone back to lust,
back to lust -
We all come back to dust.

We all come back to dust.

Sweet Corn, Fields, Forever

acknowledgements

It may take a village to raise a child, but it sometimes takes almost that many to care for and cosset a writer. Thank you to my family for lending me support - literal and psychological - as I work, making sure I eat, sleep, and get to my other jobs on time.

Thank you to Kelsey Shaver for her support and editing skills, and to the members of WORN *(Write On, Right Now)* led by Robin Deffendall whose support, critiques, and suggestions keep me on my toes.

A special thanks to my husband, Dave, for introducing me to the Thousand Islands and the magical beauty of antique boats.

And thank you to the many boat owners who've gladly shared their stories and their boats with us over the years, most recently, Ray and Ann McDowell of Pennsylvania.

Sweet Corn, Fields, Forever

about the author

R.J. MINNICK has spent a lifetime working at various jobs (she even sold Fuller Brush!) and another lifetime raising six terrific offspring with her husband.

During both those lifetimes she kept writing - poetry, reviews, short stories, nonfiction, mysteries, mainstream novels, and Christmas epics. She has credentials in national and local magazines and community news publications.

Sweet Corn, Fields, Forever is the second in her Mackenzie Wilder/Classic Boat mystery series.

R.J. Minnick lives in Fayetteville, North Carolina with her husband, two dogs, five cats and - from time to time - a child or two.

coming next in the Mackenzie Wilder/Classic Boat series....book 3

FLYING PURPLE PEOPLE SEATER

"Well, I got up here okay. And I found the boat. She's a beauty. But, well, you're not going to like this."

Those words again. My heart sank. "What is it?"

"Well, the police won't let me take it."

"The police! Why?"

She sighed a long sigh. "Well, the policeman and the marina guy went down the dock with me. The boat was kind of messed-up looking."

"Messed up? That boatsmith was supposed to take care of it, repair it, clean it up. Wait' til Charlie and I get hold of him!"

"That may take awhile, Doc. He's gone missing. The police couldn't reach him."

"What?" I asked, my voice dropping and my heart *and* stomach sinking.

"Because the boat looked messed up, I let the cop and the marina guy go on board first. Um, Doc? There was a dead woman on board your boat. The police have impounded it, and I can't leave Bateauville until they have a handle on what's going on. They'll be calling you in about a half hour, they said. Doc, what should I do?"

Dorsey Wegman is doing Mackenzie a favor by going to pick up her latest purchase, a 1936 Chris Craft cruiser she's bought from Charlie Osterhout. For some reason no one understands, the boat was moved from its traditional Lake George location to the Thousand Islands, specifically Bateauville, New York, where it was due to be cleaned up and tuned up prior to the summer season. Having tracked the boat to this village that is next door to the home of the Antique Boat Museum, Dorsey encounters some big time problems carrying out her mission.

a Mackenzie Wilder/Classic Boat Mystery

Mackenzie has to go to Bateauville for the boat after all, and soon finds herself working on another mystery involving a dead body. Only this time, she and Dorsey are on their own, in a new county, with new rules and no built-in network to fall back on.

Sweet Corn, Fields, Forever

FICTION
Printed in the U.S.
Wingspan Books